AFTER EARTH

A PERFECT BEAST

By Robert Greenberger

Batman
The Essential Batman Encyclopedia
The Batman Vault

Iron Man
Femmes Fatales

Hellboy
Hellboy II: The Golden Army

Spider-Man
The Art of Spider-Man Classic
The Spider-Man Vault

Star Trek
The Complete Unauthorized History
A Time to Love
A Time to Hate
Doors into Chaos
The Romulan Stratagem

Superman
The Essential Superman Encyclopedia

Wonder Woman
Wonder Woman: Amazon. Hero. Icon.

The Art of Howard Chaykin

Stan Lee's How to Write Comics

AFTER EARTH

A PERFECT BEAST

Michael Jan Friedman, Robert Greenberger, and Peter David

BALLANTINE BOOKS • NEW YORK

After Earth: A Perfect Beast is a work of fiction. Names, places, and incidents either are products of the author's imagination or are used fictitiously.

A Del Rey Mass Market Original

Published in the United States by Del Rey, an imprint of The Random House Publishing Group, a division of Random House, Inc., New York.

DEL REY is a registered trademark and the Del Rey colophon is a trademark of Random House, Inc.

This book contains the following short stories, previously published individually in 2012 and 2013 by Del Rey, an imprint of The Random House Publishing Group, a division of Random House, Inc., as eBooks: *After Earth: Ghost Stories: Hunted*, *After Earth: Ghost Stories: Peace*, and *After Earth: Ghost Stories: Birthright*.

ISBN 978-0-345-54054-6
eBook ISBN 978-0-345-54055-3

Printed in the United States of America

www.delreybooks.com

9 8 7 6 5 4 3 2 1

Del Rey mass market edition: April 2013

To Joan, Deb, and Kathleen,
without whom we'd get less written
and life would certainly be less fun

Acknowledgments

When we three were invited back in 2011 to help shape the *After Earth* universe, we had no idea what the experience would be like. Over the last two years, this has turned into one of the most creatively satisfying projects we've ever worked on, either individually or collectively. It has a lot to do with how generous and open Overbrook Entertainment has been to our ideas and input, letting us play in their new sandbox. While the initial storyline for the feature film came from Will Smith, it has since been added to by many people. We're the ones who were asked to take those many ideas and shape them into a timeline that was rich, varied, and deep with future story potential.

This book resulted from that timeline, selecting a vital point in the *After Earth* history that also resonated with the feature film, setting the stage without spoiling the film's fun. Along the way, we had a lot of exchanges with the OE staff, which made this a stronger story and intersects with more of the *AE* material now available for your reading pleasure.

We want to thank Will Smith, Caleeb Pinkett, Gaetano Mastropasqua, Clarence Hammond, and Kristy Creighton for their input, guidance, and support. At Random House, editor Frank Parisi had to put up with a higher than normal level of agita, for which we are appreciative.

Not *unlike the bear which bringeth forth*
In the end of thirty dayes a shapeless birth;
But after licking, it in shape she drawes,
And by degrees she fashions out the pawes,
The head, and neck, and finally doth bring
To a perfect beast that first deformed thing.

—GUILLAUME DE SALLUSTE DU BARTAS

AFTER EARTH

A PERFECT BEAST

PROLOGUE

"Zantenor! Zantenor, lost to us! Oh, mighty Zantenor, the Vermin have taken it, and we must have it back. Zantenor, lost to us . . ."

The High Minister of the Krezateen thinks he is going to lose his mind.

Outside his isolation pod, the Obsessives continue their chanting. There is no single caste in the entirety of the Krezateen society—which features as of last count 197 castes—that drives him more insane than the Obsessives.

He never knows through what process they decide which cause or issue will be the target of their attentions. Unlike many other castes, the Obsessives have no central authority, or so it seems to him. There is no council, there is no single leader, there is no meeting place. Or if there is, its location is a well-hidden secret, which would be fortunate for them. If the High Minister were aware of it, he would be eminently inclined to go there himself and burn it to the ground.

Yet somehow, even without a centralized organization, the Obsessives would no doubt find something to seize and fixate on. They would do so for however long they desired. Whether they actually bring about social change as a consequence of their fixations never seems to matter to them. They obsess because they feel like doing so, and they continue to do so until they stop.

But they have not stopped when it comes to Zantenor. They have been going on about it for years.

And years.

And *years*.

How long has it been since the Vermin took over the Holy World? Centuries, surely. During one pilgrimage long ago the Vermin had not yet arrived, and Zantenor was its normal pristine self. The Krezateen had shown up in their vast spacegoing vessels, and everything had been fine. They had orbited Zantenor; they had worshipped and prayed to the gods. And the gods had not answered, which was, as always, a good thing. Silence was good. Inactivity was good. The holy writings of the Krezateen were quite specific on that matter. If the gods accepted the offerings and felt one's prayers to be worthy, the gods would take no action against the Krezateen. If, however, misfortune befell them, the gods were making their dislike and disapproval abundantly clear.

The pilgrims had returned from their voyage and reported that the gods had been pleased with them. There had been much rejoicing on Homeworld. As was customary, the debauched celebration had lasted for a solid year, and consequently a new generation of Krezateen had been spawned, further showing the approval of the gods.

But the next visit to the Holy World had been a very different story. The Vermin had appeared.

"Zantenor lost. Lost to the Vermin. Oh, blessed Zantenor, forgive us our failures . . ."

It was impossible to determine exactly when the Vermin had shown up on the Holy World, but they had come out of nowhere, it seemed. Some believed that the Krezateen's ancient enemies, the Ventraya, had deposited them there and even cited similarities to Ventrayan technology in the design of the Vermin's vessels. But there was no way to change speculation to a certainty. The Vermin were clearly some sort of scavenger race—four limbs, tiny heads, no weaponry whatsoever built into their bodies—and they could have found some Ventrayan technology on their own and somehow adapted it to their needs.

After all, they had sensory organs on the front of their faces capable of accessing the hideous light portion of the electromagnetic spectrum, just as the Ventraya did. The Krezateen lacked such organs—eyes, the Ventraya called them—and it was good that they did. Their gods frowned on the light wavelengths. In fact, they frowned on so many things that it was difficult sometimes to keep track of them all.

But it was the Vermin that they frowned on most of all.

They were everywhere, it seemed. They had taken over entire sections of Zantenor and created nests to sustain them. The nutrient-rich ground was being used not for the gods to walk upon in their eternal contemplation but to grow food for the Vermin to consume. They were reproducing as well; during their monitoring the Krezateen identified smaller versions of the Vermin running around, filled with childish joy—as if they had any business being there.

"Blessed be Zantenor, we are not deserving of you, for we have failed to protect you . . ."

The High Minister cannot stand it anymore. *"Be quiet! Damn the lot of you; be quiet!"* he howls. His claws, a gleaming silver, open and close instinctively. Nothing would suit him better at that moment than to explode out of his pod, leap into the heart of the gathered Obsessives, and begin tearing away at them. He imagines himself in full combat fervor, clamping his teeth on the throats of the Obsessives and ripping them open, demolishing the lot of them. And as he does so, he imagines that they are the Vermin, the wretched Vermin. Would that not be glorious? To be able to tear into the Vermin in that fashion, like a mindless killing machine, like some sort of . . .

. . . some sort of . . .

"Animal," he whispers.

He closes his perception organs, and his mind reaches out.

He needs his nest brother, the High Chancellor, to

come to him immediately. Less than a few seconds pass, and the High Minister obtains confirmation that his thoughts have been received and will be attended to immediately.

However, "immediately" when it comes to the High Chancellor is very much a subjective concept. He has many things to attend to, and thus his definition of that term is different from most others. The High Minister is accustomed to this and will wait.

He decides to occupy himself by pacing in his pod. Such pedestrian concerns as gravity have no meaning within it. He moves along the curved, smooth, featureless surface up, down, and then sideways, whichever direction his whim takes him.

The Obsessives continue their chanting, nonstop as usual, but it is bothering him less and less. He supposes that he should feel grateful to them. They have sent his thoughts off in a direction that may well prove useful. So he decides that he will, for now, allow them to live and march around and chant outside his pod for as long as they are inclined to do so. He can always annihilate them later if the mood seizes him.

When the High Chancellor finally arrives, his presence is projected immediately into the High Minister's mind. The far wall of the pod peels itself aside for him, and the High Chancellor enters.

"I hope I did not keep you waiting too long." As always, his grunts and clicks are precise, as is his telepathic syntax.

"Not at all. Three days is actually rather swift for you."

"You are my nest brother in addition to all that you are for the Krezateen. Naturally I would expedite myself for you. So"—he inclines his head slightly—"how may I be of service to you?"

"I mean to discuss Zantenor."

"Ah, Zantenor," sighs the High Chancellor. He nods in the general direction of the unperceived chanting Obsessives going on endlessly outside the High Minister's pod. "Considering what you are listening to on a daily basis, I am not the least bit surprised. How do you endure it? Why do you not just eat them?"

"I'm strongly considering it, but that's not the point at the moment. We need to dispose of the Vermin."

"I readily agree. And the gods know that we have been trying. But the Vermin have proved horrifically resilient. Twice now, we have attacked them from the air. We have bombarded them with all the power at our disposal. And yet they have survived."

"Which leaves land assault."

The High Chancellor says nothing for a moment. Finally he speaks, his voice grave: "You cannot ask that of our people."

"Chancellor—"

"You cannot." His voice is so loud, so forceful, that the sides of the pod actually seem to tremble. "You know that treading upon the sacred soil of Zantenor is forbidden, nest brother. *Forbidden.* Surely you understand what *forbidden* means?"

"Of course. I—"

"It means that once you have set claw on Zantenor, you can never again return to the Homeworld. Once you die, your essence will not be allowed to join the Miasma. You will go neither forward nor back. You will be forever unclean—condemned to either remain on Zantenor, where the gods will surely abominate your presence, or else wander the stars aimlessly."

"I know all that . . ."

"So you claim. But here you are suggesting that Krezateen once again volunteer . . . or are they to be forced into it this time? Would you have them drafted into—?"

"Nest brother, enough!" howls the High Minister, and he holds up his claws as if in a gesture of surrender. "I am suggesting nothing that you are claiming! I have no desire to perceive more of our people, voluntarily or otherwise, set foot on the sacred world."

"But you said—"

"No," and he actually chuckles, something he rarely

does. "No, you said. You made assumptions that were not remotely in line with what I was considering. Yours was an energetic rant but one that was wholly unnecessary."

The High Chancellor, clearly confused, bows slightly. "My pardons, Minister. I should not have interrupted you. So tell me, then: What would you suggest? Aerial assault has failed thus far to accomplish what we need. If we do not intend to send down ground troops, then what would you have us do?"

Once again the Minister is circling his pod, but this time he is doing so with enthusiasm rather than aimless wandering. "The answer has been right in front of us the entire time. I am, frankly, embarrassed that it has not occurred to me before this. We have routinely referred to these unwanted invaders as Vermin. Animals."

"Because such they are."

"Then why not"—he pauses, apparently for dramatic emphasis—"dispose of them through the most logical means available: with animals? Send animals to kill animals."

"I don't understand." The Chancellor is shaking his vast head in confusion. "What manner of animal would you send? We cannot simply pluck animals from our ecosystem, drop them on Zantenor, and then expect them to survive. The creatures would have no chance at all. The air is different, the food sources—"

"That is exactly the point."

The Chancellor looks lost. "Obviously, Minister, you have thought this through . . ."

"We create animals to destroy animals."

"Create?"

"We have a host of data that our scientists have gathered on the Vermin." He grows more excited as he speaks. "Their strengths, their weaknesses. How their brains function, the number of hearts they have, the number of brains . . ."

The Chancellor shakes his head in incredulity. "Yes, so I've heard. One. One pathetic little heart and brain each—and those light-perception organs. It explains a great deal about them."

"And we know more than enough about the Vermin to create animals specially designed for one thing and one thing only: to destroy the usurpers who have dared to occupy our Holy World. What do you think?"

"It's brilliant. That is what I think. I am frankly astounded that no one has thought of it sooner."

"Because it is not the way of the Krezateen," the High Minister says. "We are not accustomed to having others do our fighting for us. But we are hampered by the strictures against setting foot on the Holy World."

The High Chancellor nods.

"Now, though, comes the major question," the High Minister continues. "Specifically: How long will it take? After all, my dear Chancellor, the organizing of the scientific community is under your purview. What needs to be accomplished cannot happen without your support, your dedication, and your organizational skills."

"I should point out that there are those who will argue that introducing a new life-form to Zantenor is nearly as great a crime as setting foot there ourselves," the High Chancellor says, "that we will effectively be accessories to a religious crime."

"The Vermin are the crime that is currently being perpetrated upon Zantenor. We should not be condemned simply because we are trying to put an end to that crime."

The Chancellor considers and then nods. "A valid point. You realize, however, that there are others in the Order who will not concur and may even offer opposition."

"Let them. I look forward eagerly to killing and devouring any who refuse to perceive the matter my way."

"That," says the Chancellor, "is the Minister nest brother I remember."

"Then we are in accord?"

His nest brother nods. "Very much so."

"Then again I ask—how long?"

"To develop the creature?" The Chancellor strokes his pointed chin and ponders the question. "We need to do more than study the information on the Vermin we have gathered to this point. We need to dissect it molecule by molecule. There are many directions we could take in preparing the animal. We could opt for something as small as an insect to move in vast swarms across the planet's surface. Or we could explore something so gigantic that it would crush the Vermin beneath its feet."

"Even though we have been careful not to target anything on Zantenor's surface, we have received complaints that the aerial bombardments are destructive to the planet's surface," says the Minister cautiously. "I'm not sanguine about the notion of a beast that would do even more damage."

"Very well, then," says the Chancellor. "But size does not necessarily matter. Ferocity, speed, all of these are factors to consider. Obviously, we'll have to pore over the material we have gathered on the Vermin with more scrutiny than ever before . . ."

"Yes, yes, obviously." The Minister is beginning to lose patience, but he works to maintain it because the High Chancellor is both his nest brother and a valued ally. "How long do you project the program taking?"

"Analyzing the Vermin's vulnerabilities? Developing a genetic outline?" The High Chancellor goes on and on, listing a host of necessary steps before the undertaking may reach fruition.

The High Minister stops paying attention after a while, since the High Chancellor is clearly in his own world. Finally the High Chancellor falls silent, ponders for a few more moments, and says, "About a century."

The High Minister considers the time frame and then says approvingly, "That would be acceptable. But you'd best hasten, then. A century is not all that much time."

"Indeed," says the High Chancellor. He extends a clawed hand, and the High Minister puts his own hand atop it. "Thank you for coming to me with this concept, nest brother. I will not let you down."

"I know you will not," says the High Minister. And he is secure in his confidence, for the High Chancellor knows that as generous as he is when satisfied, the High Minister can be merciless when disappointed.

The High Chancellor leaves with a sense of urgency. The High Minister is lost in thought for long moments afterward, until the chanting of the Obsessives finally recaptures his attention.

He emerges from his pod and is surprised to discover that there are only six Obsessives outside. He considers this odd; they have been making such a racket that it is hard to believe that their number is a mere half dozen.

Ultimately, it makes little difference.

When he returns to the confines of his pod, there are six fewer Obsessives outside. He finds the silence, however temporary it may be, most enjoyable.

The gathering bell clangs sonorously throughout the city. Members of the Ruling Class cannot ignore it even if they are inclined to do so. They have sworn an oath to attend it no matter when it may be struck, for its tones indicate that a time of great change is about to befall Krezateen society. At least, that is the intended purpose. Should it ring without something of sufficient moment to prompt it, the individual doing the ringing is subject to immediate execution.

The High Minister, however, sounds the gathering bell with supreme confidence. He has waited ninety-seven years for this moment (the High Chancellor, good to his word, has done his best to speed matters along).

Speculation is rife within the assembly as to the reason for this unexpected summons. Word has spread quickly that the High Minister has sounded it. There is much discussion that it has something to do with the Vermin who infest the Holy World of Zantenor, but

the formidable Warlord Knahs is making very loud pro-
nouncements that the High Minister had best not be
getting any ideas that he has any authority in the matter.

"The reclamation of Zantenor is within *my* purview!" the Warlord bellows to anyone who will listen.

Not many do. The fact that Zantenor continues to be
defiled by the tiny hands of the Vermin remains a sore
subject in Krezateen society. Indeed, there have been
many who argue that Knahs should be stripped of his
title—and preferably his head—for his failure to mount
a successful campaign that would reclaim the land in
the name of the gods.

In the place of the grand gathering, all the faction
leaders are assembled. Warlord Knahs has a prominent
place among them since his position makes him leader
of the House of War. But there are many other factions,
many other disciplines—over three hundred of them—
represented at the gathering place.

When the Krezateen address one another, it is with a
combination of telepathy and audible grunts and clicks
of their mandibles, and the gathering place echoes with
those staccato sounds ricocheting all around. The gathering place is a series of descending spirals, with the
more powerful and influential houses close to the top in
order to reinforce their station.

What is to be discussed? That is the recurring question that they think and hiss and snarl and click at one
another. *Zantenor? New tithes? Planetary disasters?
What could it be? What?*

Then conversation dwindles to a halt as something is
lowered slowly from above on a mag-lev platform. It
is a cube made of a smooth, solid black material that is
impossible to see through. The assembled Krezateen
remain silent at first, curious, and then a new swell of
conversation rises, redolent with confusion.

The High Minister monitors this with a great deal
of satisfaction. The Chancellor had been less than enthused about the prospect of this showy introduction of

his work. The High Minister doesn't care. The Krezateen are such a fractious race that before doing anything else, one has to get their attention. This, at least,
he is managing to accomplish.

The platform descends another hundred feet and
then comes to a halt, suspended there and garnering
continued discussion and speculation.

"Minister!" It is the bellowing voice of the Warlord,
echoing throughout the gathering place. "Is this what
you have gathered us for? To perform some sort of
magic trick?"

This garners a mixture of amusement and muttering.
At least nine religious factions have outlawed even the
suggestion of magic as an affront to the gods, if not to
logic itself.

"No magic," announces the High Minister to percep-
tible relief among some factions. "But instead science,
harnessed to benefit the whole of our race. I have here
the final solution to the Vermin problem."

He taps a device that dissolves the smoky blackness
of the cube, and as it happens, there are gasps throughout the gathering place as the creature within the cube
is slowly revealed.

It is huge, monstrous. Its cavernous maw opens in a
slow yawn as it licks its chops, its tongue running across
a double row of teeth. Its body is long and lean with
multiple legs that look crouched and ready to propel it
forward, presumably to strike at its prey. Its head slowly
and calmly sweeps back and forth, taking in the presence of the Krezateen but not appearing to be impressed
or agitated.

"This?" says the Warlord. "This creature is intended
to rid us of the Vermin?"

"That is the intention," says the High Minister.

The Warlord laughs. Not a chuckle or snicker but instead a loud, bold howl of derision.

The High Minister at that moment seriously considers leaping across the gathering place and tearing into
the Warlord. The odds are that it would not go well for

the Minister; the Warlord is powerfully built, one of the strongest of the Krezateen. The High Minister probably would not last very long, but that does not matter to him at that moment . . .

Softly, nest brother. The words sound within his head as the High Chancellor, a short distance away, wisely counsels him. *Do not let yourself be pulled into a needless battle. Bring them to you. Demonstrate.*

Even as his wisdom sounds within his nest brother's head, the High Chancellor is now standing and says in a flat, toneless voice, "May I ask what there is about the salvation of Zantenor you find to be so amusing? It is not as if, after all this time, you have developed a plan of any worth."

He has spoken calmly yet provocatively. The Warlord is no longer amused; his lack of success remains a sting to him. "You cooked this up, I assume," and he points accusingly at the Chancellor.

"Indeed I have."

"To what point and purpose? To unleash this . . . this *creature* upon the Vermin?"

"You have asked and answered your own question." He speaks as a parent would to an offspring, and thus his response carries an air of carefully structured condescension. Not enough to provoke the Warlord to attack but sufficient to make his point clear.

"Look at it!" The Warlord remains determinedly disdainful. "I will grant you, you have crafted a rather fearsome-looking fighting machine. Teeth that bite. Claws that catch. But it is clearly a placid monstrosity. For all the apparatus you and your genetic geniuses have provided it, it has no killer instinct."

"Really? Are you saying that you could dispose of it yourself without a weapon in your hand?"

"Unquestionably."

The High Minister knows what is coming and smiles inwardly. If there is one thing on which one can count when it comes to the Warlord, it is his insufferable ego.

"Very well." The High Chancellor maintains the air

of one who is utterly servile, eager only to please. "If you wish, I can bring the creature to the combat pit, and you may engage it in one-to-one battle."

Excellent! Excellent! It will tear him apart! The High Minister can scarcely contain himself.

He is so excited that he cannot block his thoughts from being picked up by the Chancellor. His nest brother casts him a contemptuous glance. *We do not want him dead, brother. We want him humiliated. For all his bluster, the Warlord remains a bully. And bullies are cowards. And we both know what it would do to the Warlord's standing in a society that abominates any sort of fear, much less cowardice. So be patient. A live ally can be of far more use than a dead enemy.*

He shifts his attention back to the Warlord. "I am happy to accommodate you," he says. Then, almost imperceptibly, he touches a remote control device in his pocket.

Suddenly the creature crashes against the side of its confinement. It does so with such ferocity that everyone at the gathering jumps, almost as one. Then it bares its teeth and crashes again.

"No killer instinct?" he says.

The irony is there to be seen by all. The creature is practically out of its mind with fury. It slams repeatedly against the walls of its confinement, bites at the air. Its claws rake across the clear surface, making high-pitched screeching sounds that prompt a number of Krezateen to cover their ears.

His voice soaring above the unabated howling of the frustrated creature—for it is unable to tear its perceived target apart—the Chancellor calls out, "You may now display your puissance, Warlord!"

"What's going on?" Knahs demanded.

"All I did," says the Chancellor, "is pump a small whiff of Vermin into the creature's cage. After all, such is the species it is designed to hunt and destroy—Vermin, not Krezateen. But if you are determined to demonstrate your prowess as a warrior, we wouldn't think of shaming you with an inferior adversary. So I offer to spray you with the Vermin's essence—just a bit of it. Thus exposed, you can take your place in the pit without worrying that you will be wasting your time."

There is clear satisfaction in the voice of the Chancellor and also an unmistakable hint of challenge. "This is what you want," he presses, "is it not?"

All attention is now on the Warlord. The only other sound in the meeting area is the roaring of the creature.

Only his cowardice will save him, the Minister thinks smugly to the Chancellor. *The question is: How will he rationalize it?*

Not much of a question at all, actually, thinks the Chancellor back at his nest mate.

"You," the Warlord says, "are insane if you think I am going to allow residue of the Vermin to be put upon my person. I will not have the gods abominate me so that you can provide a demonstration for your . . . freak."

And there it is, thinks the Chancellor smugly. Aloud he says, "This freak is the answer to our problem."

"Our problem," calls out one of the religious faction leaders, "is that the gods feel that our civilization is going in the wrong direction! They feel we have not been devout enough! That is why they allow the Vermin on the Holy World in the first place: to express their anger with us. And your answer is to introduce yet another life-form upon Zantenor? The moment they set claw upon Zantenor, they will be unclean! And since we sent them, we will be unclean as well!"

"Then we are damned either way!" the Minister calls out. "What would you have us do? Restrict our efforts to futile barrages and the occasional prayer?"

"The gods will show us the way!" comes another voice from the religious quarter. "We should wait—"

Enraged at such closed-mindedness, the Chancellor for a moment loses his patience. His voice thunders through the vastness of the gathering. *"The gods gave us brains to think! Resourcefulness to invent and ex-*

plore! The will of the gods resides within each and every one of us. If we refuse to take advantage of the resources the gods provide us, that is the true insult!"

It is an argument that, as far as the High Minister is concerned, is irrefutable. That should be the end of it.

Instead it is only the beginning.

For years it goes on. For years, a debate that for a time seems as if it will crack the entirety of Krezateen society apart. Ultimately the decision comes on one raucous day after a debate that lasts nineteen straight hours. It is decided that the Unclean—as the creatures have come to be known simply through repeated use of the adjective—will be unleashed upon the sacred world in order to annihilate the Vermin.

The High Chancellor remains furious over one compromise that he has to make. To him, the most devastating aspect of the creatures is that they will propagate themselves. He has labored long and hard to make them as fertile as possible. Their desire to procreate will be second only to their compulsion to hunt and consume Vermin. But the religious factions simply will not bend: The notion of something crafted by the Krezateen breeding on the Holy World is to them simply too much of an abomination.

Most frustratingly, even the High Minister refuses to support his nest brother. "The creatures are intended to have a specific purpose," he says. "They are to rid the Holy World of an unholy life-form. But if they breed as quickly as you propose, then once the Vermin are gone, the home of the gods will be overrun by monsters of our own making. Can you guarantee that the gods will perceive that as any better a situation?"

"I would not presume to guess one way or the other how the gods would react to anything," says the High Chancellor.

So it was that he and his team had to reconfigure the

creatures so that they would be genderless and incapable of breeding. Of course, what will happen through the hand of nature once the creatures are unleashed upon the land, even the High Chancellor cannot predict. But he, at least, will have done all that he can. The rest struggles in the claws of the gods.

The High Chancellor could easily do without the absurd festivities that have been crafted to celebrate the launch. *That* he considers something of an affront to the gods. The High Chancellor has always believed himself to be an austere individual, and he considers the launch a solemn occasion. For the first time in a long time, the Krezateen are taking a positive step to take back their Holy World. Why saddle the event with gaudiness?

No reason. No reason at all. But they do it anyway.

Yet another compromise that he has lost.

Well . . . at least he will be along on the journey to monitor firsthand the effectiveness of the creatures (he never uses the term *unclean* in his musings. The term offends him even if he has learned to tolerate it).

Are you almost here, nest brother? The sound of the High Minister's voice echoes in his head. The High Chancellor assures him that he has nearly arrived as he moves through the elevated maze of roads that constitutes much of the surface of the Homeworld. One of the roiling rivers of lava upon Homeworld's surface surges far beneath him. Heat billows up like a fist. He ignores it. He has bigger things to worry about.

He has almost reached the launch site. The vessel that will carry them to Zantenor is not, of course, there. It is in orbit around the Homeworld. Instead, there is an array of shuttles that will lift off and carry the High Chancellor and the High Minister to the transport vessel. It is a standard-issue pilgrimage ship, capable of transporting two hundred Krezateen in one trip. However, this crew load will be far less: only the High Chancellor and the High Minister and a complement of scientists to observe how the creatures perform against the Vermin. If things go the way the Chancellor is hoping, they will return home with reports of success.

Sure enough, there are the shuttles, placed on a huge round platform. He and the Minister embrace quickly, patting each other on the back. "We are accomplishing great things today," says the Minister. "It could not have been accomplished without you."

"You are absolutely right," the Chancellor replies.

There are speeches then. Speeches and blessings and endless prayers. The heads of seemingly endless factions step forward one at a time, each trying to outdo the other in his religious fervor. The Chancellor finds it bleakly amusing considering how many of them had offered protest and resistance when the project was announced. Obviously they have come around. It has been the Chancellor's experience that that is often the case: Massive resistance to new ideas is followed by an eventual embracing of them.

After what seems far too long a time, the shuttles are on their way. They arc gracefully skyward toward the ship that is waiting for them.

The creatures have been loaded aboard. They are safely secured, in suspended animation, inside a smaller vessel—a drop ship—within the larger ship's hold. Once they get within range of Zantenor, the drop ship will descend upon the holy planet and its contents will be unleashed upon the unsuspecting Vermin.

The High Chancellor, the High Minister, and the rest of the crew likewise will be slumbering for the duration of the trip, which will require eighteen years to complete. The ship's automated systems will revive them once they are within range of Zantenor. And then . . .

. . . *and only then* . . .

. . . will it be possible for them to recapture the approval of the gods.

Minutes later, the shuttle delivers them to the pilgrimage vessel. The High Chancellor and High Minister enter. Excitement is beginning to pound within the Chancellor's chest cavities. He has never had the honor of making a pilgrimage, and his time has been running out. Long-lived he may be, but even he and his nest brother will not last forever, and he might not live long enough to be part of the next pilgrimage.

So instead he is part of not a pilgrimage but a great scientific adventure. What does it matter, the pretext? He will be traveling within range of the planet of the gods, and he may actually oversee its liberation from the Vermin. Is that not a prospect to be—?

A chill suddenly strikes his spine. He sees by the Minister's reaction that he is responding likewise.

The Warlord and his soldiers are standing there within the ship to greet them. "Welcome aboard, Honored Ones," Knahs says with what he no doubt considers to be some sort of suavity.

"What are you doing here?" the High Minister asks him fiercely.

The Chancellor is equally outraged. "This is a scientific mission."

"This is a battle. A battle that is part of a much larger war," the Warlord informs them. "If a military situation presents itself, it will be the job of my soldiers and me to be prepared for it. Furthermore"—he smiles maliciously—"we wish to make certain that the results you present to our people are accurate representations of what actually transpires on the Holy World."

"This is intolerable," declares the High Chancellor.

"Very well," says the Warlord with an indifferent shrug. "You are free not to tolerate it. The shuttle can readily take you back to Homeworld." He gestures toward the entranceway through which the Chancellor has just come.

The High Minister trembles with indignation, but once more the Chancellor speaks to him in a soothing manner.

Let him have this small triumph, brother. The greater triumph will be ours, and he will ultimately destroy himself. I know his kind.

We both do, agrees the High Minister, not without effort.

The Chancellor just hopes that he is correct. And he also hopes that, considering all that is being done to placate the gods, the gods will make it worth their while.

CHAPTER ONE

576 AE

"Think they're getting tired of eating dirt?" asked Meredith Wilkins, Prime Commander of the United Ranger Corps of the planet Nova Prime.

"It builds character," said Commander Elias Hāturi, her right-hand man. He took a noisy bite of his Nova Prime apple, which had been grown from the seeds humankind had brought with it from Earth.

"The grit's good for their digestion," added Commander Bonita Raige, a short woman with close-cropped blond hair except for a white patch in the back from a field injury. She had been advising the Prime Commander for years but had joined Wilkins's staff only recently.

On several screens before them, three color-coded squads of armed Ranger cadets were scrambling across a craggy red stretch of desert, each one trying to obtain a strategic advantage without being seen by its opponents. The squads had started out with a dozen cadets apiece in this mock battle, but they all had felt the toll of one skirmish after another.

There were no real injuries, of course. Just a color change in a light-sensitive disk worn on the back when it was hit by an adversary's laser beam. Anyone so tagged had been forced to leave the game.

Blue Squad had taken the worst of it. Led by Erdmann, the most experienced of the cadets, the squad nonetheless had gotten caught in a most costly ambush. Erdmann had only two subordinates left.

Green Squad hadn't fared much better. It had sustained seven casualties, including Cheng, its mission leader. Earlier in the day, Cheng had made a heroic sacrifice that allowed her squad mates to escape. Wilkins didn't hold out much hope for the five remaining Reds. In her experience, squads didn't last long once they lost their leader.

Red Squad, at this point, had to be the odds-on favorite to win the exercise. It still had nine cadets to its name thanks to the canny leadership of Lucas Kincaid, a lean, strong kid with aquiline features. Wilkins had had her eye on Kincaid ever since he'd signed on. The kid had a knack for getting others to follow him and buy into his strategies, which were always calculated to eliminate his opponents.

So far Kincaid had done just that. With Blue on the run, victims of his most recent assault, Kincaid was turning his attention back to Green. Unfortunately for its chances, Green had retreated into a deep, high-walled valley.

As Wilkins watched, Kincaid took advantage of Green's error by following them in. First he fanned his cadets out on either side of him, filling the narrow confines of the valley. Then he marched them in pursuit of Green on the double. At this rate, they would catch up with the Green Squad in no time, and Red's nine-wide formation would prevent any of the enemy from escaping their net.

"What do you think?" she asked her commanders.

"He knows what he's doing," Raige said.

"Has all along," observed Hāturi, who was big and barrel-chested. He tossed his apple core into a waste aperture in the wall. "Then again, he's a Kincaid. He didn't exactly come from nowhere."

The name Kincaid, Wilkins reflected, had been an important one in the four-hundred-year history of humankind on Nova Prime. Kincaids had been key figures in the Rangers, in the science corps led by the Savant, and even in the religious order led by the Primus. It was good to see that young Lucas had inherited the best of his family's genes.

Wilkins turned to Raige. "You have a nephew in the games, don't you, Bonita?"

Raige shot a look at the Prime Commander. "You know I do."

His name was Conner. Unfortunately, he hadn't distinguished himself the way the Kincaid boy had—far from it. But he hadn't been eliminated from the game, either.

"Maybe he has a little promise after all," Wilkins allowed.

That would be good, considering the Raiges had been around since the exodus from Earth as well. In fact, the very first Prime Commander had been a member of the Raige clan, and the family was still well represented in the Rangers—not only by Bonita but also by her husband, Torrance, and her brother, Frank, Conner's father.

Some of the colony's best times had taken place when the Raiges and the Kincaids were acknowledged rivals, vying to see who could contribute the most to the Rangers. Not that Wilkins expected that sort of thing to happen on her watch. To that point, Lucas Kincaid had demonstrated pretty clearly that he *had* no rivals.

"Red's going to win this," Hāturi concluded.

"Let's see if Green has any idea of what's going on," Wilkins said, bringing up a view of the valley that seemed likely to include the Green Squad.

Unfortunately, Wilkins's video feed was blocked by some of the projections on the valley walls. She manipulated the controls on the panel in front of her, trying to get a better angle. Finally, she found one that wasn't obscured.

"There they are," Hāturi said, pointing to what was left of Green Squad.

Wilkins nodded. "And they have no inkling that Red is narrowing the gap." It was disappointing. These were supposed to be seasoned cadets. They were supposed to know what they were doing at that point.

Then Raige said, "I only count four of them."

The Prime Commander counted. "Four," she echoed. "Who's missing?"

It only took her a moment to figure it out. "Your nephew, Bonita." Conner Raige was nowhere to be seen.

"Where is he?" asked Hāturi. He turned to Wilkins. "With your permission?"

"Go ahead," she said.

Hāturi ran through every view they had of the valley. Conner Raige wasn't on any of them.

"Want me to check his transponder?" Bonita Raige asked, her fingers hovering over a control panel. A tap would trace the emergency beacon woven into Conner's uniform.

"You worried?" asked Wilkins.

Raige shook her head. "No." Though she might have been, just a little.

"Then," said the Prime Commander, sitting back in her chair, "let's see how this plays out."

The more Wilkins watched, the more she wondered. Then she saw Conner appear as if by magic, and she stopped wondering. The cadet had come out of the ground behind Red Squad, where nobody—including Red, apparently—had expected him, and he began picking off the Red cadets one by one.

"Well, I'll be damned," Hāturi said.

Wilkins was watching Conner execute what might have been the cleverest and most audacious maneuver she had ever seen in a war game. Before it was over, Kincaid and all the rest of his Red Squad cadets had been hit with beams from Green Squad's practice pulsers. A screen to the Prime Commander's right flashed nine names, one after the other, denoting that the Reds were no longer live participants in the exercise.

When the show was over, Wilkins smiled and said,

"That was pretty damn impressive. And he wasn't even the leader of record."

"It's in the blood," Bonita Raige said, keeping a straight face though her heart was bursting with pride.

The Prime Commander nodded approvingly. "Apparently so. Quite a nephew you've got there."

Conner Raige hadn't had such a good day in a long time.

He acknowledged that fact, if only to himself, as he led his team between two of the metal spires that supported the rust-colored fabric structure of his cadet barracks. Once under the smart fabric roof, he felt the temperature drop and was grateful. It was a relief to get out of the fiery suns of Nova Prime, which he had been forced to endure for the last several hours.

Conner wasn't just hot. He was tired, bone-tired, as tired as he had ever been before. But it was a *good* tired. His headgear, tucked securely under one arm, usually felt like a burden to him. But today it was a tangible reminder of what he and his Green team had accomplished.

He could still see the looks on the faces of the Reds as they whirled about, having come to the realization— too late—that there was someone lurking behind them. Looks of surprise. Looks of embarrassment. Looks that said it wasn't fair for them to lose the competition at the last moment when they had been winning it all along.

Conner would hang on to that memory for a while. That much was certain. After all, it wasn't often he did something he could be proud of.

That was one of the problems with being born into a family of legends. Everything he did was measured against what other Raiges had done, all the way back hundreds of years to the time of the Exodus from Earth. No one in the colony ever came out and told him that, but they didn't have to. He could see it in their eyes.

That's pretty good, they would be thinking, *but not as good as what your great-great-grandfather did. Or your grandmother on your dad's side.*

Or your father.

Conner's bunk was at the far end of the barracks, one of several dozen beds arranged in perfectly neat, uncluttered rows and columns. When he reached it, he hung his headgear on a hook protruding from his bedpost. Then he swung himself around the post and plopped himself down on the mattress.

All around him, he could hear members of his Green team doing the same. It felt good to lie down as he watched the barracks roof undulate under the press of an afternoon wind. He closed his eyes, and again he saw the faces of the Red team.

And he found himself smiling.

It felt funny, as if the muscles in his face weren't used to it. But then, smiling wasn't something Conner did a whole lot these days. In fact, it was something he probably hadn't done at all since he had become a cadet. But he was doing it now. And why not? He had earned it, hadn't he?

Damned right, he thought.

Naturally, he wasn't going to say that out loud. He wasn't going to say anything that could be considered a taunt of Red Squad. But a private little grin? He could certainly be permitted that.

Just then, Conner heard someone whisper something. He couldn't make out the words, but the tone was a familiar one. Opening his eyes and turning in the direction of the whisper, he saw two of his Green teammates. One was a guy named Augustover. The other was a woman named Ditkowsky.

They were frowning at him. Just for a moment, of course. Then they went about their business.

Not that he hadn't seen them shoot him disapproving looks before. And it wasn't just Augustover and Ditkowsky who had done so. At one time or another, a lot of other cadets had done the same thing.

Conner didn't get it.

If one of *them* had turned around a war game and transformed defeat into victory, he would have patted that cadet on the back and congratulated the hell out of him. He would have sung his praises. But no one was congratulating Conner.

He sighed and allowed himself to fall back against his mattress. *What the hell . . . ?* He had understood the attitude of the other cadets when he first arrived, especially after he screwed up not just one time but a couple. His dad had told him that new cadets were treated like garbage, that they had to prove themselves before they got any respect.

But what he had done that morning in the desert should have made up for the screwups. It should have more than made up for them.

So why are they still giving me the stink eye? he wondered.

He had the answer, and it was a bitter one, before he had even finished asking himself the question: *Because I'm a Raige, even more so here than in the rest of the colony. Because no matter how hard I try to be a Ranger, no matter what I accomplish, nothing will ever be good enough.*

The hell with them, then, he thought. *The hell with all of them.* He would do what he had to do on his own, without their approval.

As he thought that, he heard a murmur run through the barracks. Curious, Conner picked up his head and saw the tall, gray-haired figure of Prime Commander Wilkins negotiating a path through the barracks.

Suddenly, every cadet in the place was standing at attention, Conner among them. He wanted to sneak a peek at Wilkins's expression, maybe get a sense of what she was doing there, but he couldn't. He had to look straight ahead.

There were a few moments when all he could hear were the clacks of Wilkins's heels on the hardwood floor beneath them. Then the Prime Commander said, "At ease."

Conner relaxed and turned his head. Unfortunately, Wilkins's iron features didn't give much away. But then, that was always the case.

"I just spent several hours watching you cadets compete out there," she said. "You deserve feedback and you deserve it now, while everything that happened is fresh in your minds."

Conner wouldn't have minded getting that feedback later, after he had gotten some rest, and he was sure his fellow cadets felt the same way. But no one said so. After all, it was the Prime Commander.

"In some ways," Wilkins said, "you acquitted yourselves well. But not in *all* ways. All three teams made costly mistakes. In the context of a war game, you have a chance to learn from those mistakes and make improvements. But when you've completed your training and become Rangers—and as you know, that won't be the outcome for everybody in this barracks—you won't have the luxury of making mistakes. Because if you screw up as a Ranger, you'll pay with your life or the lives of your squad mates."

She looked around the barracks. "Keep that in mind as you prepare for the next round of the war games, which will commence exactly one week from today."

The cadets were absolutely silent in the wake of the announcement, but Conner could hear their groans in his head nonetheless. They weren't supposed to have engaged in war games again for six months. A week between games wasn't much at all. It was almost nothing.

He couldn't remember any other cadet class having that kind of burden placed on it. *So why us?*

He wondered if it had anything to do with the criticisms he had heard were being leveled against the Rangers lately. Not from anyone in particular, but an undercurrent of them. The other cadets had noticed. And if *they* had noticed, it was a good bet that Wilkins had, too.

If the Rangers were under fire, Wilkins might be thinking, they had to be more careful than ever not to make mistakes. Hence the new round of games so soon after the last one.

"Any questions?" asked the Prime Commander. There weren't any. "Then you're dismissed."

Everyone went about his or her business. In most cases, that meant hitting their bunks again. Certainly it did in Conner's case. But he had barely gotten comfortable before he saw that Wilkins hadn't left the barracks. In fact, she was standing right over him, eyeing him without expression.

"Cadet Raige," she said, "you are not dismissed. Walk with me."

"Yes, ma'am," said Conner, swinging his legs out of bed. He got up to follow Wilkins, the eyes of the other cadets on him. *What the hell have I done wrong now?* he thought.

CHAPTER TWO

The Rangers' ruddy sandstone command center, which housed the Prime Commander's office, looked like just another piece of the desert landscape. It was in the middle of the Ranger compound, past the other cadet barracks, the mess hall, and the armory.

Wilkins didn't say a thing to Conner until they reached her office and went inside, and even then all she told him was, "Close the door."

He did as he was told. Then he waited for his superior to take a seat behind her desk.

Finally, she looked up at him and said, "Cadet Raige."

"Yes, ma'am," he replied, so curious that it hurt.

"That," she said, "was quite a spectacle out there this morning. One of the few bright spots, in fact, in what was frankly a mostly unimpressive war game."

Conner bit back a smile as hard as he could. It was one thing to look pleased with himself in the barracks and another to do so in the Prime Commander's office. "Thank you, ma'am."

"Where did you come up with that strategy?"

Strategy? The word implied that he had thought in advance about what he had done. But he hadn't thought about it at all.

"I just went with my gut," he said.

The Prime Commander's eyes narrowed ever so slightly. "Your gut?" She didn't look satisfied.

"I just knew what it would take to lure Red Squad

into a trap," Conner ventured, hoping it would sit better with Wilkins. "And I did it."

But Wilkins's expression didn't change. "You just *knew*."

He tried a different approach, one he thought she would want to hear. "I come from a long line of Rangers, ma'am. My dad, Frank Raige . . . I believe you know him."

"I do," she confirmed.

"And there's my uncle Torrance and my aunt Bonita. And everyone else in our family that's served with the Rangers for the last six hundred years. I guess some of what they know rubbed off on me, um, a little."

"And that's your explanation?" Wilkins asked.

Obviously she didn't like that one, either. She was looking for something else, but he didn't know what. "Yes, ma'am," was all he could say.

"Well," said the Prime Commander, "you're a superior tactician, Cadet Raige. That much is clear. But you'll never get a chance to put your abilities to work on behalf of the colony until you can articulate the thinking behind your tactical choices. At least not as long as I'm in charge. Because what may seem like blind instinct to you is actually an application of intellect. It's that intellect I'm interested in, and it's what you should be interested in as well."

"Yes, ma'am," Conner said again, though he didn't necessarily agree with the intellect part. To him, instinct was more important than intellect. In fact, instinct was the number one quality that made someone a good Ranger.

Whether the Prime Commander thought so or not.

"With that in mind," Wilkins said, "I would like you to write a formal battle plan that tells me precisely what you did to Red Squad and how you did it, step by step by step. And I would like you to turn it in to me by noon tomorrow. Is that clear?"

Conner thought she was kidding. He *hoped* she was

kidding. But the longer she looked at him, the more certain he was that she was dead serious.

"Yes, ma'am," he said a third time.

But in his mind, he was reeling. *A formal battle plan? By noon? Is she out of her mind?*

"Good," said Wilkins. "And by the way . . . I know your family's a distinguished one. But we have to make our own legacies in life. Yes?"

"Yes," Conner said, though that sounded even *harder* than living up to his family name.

"You're dismissed, Cadet Raige."

"Thank you, ma'am."

As Conner left the command center, he was already wrapping his head around the magnitude of the task. *If I stay up all night, I can finish it on time. At least I think I can.*

He would have loved to get a decent night's sleep after spending most of the day broiling in the desert. *Doesn't look like that's going to happen,* he thought bitterly.

Worse, he had a feeling that Wilkins was setting a precedent. Was he going to have to write a battle plan every time he led a team? That would be hell. What he had always liked about the Rangers was having a chance to act *without* thinking.

"Hey, Raige!"

Conner turned and shaded his eyes against the brazen sunlight. His pal Blodge was jogging his way, raising little puffs of dust from the red ground.

"Hey," Conner said in return.

Blodge, whose real name was Raul Blodgett, was a big guy with a round face and a brush of red hair. He had signed on as a cadet the same day Conner had, had gone through all the exercises Conner had. Except Blodge was one of the more popular guys in his barracks. People just naturally warmed to him the same way they didn't just naturally warm to Conner.

"Everything all right?" Blodge asked. "I mean, you won the exercise, right? At least that's how it looked to us poor jerks on the Blue team. Looking at that face, I'd think you were the one who lost."

Conner grunted. "That all depends on how you look at it."

"You kicked Red's butts, right? And Kincaid's butt in particular. How else *can* you look at it?"

"Wilkins wants me to write a detailed battle plan explaining how we did it."

Blodge's face puckered with sympathy. "Ouch. Sorry about that."

"Yeah," said Conner, "so am I."

The day Frank Raige flew his first Kelsey flier was the day he found out who he was.

On the ground, he had always been a little impatient with himself, a little fidgety. As hard as he worked, he always felt he could work harder, make himself into something better.

In the air, he *was* something better.

"How's she feel, Captain?" his flier technician, Smitty, asked over the craft's intercom.

Like the wind, Frank thought. The flier, a long black dart, was running perfectly. But what he said was, "Like she's going to fall apart any minute. You get rid of those mechanics of yours and tell them it was my idea."

"Meaning: They're doing a great job, keep up the good work," said Smitty, who had become familiar with Frank's antics over the decade they had worked together. "Got it, sir."

Frank looked down at the desert below him. It sprawled, all gold and rust glinting in the light of first sun. To his left, hundreds and hundreds of kilometers to the north, the land rose and took on a coat of rich green fir forest. To his right, it stretched south to the unseen Thermopoulos Sea. It was a beautiful world. At times like these, he was grateful to the pioneers who had steered humanity to Nova Prime instead of somewhere else.

"Planning on getting back soon?" asked Smitty. "Laura's asking when I'm going to be home."

"I'm coming about as we speak," Frank told him.

He had a habit of getting carried away when he was in the air. He didn't want to apologize to Smitty's wife yet again for keeping her husband at work an hour after his shift was supposed to have ended.

As Frank banked, the land below him seemed to tilt and spin about. The flier responded perfectly, adjusting for the wind without a hitch. It was a pleasure to test something so well designed. But Frank wasn't going to be any more forthcoming with his praise when he spoke to his engineers than when he spoke to his mechanics. If he did, they probably would faint dead away.

As the outskirts of Nova Prime City slid toward him, he could see the research center where his wife, Rebecca, would be bent over her microscope, seeking a cure for Ressler's Disease, one of the more vicious bacterial mutations humanity had encountered since it had landed on Nova Prime. He could also see the red-clay obelisk erected as a monument to the four hundred thousand colonists who had survived the long, hard passage through space.

And he could identify the barracks where his son, Conner, was probably stretched out on his bunk, catching up on shut-eye after taking part in the Prime Commander's war games. Frank knew what that was like, having participated in the games when he was a cadet.

All he wanted in life was down there in Nova Prime City. As much as he loved flying, he loved returning to his family even more.

"Got a visual on you, Captain," Smitty reported. "All clear for landing."

"Roger that," Frank said.

The flier landed as smoothly as it handled in the air. In moments, it had coasted to a halt. Frank turned off his flight systems one by one. Then he removed his harness and opened the hatch. Immediately, he felt the hot, dry air of the desert wash over him. Some people preferred air-conditioning, but Frank liked the heat.

Smitty came running over with a comm unit in his hand.

"What's up?" Frank asked.

Smitty handed him the communicator. "It's Prime Commander Wilkins, sir. She called as you were landing."

He put the comm unit to his ear. "Yes, ma'am. Raige here."

"At ease, Frank. It's just the two of us."

He grew concerned. If this wasn't an official call . . . "Everything all right?"

"You mean, is Conner all right?"

"Well . . . yeah."

"That's why I called, Frank. I've got good news."

He exhaled a breath he didn't know he'd been holding. "That's the kind I want to hear."

"We just finished our war games, though we're going to reprise them in a week's time—an object lesson. But I'm happy to tell you that Conner distinguished himself even if no one else did. Hell, he pretty much carried the day for Green Squad all on his own."

Frank felt his throat tighten up. Though he was beef jerky on the outside, he'd always been a softy when it came to his family. "That's great. What did he do?"

After Wilkins filled him in, she added, "I told you he's been having some trouble finding himself. After this I expect he'll find his rhythm."

"I sure hope so. You didn't pat him on the back too hard, I expect."

"You know me better than that," said Wilkins. "He's in the study center now trying to pull together a battle plan based on what he did purely out of instinct."

Frank smiled to himself. "Good. Can't hurt to make him think. And the other cadets won't see him gloating."

"Or getting too many kudos from the brass. Nobody

likes a teacher's pet—especially when the teacher's a Prime Commander."

He understood the reference. Wilkins herself had been a cadet deserving of that kind of recognition. But the Prime Commander at the time—Frank's father, Joshua Raige—had been wise enough not to praise Wilkins too much in public.

"I'm happy to see the lesson rubbed off," Frank said.

"Your dad didn't give *you* too much recognition, either."

"How would that have looked?" Frank asked. "The only thing worse than being the teacher's pet is being the teacher's son."

"He knew what he was doing, all right," Wilkins said. "I miss the old goat."

Frank nodded to himself. "So do I."

As much as he liked shooting the bull with Wilkins, he knew she had a lot on her plate. The last thing he wanted to do was distract her from her work even if they *were* old friends.

"I appreciate the report," he said. "But right now I ought to—"

"Hang on a moment, Frank. I know I've asked you this before, but I could sure use you at the top. Elias will be retiring soon, as you know, and as far as I'm concerned, a Prime Commander can't have enough Raiges on her staff."

He was flattered, as always, but he needed a promotion like Nova Prime needed another desert. He had joined the Rangers to be a flier, not a desk jockey.

"It's getting a little hard to hear you," he said. "Must be a sunspot or something."

"Don't give me that," said Wilkins. "If you're too scared to move up the ranks, just say so."

Frank chuckled. "That's me, ma'am, shaking in my britches. You have a good day, now. Call me any time with news like that."

"I hope to. Wilkins out."

* * *

Damn, Conner thought as he sat in the stillness of the cadet study center with the second sun dropping toward the horizon. He sighed and tapped his forefinger on the desk next to his keypad. Then he thought it again: *Damn.*

Wilkins probably hadn't thought she was asking very much from him. After all, a lot of war game maneuvers were plotted out *before* they were executed. But Conner hadn't done that—far from it. In fact, his Greens had been on the razor's edge of losing the game until he came up with a new approach on the fly.

Right from the start, Lucas had led his Reds as if they were a pack of hungry wolves. They had forced Conner's team to retreat not once but three times. They had gotten the Greens to split up into pockets of resistance, each one cut off from its comrades, and then they had eliminated the pockets one by one.

Of course, Conner should have recognized such an approach in advance. He had known that Lucas had to be first all the time, even if it was just on the line to get into the mess hall, and didn't care who he had to push out of his way. Hell, everyone knew that.

So it wasn't so hard to anticipate that that was how Lucas would command his forces. With aggression. And as a tactic, it had come close to working. The Greens were down to five cadets, hounded as a group by Lucas's greater numbers, when it finally occurred to Conner to turn Lucas's aggressiveness against him.

It had been no more complicated than that. *Just turn it against him.* That was what Conner had told himself.

How could the Greens do that? For the most part, by continuing to do what they were doing already— retreating. That was the trap. But to spring it, one of the Greens would have to get behind the Reds and pick them off from the rear.

Because once you're behind somebody, the advantage is all yours.

But it was easier said than done. Lucas's cadets had been smart enough to fan out from one side of the valley to the other. The Greens would find it hard as hell to sneak around them.

That was why Conner had decided he wouldn't take that route.

He would have gone *above* them, except there weren't more than a couple of trees in the area, and the ones that existed weren't sturdy enough to hold his weight—and even if he had been lucky enough to find one that could, it wouldn't have had enough foliage to hide him from sight.

Forced to discard the options of going around or over Lucas's cadets, Conner pursued the only other course of action open to him: going under them.

The idea had sounded dumb at first, even to Conner. The Greens didn't have time to stop and dig a hole—not with the Reds just a few minutes behind them. But there were holes that had been dug long before the exercise started if one knew where to look.

And Conner knew.

After all, he had been obsessed with the planet's animal life since he was a little kid. If it ran, crawled, climbed, flew, or swam, he had long ago become an expert on it. And what kind of expert wouldn't have known that kangaroo rats dig deep, far-ranging burrows underground?

Back on Earth, before the ships took off with genetic samples of every creature that could be collected, kangaroo rats had been small—about a foot long, including the tail. But on Nova Prime, with the help of geneticists, they were bigger and stronger. Conner was grateful for the change. Without it, he might never have been able to find a burrow when he needed one. After collapsing it with a few stabs of a fallen branch, he had concealed himself with a few heaping handfuls of dirt and debris while the other Greens continued to retreat.

There was a tense moment when Lucas's cadets

marched through, their eyes trained ahead when they would have done much better at that point if they had looked down. One of them came within a meter of Conner, nearly stepping on his hand.

Then they were gone, and he was free to go after them one at a time. With a little luck, he had thought at the time, he could get a few of them before they caught on to what he was doing. As it turned out, he had *more* than a little luck.

He had enough to even the odds before Lucas or any of the other Reds realized what he was doing. And by that time, it was too late for them. Their opponents doubled back suddenly, surprising them, and Conner continued to harass them from behind.

But to break it down on paper, move by move? It wouldn't have any meaning. After all, it wasn't the *moves* that had won the day for the Greens. It was the way they were executed.

How do you chart that? Conner thought. If anything, it was Lucas's strategy the Prime Commander should have asked for. Now, that was something Conner could chart—and wouldn't mind doing so now that he had managed to find a way around it. He sat back in his chair and massaged the bridge of his nose with his thumb and forefinger.

In a few hours, his fellow cadets would be enjoying a day off. Blodge had said he was going to spend it hiking in the mountains, with his girlfriend, no doubt. Gold had signed up to go hang gliding. Mphalele had tickets for a concert in Chen Valley . . .

Conner stopped that train of thought. Only officers made up battle plans. If Wilkins had asked what she'd asked, she must have thought Conner was officer material. He wondered what his uncle Torrance would say to that. He wondered what his aunt Bonita would say. And his father . . .

Frank Raige had never told his son he had to become a Ranger. But the day Conner had signed up, he had seen his father smile as he'd never smiled before. His father had never said he was proud because that wasn't his way.

But he *had* been proud.

In the days and weeks that followed, Conner hadn't given his father or anyone else a lot to be proud about. He'd shown up at the wrong places at the wrong times. He'd overslept a morning drill. He'd even gotten into a fight with another cadet over something so trivial that he couldn't remember what it was.

So if Conner had to sacrifice a little sleep or forgo a day off, he would do that. He would do whatever it took to make his family proud of him. Even if it didn't make the least bit of sense to him.

With a sigh, he started typing. *If I don't stop to eat anything*, he thought, *I might be finished by noon, after all.*

CHAPTER THREE

Trey Vander Meer cleared his throat and signaled to his engineer. Then he spoke, basking in the sound of his honey-smooth voice as it filled the broadcast studio.

"Hello, Nova Prime. This is Trey Vander Meer, looking out for your interests when no one else will. Today's conversation is about the semiannual Ranger cadet training exercise known as the war games.

"In case you didn't know, the first round of games are over—though there will be another round, a punishment of sorts. Either way, who cares, right? What does a Ranger exercise have to do with you and me? Quite a bit, actually. You see, with the first of the war games behind us, we're one step closer to minting a whole new class of Rangers, swelling the ranks of what is undeniably the most bloated organization on the planet. That's right, you heard me—bloated, as in swollen. Puffed up. Bigger than necessary.

"Friends, we didn't need the Rangers we had already. Now we're on our way to having even more of them thanks to a rather costly set of exercises. In fact, only the Rangers' Prime Commander Wilkins knows exactly how costly because she's not sharing that information with you and me—the people who happen to pay her salary in case any of you may have forgotten.

"But this, as they used to say back on Earth before the Exodus, is only the tip of the iceberg. The Rangers consume a tremendous amount of our colony's resources to manufacture weapons, maintain barracks, produce and clean uniforms, keep their aircraft aloft, and so on. They also operate an increasingly sophisticated command center that we seem to be rebuilding—excuse me, *upgrading*—every few years. Our valuable resources would be better spent addressing the problems caused by the drought, from which we're still recovering in so many ways.

"I know the Skrel are out there somewhere in the vastness of the universe. I know they gave us some good licks when they showed up before—and if you've listened to this program in the past, you know that no one honors the casualties of those attacks more than I do. But for the last couple of hundred years we have strengthened our defenses against airborne threats. We have honed our F.E.N.I.X. tech. We have what seems like a million satellites scanning the stars. In my opinion, these are all good and proper uses of what we have. But honestly, can anyone out there even begin to tell me why we need so many Rangers?

"I don't want to hear that we're worried about the Skrel. They got their noses bloodied twice; they'd be crazy to come after us a third time. And our unmanned probes—one every week, it seems—haven't turned up any evidence of other intelligent life. So why do we keep pouring credits into the Rangers? Why do we need to build faster and faster aircraft? It may appear that our resources here on Nova Prime are unlimited, but I assure you that they're not.

"I don't have to remind you that we already ruined *one* world by mismanaging her ecosystem, by raiding her pantry until it was bare. We cannot afford to let that happen again. We as a species cannot do to Nova Prime what we did to Earth. I, for one, will not permit it.

"As a society, we need to have this dialogue, my friends. We need to reexamine our priorities. The Prime Commander must listen to the will of the people for a change rather than the will of the military yes men with whom she surrounds herself. She may think we'll stop asking for this, but we won't. We'll keep asking until we put our colony back on the forward-looking track it deserves.

"Think about it, Nova Prime. I know I will."

The red light on the wall in front of him flickered off, and Vander Meer sat back in his chair. Ken Pham, the show's producer, came out from behind his control panel and sat down beside the radio host, who dabbed at the sweat on his brow with one of the blue polka-dot handkerchiefs he'd gotten as a birthday present from his wife.

"Nice job," Pham said. "You nailed it on the first take."

"Don't I always?" asked Vander Meer.

"Actually, no."

Vander Meer chuckled. "Well, then, *almost* always. The show will hit at the usual time?"

"Right on schedule," Pham assured him.

"No editing?" Vander Meer had been displeased in the past when Pham or some other producer took liberties by omitting some of his material.

"Not today," said Pham.

"I am agog," Vander Meer said.

He unfolded himself from his chair. He had always been tall and reasonably slender, but lately he had developed a paunch that he blamed on weak stomach muscles. The truth was that he liked to eat, particularly in the colony's finer restaurants, but didn't like to exercise a great deal. And it wasn't only his middle that was giving way. His hair had started to thin as well, spurring him lately to massage in ointments to stimulate follicle growth. Still, it was a race to see which would win out: the advance of his regrowing hair or the recession of his natural hairline.

Vander Meer hated aging. He hated looking at the jowls he had to shave each morning. He hated the constant reminders from his family to stop at seconds, not thirds at dinner. He would have given anything to have the metabolism he had enjoyed when he'd first begun broadcasting twenty years earlier.

It was then that he had made a name for himself as a journalist, covering the secession battle between Nova Prime City and New Earth City. That was back in 553 AE. His reportage on the conflict gained colony-wide attention, and he rose through the ranks until he was finally invited to become a commentator, for which he used his field experience to reflect on social trends. But one trend in particular had caught his eye.

Over the years, Vander Meer had noticed how cavalierly the Rangers conducted their business not only before the secession fight but afterward. He had seen how they took their funding for granted, as if they were entitled to it by virtue of the work they had done in the distant past.

The Rangers irked him for reasons he couldn't even explain—maybe because he once had wanted to be a Ranger himself but never had gotten to the point where he was physically fit enough. But more and more, judiciously so that he wasn't simply dismissed as a crank, he had ramped up his criticism of the Corps and its place in society until he could lambaste them as he had today. *Let's see what they have to say about Trey Vander Meer now,* he thought.

The show over, Pham got up and touched several pressure-sensitive controls on the studio wall. At the same time, the lighting dimmed and systems switched over to standby.

"You know what I'd like to do?" asked Vander Meer, toying with a thought.

"What's that?" asked Pham.

"Get Wilkins on the program with me. People would tune in then; I can tell you that."

Pham considered the idea for a moment. Then he said, "I'll see what I can do."

"Excellent," Vander Meer said. "Let me know how it goes, will you?"

"Sure. And let *me* know if you hear about anything good to read." Pham held up an electronic tablet that he carried with him wherever he went. "Seems there's a dearth of good things to read these days."

"It's a deal," said Vander Meer. "Now, home for lunch. Family awaits."

Leaving the studio, he entered the hot, dry air that was the hallmark of Nova Prime. The survivors of a dying Earth had settled in this spot in the foothills of red-clay mountains because it offered protection from the weather and had rivers for the colony's water needs. There had been cooler areas on the planet's surface, but settling them would have meant cutting down trees or otherwise tampering with the planet's ecology, and that was something humankind would never do again.

So they had settled *this* area, and things had worked out rather well. Except for the heat, of course. And the dust. And the occasional severe thunderstorm.

Vander Meer's home was only a couple of kilometers from the studio in an exclusive, newly constructed enclave made up of just seven residential structures. Most of the better parts of Nova City were older, some dating back as far as the arrival on Nova Prime, and were tucked into the foothills of the mountains.

This one was the exception. But Vander Meer didn't mind. His neighbors were all doctors, teachers, or artists, and ideas seemed to flow freely and easily in their little pocket of the colony. He loved that about the place. After all, he was nothing if not an intellectual.

And yet, since he had begun inserting more controversy into his broadcasts, his neighbors had begun looking at him differently. Or rather, some of them had. Others agreed with him, of course. Those were the ones who shook his hand when he saw them, or slapped him on the back, or made encouraging remarks. He was striking a chord, no doubt. And if he could get Wilkins on the program, it would resonate even louder throughout the colony.

Still salivating over that possibility, Vander Meer arrived home. It was a modest structure in which he lived, the same red color as the desert and just big enough for him, his wife, and his three children—although he expected that it would feel larger when his oldest began classes in New Earth City in a few months' time. Maybe then there might be some peace under his roof.

"Did you do it?" his son Skipper asked as Vander Meer crossed the threshold. Skipper was only six, but he had absorbed his father's antipathy for the Rangers.

"Do what?" asked Vander Meer as he picked the boy up in his arms. "Take the Rangers down a peg?"

"Tear them apart, Dad. That's what you said you would do—tear them apart!"

Vander Meer smiled. "I didn't *say* I would tear them apart, son."

"Yes, you did," said Vander Meer's older son, Michael, who had shown up in the hallway behind Skipper. "That's *exactly* what you said."

Michael, who was eighteen, had enjoyed a growth spurt lately and was now even taller than his father, a fact that made Vander Meer uncomfortable, especially since they often took opposite sides of an argument. For instance, Michael didn't think the Rangers should have their budget pared down. He thought they still served an important purpose in the colony. The conflict between father and oldest child had made life at home increasingly difficult. Fortunately, Skipper was there to balance things out.

"Okay," the boy said impatiently, tugging on Vander Meer's shirtfront, "so what did you say in your broadcast?"

"That the Rangers are a burden we should no longer have to bear," Vander Meer said, looking at Michael.

The teenager rolled his eyes. "Great. I can't believe you're my father."

"Michael's fighting with Dad again," Skipper called into the kitchen, where his mother was preparing lunch.

"We're not fighting," Vander Meer said, putting Skipper down on the floor. "We're just talking."

He watched Michael retreat to the family room, where the boy plunked himself down on the couch and activated a holographic game. He wore his light brown hair long and pulled back in a braid that was held together with a decorative clasp carved from stone. He also had taken to sporting a shamrock-shaped ear cuff made of a metallic alloy in accordance with the latest Celtic fashion.

Was I ever like that? Vander Meer asked himself. He didn't think so.

Moving on, he entered the kitchen, where his wife was tossing a salad. He moved close to her, pushed aside a lock of blond hair, and whispered in her ear, "Save me, Natasha."

"Sorry," she said, "you're on your own."

Natasha, a good-looking woman for her age, was more than Vander Meer deserved, and he was the first to say so. He prayed she would never come to her senses.

"As usual," he said good-naturedly, and helped her bring lunch to the table.

Skipper pulled a chair out and sat down eagerly. Lunch was his favorite meal, after all. A moment later, Michael joined them.

Vander Meer noted that the table was set for four and wondered where his daughter might be. "Elena's at . . . ?" he asked.

"Dance," said his wife.

He remembered now. "Right. Dance."

Briefly, they said grace. Then Natasha doled out the gazpacho while Vander Meer sliced the bread and the boys took salad from the bowl in the middle of the table.

"So what does the afternoon hold for you?" Vander Meer asked his wife.

"I have to finish the quarterly review," she said.

"Do you have to go back to the office for that?" he asked.

"No," she said, "I can do it here at home." She buttered her bread, broke off a piece, and popped it into her mouth.

Skipper, by contrast, ripped a piece in half and slathered it with butter.

"There's more to the meal than bread," Vander Meer reminded the boy.

"Right, Dad," said Skipper, talking around the bread in his mouth.

Natasha concealed a smile behind her hand. Vander Meer saw it and shared it with her. Then, seeing that Michael was staring off into space, he asked, "What about you, Number One Son?"

Michael glanced up at him. "I need to finish picking up school supplies. Then I'm getting together with Olivia."

"Ah, the fair and enchanting Olivia," Vander Meer said with a smile.

"Even *she* agrees with Dad about the Rangers," Skipper said.

"She does not," said Michael, shooting a glance at his brother. "She doesn't even listen to him."

"That's a lie," Skipper said, his voice rising in both pitch and volume. "She told me she did."

"She was just being nice," said Michael.

"Funny," Vander Meer said. "I thought everyone listened to my commentaries."

"Actually, that's not the case," Natasha said.

Vander Meer pressed his hand to his chest as if he had been stabbed. "You, my dear, wound me."

"You, my dear," said his wife, "can get carried away sometimes. Remember, last year you took Flint to task for his water purification project."

"Didn't I make sense?" Vander Meer asked.

"Of course you did. And you got him to appoint a committee."

"Which I watched closely."

"Which approved the project."

"At least I kept Flint honest," Vander Meer said.

Natasha turned to Michael. "Skipping dinner or bringing her here?"

"Skipping," said Michael. He turned to his father, his face reddening. "And I'll keep on skipping till Dad realizes how wrong he is. The Rangers keep the peace. They have to stay state of the art. I don't understand your problem with them, I really don't."

Vander Meer let his son finish, desperate not to let this be another ruined meal. He wanted to respect Michael's point of view. *At least he has one,* he thought. Too often, Vander Meer felt, the younger generation was self-absorbed and apathetic. So he held his tongue and waited until Michael took a mouthful of soup.

Then he said, "When you can discuss this with me without our blood pressures rising, we'll talk."

Michael grunted. "Sure we will."

Vander Meer frowned. *Patience,* he thought. *He'll come around . . . eventually.*

Elias Hāturi barged into Meredith Wilkins's office and bellowed, "I want to get my hands around his neck! Just for a minute!"

The Prime Commander knew exactly what he was talking about. She had just finished listening to Vander Meer's commentary on the Rangers, in which he had pretty much challenged her to defend her position. It felt to her as if the temperature in the room had risen in the last few minutes. Forcing herself to remain calm, she turned off her monitor and leaned back in her chair. No doubt, other journalists would be calling to find out her reaction, and she wasn't entirely sure yet how she wanted to handle this.

"Well?" said Hāturi.

She held up a hand. "Calm down, Elias. There will be no strangling on my watch." She rose and walked over to a side table where a pitcher of cool water suddenly looked very inviting. "Besides," she said as she poured, "I want that privilege when the matter is settled."

"How can this be settled? You know what he's like.

He's done this before. He's just going to beat you up until he gets his way."

"Or he gets himself swatted," she said.

Hāturi slumped into a chair. "And how are we going to do that?"

Wilkins sat down again as well. "I have to think about it."

But she didn't have the luxury of thinking for long. The media wouldn't allow it. Times like these, she was thankful she never had married or had children. There were some burdens she felt more comfortable carrying alone.

An adjutant knocked politely on the door, which was still open.

"Come in," Wilkins said.

"Ma'am," said the adjutant, "there's a gentleman named Ken Pham outside to see you. He says he produces Trey Vander Meer's program."

Wilkins and Hāturi exchanged surprised glances. Then she said, "Send him in, please."

Pham entered in a freshly pressed suit with his shirt open at the collar. Wilkins had met him before, though she would be damned if she could remember the circumstances.

"How can I help you, Mr. Pham?"

"I need a good novel to read, to be honest," he said.

"That's a little beyond our purview," she said evenly.

"Did you happen to hear Mr. Vander Meer's commentary today?" Pham asked.

"Sure did. Come to collect my resignation?"

He chuckled politely, appearing unperturbed by the barb. "No, but I am here to ask about a follow-up."

"You want a rebuttal?"

"Sure, if you have one. But I'd prefer to invite you to appear on the show. Let's air both sides of the discussion and let the people make up their minds."

Wilkins paused to consider the offer. Rather than let Vander Meer beat the drums on this for days or weeks, a public discussion might actually bring the controversy to a quicker close, preferably with the Rangers coming out on top.

She considered the matter from all angles, trying to sniff out a trap. She couldn't find one. "When?"

"As soon as possible," said Pham. "What's your schedule look like?"

"I'm busy every moment of the day, seven days a week," she said. "After all, I'm the Prime Commander of the Rangers, and the Rangers have a lot to do, contrary to what you may have heard in your studio. But I'll do my best to make some time."

"That would be great," Pham said. "I'll wait to hear from you." And he left just as Wilkins's adjutant appeared at her door again.

"Yes?" she said.

"Sorry to bother you, ma'am, but Cadet Raige is here to see you. He says—"

The Prime Commander didn't let him finish. "Let him in."

A moment later, Conner Raige walked in with a tablet in his hand. He looked bleary-eyed. But then, he would have been up all night if he'd finished the task she set for him.

He handed her the tablet. "As you asked, ma'am."

She nodded. "Thank you, Cadet Raige. Get yourself some sleep. You look awful."

Raige nodded. "Yes, ma'am. Thank you, ma'am."

"And don't pay any attention to Trey Vander Meer," she said, though she was really just venting her frustration. "His latest commentary is decidedly *not* conducive to a good sleep."

The cadet looked at her, obviously lost. "Ma'am?"

"Never mind," she said. "Dismissed."

Wilkins waited until Raige was out of earshot. Then she picked up the tablet he had given her, considered it for a moment, and turned to Hāturi. "Well, Commander, it looks like it's *my* turn to draw up a battle plan."

CHAPTER FOUR

Conner hadn't known what the Prime Commander was talking about when she mentioned Trey Vander Meer. But he rectified that as soon as he returned to his barracks.

Wilkins was right. Vander Meer's commentary wasn't conducive to a good sleep at all, at least not if it was a Ranger who was listening to him. And, Conner discovered as he played the commentary on one of the data stations set up in the center of the barracks, Vander Meer had tacked on a bonus commentary for net viewers.

"Things change," he said in a honeyed voice laced with an unmistakable arrogance, "often without our realizing it. And when they do that, we have to change, too. We have to live in the present, my friends, not in the past.

"We used to try to cure illnesses by bleeding people with leeches. We don't do that anymore. We used to think it was all right to pollute Earth's atmosphere. We learned our lesson. Now we're spending a disproportionate amount of our colony's resources on the Rangers."

His teeth grinding, Conner forced himself to continue listening.

"Even though we haven't had a problem with the Skrel for hundreds of years, even though we have enough early-warning satellites to build our own moon, even though crime is at an all-time low. Need I go on?"

"Hey," said a familiar voice behind Conner's back, "shouldn't you be asleep?"

Conner turned and looked back at his pal Blodge. "And shouldn't you be hiking in the mountains?"

"I was. Then Julie twisted her ankle—nothing terrible but annoying enough for us to head back. What are you watching?"

Conner scowled. "Vander Meer."

Blodge chuckled sympathetically. "Right. That guy."

"I don't get it. How can anyone think the Rangers are obsolete?"

Blodge dismissed the question with a wave of his hand. "Don't listen to him, Conner. He's out of his mind."

"What if someone had decided the Rangers were obsolete before the *first* Skrel attack? Where would we be then?"

"He's just making noise, man."

"But people *listen* to his noise," said Conner. "They think he's got a point."

"Who cares what people think? It's not like there's anything we can do about it."

"We can speak up. Maybe that's not much, but it's something. We can make it clear to people the Rangers are still needed."

Blodge smiled. "Sure . . . if anybody asks us."

Unfortunately, Vander Meer's was the voice everybody wanted to listen to. Conner shook his head. Couldn't they see how dangerous his advice was?

He wondered what his dad thought of Vander Meer. He would make a point of asking him the next time they spoke, but he had a feeling he already knew. Frank Raige took pride in being a Ranger, in coming from a long line of Rangers.

He wouldn't have much use for a know-nothing loudmouth like Vander Meer.

Prime Commander Wilkins was usually the first of the colony's three leaders to attend their monthly tripartite meeting. This time, an unexpected demand for her attention made her the last one.

As she entered the conference room, she saw Primus Leonard Rostropovich and Savant Donovan Flint sit up abruptly in their chairs. People did that when they'd been caught at something, she noted.

"Starting a conspiracy?" she asked.

Flint, a slender man with thinning blond hair and an even blonder mustache, laughed, albeit a little nervously. "You caught us, Commander. We were going to scheme behind your back to redesign those rusty brown uniforms you Rangers insist on wearing."

"They're a tradition," Wilkins said. "The first Rangers to set foot on Nova Prime wore them, and we'll keep on wearing them as long as there are Rangers. But that's not what you two were whispering about."

The Primus, an austere individual with a sharp widow's peak and a prominent hawklike nose, sighed. "Very well. We were trying to spare your feelings, but if you insist." He smoothed the front of his brocaded brown robe, a fancier version of what his augurs wore. "You've heard Trey Vander Meer's latest broadcast?"

Wilkins stiffened. "I have. And I'm addressing it."

"In what way, if I may ask?" said the Primus.

"I'm appearing on his program to . . . discuss it with him."

Rostropovich frowned. "Not the tack I would have taken."

"I meet problems head-on," said the Prime Commander. "I am, after all, a Ranger."

The Savant and the Primus exchanged glances. "But you're not just a Ranger," Flint said. "You're also a member of this world's governing body. So whatever you do as chief of the Rangers reflects on our offices as well."

"And you think I'll reflect on us poorly?" Wilkins asked.

"To be blunt," said the Primus, "and I know you would want us to be so, you have already done so."

"By accepting his invitation?" asked the Prime Commander.

Rostropovich nodded. "Precisely."

"All I want to do is present the facts," Wilkins said. "That'll end his little rant once and for all."

"I think you underestimate Mr. Vander Meer," the Primus said. "He's become quite the popular commentator. His rhetoric may leave something to be desired, I'll grant you that. But he does seem to tap into what's on people's minds."

"And if he twists your words just right," said Flint, "we could be facing a bigger problem than we had before."

"Quite a bit of confidence you've got in me," Wilkins said. "I'm flattered."

"You're on Vander Meer's turf," Flint reminded her. "He knows it better than you do. As a strategist, you know how much of an advantage that gives him."

The Prime Commander scowled. "What would you have me do? Not show up? That won't look very good, either."

"That's what we were talking about," said the Primus. Again, she saw the exchange of glances. "It would be more difficult for Vander Meer to come out on top if all three of us were to attend his program."

"All three . . . ?" Wilkins said.

Flint leaned forward in his chair. "It'll be a lot harder to make you look like a wastrel if we all weigh in on the Rangers. You know, talk about how valuable they've been over the years."

The Prime Commander hesitated. Flint had a point. And although her ego told her that she could—and should—handle Vander Meer on her own, it wasn't about her. It was about the Rangers.

"You see the value of what we're proposing?" asked the Primus.

Wilkins nodded. "Thank you."

"No need," Rostropovich said. "I'm certain that you would do the same for me were our positions reversed."

The Prime Commander wasn't so sure about that. Nonetheless she said, "Naturally."

Conner had just come back from a five-klik run with Red Squad. Cheng was back in the leader's position, showing him that Wilkins hadn't completely changed her mind about him yet. He heard Lucas Kincaid having a heated discussion with Danny Gold. Gold, a tall, thin fellow, was one of the few cadets besides Blodge who hung out with Conner now and then, and so Conner felt himself on Gold's side even before he knew what the conversation was about.

"Really?" Lucas said. "Name one."

"There's the black market," Gold said.

"Right. And is that why you signed up to be a Ranger? So you could bust a bunch of kids?"

"Of course not," Gold said. "But—"

"But that's what you would be doing," said Lucas, doing what he always did—going for the jugular—on the battlefield or anywhere. "The guys who run those warehouses are no older than your little sister."

"What they're doing is illegal."

"So stop them. But do they need Rangers to do it? That's the question."

"What about aliens?" asked Gold.

Lucas turned to him. "What about them?"

"We were attacked once. It can happen again."

"Come on," he said. "You know how long it's been since the Skrel showed up here?"

That was when Conner figured out what they were talking about. It was like listening to Vander Meer all over again.

"I don't know," Gold said.

Lucas laughed. "Well, I know. It's been over three hundred years. That's before your great-great-great-grandfather was born. And not a sign of them, not even a comm bleep. You seriously think we'll ever see those buggers again?"

Gold shrugged his bony shoulders. "We might."

"We might also grow wings and fly to a moon. But we won't. We've seen the last of the Skrel—you can bet your last credit on it."

Finally, Conner couldn't take it anymore. "You sound like Vander Meer," he called out, his voice ringing throughout the barracks.

In its wake, there was silence. Then Lucas turned to him and said, "What?"

"You heard me," Conner said.

Lucas walked over, his boot heels clacking on the barracks' wooden floor, until he was looking down at Conner. "First of all," he said, "I wasn't talking to you. Second, I don't appreciate being compared to a muckraker like Vander Meer."

Conner looked up. "Then don't spout the kind of garbage Vander Meer spouts. That talk about not seeing the Skrel for hundreds of years—what is that? You think we're safe here? You think Nova Prime doesn't need the Rangers anymore?"

Lucas bent down, planted his hands on his knees, and smiled an oily smile. "I'll tell you what, Raige. When I want your input, I'll ask for it. Till then, shut your mouth."

Conner felt his face grow hot as he returned Lucas's scrutiny. "Or what?"

"Or I'll shut it for you. Understand?"

Suddenly Conner was on his feet, a clump of Lucas's uniform in each fist, shoving the other cadet backward step by step. Lucas slammed into the bunk behind him—hard. Then he recovered and shoved Conner back.

"You want a piece of me?" Lucas snarled between clenched teeth. "Any time, Raige! Any time and any place!"

"How about here and now?" Conner asked.

Before he knew it, Lucas had accepted his invitation

by taking a swing at him. Conner was ready for it. He knew it was coming. But Lucas was so fast, he still got in a glancing blow to Conner's jaw. It stunned him for a moment. But it was just one shot. Conner wasn't going to go down so easy.

As Lucas tried to follow his first punch with another one, Conner ducked out of harm's way. Then he hit Lucas with an uppercut that snapped his head back. Stunned, Lucas couldn't avoid Conner's next blow or the one after that. Lucas reeled backward, looking helpless. Conner went after him, all his frustration and self-doubt coming to a boil.

Maybe he wasn't the best Ranger candidate who had ever come down the road. Maybe he wasn't what everybody had expected from a Raige. Maybe he'd find he wasn't even Ranger material. But he was better than Lucas Kincaid and his stupid traitorous remarks, and he was going to prove it once and for all. One more punch would do it.

But as Conner threw it, his target disappeared. Without an impact to stop Conner's momentum, it carried him forward, leaving him defenseless against the left hook that hit him in the side of the head and sent him staggering or the right hand that rattled his jaw, flooding his mouth with the metallic taste of blood. He got his hands up and retreated a couple of steps and would have retreated one more if he hadn't felt a bunk behind him. Almost too late, he saw Lucas go for him with another right.

He twisted to avoid it and then got in a shot underneath Lucas's eye. It seemed to blind Lucas for a moment, which was all the opening Conner needed. Putting everything he had behind his next punch, he sent Lucas sprawling. Before Lucas could get up, Conner was on top of him, pinning him to the floor with his knees.

He pulled his fist back, aiming to end the fight then and there. But before he could do so, he felt someone clamp on to his wrist.

Who?! he thought. Which one of his fellow cadets?

But it wasn't a cadet, he realized. It was Tariq Lennon, the swarthy, square-jawed officer in charge of cadet training.

"Atten-shun!" someone bellowed.

As one, the cadets stiffened to attention, hands at their sides. Conner and Lucas, still facing each other, dropped their fists and did the same.

Without a word, he looked the combatants up and down. There was quite a bit of blood on them, and he didn't seem to miss any of it.

"Well, now," he said at last, "here's something interesting. I thought I heard a commotion in here. But when I walk over to check it out, there's no commotion at all. Just you two standing here, looking at each other like the best of buddies.

"Which would be fine, except you're *not* the best of buddies. So I find myself wondering what kind of comradely impulse made Cadet Kincaid here feel compelled to pay Cadet Raige a visit."

"Nothing, sir," Conner said.

"Just passing by, sir," said Lucas.

Lennon smiled. "Just passing by. Of course. No problem?"

Kincaid glared at Conner. "None, sir."

"No problem at all, sir," Conner said.

"I see," said Lennon. "And yet you two seem to have pounded each other half to death. So there must be a problem." He turned to Conner. "Cadet Raige?"

Conner couldn't fail to answer a question directed right at him. He thrust his chin at Kincaid. "The cadet here was repeating that Vander Meer crap about the colony investing too much in the Rangers."

"Really," Lennon said. He looked at Kincaid. "Is this true?"

The muscles fluttered in Kincaid's jaw. "It is, sir."

Lennon turned to Conner again. "Well, Cadet Raige, it just so happens *I* agree with Trey Vander Meer, too."

What?! thought Conner, feeling as if the world had been pulled out from under him. Lennon was a commanding officer in the Rangers. How could he side with that loudmouth on the radio?

"I don't see how," he said.

He hadn't meant to say it. It just came out.

"I beg your pardon?" Lennon said, moving closer to Conner until their noses were almost touching.

Conner had a choice. He could take back what he had said and pacify his commanding officer. That would be the wise choice; no question about it. Or he could go the other way, which was the path he found himself taking.

"What I said, sir," he replied evenly, "was that I don't see how."

Lennon's eyes narrowed to slits. "You don't see how I could agree with Trey Vander Meer?"

Conner steeled himself. "Yes, sir."

"And why is that?"

There was no going back now. "Because he's the enemy of everything the Rangers stand for, sir."

"The Rangers," Lennon said, "don't have any enemies in this colony, Cadet Raige. We're all in this together. The sooner you get that through your head, the better."

Conner bit his lip. He knew how dumb it would be to disagree with Lennon, how abysmally stupid. He did it anyway.

"Sir," he said, "the Rangers do have enemies, people who would like to see the Corps whittled down to nothing because they believe it doesn't serve a purpose anymore. And Trey Vander Meer is one of them."

Lennon's eyes widened. "That's your opinion? Because I'm pretty sure cadets haven't earned the *right* to have opinions. You're a cadet, aren't you?"

"Yes, sir," Conner answered.

"You haven't been promoted without my knowing it?"

"No, sir."

"But you do want to be promoted someday, don't you? Before you're too old to pick up a real pulser?"

"I do, sir."

"Then you'll keep your *opinions* to yourself. Do you

understand? Or do I need to be Trey Vander Meer to get your attention?"

"Yes, sir," Conner said. "No, sir."

Lennon glared at him a moment longer, a reminder of who was in charge. Then he turned and left Conner and Lucas standing there.

It was clear to Conner that Lucas wanted to go at it again, maybe as much as Conner himself did. But after what Lennon had said, that wasn't going to happen.

With a curl of his lip, Lucas walked away. A bunch of cadets went with him. After all, Lucas—unlike Conner—had been a model cadet from the time he had arrived in the barracks; that was why he'd been named leader of Red Squad. People gravitated toward a leader.

The only cadet who came over to Conner was Blodge. "Nice going," he said, apparently without irony.

"Nice?" Conner echoed. He sat down and let his head fall into his bloody-knuckled hands. "I'm such an idiot."

"No," Blodge said, sitting down beside him, "you're not. You stood up for what you believed."

"To my commanding officer!"

"Maybe he'll respect you for it."

Conner shook his head. "Did you see the look on his face? That wasn't respect. Anger, maybe. Disgust. But definitely not respect."

"Listen," Blodge said, "whatever it was, he'll forget about it. He didn't get to be the officer in charge of cadets by holding grudges against them."

Conner glanced at him. "How do you know that?"

Blodge reddened. "I just . . . I mean . . . all right, I don't. But it makes sense, doesn't it? He would have to be an evenhanded guy for him to rise that high in the Rangers."

It did make sense. But that didn't mean it was true.

Conner sighed. He finally had made some headway with Wilkins. He finally had begun to distinguish himself the way a Raige would be expected to. And now . . . this.

"Thanks for trying to cheer me up," he told his friend. *Even if it's not working very well.*

"Hey," said Blodge, "what are friends for?"

As he crossed the barracks to return to his bunk, Conner heard a roll of laughter. He traced it to Lucas and a half dozen cadets who'd gathered around him.

They're laughing at me, Conner thought.

The funny thing—the *really* funny thing—was that he and Lucas had been friends at one time. In fact, when they were five or six, they were best friends— even pricked their fingers so they could become blood brothers. No one had told them that the Raiges and the Kincaids hadn't traditionally gotten along. Not even Conner's dad, who was otherwise big on history lessons. No one had said, "Hey, Conner, stay away from that kid. His ancestors have been our rivals for the last six hundred years."

So Conner looked for Lucas whenever he went to the playground near his house, and Lucas looked for him, and they shared many an adventure together in the jumble of red rocks nearby. More often than not, they pretended that they had crash-landed on an alien world and had to survive in its hostile environment until help came.

They played cageball. They played football. They decided that Conner was better at one and Lucas at the other, though Conner couldn't remember anymore who was better at what. Then, like a lot of kids, they drifted apart. Conner wasn't even sure when it happened. He just found himself playing with new friends and saw that Lucas was doing the same, and before Conner knew it they were like strangers.

Those who knew them in those days assumed their family histories finally had come between them. But that wasn't the reason Conner and Lucas stopped being pals. In fact, Conner hadn't even known about their families' rivalry at the time.

Anyway, when Conner was eleven, Lucas and his family moved to a house on the other side of the colony, and Conner didn't see much of him after that. Or, given the way kids' faces change as they mature, maybe he had seen Lucas after all and didn't know it. He didn't even recognize Lucas on their first day of cadet training, not until the roll was called and Lucas's name came up. At that point, Conner wasn't harboring any ill will toward Lucas. Just a certain curiosity.

But ill will had entered the equation pretty quickly. And Conner couldn't imagine it going away anytime soon.

Contrary to what people liked to say, Frank Raige wasn't always on duty. Sometimes he was lounging, watching a replay of the scholastic football championship from the night before.

Not that he was as rabid a fan as his sister-in-law Bonita. She was what he called "off the charts." But like anyone else, he sometimes liked to just relax.

He was just watching the first half of the game come to a close when the comm unit beeped. He answered the way he always did, on the job or off: "Raige."

"It's Meredith," said the voice on the other end.

Even in her most casual moments, the Prime Commander didn't give away her feelings. Sometimes that was a good thing. At the moment, Frank had a feeling she was calling about Conner again; it could only be bad. After all, Wilkins had already said that Conner had turned the corner. The news couldn't get any better than that.

But it could get worse. "What is it?" he asked more abruptly than he had intended.

"I'm calling about Conner. I wish it was good news, but it's not."

Frank's heart sank in his chest. "What happened?"

"He got into a fight with Lucas Kincaid. They'd had words before, but this time it blossomed into a knock-down-drag-out. Or rather, it would have been if Tariq Lennon hadn't broken it up."

Frank saw Rebecca come into the room, a smile on her face. It vanished as soon as she looked at him.

"I don't suppose there's any chance Kincaid started it?" he asked. It was as close as he would let himself come to giving his son the benefit of the doubt.

"Not from what Lennon said. Apparently, Conner accused Kincaid of parroting Trey Vander Meer." Wilkins sighed. "Can't say I blame him for being sensitive to Vander Meer's vitriol."

Frank couldn't, either. Vander Meer's unrelenting criticism of the Rangers had him on edge as well.

"But that's no excuse for fighting with his fellow cadet," he said. "Especially a Kincaid."

The Raiges and the Kincaids had been rivals since before humanity had landed on Nova Prime. Sometimes that had brought out the best in both families. Other times it had brought out the worst. When that happened, it created cracks in the Corps. But this was no time to let those cracks turn into schisms. The Rangers had to present a united front if they were going to weather the storm of public opinion sweeping across the colony.

"Do you want me to talk to him?" Wilkins asked.

Frank considered it for a moment but *only* for a moment. "Nobody ever became a good Ranger by receiving special treatment. He's going to have to figure things out on his own."

"That's my take on it as well. I just wanted to make sure we were on the same page."

"Thanks for calling," he said.

"Sure thing, Frank."

Only after he put the phone down did Rebecca say, "What?"

"You're not going to like it," he said.

CHAPTER FIVE

"So you're okay?" asked Lyla Kincaid.

Her brother nodded on the other end of the vid connection, his face looking like he'd volunteered it for pulser practice three days in a row. "I'm fine."

"Was it really Conner Raige? Didn't you two used to be friends?"

He shot her a dark glance. "*Used* to be."

"Right. But not anymore, I guess."

"Not anymore."

"So what did you fight about?"

He shrugged. "Nothing."

"Makes sense," Lyla said. "Good thing it wasn't about something. Who knows what would have happened then."

What a creep, she thought. Were she and Lucas really related? It was hard to believe sometimes.

Despite her concerned-sister questions, he'd said nothing at all. And unless she prompted him, he wouldn't ask a thing about *her* work. No "How's it going?" No "Any progress?" No indication that he even *knew* what she was working on. The only work he cared about was his own. That was the way it had been since the day he became a cadet. No, even before that.

My training. How often had she heard that phrase? As if no one else could make a valuable contribution to civilization. As if the only people who had ever done anything worthwhile in the entire history of Nova Prime were the damned Rangers.

Well, the Savant's corps of engineers had made some pretty sizable contributions, too. Not that she needed her brother to start reeling them off. It would just have been good if once—*once*—he could have said, "How's that hearing device going? Are you having any luck? Or are you pouring your heart and soul into it just for the hell of it?"

"Well," she said, "take care of yourself, all right?"

"Sure," he said, and terminated the connection.

Lyla let out an exasperated sigh. *Such a creep.*

Conner didn't often find himself in a place like O'Hara Street. He knew a couple of things about it, though. One was that it was named after a former Prime Commander of the Rangers who had presided over a difficult time in the colony's history. The other was that it was a busy thoroughfare, probably the busiest in Nova City, full of restaurants and shops and such.

Conner preferred open spaces, places where he could hear the wind if he listened closely enough, places where he could feel the rhythms of the planet and all the different forms of life that humanity had brought to it. But Blodge had wanted to visit O'Hara Street, and he had asked Conner to go with him. So there they were, navigating their way through the flow of colonists in either direction.

"You've got to love this place," Blodge said.

"Absolutely," Conner said, trying to work up some enthusiasm.

"The sounds, the smells . . ."

"All of that."

"I'm in the mood for crab balls. You?"

"Sure," said Conner, who was actually quite partial to crab balls. "I, uh, didn't know they have them here."

"Pal, they have *everything* here."

Suddenly, a couple of kids slid past them on colorfully decorated gyro boards, one of them bumping Conner's arm as he went by. Conner's first impulse was to turn and shout something at the offender, but he restrained himself. He had been that age himself not so long ago.

When had he become such a curmudgeon?

"Hey, Con," Blodge said.

He had stopped in front of a jewelry store. The necklaces in its window, made of rare colorful stones found in deep mountain caves, glittered wildly in the afternoon sunlight.

"Jewelry's good," said Blodge, who had brought him to O'Hara Street. "Don't you think?"

"For what?" Conner asked.

"For Julie."

"Your girlfriend?"

"You know another Julie?"

"Well . . . no."

"So that's the one." Blodge jerked a thumb over his shoulder. "Jewelry?"

Conner shrugged. "Why not?"

"All right, then." Blodge turned back to the items in the window. "A necklace, you think?"

Conner wanted to be helpful. "How long have you been going out? A year?"

"Almost two years. Where have *you* been?"

"Two? Really?"

"Really. So . . . a necklace? Or maybe something more serious?"

Conner wanted to give his friend good advice. The problem was that he was ill equipped to do so. "I may not be the best person to ask."

"Why?" asked Blodge. "Because you've never gone out with a girl for more than . . . what? A couple of months?"

"Well, yeah."

"But you've gone out with a whole lot of different girls, right? You must have learned something about them."

Conner frowned. What had he learned? Nothing he could articulate.

"Okay, then," Blodge said. He glanced at the jewelry display. "A necklace. But a really nice one."

Conner felt relieved.

"Come on," said Blodge, taking hold of his friend's arm and pulling him up the steps. "You can help me pick it out."

"Right," Conner said, wishing he were somewhere else but determined not to let his friend know that.

He was halfway up the steps when he heard a cheer. Glancing back over his shoulder to see where it had come from, he noticed a knot of people—fifteen or twenty of them—that had gathered in the street. Conner wondered why and stopped to see. Again he heard the roar.

"What is it?" asked Blodge, looking back at him.

"That," said Conner, pointing.

"It's just a bunch of people."

But something about it made Conner want to know why they had gathered. "Come on," he told Blodge, making his way back down the steps.

"Sure," said his friend, allowing Conner to pull him along. "Why not?"

As they got closer, Conner saw that someone was standing in the middle of the crowd. Someone tall, with a thatch of pale yellow hair. Someone who looked painfully familiar.

Trey Vander Meer, he thought.

"Hey," Blodge said, "that's—"

"I know," Conner said.

"Why do we continue to support the Rangers?" Vander Meer asked the crowd. "In this day and age, what's the point?"

It had been hard for Conner to tolerate Vander Meer's garbage when he'd heard it on a computer. Hearing it in person made it twice as hard.

"Come on," Blodge said, tugging at Conner's sleeve. "He's just going to tick you off. Let's go."

But Conner wouldn't budge.

"The answer I've come up with," Vander Meer said,

"is that they've always been around. We've gotten used to them, like a pair of old shoes. We may not need them anymore. We may have lots of other places to put our resources where they'll do more good. But out of habit, we keep them around."

Conner felt his teeth grind.

"Con?" said Blodge, tugging harder.

Conner ignored him.

"Do we need someone to say that's wrong?" asked Vander Meer. "Well, friends, I'll say it. I'll shout it from the rooftops. The Rangers are obsolete. They're a waste of credits. And the sooner we accept that, the better off we'll be."

Conner couldn't stand there anymore and let Vander Meer's rhetoric go unchallenged. He had to say something.

What he said, loudly enough for everyone to hear, was, "You're wrong!"

That drew everyone's attention.

"We're not obsolete, and we're not a waste of credits," Conner continued. He moved across the street. "We're as necessary now as we were the day the Skrel attacked, when the Rangers were all that stood between the colony and annihilation."

Vander Meer looked back over his shoulder and smiled. "Ah, one of our men in uniform." He turned to Conner. "Happy to make your acquaintance, Cadet . . ." He leaned in to peer at the name on Conner's uniform. "Ah, Cadet Raige. I believe I know that name."

"It doesn't matter what my name is," Conner said. "All that matters is that you're plowing this world under with your garbage."

"My garbage!" Vander Meer echoed. "That's some strong language, Cadet Raige. What exactly is your objection to my speaking my mind? Don't you believe in free speech?"

Conner saw what the older man was doing. "This isn't about what I believe. It's about the safety of Nova Prime. Without the Rangers, there is no safety."

"History shows otherwise," Vander Meer said. He looked around, playing to the crowd. "We haven't had an incident in hundreds of years—or did I miss something?"

People laughed.

"And when we do have an incident, as you call it?" Conner asked. "Are we going to start the Rangers up from scratch? You think whoever attacks us will give us time to do that?"

"You look like a smart kid," said Vander Meer. "Why don't you go back to your bunk and apply some of that math you learned in school. Take the Rangers in your Corps—the ones who aren't doing a whole heck of a lot for us, which is pretty much all of them—and multiply that number by a hundred and twenty thousand credits, which is what it costs us to maintain each of them for a year." He turned to the crowd. "A hundred and twenty thousand credits, my friends, at a time when many of us are still reeling from the drought and its attendant supply shortages. A hundred and twenty thousand credits for each and every Ranger. And for what?"

"For peace of mind," Conner said, interrupting him. "For the security of knowing we'll be ready if a threat does materialize. For insurance that no matter what, Nova Prime will be as safe a place for your children as it was for you and me."

As Conner spoke, he saw people begin to nod. At the same time, Vander Meer's expression changed. His eyes lost their humorous glint, and his mouth became a thin, hard line.

But only for a moment. Then he seemed to remember where he was, and his smile came back as big as before.

"You're quite the phrase turner," he told Conner. "But the truth is that the Rangers are an anachronism, a relic of times past. We need them about as much as we need quill pens, or eyeglasses, or gasoline-powered transports."

"That's your truth," Conner said. "Not mine. And

not theirs." With a sweep of his arm, he included those who had gathered around them. "We know better."

"You think you do," Vander Meer said. "But hey, by all means go on deluding yourself. Some of us have something to accomplish today—as you'll come to understand if you tune in to my program in less than an hour." And with a loud chuckle, he walked off.

With that, the crowd began to dissipate. But not before a few of the onlookers cast appreciative looks in Conner's direction.

"Wow," Blodge said, genuine admiration in his voice, "you really told him off."

Conner smiled to himself. "I did, didn't I?"

"Without a doubt. I'm proud of you, Con. Now, that necklace . . . ?"

Conner felt so good about himself that he didn't even mind following his friend into the jewelry shop.

Cecilia Ruiz had been on her way to the jewelry store on O'Hara Street when she saw the crowd gather in the middle of the road.

It took her a moment to realize that the focus of the crowd was Trey Vander Meer, the news commentator. She didn't have much time to listen to the media, but everyone knew Vander Meer.

Even if not everyone necessarily agreed with him.

Come on, she thought. *You came here for a reason.*

But it was hard not to be drawn into the crowd, hard not to pay closer attention to what the man was saying. Of course, she didn't like the idea of the Rangers getting downsized. Not at all.

So say something, she thought.

But she had enough on her plate without getting involved with a damned celebrity. Besides, she wasn't much of a public speaker. She would probably just make a fool of herself.

And there was the jewelry store standing there, waiting for her. The jewelry store she had to go into but dreaded going into, because it was her mother's bracelet she had come to pawn there. *My mom's bracelet, for godsakes!* But she was a mom now herself, and she and her family needed the credits.

And the guy who owned the store was known for his honesty. If she was going to pawn the bracelet her mom had loved and cherished when she was alive, the bracelet she had handed down to her only child, at least she'd get a decent price for it.

Not that she had a choice in the matter. *I've got no choice, no choice at all.*

But before she could go into the store, a Ranger cadet made his way through the crowd and confronted Vander Meer. Did a damned good job of it, too. And the longer Cecilia listened, the better she felt.

It seemed somebody could speak up, after all. Somebody could take a stand and in doing so make people like Cecilia feel a little less helpless. It came as no surprise to her that the kid was a Raige. Raiges had never been shy about speaking their minds, had they?

Finally, the argument broke up, with Vander Meer retreating. Cecilia's spirits were buoyed a little as she eyed the jewelry store again. But before she could get to the steps, she saw the Raige kid and his friend go up them.

Cecilia hung back and waited some more, pretending to window-shop on O'Hara Street when the truth was that she couldn't afford anything in those windows. After all, it was hard enough for her to think about pawning her mom's bracelet without having to do it while someone was watching.

Trey Vander Meer straightened the lapels on his new green suit, put the unexpected and slightly jarring incident on O'Hara Street behind him, and waited for the red light on the studio wall to go on. As soon as it did, signaling that his show had started, he turned to the camera and began speaking.

"Welcome, friends, to an unprecedented conversation with our three most important voices on Nova Prime," he said. "Over the last few weeks, the size and scope of the Rangers' role on our world has become a topic of heated discussion in the workplace, at home, and in houses of worship. But until now, we haven't heard from our leaders. You know who they are, so let me get right to it."

He turned to Wilkins. "Prime Commander, let's start with you. What is the current mission of the Rangers?"

Vander Meer settled back in his plush chair and spared a glance at the small studio audience—his wife and two older children included—that had been gathered so that the cameras could capture its reactions. He was happy that at least part of his family could be there to witness in person this historic exchange and, of course, his role in it.

Wilkins, looking every bit the professional in her all-white dress uniform, looked her host in the eye as she considered the question. "My mission is to keep you and your family alive. Should this studio catch fire, who will clear the area and allow the firefighters to do their work? Should your home be robbed, who will investigate and apprehend the burglars? What if there's a flood? An epidemic? The Rangers maintain the peace and security of this world. We're fortunate to be a growing population, Mr. Vander Meer, adding new communities and cities with every passing generation. But make no mistake, they all need protection."

Vander Meer nodded while she spoke. Then he leaned toward her casually, friend to friend as it were. "Protection from what, exactly? Not from what you've just listed or you'd be demanding a lot less in terms of our resources. I think you'll agree that we've had nearly three centuries of peace, and yet you continue to refine your weapons and your other pieces of equipment. How can you justify that?"

"As I just said, Mr. Vander Meer, we have a growing population. We must increase our Corps and our investment in technology to match it. Or are you suggesting a population of over three million people requires *fewer* Rangers? Have I missed something about human nature?"

Seeing he wasn't making any headway with that approach, Vander Meer opted for another one. "Let's turn to our expert on human nature, then, and ask the Primus his thoughts."

"Thank you, Trey," Rostropovich said. Like Wilkins, he looked freshly pressed without a hair out of place. Vander Meer also thought the Primus was wearing some eyeliner and smiled inwardly at the man's vanity.

Maybe that's a topic for another day, he thought. *The vanity of the Primus . . . Is he truly the man we want to shape our values?*

"The issue you raise," the Primus continued, "is a complex one, to say the least. Originally, the Rangers were formed to ensure that the arks were built and that we could save humankind. We've continued to look to them since then, whenever times grew bleak. They have maintained the peace during drought and other natural disasters. They've kept us from harming ourselves and our neighbors. And they have done all this remarkably well."

Blah, blah, blah, Vander Meer thought. His studio audience was looking bored. He was about to cut the Primus short and pose a question to Flint.

"But," said the Primus, "the question before us is about today and not yesterday. Our resources are not unlimited. It appears prudent that we periodically stop and reexamine how those resources are allocated. You have spoken of downsizing the Rangers, Mr. Vander Meer, so we can fund more worthy projects. I believe there may be merit to this approach."

Vander Meer wasn't expecting him to say that. Neither was Wilkins, judging by the way her mouth had fallen open.

But she was a Ranger. She was trained to respond to sneak attacks. "I'd like to think planetary security is a worthy project," she shot back.

"Aren't the satellites doing the bulk of that work?" asked the Primus. He turned to Flint. "Savant?"

Flint looked uncomfortable. Very uncomfortable. He glanced apologetically at Wilkins, but he answered. "The satellite scans have shown nothing other than routine star static for centuries."

"As I thought," Rostropovich said. "Perhaps it is time to reconsider our priorities."

"What's more important than our security?" Wilkins asked.

"Our souls, for one thing," the Primus replied coolly.

"But until they ascend," the Prime Commander pressed, "shouldn't we try to prolong their mortal tenure?"

"My augurs," Rostropovich said, "indicate that the people are questioning our decision to place so much emphasis on the Rangers at the expense of other possibilities."

"We keep the peace," Wilkins insisted. "We're the first responders. We're there for accidents, fires, thefts, and the occasional bombardment from aliens who have some grudge against us for existing."

"All well and good," Vander Meer said, jumping in. "But as the Primus notes, we have other needs on Nova Prime, and—as we've pointed out more than once now—those aliens you speak of haven't been seen for hundreds of years."

He smiled at Rostropovich, unable to believe his luck. Who would ever have thought that the Primus would take his part, effectively stabbing Wilkins squarely in the back?

"The only logical course," Vander Meer said, turning back to the beleaguered Prime Commander, "is to reduce our commitment to the Rangers and reapportion the savings. And to do it now."

The studio audience nodded in agreement. Vander

Meer celebrated inwardly. *I've barely had to say a thing,* he thought. *The Primus has said it all for me.*

As soon as Vander Meer's program was over, Wilkins scowled at Flint and said, "Thanks."

He held his hands out. "I'm sorry. What was I supposed to say?"

What indeed? Wilkins asked herself. Flint hadn't had much choice, the way the question was posed. But Rostropovich . . .

She turned to the Primus. But he had already risen from his seat and headed for the studio's exit.

"Prime Commander," said Vander Meer, approaching her with his hand out to shake hers. "I want to thank you for coming. It was a most—"

Wilkins never heard the rest. She was too busy pursuing Rostropovich, weaving her way among the members of the studio audience who had gotten up in order to speak with her and her colleagues.

The Primus walked through the doorway and out to the street beyond it. But it wasn't difficult for Wilkins to catch up with him. Rostropovich had never been one to take part in exercise.

"I want to speak with you," she said.

"We've already spoken a great deal this morning," he replied. "What else need be said?"

"You ambushed me," she snapped, her eyes full of fire.

"Ambushed?" He shrugged off the accusation. "I expressed what was in my heart."

"If you felt that way, you should have told me so in advance."

"Maybe you can command your Rangers what to say and when to say it. You don't have any such authority over the office of the Primus."

"Of course not—because you set an example for everyone. An example of fairness. An example of *trust-worthiness*."

The Primus harrumphed. "I did what was necessary. Had I warned you of my intentions, you would have prepared a response. This way, your position was exposed as one of greed and self-interest."

The Prime Commander felt her face grow hot with indignation. "Greed? Because I want to protect Nova Prime?"

"Because you don't need the resources you've demanded in the past, and you know it. Now some small portion of those resources will go elsewhere. It is hardly a tragedy."

Wilkins nodded. "I misjudged you."

"No doubt," said the Primus.

The Prime Commander watched her colleague walk away. Resentment burned inside her. She had allowed Rostropovich to catch her by surprise, to outmaneuver her. She had permitted him to strip their world of its defenses.

She hated him for his smugness, for his lack of ethics. She hated him for the blindness that would put the citizens of his world at risk. But the Ranger in her knew that she had only one person to blame for what had happened in Vander Meer's studio: herself.

CHAPTER SIX

Lyla was accustomed to being the only spectator at the North Side cageball court on Monday afternoons, when it was full of running, jumping twelve-year-olds noisily trying to put a ball in a basket. It was rare that she had to share the fence with someone.

But this Monday afternoon seemed to be an exception. Farther along the fence, a couple of cadets stopped in the brazen sunlight to watch the game. She wondered if they knew her brother. *No doubt.* Lucas was, after all, Lucas.

One of the cadets was pretty good-looking, she noticed. Tall and broad-shouldered, he looked like he wanted to step onto the court and take a few shots himself. The other one was tall, too, but stockier, with a shock of red hair.

After a moment, Lyla noticed them looking at her. Talking about her, too, if she wasn't mistaken. Feeling a blush coming on, she turned away.

Why? she asked herself. Why not just return their scrutiny, maybe even walk up to them and introduce herself? Or—God help her—go so far as to ask the good-looking one out?

Because if she went up to the guy and opened her mouth, her throat would close like a vise and nothing remotely intelligible would come out. *That's why.*

Lyla had always been shy as a child. Some people got over their shyness after they put their teen years behind them. In her case, the problem had gotten worse.

That was why she buried herself in lab work: because it was easier than socializing with actual human beings. She was fine in the company of her colleagues, people in whom she had no romantic interest. *Absolutely fine.* But someone like the cadet standing along the fence . . . no way. If she tried to talk to him, her heart would start beating so hard, it would crack a rib.

So I'll just stay where I am, she thought, *and watch the game. And maybe the guy will go away.*

But he didn't. In fact, he started walking in Lyla's direction.

She swallowed hard. *Don't look at him,* she told herself. *Just watch.*

"Excuse me," the cadet said, "but I've got to ask. Are you a cageball fan?"

She shook her head, pretending to remain intent on the game. *Just pretend he's a colleague, inquiring about your work.* "Not exactly. I'm an engineer. I've been working on a hearing device." She pointed through the fence at one of the kids on the court. "A couple of months ago, I implanted one in that kid over there."

His name was Pietro, and he was far and away the best player on the court. Not that she was biased or anything.

"And now he can hear?" asked the cadet.

"Perfectly," Lyla said, unable to keep a note of pride out of her voice.

"That's great."

Funny. There was something about his voice she found familiar. *Probably my imagination.*

"So you came down to watch him?" the cadet asked.

"It was part of our deal. If he let me put in the device, I would watch him play one time."

"And this is the time?"

Lyla smiled. "Actually, this is the *tenth* time. It's gotten to be a habit with me. I'm here every Monday afternoon, no matter what."

The cadet laughed. "I guess my friend Blodge was right."

She turned to him, wondering what that might mean. *Is this one of those deals where a guy talks to you on a dare?* "About what?"

"I need to laugh more. I get a little intense sometimes."

"I can't picture you being intense."

He laughed again, and all of a sudden she realized that they were having a conversation. *A real-life, honest-to-goodness conversation.* It was crazy, but there it was.

They watched the kids go back and forth a little more. Pietro couldn't have looked happier. Every time a teammate called something to him, he turned in response.

Lyla felt better about that than she'd ever felt about anything in her life. Although talking to a dashing young cadet, actually *talking* to him, might come in a close second.

"I used to play a little cageball myself," he said. "My dad played it, too. He was better than I was. But I still liked it."

"You don't play anymore?" Lyla asked.

The cadet shook his head. "Too busy trying to be a Ranger."

There was something about the way he smiled, sort of joking but serious at the same time, that seemed familiar—even more so than his voice. Lyla got the feeling that she had met the cadet before.

Then she thought, *No. A guy who looks like he does? I'd have remembered him without a doubt.*

"Anyway," he said, "my name's Conner. Conner—"

Oh, my God, she thought.

That was why he seemed familiar—because he *was.* Because he had been Lucas's best friend when they were kids. Because he was the one who had had a boxing match with her brother right in the middle of their barracks.

"Raige," she said, interrupting him.

He looked surprised. "Yeah. How did you know?"

"I'm Lyla Kincaid," she blurted. "That's how." Then

she walked away as fast as she could even though Pietro would glance at her spot at some point and wonder what had happened to her.

She would explain it to the kid later. *Conner Raige. Doesn't it figure?* She had felt so comfortable talking to him, so at ease with herself. And out of everybody he could have been, everybody on the planet, he had turned out to be . . .

Conner Raige.

"From time to time," the Primus said, his voice echoing impressively, "the world gets remade. Sometimes it is done for us. Sometimes we do it ourselves. Back on Earth, we were foolish. We destroyed God's creation, our home. But we were given a chance for redemption, brothers and sisters."

The Primus cast his gaze over his congregation. Most of the time, his goal was simply to comfort them so they were better equipped to face life's trials. This time, he had an entirely different agenda in mind.

"Before the Earth died, we were permitted to slip its bonds. But we needed to do so in an orderly way. The Rangers provided that order, and for half a millennium they have continued to provide it. Twice they repelled hostile forces that sought to cast us from this new world of ours, this second paradise. They have tended to the sick, to the injured, to the wronged. For that, we owe the Rangers a measure of thanks.

"However, it is time to remake the world again. The hour of our need has come and gone. A more modest Ranger Corps is required to meet our more modest needs."

Rostropovich paused and let the words settle like fine incense over the crowd. His most trusted augurs were mixed in with the congregation. They led the murmurs of agreement. What was more, cameras and sound equipment were carrying his message from building to building, city to city.

True, it was Trey Vander Meer who had unleashed the first salvo at Wilkins and the Rangers. But the Primus had known an opportunity when he saw one, and he would use it to expand his power as far as he could.

After all, the Rangers had had their day. It was high time that Nova Prime embraced a different sort of leadership, one that focused on the spiritual rather than the mundane.

"We still need a force," he allowed, "to maintain the peace and ensure that the laws of this world are followed. We still need someone to protect the streets, inspect the goods being manufactured, and respond to natural disasters. But for these purposes, the size of the Ranger force is an untenable one.

"A debate has sprung up among the people. Many say that the Rangers should be downsized, made more efficient. While no change has been made as yet, I have listened. I have heard from my augurs and from you, my brothers and sisters in faith.

"I want to move the dialogue forward. That is why I suggest today that Prime Commander Wilkins submit a plan for the reduction of her forces—and the decentralization of the Rangers as an institution. A series of small police forces, one in each community, would still keep us safe. They could respond even more rapidly than the Rangers do today to local threats. Or if necessary, they could work together, brothers in arms, to deal with larger challenges.

"Such a reorganization would also mean that services formerly supplied by the Rangers would be supplied instead by the augury or the Savant's engineers. However, we would be willing to make that sacrifice.

"Of course, once the Rangers are disbanded, there would be no Prime Commander. Our tripartite form of government would become bipartite. It would be a welcome simplification of what is sometimes an unwieldy process.

"Mind you, I propose this reorganization with no malice toward the Prime Commander. I continue to hold her in the highest regard, as I do all the Rangers. But now is the time to embrace a new way."

The Primus was gratified to see a sea of heads bobbing in accord with his message. Everything was proceeding as he had hoped.

Watching the Primus's sermon from her office, Meredith Wilkins bit her lip. Sitting beside her, Bonita Raige looked like a coiled spring.

"The bastard," Bonita said.

"That's disrespectful," said Wilkins. "He's the spiritual leader of the colony, remember?"

"And he's a bastard," Bonita insisted.

Wilkins nodded. "Damned right he is."

She forced herself to watch the sermon to its unsavory conclusion. As far as she could tell, it was well received—as all Rostropovich's addresses were received. He was that kind of speaker.

Then came the obligatory press conference on the steps outside the congregation hall. "We are fortunate," the Primus said to the journalists who had gathered around him, "to have survived Earth's destruction. Nova Prime has been our redemption—and the Rangers have been God's instruments in that redemption. For that, we owe them a debt of gratitude.

"However, there is a time to reap and a time to sow, a time when we must take up arms and a time when we must lay them down. While we can never cease being cautious, our safety has been assured. Should we not free our brothers and sisters in the Rangers to do other work that will let us flourish as a colony? Might this not be the time to turn our swords into plowshares?"

Abruptly, Wilkins cut the signal.

"He's taking it to us," Bonita noted angrily. "Not only calling for a reduction in the number of Rangers but the elimination of the Prime Commander from the tripartite agreement. I don't know who's the trickier bastard, Vander Meer or the Primus."

"Vander Meer is just a showman," Wilkins said. "It's the Primus I have to watch. His opinion and influence . . . well, I don't have to tell you. I hate to say it, but we have to throw him a bone."

Bonita glanced at her. "You mean reduce our forces?"

"Not yet. But something. Call a meeting of department heads. Tell them I want to hear cost-cutting suggestions. Make it first thing tomorrow."

Bonita nodded. She didn't look happy.

But then, Wilkins wasn't happy, either. The idea of skimping on security went against everything she had ever been taught, everything she believed in. She wished there was another way.

Unfortunately, she didn't see any.

When Conner was called into Lennon's office in the command center, all kinds of thoughts went through his head.

First, he thought he was going to be disciplined after all for fighting in the barracks. But if that were the case, Lucas would have been summoned to Lennon's office as well, and Lennon had sent only for Conner.

Next, it occurred to him that Lennon wanted to apologize for making his response to the fight a personal diatribe. After all, Conner was entitled to his beliefs, and Lennon had reamed him for them. But he rejected that possibility even more quickly than the first. Lennon wasn't the sort to apologize for anything. Ever.

The third notion that came to mind was that Lennon was going to promote Conner to squad leader for what he had done during the war games. Not because he wanted to but because Wilkins had ordered him to.

In the end, Conner found out that his superior had *none* of those things in mind. "So," said Lennon when

Conner arrived, "when was the last time you stood satellite duty?"

"I haven't *ever* stood satellite duty, sir," Conner said.

Lennon smiled. "Well, Cadet, there's a first time for everything." He told Conner when to report and what to expect. "Details on your tablet in case you've got any questions. Dismissed."

It might have been the quickest conversation the command center had ever seen. *Satellite duty,* Conner mused as he walked out of the building.

He was recalling what he had heard about such an assignment when he saw a familiar face waiting for him outside the command center.

"Dad?" he said.

It was a surprise, to say the least. Frank Raige hadn't visited his son the whole time Conner had been in training. They had gotten together those times when both he and Conner went home on leave but never once when Conner was on duty.

His father couldn't have shown up at a better time. "Listen to this," Conner said. "You know what that lowlife Vander Meer's been saying about—"

"I heard," said his father.

His response was clipped, abrupt. It brought Conner up short, making him wonder why Frank Raige would react that way.

He thinks I let Vander Meer's comments go, Conner decided. *He thinks I looked the other way.* "Don't worry," Conner said, "I put Vander Meer in his place. I didn't let him get away with that garbage."

"That's the problem," said Frank Raige. "You didn't let him get away with that garbage. Since when are you the official spokesman for the Rangers?"

For a moment, Conner thought his father was kidding. His dad would do that sometimes—pretend to be deadly serious and then break out into the world's biggest grin. But not this time. Frank Raige's eyes looked like they had been chiseled from rock.

"I—I'm not," Conner stammered. "But I couldn't—"

"But nothing," his father said. "There's a chain of command in the Corps. You know that, right? It starts at the top and it works its way down, and it's been there since long before either of us was born. Some people in that chain, usually the ones with the most experience, are authorized by the Prime Commander to speak on behalf of the Rangers—and others are not. You are one of those who are not."

Conner felt his throat constrict. He couldn't remember the last time his dad had spoken to him with an edge in his voice. He was angry; that much was clear. Angry and embarrassed.

The worst part was that Conner didn't deserve it.

The Rangers would never in a million years make an official response to Vander Meer's crap. If Conner hadn't opened his mouth, those people in the plaza would never have heard the other side of the argument: the Rangers' side. They would have accepted everything Vander Meer coughed up without exception.

Conner started to say so.

But before he could get two words out, his father held up a hand. "The Prime Commander makes that decision, not you. If she wants to say something, that's her business. And if she doesn't, that's her business as well."

"But Dad," Conner asked, "how would the Prime Commander even have known what Vander Meer said? She wasn't there—I was."

"It's not your problem," said his father. "Someone else's, maybe, but not yours. Your problem is acting like a Ranger, and you're nowhere near a solution from what I can see. You get into fights in your barracks, you insult your commanding officer, and you mistake yourself for the Prime Commander. You're part of a family that's been a credit to the uniform since before we came in sight of this planet. *Act* like it."

And that was it. There was no room for protest, no room for argument, nothing else that could be taken into account. Conner was supposed to listen to Vander

Meer's nonsense and remain silent regardless of how untrue it was.

"You read me?" asked Frank Raige, his gaze still hard and unyielding.

Conner did his best to contain his disappointment. "Yes, sir. I read you."

His father nodded. "Good."

Then he turned around and walked away. As if they weren't related, as if they had never even met before.

Conner knew his fellow cadets would be standing around looking at him even though they were pretending not to do so—looking and listening. He didn't give them anything more to talk about. He just made his way back to the barracks as if nothing had happened.

It hadn't been easy being a cadet all these months, but at least he had known that his family was behind him, that if push came to shove, they would support him as they always had. *Unconditionally.* Now he had learned otherwise.

To that point, Conner had worshipped his father. It was shocking to hear the object of his worship tell him to shut up and obey orders, even if it wasn't in so many words.

All right, Conner thought. *I can do that.* He would shut his mouth and keep it shut.

No matter *what* he saw.

Bonita Raige was tired and miserable when she got home. But she wouldn't be able to sleep; she was pretty sure of that. She needed to talk, to work out some of the anger that was churning around inside her.

Her husband, Torrance, was sleeping already when she entered their bedroom. Had she been a considerate wife, she would have slipped in beside him as quietly as she could and allowed him to go on sleeping.

Consideration be damned, she thought.

"You awake?" she asked.

"I am now," he replied. He sat up in a shaft of the moonlight coming in through the skylight. "What's up?"

Bonita was reminded of how handsome her husband was. Tall, broad-shouldered, brown-eyed, and brown-haired, he was the spitting image of his father, a good-looking man in his own right. Torrance's brother, Frank, with his craggy features, was a throwback to their grandfather. As far as Bonita was concerned, Torrance had gotten the better of the deal.

Which meant that she had, as well.

"Did you hear the Primus?" she asked.

"I did," he said.

"And?"

Her husband shrugged. "It's all politics, Bon. It'll sort itself out."

She stared at her husband in disbelief. "Wow, that's it? Just politics as usual?"

"It's not?"

"Not to me. It's the future of the Rangers Rostropovich is talking about. And Vander Meer; I could kill that—"

"Hey," Torrance said, laying his hand on top of hers, "calm down. We're all just cogs in the machinery. The Primus, Vander Meer . . . they think they're more than that, but they're not. They're cogs, too. The machinery . . . it's been in place for hundreds of years. The Rangers have done a good job. We're not going anywhere."

"How can you be so certain?" Bonita demanded.

"History. You think this is the first time someone's gone after us? And here we are, still standing. There may be changes, modifications . . . but the Rangers will endure. So go to sleep, will you?"

His complacency ate away at her. On another occasion, she might have listened to him anyway. But not this time.

She got up and walked into the next room.

"Bon?" he called after her. "Bonita? Where you going?"

"Back to work," she muttered, and left the house.

CHAPTER SEVEN

Meredith Wilkins paced the conference room as her department heads filed into her office, which had been stocked with additional chairs. Once the last of them settled into a seat, she sat down as well and began.

"Elias," she said, turning to Hāturi.

Hāturi activated the portable holo display device he had planted in the middle of the room. Suddenly a complex of charts and images of tools, weaponry, and aircraft was floating above the meeting.

"We've been criticized for siphoning off too many resources from the colony," she said. "So as a show of good faith, we're going to cut our demands to the bone. That's why I called you all here: to help me decide what we absolutely must have and what we can do without."

"Well," said one of her assembled officers, "we can slow down the modernization of the flier fleet. Instead of upgrading every ten years, we can make it every fifteen."

"Of course," said another officer, "that will mean revisiting the manufacturing process. If we're going to wait fifteen years to replace fliers, they need to be built to last twenty."

Wilkins hated to equip her pilots with anything less than what was the state of the art. Frank Raige wouldn't be happy.

"What else?"

"We've been talking with the Savant's team," said a third officer, "about ceding satellite monitoring to them except for periodic checks. That'll save us on personnel."

"By how much?" a fourth officer asked with an edge to his voice. "And how long will it be before we're relieved of satellite duty completely?"

"He's right," said the second officer. "You give the Primus a hand, he'll take an arm. He won't stop till we're too small to matter."

Wilkins held her tongue. This was what it felt like, she guessed, to be nibbled to death by a thousand insects. *A layer at a time gets stripped away until I wake up one day and there's no one left to command.*

But she didn't have a choice. If she was going to preserve the Rangers, she had to do this. "Next?" she said, and waited to hear the next cost-cutting suggestion.

Looking at his sister, Frank Raige was reminded of what his mother had been like when she was alive.

Rosaria Raige had been a slender woman with bright blue eyes and auburn hair, just like Frank's older sister, Theresa. She had been quiet and thoughtful, just like Theresa. And like Theresa, she had been a voice of spirituality in the family.

An unwelcome voice at times but one that none of them would dare deny: not Frank's father when he was alive; not Frank's younger brother, Torrance; and not Frank himself, even when he was old enough to have his own family.

It was that last quality that came to Frank's mind as he met Theresa's gaze across a scarred wooden table in an old-fashioned Irish tavern called Tir Na Nog. "Bad day?" he echoed. "These days, they're all bad."

His sister, who was still wearing her brown augur robes, looked sympathetic. *Just like Mom,* he thought. "Sorry," she said.

They had been close as kids despite all their obvious differences. Frank was tall and broad where Theresa was petite. He had been rough and tumble where she was reserved. But separated only by a couple of years and older than Torrance by half a dozen, they had been coconspirators growing up, most notably in the "Frankie Has Run Away from Home" caper, in which his sister swore she had seen him take off for the mountains when he had been hiding in the broom closet all along.

Unfortunately, they weren't coconspirators anymore. "Don't be sorry," he said. "You're not the one bad-mouthing the Rangers on the vid."

But the Primus was, now that he had made it clear he was siding with Trey Vander Meer. Frank left that part out.

Theresa patted his hand. "I know. That seems to be all anyone wants to talk about."

"I'd rather it be about who serves the better sandwich, us or New Earth City. Or some hybrid flower that fights chromosome damage like the one that engineer came up with last year. Anything but the Rangers."

Theresa took a sip from her cactus ale. That was one thing Frank and his sister still had in common—a love of good brews—and Tir Na Nog had as good a beer list as anyone this side of Earth.

"I understand," she said. "But we're all in the public eye, aren't we? Even augurs get their share of criticism."

Not really, he thought. "Vander Meer's not just in the public eye. He's in the public ear."

"He's got a right to say what he wants," Theresa reminded him.

"Except we listen even when we should know better." He looked to a waitress passing by with a tray and three glasses, each one beaded with perspiration and topped with sudsy foam. "Are we crazy?" he asked her on a whim.

She flashed a smile and said, "No more than the other customers. Get you a refill?"

"Not me," Theresa said.

"I'd like one," said Frank. He drained the last of his beer and passed the waitress his empty mug.

"Do you think Wilkins will give in?" his sister asked.

He shook his head. "I don't know."

Mainly because he hadn't asked. And he wouldn't. Wilkins could handle the situation without any help from him.

"What about the augury?" Frank asked. "What's the drone?"

Theresa seemed to hesitate. But then, his sister wasn't one for confrontation. But if she didn't want to answer, it meant the colony's priests had turned against the Rangers, too, just like their Primus.

"It's okay," he said.

"Frankie," Theresa protested, "it's not a simple answer. Of course there are some who agree with Vander Meer. But not everybody."

Frank looked at his sister, as much an augur as any who had ever taken vows, and still couldn't believe their father had allowed her to take her life in that direction. Joshua Raige had still been the Prime Commander when Theresa had sat him down one night after dinner and gently explained why she had decided to become an augur.

Joshua Raige had expected all three of his children to join him in the "family business." But Theresa was firm in her resistance to the idea. She didn't have the instincts to be a soldier, she said. She was made for more spiritual pursuits.

Bitterly disappointed, Frank's father had blamed his wife for their daughter's decision. In fact, it came close to breaking up their marriage. On his deathbed, Joshua Raige had said he accepted Theresa for who she was, but Frank never believed he meant it.

"Frank?" Theresa said, bringing him out of his reverie.

"Sorry," he said, focusing on her again. "I was—"

"I *know* what you were doing. It's not the first time

I've seen that look in your eye. You're thinking about Dad and what he thought about my joining the augury."

"Here's your refill," the waitress said.

As she breezed by, she plunked down Frank's beer. *None too soon,* he thought. He could buy time by taking a swig before he responded to his sister's observation.

"I was," he said finally, putting his beer down on the table. "To be blunt, he wouldn't have liked Vander Meer any more than I do. And he wouldn't have liked any Primus who stood with Vander Meer."

Theresa nodded. "Probably not. But he's our Primus. And as an augur, I'm bound to look to him for spiritual guidance."

There was a moment of silence between them. An uncomfortable silence. Then Theresa asked, "So what's happening with my nephew?"

He managed something like a smile. "Conner could be better. But he'll get the hang of it. As Torrance likes to say, it's in the blood."

"Would you like me to talk with him?" Theresa offered.

"Not necessary," Frank said, maybe a little too quickly.

And they sat there, together in some ways yet so far apart in others.

INTERLUDE

The High Minister awakens and is—to some degree—surprised. When he had settled into his sleep pod for his embarkation on this great adventure, he had considered the possibility that he might never awaken from his forced slumber.

Warlord Knahs, as far as the High Minister was concerned, was perfectly capable of sabotaging the sleep chambers of him, his nest brother . . . indeed, just about anyone who posed a threat to his ambitions, whatever they might be.

Yet here is the Minister, hale and hearty. And he senses the stirring of his nest brother as well a short distance away.

The sleep pod seeps open. Mist wafts from it, and the Minister is jolted as he feels the warm air from the ship's atmosphere mixing with the cold in every part of his body. He stretches, shivers, and then braces himself as he emerges from the pod. He extends one clawed foot, then another, and carefully eases his full weight onto them. His knees buckle, and he almost spills onto the floor but catches himself at the last moment, clinging to the pod to keep himself upright.

There is a loud thud close to him. He turns and—as much as he hates to admit it—is somewhat amused as he perceives his nest brother sprawled flat on the deck. Apparently the High Chancellor's reflexes are a bit slower than the Minister's.

"You are smirking," says the Chancellor in a foul temper.

"It is not my fault if you do not appreciate the amusement of it."

The Chancellor's only response is a grunt.

As soon as the two of them are secure and on their feet once more, they check on the welfare of the scientific crew, who are adapting to their emergence from their years-long coma. They then head down to the command center. Neither of them is surprised to perceive that the Warlord and his followers are already hard at work.

The Minister knows this for what it is: a pompous effort to appear indispensable. Of course, the ship is fully automated. There is nothing that either the Warlord or his people are going to bring to the vessel's operation. Yet they busy themselves like walking redundancies, making sure every system is operating as it should.

"How kind of you to join us," says the Warlord with a sneer. "We reached the outer rim of the Holy World's solar system some time ago. We were beginning to worry about you. After all, the strain of extended flight is not for everyone."

"Your consideration is appreciated," replies the Minister, who cannot resist adding, "even if your presence here is suspect."

And suddenly the Warlord's mind rips into the Minister's with volcanic force.

It is an insane breach of Krezateen protocol. Although nest brothers such as the Minister and the Chancellor communicate with each other routinely, if another is going to engage in telepathic conversation, it is absolutely mandatory that a preliminary probe be made, permission be acquired.

Warlord Knahs does not bother with such niceties. Instead, the sheer force of his personality hammers the Minister, so much so that he staggers. He becomes instantly aware that the link is three-way: The Chancellor is hearing it as well.

My presence here is entirely your responsibility. Ever since the presentation of your monstrosity to the assemblage, my bravery has been questioned. You have undermined my honor, and I will retrieve it. And when these creatures fail—as they inevitably will—then you will all see what a true Warlord can do.

"Warlord, we are ready to block the feed of their security satellites."

The Warlord's first officer reports as stoically as he can, but the excitement in his voice is readily apparent, almost as palpable as it was when their vessel sighted the Holy World's system in the first place.

He has obviously never been on a pilgrimage, either, thinks the Minister.

The Warlord releases them from the hammerlock of his mental hold. Then he says out loud, "Good. Let's get this over with."

The technology required for obscuring their arrival from the Vermin is simple, mostly because the Vermin's technology is so hopelessly primitive. It is in the power of the Krezateen—with their eight fully armed vessels—to simply blow the Vermin's satellites out of space, but that would trigger alarms. This way, it will take the Vermin time to realize that something is wrong—something other than natural signal interference such as solar radiation. The Krezateen will have all the time they require.

For a moment, all is silent in the command center. Then the first officer says, "Satellite feeds are blocked."

Knahs raises his arm in a gesture of disgust. "Take us in, then."

A cheer goes up among the Krezateen, for they know they have taken the first step in the elimination of the beings that have befouled their Holy World. Soon they will enter Zantenor's atmosphere and discharge their lethal cargo, as will all the other vessels in their fleet.

The High Minister cannot resist taking a dig at his

old rival. "You seem less than enthused, Warlord. A great day dawns for the future of the Krezateen—a day in which we take back our Holy World."

"Animals are taking actions meant for warriors," the Warlord tells him. "We shall witness their efficacy."

"Yes, we will," says the High Minister. "And perhaps by the end of this endeavor, it will be you, Warlord, who will come to have more respect for what science can accomplish."

"Do all that you wish with your brains," says the Warlord with studied indifference, "while I stick with my arms, and we shall discover who is ultimately triumphant."

Yes. Yes, we will, the High Minister thinks to himself, but not anywhere near the telepathic range of the Warlord.

CHAPTER EIGHT

Vander Meer couldn't have been happier about the way his shows had gone lately. But his happiness was punctured as soon as he walked into his house and felt the sting of his daughter Elena's greeting.

"Too far, Pop," she snapped angrily, reading something from her tablet rather than looking up at him. "*Way* too far."

"Good afternoon to you, too," he said, smiling sweetly despite the rebuke. "And in what exactly did I go too far?"

"You know what I'm talking about," Elena said.

She criticized him a lot these days. Even more than her brother Michael, and in a more unrelentingly confrontational way.

"Whoa," said Vander Meer, patting the air. "If you've got something on your mind, let's talk about it."

"That's the problem," Elena told him. "You talk. You don't listen."

Vander Meer sighed.

He and Elena disagreed on just about everything these days. And she was only thirteen. What was it going to be like when she got older?

"Okay," he said. "I'm listening. In fact, I'm all ears."

It was a joke she used to enjoy. "You're *not* all ears," she would say. "You've got arms and legs and a nose and a mouth . . ." and then she would break into giggles.

Not this time. And maybe never again, he reflected, feeling a pang of loss. His baby was growing up.

"You're treating the Prime Commander like a criminal," Elena said in an accusatory tone.

Finally, she looked up at him. Blond and blue-eyed, she was nothing short of adorable, and years of dancing had left her well toned. He despaired that the boys were already noticing her.

"Am I?" he asked.

"Yes. She's just trying to do the right thing, and you're killing her for it. All for the sake of your ratings."

Thirteen and already wise in the ways of a wicked world, Vander Meer thought. *Why couldn't kids hang on to their innocence anymore?*

"Tell you what," he said. "I'll reconsider the way I treat the Prime Commander. No promises, but I'll give it some thought. All right?"

That seemed to pacify her. A little, at any rate.

Just then, Vander Meer spotted something on her right middle finger: a new ring, one he tried to identify but couldn't.

"Where'd that come from?" he asked his daughter.

"Class. I told you."

"No, the ring," he said, pointing.

Elena blushed. "It's a Claddagh ring."

"A what?"

"It's ancient Irish. A symbol of . . . lasting friendship." The blush deepened.

"Where'd you get it?" he asked.

"From a friend."

"What friend might that be?"

His daughter hesitated, twisting the ring around her finger. Thrilled that he'd managed to change the subject, Vander Meer didn't rush her. Finally, she got out one word—one name.

"Derrick."

"Have I met this Derrick?"

"Pop, he's been in my classes since we were five," she said, clearly exasperated.

"Which one is he? The blond one?"

"That's Pavel."

"The redhead?"

"Eric? Or Clive?"

"I guess neither. Okay, so who or what is this Derrick?"

"He's the black-haired guy who always sits near me in class because our names fall one after the other."

"Derrick . . . ?"

"Ungar."

"Derrick Ungar. Do I know his parents?"

"No, but they know you. And like me, they don't approve of the way you're attacking our leaders. They say you're disrespecting the system."

Here we go again, thought Vander Meer.

"The system is hypocritical," he said, patiently and not for the first time. His distaste for the colony's judges was another hallmark of his show, one that he hadn't revisited in a while. "It's difficult to give it less respect than it deserves."

"That's not what Derrick's parents say. They say the system is as good as the people who run it."

"Elena, sweet pea, it's never that cut-and-dried. There are shades of gray, nuances that need to be explored."

"Don't you mean exploited?" Michael asked as he walked into the room.

"Ganging up on your father?" Vander Meer asked his son.

"Just joining the conversation," the boy said. "I thought you were in a listening mood."

"Apparently I'm not the only one."

"I heard you talking from the other room," Michael said. "It was hard not to."

"So," Vander Meer said, trying to change the subject again, "what's your take on Elena and this Derrick?"

The boy glanced at his sister. "Ungar's okay, I guess. He can't throw worth a damn, but he's good at defense."

"Michael . . . !" Elena whined.

"I'm kidding." He turned to his father again. "Besides, I'm not letting Dad off the hook so easily."

"You just push too hard," Elena told her father.

"That's right," Michael said. "You need to ease up."

Vander Meer had to chuckle. It was the first time he'd experienced the singular delight of his son actually telling him what to do.

"I'll have you know," he said, "that people *love* me. What makes you right and them wrong?"

"You and the Primus have them so stirred up, they can't think for themselves," said Michael.

"When did you become a sociologist?" Vander Meer asked.

The good news was he had smart kids. The bad news was he had smart kids. They were formulating interesting and thoughtful arguments, but they were irritating him as well. Pride and anger fought for control of his tongue.

"I'm not," Michael said. "But I don't have to be to see what you're up to."

"That's right," Elena agreed.

Suddenly, Vander Meer had a yen to take a walk.

Conner sat in the command center's satellite data room, a surprisingly small enclosure with thirty or so large holographic screens, each one displaying information fed by one of the colony's vast orbital array of signal receivers. He could hear his father saying, "Every cadet has to stand satellite duty some time or another."

He could still see the look on Frank Raige's face outside the command center, and it still stung to hear his dad say what he'd said, though not quite as much as when it first happened. But Conner was still determined not to say anything out of line.

Not to say anything *at all* if he could help it.

He read the last line of data on one screen, then moved on to the next one in the methodical sequence recommended to him by the bleary-eyed female engineer who had sat in his seat the night before.

Conner could hear his mother, too, adding, "You've got to pay your dues."

His parents had made those remarks in a restaurant the day before he entered cadet training, at a special dinner in his honor attended by his aunt Bonita and his uncle Torrance. But Conner hadn't understood why they felt compelled to mention satellite duty when there were so many other aspects of his training they could have brought up.

Only a few minutes into his shift, he understood.

There were thirty screens, after all. He probably could have glanced at each of them and been done with it. Certainly, no one would have known. But Conner wasn't like that. If Lennon had given him a job, he was going to do it.

Especially if Trey Vander Meer had pressured the Prime Commander into shifting the primary responsibility for monitoring satellite data to the Savant's engineers. The Rangers would take only one two-hour shift a day now: this one.

All the more reason for Conner to pay the utmost attention every minute of his shift. If the Rangers were going to get only one peek at the data each day, it was more important than ever that that peek be a thorough one.

Not that he was surprised that none of the screens he had studied had anything alarming on them. The colony would have need of the Rangers one day, but he didn't necessarily think *today* would be that day.

Fortunately, the system was a simple one to understand. Each satellite had a set of dimensions programmed into it that approximated the size of the Skrel craft from the aliens' first attack five hundred years earlier. If an object entering the atmosphere of Nova Prime came anywhere near those dimensions, the satellite would transmit an alarm to Ranger facilities throughout the colony.

If the object was smaller, the satellite in question would simply record the passage of the object and add the data to its logs. Anything that size would burn up in the atmosphere, anyway.

The second thing every cadet had to know was that a given satellite monitored only a section of the atmosphere, with very little overlap between satellites. Therefore, a meteorite that was observed by one satellite probably wouldn't be observed by another, and in no case would it be observed by more than two satellites.

Simple, Conner mused.

But whoever was on monitor duty wasn't supposed to wait for an alarm. He or she was supposed to be alert for anything. Otherwise, why involve a human being in the process at all?

So Conner did his job, tedious as it was.

It wasn't until he came to the twenty-sixth screen that he noticed something unusual. Or, at least, something he thought was unusual: The screen didn't show anything entering the atmosphere of Nova Prime. Of course, that was a good thing. But it seemed strange for the screen not to have recorded anything, not even a little debris. He made a note of it in his report file, then moved on to the next screen and discovered that one didn't have any entry data, either. *Well,* he thought, *that's a coincidence.*

The twenty-eighth screen had a record of some debris, as did the one after it and the one after that. But not screens 26 and 27. Just for the heck of it, Conner checked the data from the previous shift. Both screens showed small amounts of debris entering the atmosphere over time. But not now. He ran a diagnostic on screens 26 and 27. They were working perfectly in all respects, just not showing any entry objects.

Conner sat back in his chair and massaged his chin. It was probably nothing, but just for the heck of it he went back to see when those screens had last shown any debris.

He leaned forward.

Seventeen minutes and twenty-two seconds before

the end of the previous shift, both screens had stopped showing any incoming material. Seventeen minutes and twenty-two seconds exactly.

Before that, both of them had registered small amounts of debris. Then, at exactly the same time, they had stopped. And neither of them had shown anything since that time.

Can't be, Conner thought.

He ran another diagnostic just to make sure he hadn't screwed up the first one. It didn't turn up any problems. The screens were fine.

I've got to tell Lennon, Conner thought.

No, said a voice inside him. *Remember what you told Dad? You were going to keep your mouth shut.*

So much for that promise.

Conner lingered at the console only long enough to log out, his fingers flying over the command pads. Then he was out of his seat and heading for the door.

CHAPTER NINE

Conner had been watching Lennon go over the satellite data on his data pad for the last five minutes. It hadn't been easy for the cadet to remain quiet, but he wanted Lennon to be able to concentrate, to appreciate the potential magnitude of the threat. Unfortunately, Lennon was the guy he had mouthed off to not so long before. But Conner had known he would have to face him eventually.

Besides, he had no choice in the matter. If he was right about the data, there wasn't any time to waste.

Finally, Lennon looked up. "So you think . . . what?" he asked of Conner. "That we're being invaded by someone?"

He said it as if it were a joke. As if the colony had never before been attacked by a species from another planet.

"I don't know, sir," Conner said, "but something's going on. That much is obvious."

Lennon smiled. "It's not obvious to *me*, Cadet. I'll grant you that the data deserves further study. But let's not forget that these data receivers malfunction from time to time."

"I ran a diagnostic, sir."

"The diagnostics malfunction, too," Lennon said. "Trust me; I've seen them do it on a dozen different occasions."

"Sir, it still warrants a—"

"An all-points alert? Let me tell you something,

Cadet." He jerked a thumb over his shoulder. "There are people out there who have put us under a microscope, and those people are just waiting for us to do something stupid. Because as soon as we do, they're going to point to it and say, 'You see? Those Rangers are a bunch of Chicken Littles crying that the sky is falling. We can do fine without them.'

"Now, it may be that those satellites stopped receiving data for some nefarious reason. But my gut is telling me that it's nothing of the sort—that in fact, it's nothing more than a harmless coincidence. Worthy of investigation? Sure. But if we panic and declare a state of emergency and we're wrong—that could be the end of the Rangers. And I'll be damned if I'm the guy that brings that end about."

"But sir," Conner said, "what good are the Rangers if we can't do the job we're supposed to do?"

"That's a good question," Lennon said. "Here's another one: What will this colony do without the Rangers when a *real* danger rears its head?"

But what if this is *a real danger?*

That was what Conner was going to ask. It was right there on the tip of his tongue. But in the end he held back. He could see by Lennon's expression that it wasn't going to do him any good.

"Thanks for your vigilance, Cadet," Lennon said. "You're dismissed."

It took all of Conner's willpower to say, "Yes, sir," and return to his post.

Frank Raige was just taking his flier up for a routine bounce when his comm board lit up and he heard an urgent voice over his intercom: "Something's falling out of the sky! No—there's more of them—eight altogether! Forty thousand cubits apiece, best I can make it out! Doesn't look like anything we've ever seen before! Repeat—"

Frank didn't need to hear any more. Harl Jones had as much airtime as Frank did. If he was sounding the alarm, it wasn't for nothing.

But . . . falling out of the sky? *Eight of them?* It had been hundreds of years since anyone had had cause to say that. For all the Rangers' talk about invaders, no one really expected to get a report like that.

Yet there it is.

Just then, Frank's communicator pulsed. He glanced at the readout and saw that it was Conner calling. But the veteran had no time to answer. He took note of the coordinates his colleague had sent, applied max thrust, and felt himself slammed back into his seat. The world—city, mountains, desert, everything—went by in a blur.

Moments later, he eyeballed what Jones was talking about. They were only a few kilometers outside Nova City, out on the flats. Big, gray, insect-looking things. *Skrel?* he speculated, recognizing how closely they resembled the aliens' ships the last time they had appeared over Nova Prime.

A flier—Harl's, apparently—was circling the vessels, no doubt in an attempt to get more data. *And taking a chance,* Frank thought. He didn't see anything on the ships that looked like a weapons array, but it was hard to tell.

Frank got on his intercom. "Back up, back up!" He transmitted the coordinates for good measure even though Harl had done that already. Then he went in for a closer look.

The vessels looked sturdy if not particularly aerodynamic. They weren't as gray as he had thought; there was an iridescent streak running through the material of their hulls, rainbow-colored like oil in sunlight. And they had plenty of nooks and crannies, enough to conceal whatever its makers had wanted to conceal.

Were they full of Skrel? An invasion force—or part of one? And were there other vessels like it dropping from the heavens elsewhere on Nova Prime?

Back at headquarters, Wilkins would have been apprised of the situation by now. She would be asking herself the same questions—and coming up with the same answer Frank had come up with: *Don't know.*

At least not yet.

Half a minute later, another couple of fliers joined them. Within the minute, there were a half dozen of them altogether. By then the vessels were only a few hundred feet from the ground.

Waiting to see what they were up to, Frank held his fire and made sure the others did the same. But he kept his sights fixed on the ships all the same.

"Raige?" It was Wilkins's voice.

"Right here, Commander."

"What's our sitch?"

"They're descending. Slowly. No sign of hostile intent. Yet." Frank watched for the slightest movement along the vessels' surfaces. "Where did they come from? And why didn't we catch them before this?"

"We're trying to figure that out now," said Wilkins.

Suddenly, a set of bay doors opened beneath one of the vessels and dropped something—something long and gray and featureless. A moment later, the thing hit the ground—and broke open, releasing its contents.

An animal, as far as Frank could tell. An animal, the likes of which he had never seen before, crawling from the debris. He didn't get it.

Animals falling from the sky . . . ?

Then the other ships started dropping the same kind of long, gray objects. And wherever the things smashed into the surface, they discharged the same kind of animal.

Frank swore to himself. "You seeing this, Commander?"

"I am," said Wilkins, "and I don't like it."

The objects came down in quick succession, like hail, destroying themselves in one impact after another. Then the hail stopped—just like that—and the alien vessels began ascending, as if their job was done. Frank and his fliers couldn't follow them—they weren't built for higher altitudes. Besides, their priority was what the vessels had discharged.

"What are those things?" Wilkins asked.

"Damned if I know," Frank said.

He caught a glimpse of fish belly–pale hides, blue-gray streaks, heavy-duty claws, huge maws full of sharp teeth. The creatures hesitated a moment, then charged in the direction of Nova City, one after the other.

"They're not goodwill ambassadors," Wilkins concluded.

But Frank already had decided that for himself. "Take them out," he ordered the other pilots, and went after what he couldn't help seeing as a herd. He didn't need his autotargeting function, especially with the beasts clustered so closely together, but he used it anyway. As soon as he had one of the creatures in his sights, he fired.

His pulsers scorched the air with a silver-blue fusion-burst stream that obscured its target with the ferocity of its assault. *Direct hit,* he thought, consulting his instruments. One down, a bunch to go.

Then he realized that the creature he'd hit hadn't been killed by the pulser stream. Hell, it had hardly slowed down.

He fired again, his stream one of many plunging into the midst of the beasts. And again his target seemed barely fazed by it.

All around him, his fellow pilots were getting the same results. They were bringing the lightning and had nothing to show for it.

What the hell . . . ?

"Orders?" asked Harl Jones, his voice full of frustration.

"Keep firing!" Frank growled. What else could they do?

Especially with an innocent Nova City looming ahead in the lap of the red-clay mountains, its outermost precincts visible now with the naked eye.

CHAPTER TEN

On a series of holographic sections floating in front of her console, Wilkins watched the swarm of red blips representing the unidentified creatures traversing the landscape between the crash site and the outskirts of Nova City.

They were three kilometers from the colony and closing. And none of the blasts Raige and his fliers were raining down on the beasts seemed to have any effect on them.

Wilkins touched one of the pads on her console. "Commander Arroyo," she said, addressing the officer she had placed in charge of the city's F.E.N.I.X. defenses just months earlier, "I want you to take those things out."

"Acknowledged," said Arroyo. "Targets acquired. Firing."

On Wilkins's screens, the city's F.E.N.I.X. projectiles leaped from powerful cannons sunk deep into the natural crevices in the mountains. This was the tech that had stopped the only other invaders Nova Prime had ever faced. Stopped them cold.

For a moment, Wilkins allowed herself to believe that the projectiles would do the same thing to the beasts. She pictured the F.E.N.I.X. pods hitting their targets, latching on to them, penetrating them with shape-changing projections. And in fact, that was what they did whenever they smashed into their targets.

But the beasts weren't airborne craft. They seemed to

have the finely honed sensory apparatuses and the reflexes to spot and elude the projectiles. Despite Wilkins's hopes, the F.E.N.I.X. pods never hit a single target. The creatures just kept coming.

And then it was too late. They were too close to the city for the cannons to unleash additional projectiles. Too close to it—and then *inside* it.

Wilkins felt a pit open in her stomach. "Cease fire," she snapped.

"Ceasing," Arroyo said, sounding every bit as frustrated, every bit as horrified as the Prime Commander.

Wilkins forced herself to think, and when she did, it made a grim kind of sense that their F.E.N.I.X. tech wouldn't be able to stop the creatures. If it was the Skrel, if they had come back after all those years, would they have done so if they couldn't beat the colony's defenses? Would they have bothered if they couldn't defeat the F.E.N.I.X. projectiles humanity had thrown against them hundreds of years earlier?

Wilkins consulted her instruments. There were . . . what? Two dozen, three dozen of the creatures? And they were inside Nova City, where they could destroy at will. Because she had gotten a glimpse of one or two of the things, and she was very certain that they were there on Nova Prime to destroy every human being in their path.

"Prime Commander?" It was Frank's voice. "We're pursuing the creatures as best we can. But it's hard to get a read on them with all the buildings in the way. People, too. And even when we hit them—"

"Acknowledged," Wilkins said. "Do your best, Frank."

She still didn't know how the alien vessels had gotten through their satellite grid, but she would find out. And she had to get a squad out to the alien craft. There might be answers on it.

But Wilkins's main concern was stopping the creatures. If Raige's fliers couldn't stop them, her only other option was to meet them on the ground. *In the streets*.

And she didn't much like that approach, either. Ground

forces would have the same pulsers the fliers had. Their only advantage would be that they were closer to the monsters and could hit them with more force.

But that would also mean the monsters were close to *them*. She cursed under her breath. "Elias!"

Her colleague was at her elbow in an instant. "Prime Commander?"

"Look at the buggers' entry points into the grid. We need squads set up to intercept them. Make sure they communicate with the fliers in case we spot some of the creatures from above."

"Acknowledged," Hāturi said, already on his way.

Within moments he was at the deployment screen, assigning Rangers on the basis of their proximity to the new posts. A moment later, Bonita joined him.

They began clustering their personnel in teams of six, seven, or eight, led by the highest-ranking Ranger available in each area. Wilkins was pleased about how smoothly they appeared to come together. It was that kind of teamwork that might mean the difference between life and death.

Rangers in New Earth City were forming squads as well. The reports she was receiving from Commander Bartlett told her as much. But as far as she could tell, none of the creatures had headed that way. *Why should they?* Nova City was much closer, a much more convenient hunting ground.

Just then, a message came in from Bartlett. It was reflected on one of her screens. *Should I send reinforcements?*

"Not necessary," she replied, depending on her software to translate the words into text. "At least not yet."

Another of Wilkins's floating screens showed her a report from Commander Lennon. He and his cadets were taking to the streets as well, but not to fight the invaders. Their job was civilian control.

Because as it stood now, every human being in the city had to be considered a target.

* * *

Ken Pham looked stunned when Vander Meer said he intended to go on with the day's broadcast. "You understand we've been invaded, right?"

"And now we need to reassure people," Vander Meer said. He was deadly serious.

The news bulletin to which he had woken—the one that spoke of the alien vessel—had sent a thrill of fear through him. Then he saw the advantage in reporting on this historic event. All his journalistic instincts firing at once, he skipped half his morning routine and rushed for the studio while the rest of the family headed for a shelter. They had begged him to stay with them, of course.

But he couldn't. Immortality awaited.

Vander Meer had studied journalism, though his detractors had often suggested otherwise. He recognized that the great shapers of opinion in the past had been the ones who had covered events like this one. There was Murrow during World War II and McCracken during the departure from Earth, and now it was *his* time.

"I have to keep them informed," he added. "In touch with what's going on."

"Don't you think the Rangers are doing that?" asked Pham. "Why are you so fired up to be on the air?"

"I need to play my role, be part of history," he started to reply, and realized how pompous he sounded, even to himself. "I can't just hide in a bunker, Ken."

His producer let out a sigh. "Me, either, I guess." He began warming up his control panel.

Vander Meer smiled. "I know. You'd rather be reading under a tree."

"Is that too much to ask?" Pham touched one last screen. "All warmed up and ready."

Vander Meer automatically looked down to make sure he was presentable. His navy blue and gray suit—the next outfit in his rotation—seemed fine, pressed and clean. He glanced up, saw the live light blink to life, and began.

"My friends," he said, aware of the importance of each word, "the attack is real. We are all in danger. But we have practiced for just this occurrence, haven't we? All you have to do is find shelter and then look after yourself and your loved ones.

"My sources inform me that there are just a few dozen of these creatures and that the Rangers vastly outnumber them. They are overhead in their fliers, blasting the monsters to pieces. They're in the streets, hunting the monsters down. I assure you, we will prevail.

"One has to wonder, though, about the timing of such an attack. Just as Prime Commander Meredith Wilkins began to dismantle the Rangers, here comes a threat to our very existence. Now, my friends, I am not suggesting in the slightest that Wilkins conjured up a threat to scare us and, in doing so, to protect the Rangers' position in our society. But it does all seem rather . . . how shall I put it? *Convenient?*"

Pham looked horrified at the suggestion that Wilkins had somehow arranged the attack as a way to protect her job. But his horror was short-lived, because messages were starting to pour in from listeners.

Vander Meer nodded approvingly. "While you are staying safe," he continued, "I will try to find answers for you. In fact, I will be broadcasting on a regular basis so you can remain informed as to what is *really* happening out there.

"This is Trey Vander Meer, back as soon as I have more news."

As soon as the signal ended, Pham shot out from behind his console. "Are you nuts? Do you intend to go out into the streets now and interview one of the beasts? Maybe stop a Ranger on patrol and ask him about Wilkins?"

Vander Meer ignored the questions and picked some lint off his pants. "What was the response?"

Pham blinked and checked his board. "They think

you're on to something. Metrics show seventy-three percent believe you're asking the right questions."

"Excellent. Well, then, maybe I should check in with the Prime Commander and see what *she* has to say."

"You go over there, she's as likely to lock you up as anything else," said Pham.

Wilkins was still reading screens and responding when she noticed Bonita standing next to her. "Commander?" she said.

"I should be out there," Bonita said.

Wilkins grunted as she watched the alien creatures fan out from their points of entry into the grid. "With an injury that almost killed you once."

"I've got a clean bill of health," Bonita insisted. "And the Rangers are going to do a better job if they have another experienced officer out there."

Wilkins couldn't argue that Bonita was one of the best squad leaders she had ever seen, or that she had tested off the scales in tactics, or that they needed people in the streets who knew what they were doing.

Of course, she wanted to protect Bonita, a friend as well as a colleague. But under the circumstances, she had to grant the woman's request. Anything else would be a dereliction of her duty to the colony.

"All right," Wilkins said. "Against my better judgment."

She already had put Bonita's husband, Torrance, in charge of a squad. She hated the idea of having two members of one family on the line like that. But that was the job they had chosen in life.

"Yes, ma'am," Bonita said, her eyes bright. She was eager to get back into the thick of things. But she would also keep her head about her. Wilkins was sure of that.

"You won't regret it," Bonita assured her. And she left the room without another word.

Wilkins frowned. Letting Bonita join the patrols hadn't been an easy decision. But she had a feeling she'd have to make harder ones before the day was through.

Frank Raige wished he could drop another pulser barrage on the creatures as they rampaged through the streets of Nova City.

But it didn't make sense. The creatures already had taken everything his fliers could dish out and barely even slowed down. The only ones Frank would be hurting with a fusion-burst barrage would be his fellow human beings.

The same human beings who were taking shelter as fast as they could, having been warned by the city's civilian defense system. But Frank could see from his vantage point that his fellow Novans weren't responding quickly enough. Despite the drills the Rangers had conducted periodically, few people seemed to know where to go or how to get there. Too many of them were milling in the streets, unaware of how close the alien monsters were or how quickly they would be upon them.

As Frank watched, his stomach tightening so much that it hurt, one of the creatures ran right into a knot of confused colonists. Before any of them knew what had hit them, the thing cut a swath through them with its foreclaws, sending bodies flying into the buildings on either side.

Some of the people got out in time. But the others . . . Frank's jaw clenched at the sight of how badly the creature's victims had been ripped apart. It clenched even harder when he saw the beast shove its maw into the bloody remains.

An infestation had been unleashed in Nova City. An infestation the likes of which no one had ever seen before.

And there was nothing Frank Raige could do about it.

* * *

Bonita Raige hadn't been in the field in what felt like forever, and so she didn't feel fear at the prospect of facing the creatures from the stars. Instead, she experienced a weird sense of lightness, almost like elation.

Having made it to the city's South Armory in no time flat, she was part of a mob of Rangers, each one grabbing a set of body armor, pulsers, and comm gear. Once she had slipped on everything she needed, she paused for only one thing.

Tapping the appropriate studs on her wristband, she called her husband and left a message. "Torrance," she said, "I'm back! Wilkins is sending me into the field!"

She could imagine Torrance's response: *"You want me to be happy she's sending you into action? Are you nuts? Is she nuts?"*

He would be concerned about her injury, of course. All it would take was one good shot to her head and Torrance would be a widower. And that was the way he would look at it, maybe even the very words he would choose.

But Bonita was a good squad leader. And the colony needed her.

Torrance would have asked her to think it through, to reconsider. But if she did that, the alien creatures would be in the center of town feasting on the people she was supposed to protect. So no, she couldn't think it through. She had to act.

Bonita wished she could tell him that everything would be all right and know that for sure. But she was a Ranger. The first thing they had told her when she was a cadet was that nothing was for certain.

Nothing.

CHAPTER ELEVEN

Conner and his fellow cadets stood on either side of the shelter doors, covering the street with their pulser rifles, while a steady flow of their fellow citizens filed into the sanctuary.

"Easy," said the Ranger in charge of their squad, a thickset woman named Eckersley. "No need to trample anybody. We're here to protect you."

But Conner had heard the reports. The creatures couldn't be stopped with just a fusion burst. Hell, no one knew if they could be stopped at all.

Skrel, he thought.

It was hard to believe, even for the guy who had gotten the first whiff of them. But the squad of engineers dispatched by the Savant to inspect the wreckage of the alien ship confirmed it. They found the same insignia on the side of the vessel that their ancestors had seen on the Skrel ships that had descended on the colony hundreds of years earlier.

Smaller, yes. Harder to identify from a distance. But definitely the same insignia.

The Skrel were back. Except this time they weren't attacking with ships. They had gone a different route.

Conner had heard stories . . .

No, he thought, driving them from his head. There was no time for speculation, no time for fear. There was only the task at hand.

He was a Ranger, and he had a job to do.

* * *

Wilkins saw Hāturi enter her command headquarters with an older man, a fellow with a thick head of gray hair pushed back from a broad forehead. He wore a white lab coat with the Savant's emblem sewn on the right breast.

"Commander Wilkins," Hāturi said, "this is Jean-Pierre Rambaldi, on loan from the Savant. He's a *zoologist*."

"At your service, Commander," Rambaldi said in a cultured voice.

Wilkins couldn't help glancing at the holographic screens around her, all of them showing her Rangers in action. Some were chasing the beasts; some were tending to the wounded. Some were covering the dead with fabric. The death count was rising way too quickly. She needed to know more about the enemy, and from what the Savant had told her, Rambaldi was their best bet in that regard.

"So," Wilkins said, "what do you know about the beasts so far?"

"Keep in mind," said Rambaldi, "that I've only seen as much as you have, Prime Commander. I've not had the chance to examine one of the creatures first-hand. I would need a corpse to obtain more definitive answers."

"I get that," Wilkins said. "Tell me what you know."

Rambaldi nodded. "First of all, they're sightless."

Wilkins was surprised. They had done what they'd done without *eyes*? "How do you know?"

"We've yet to identify sight organs in any of the magnifications we've studied. Such organs, you see, would have to be in plain sight in order to be useful. And none are."

It made sense. "So how do they track us?"

"They seem to be driven primarily by sense of smell.

Certainly not the first species we've encountered that depends heavily on the olfactory sense. But don't assume that their sense of smell, or any other sense, works the way ours does. These are alien creatures. Even that which seems familiar about them may be wildly *un*familiar."

"They're also impervious to pulser blasts, from what we've seen."

"Yes, though we're not sure how. After all, pulsers pack quite a punch. Again, if I had a carcass to dissect . . ."

"What else?" Wilkins asked.

"The talons on the creatures' limbs appear to be composed of a form of keratin, not unlike our own fingernails. But those talons are exceedingly sharp and exceedingly hard. Unbreakable for all intents and purposes."

Wilkins nodded.

"They're quick, too," Rambaldi observed.

The Prime Commander grunted. "Tell me about it. We've clocked them at almost eighty kliks an hour."

"Upward of eighty-five, actually. Slower when they try to maintain a steady speed for a longer period of time, but not much. Seventy, perhaps."

"Okay, so we can't outrun them," Wilkins noted.

"They don't tire, either. We've not seen them pause for rest. No sooner do they consume one kill than they begin seeking another. Based on that information, I would say they have very aggressive metabolisms. They convert their sustenance into energy much more quickly than anything we have seen before."

"Don't they have to sleep sometime?" Wilkins asked.

"I wouldn't rule it out," said the zoologist, "but we haven't seen it."

"Any guesses as to how strong they are?"

"Strong enough to leap several meters at a time in any direction."

Wilkins nodded. That fit with what she had observed. Unfortunately, she had yet to hear anything she could put to good use.

"I know," Rambaldi said. "It's frustrating. But they have weaknesses, I assure you. We just have to identify them."

The Prime Commander's attention was drawn to the holograms again. She watched one creature lope away from a human body it had picked clean. It moved easily, fluidly, not pausing once to sniff the air. If it depended on its sense of smell, it did so with confidence.

"We've been speculating," Hāturi said, interjecting, "as to whether these monsters are the Skrel themselves or some other species. What do you think?"

"Based on what we've seen of the Skrel craft—I'm speaking of their first attack, of course—these creatures are probably too big to be members of the same species." He lowered his voice as if he were talking to himself. "They remind me of an alien version of the *Ursus arctos horribilis*."

"What did you say?" Wilkins asked.

Rambaldi smiled a grim smile. "That's the formal name for the grizzly bear. Something about the creatures' gait, their size . . . reminds me of *Ursus arctos horribilis*."

"Doesn't matter what we call them," Wilkins said. "What matters is that we find a way to stop them."

Bonita could take care of herself.

Torrance Raige fixed on that truth as he led his squad of six seasoned Rangers through the most densely populated residential section of Nova Prime City. The doors there were all closed, the windows boarded up with everything from plastic to sheet metal. Since dawn, when his patrol had begun, he had spotted just a few people hurrying here and there for supplies. Not that there were any food markets open. They all had closed as soon as word got out about the Ursa. Torrance grunted. Some scientist had come up with the name only the day before,

but that was what everyone was calling the creatures—
Ursa.

It seemed to him that the word *Ursa* should describe just one of the beasts, but the scientist used it to describe all of them. *Leave it to an egghead to complicate things,* Torrance thought.

He hoped people's pantries were better stocked than his own. Neither he nor his wife had been much for shopping trips. One of them had always brought something home on the way back from work. Now there was no place to go for food. The city had an eerie quiet to it, a bizarre and unsettling emptiness. If Torrance hadn't had access to Ranger supply depots, he didn't know *what* he would have done.

Gone to Frank's place, maybe. Or Theresa's. For someone who lived alone, Theresa always seemed to have a lot of food on hand.

First sun was halfway up the sky, rapidly warming the air, and they still hadn't sighted any Ursa. At first, Frank and his fliers had made it fairly easy to keep track of the things, for all the good it had done. But after their initial feeding spree, they had been harder to locate. It was as if they knew they were being watched from above and had found places to hide from that surveillance.

So they can be anywhere, Torrance thought. *Anywhere at all.*

An intersection loomed ahead. Torrance gestured for two of his Rangers to check it out. He and the others stopped in their tracks. Valley and Abalo, both third-year Rangers, moved ahead and secured the crossroads. Only after they looked around and signaled the all-clear did Torrance and the others advance.

Valley and Abalo remained there until their squad mates had negotiated the intersection. Then they rejoined the group.

It was the procedure they had followed ever since they had left their barracks. Tedious, without a doubt. But

they weren't in a hurry. They had
careful, which was always preferable

On Torrance's left, Mayweather and
on window coverings to make sure they
*Not that it'll matter if the Ursa really go to
them.* But as far as they had heard, none of the cre___res
had tried to pry the humans out of their homes. *At least
not yet.*

Then again, there had been plenty of humans around
to hunt in the beginning. Now, with so few of them
around, the Ursa might change their tactics.

"Good here," Mayweather reported.

Torrance nodded. Then he turned to Rios and Le
Clos on his right side. "Same here," said Le Clos.

Torrance was about to nod again when something
told him to look not left or right but *up.*

Suddenly a shadow passed over him, and he discharged his weapon at it. The long, pale form absorbed
the flash of fusion-burst fire but seemed unperturbed by
it. Then the thing was among them, reaching for Torrance with a razor-taloned paw.

He had a moment to see its face, if it could be called a
face. No eyes, just as they had been told. Just a gaping
black mouth ringed by a double row of sharp bone-
white teeth. Words popped into Torrance's head: *quick
but not agile.* Testing the theory, he dived to his right,
rolled, and came up mercifully unscathed.

By then, his squad had begun blasting at the Ursa
from six different directions, each one careful not to get
caught in line with anyone else's energy bolts. The monster writhed under the barrage, clearly annoyed by it,
maybe even hurt a little. Rios must have thought so
because he tried to move in a little closer to increase the
intensity of his beam. *Too close,* Torrance thought. He
had already opened his mouth to order Rios back when
the Ursa lashed out and disemboweled the Ranger with
a sweep of its talons.

God, thought Torrance.

His stomach churned at the sight of Rios lying there,

...nsides spilled out on the ground in a red ruin, but he couldn't allow himself to be slowed down. He still had five Rangers to keep alive. "Maintain your positions!" he roared. "Don't let up!"

However, considering there were now only five Rangers left alive to fire at the thing, they had *already* let up. The Ursa snapped its head from side to side as if looking for another target, another human it could rip in half. Its legs bent as if it were gathering itself.

"It's going to spring!" Torrance bellowed.

The only question was in which direction. It was answered a moment later as the monster went for Torrance. As before, he hurled himself out of the way. But this time he didn't get away as completely as he had the first time. He felt a fiery pain deep in his thigh, ripping through flesh and muscle, dragging a groan out of him. As he rolled to a stop, he raised his weapon, pain and all. But the Ursa didn't seem interested in pursuing Torrance. Free of the ring of silver-blue fire that had surrounded it, it scooped up a mouthful of Rios's remains and bounded away.

"Pursue?" asked Valley.

"No," Torrance said. *Not with the squad diminished.* "Stay here. Just send a comm report on ahead."

"Yes, sir," said Valley, and activated her naviband.

As the Ursa turned a corner and disappeared, Torrance took stock of his squad mates. They were all pale, all sweaty with fear and revulsion. And it wasn't just from the way the thing looked or smelled or what it had done to poor Rios.

It was the alien-ness of it. It was the feeling that it had come from somewhere humankind had never known, both literally and figuratively.

As Torrance came to that understanding, Mayweather dropped to his knees beside him and flipped open an emergency medical kit. Taking out a compress, he pressed it against Torrance's leg to stop the bleeding, which was substantial. Torrance's entire pants leg had been dyed crimson.

Morales approached Rios, or what was left of him. "Help her," Torrance said, gesturing for the others to pitch in.

As badly as Rios had been ripped up, they couldn't just leave him there. He was a Ranger, after all. They had to pick up what was left of their comrade and take it back with them.

"It's deep," Mayweather said. He had picked up the compress to inspect his superior's wound. "We'd better get you to a medicenter."

Torrance laughed bitterly. "Assuming we can find one that's still open."

When Lyla Kincaid got the message on her home screen that the Savant wanted to address every engineer on the planet, it came as no surprise to her. After all, the colony was in crisis mode. It only made sense to enlist the expertise of Nova Prime's science corps in the defense effort. Lyla and her colleagues were nothing if not problem solvers, and the Ursa represented the biggest problem the colonists had faced in centuries.

What *did* surprise Lyla was the sight of Leslie Vincenzo's long, stern face filling the screen instead of Donovan Flint's. Though Vincenzo was nominally Flint's second in command, she seldom seemed to step outside her office.

I guess she made an exception this time, Lyla thought.

"I don't need to tell you how serious the problem is," said Vincenzo. "The Ursa, as they've come to be known, are destroying us one by one, and the Rangers, despite their best efforts, haven't been able to stop them. That leaves it up to us to devise a solution."

The mention of the Rangers made Lyla think of her brother. Last she had heard from him, he was going out on a civilian control mission. She forced herself to believe that he had come back from it.

"For hundreds of years," Vincenzo continued, "fusion burst was all we thought we needed. Then came the first Skrel attack, with its shielded ships, and we had to come up with an alternative to fusion burst. That was when we invented F.E.N.I.X. tech."

Lyla knew a lot about F.E.N.I.X. tech, including what the acronym stood for, which many in the colony seemed to have forgotten. The first two letters, *F* and *E*, were the chemical symbol for iron since iron atoms were the basis for the device's nuclear power. The last three letters stood for "Novan Instrument of Execution."

But then, she had reason to know more about F.E.N.I.X. tech. It was her ancestor, Jack Kincaid, who had invented it hundreds of years earlier, employing magnetic fields to transform a projectile made of thousands of steel filaments into different shapes that in sequence could penetrate a Skrel craft and then tear it apart from within, shields or no shields.

"Unfortunately," Vincenzo said, "neither technology seems to work very well against the Ursa. On occasion we seem to be able to frustrate the creatures with our fusion-burst hand weapons, but with our limited ordnance we can't muster the force necessary to damage them. Our F.E.N.I.X. projectile cannons failed to take down any Ursa outside the city limits, and we can't use F.E.N.I.X. tech in the streets. Even if we miniaturized the cannons, there's not enough time for a projectile to morph at close range.

"So we need something new: a weapon designed not to repel Skrel spacecraft but to kill or at least disable an Ursa. It must take into account not only the creature's anatomy but also its behavior—its hunting style. And it must lend itself to a mass-production schedule that makes use of what manufacturing resources we have, or can reasonably expect to have, at our disposal."

"Is that *all*?" Lyla said out loud.

"You've all been working on projects with defense implications," said Vincenzo, "at least in theory. I want you to focus on those implications and give me something that can be used with consistent effectiveness at a distance of ten feet or less. I'd give you a deadline, but I don't think I need to step up your sense of urgency in this case. Colonists are dying every day, and you don't want your loved ones to be among them."

But no pressure, Lyla thought.

She imagined her fellow engineers thinking the same thing—but not for long. Being the problem solvers they were, they already would have begun to look at the projects they were working on in a new light—in terms of whether they could be repurposed to kill Ursa.

Just as Lyla was doing, only she was giving the Savant's deputy half her attention.

"What are you waiting for?" Vincenzo asked. "Get going. Your colony needs you."

Lyla didn't need to be told twice. Her lab was just a couple of blocks away. She could call for a Ranger escort, but there would be engineers all across Nova City doing that. The drain on the Rangers' already stretched resources would be considerable.

I'm young, Lyla thought. Her lab was close. She could go it alone.

CHAPTER TWELVE

Days passed and Trey Vander Meer knew what people would think of him.

They would think he was crazy for venturing out of his house to broadcast a special edition of his program when the streets of Nova City were full of biological killing machines. And maybe he *was* crazy.

But he was also driven by the notion that the people of Nova Prime *needed* him—needed him now more than ever. He felt like a hero braving the trip to his studio to keep their spirits up. After all, who else would do it? Not an official source like Wilkins, certainly. She might be fine for the Rangers, but her bedside manner was nothing like Vander Meer's.

And there was plenty for the people to be upset about. The death toll continued to rise, albeit more slowly now than at first, each death stirring the coals of the colony's fear and keeping men and women from finding comfort or rest. Children woke screaming from nightmares. Insomnia plagued the adults.

Nor was it all the Ursa's fault. Food and water were becoming tougher and tougher to come by. The demand for a safe delivery method was growing. In fact, Vander Meer had prepared notes for a commentary on that very topic. He wanted to hold the government accountable for its failure to maintain some kind of infrastructure during the crisis.

Yes, the people needed him. And when it was all over, he would get credit for his heroism. He had no doubt of that. He would be remembered as the one who bolstered the colony's morale in its darkest hour.

Of course, there hadn't actually been any Ursa sightings in his neighborhood. Therefore, the odds were good—no, *very* good—that he would get to his studio and back without coming within three or four kilometers of the monsters. But that was a detail that could be left out of his autobiography.

"Trey," said his wife, her face streaked with tears, "I wish you wouldn't—"

He held up a hand to stop her. "My dear, we've already had this conversation. You agreed that I should go."

"I gave in," she said. "That's not the same."

It wasn't easy to leave her like this. But he was sure that other great journalists had made sacrifices. He would have to do the same thing, tears or no tears.

Vander Meer took one last glance at his children, who were sitting together in the family room, watching the official Ranger feed because there was nothing else to watch. *I'll change that,* he thought. *And in the process, I'll show Michael and Elena that their father isn't the ghoul they thought he was.*

Elena had been the most anxious of them, of course. She wanted to be with her boyfriend, but Trey and Natasha had refused to let her go. She was reduced to speaking with Derrick through the vid system despite the difficulty of finding a measure of privacy for their conversations.

"I'll be back soon enough," he assured Natasha. "See you then, my love."

Then he unsealed the door and cracked it open, looking straight, then left, and finally right. The streets were quiet, not a bird or insect in evidence. If anything, the utter silence was a bit unnerving. Nova Prime City had a distinct sound, a sound filled with life, and it was absent now.

"Lock it," he told his wife, feeling a sudden chill. Then he stepped outside and closed the door behind him.

He waited a moment for Natasha to do as he had asked. When he heard the last of the dead bolts they had added slip into place, he was satisfied. Taking a deep breath, he began his walk to work. It was a hot day. Before he had gone fifty meters, he was sweating. By the time he completed his journey, he would be a dishrag. Good thing he had a change of clothes waiting for him at the studio.

Vander Meer had barely reached the end of the block when he heard the growl. It wasn't the kind a dog made. It was too deep, too prolonged. *Ursa,* he thought.

But there wasn't an Ursa around, at least none that he could see. Then he realized that the growl was coming from behind his neighbor's house. The house right next to *his*!

I've got to get back home, he thought.

But he couldn't move. He was frozen in place, rendered unable to speak or even breathe by the terror that took crushing hold of him. As he stood there, helpless, he saw the Ursa after all.

It was slinking along the side of his neighbor's house. Nor was he the only one who had spotted it. From behind not only his door but others as well, he heard the rising swell of panicked voices. He could imagine the debate—run or stay put—each answer bringing its own complications and dangers.

I have to find a place to hide, he thought. Otherwise, he would be the easiest prey the creature had ever had. But he couldn't ask someone to open a door or a window for him to find safe haven in that person's home. He could feel cold sweat run down his back like a river, and his heart was beating so hard that it hurt.

Before he could figure out what to do, he heard another sound—not a growl but a human scream. And it was outside, not muffled by protective walls. The scream of a little girl. And there was a word in the scream, a word he could make out all too well: *"Dad!"*

It took him only a fraction of a second to process that it was Elena's voice, which made no sense since she had been inside the house when he'd left. He had hugged her good-bye after breakfast. She was safe.

Then it came to him: the boy! He lived a couple of blocks away. She had waited until Vander Meer was gone and then slipped out the back door.

Again the scream, this time louder and longer and higher in pitch: *"Dad!"*

It was mingled with the Ursa's growl as it moved back along the side of Vander Meer's neighbor's house, retracing its steps, and vanished around the corner into his neighbor's backyard.

Time slowed for Vander Meer. He imagined that he could see the Ursa catching sight of his daughter. There would be nowhere for her to hide back there. He had torn down the swing set months earlier, having seen that even Skipper was too big for it. Not even a shed, though he had planned to erect one after Michael's birthday.

Elena! he thought, tears running down his cheeks. She was trapped outside the safety of the house. Although she might try to plead for her brother to let her in, Michael wouldn't do so—not when he knew full well that it would expose him and Skipper and Natasha to the same danger.

Vander Meer heard screams of pain. His baby was being killed, torn apart, and he couldn't move to help her. He *couldn't* no matter how hard he tried. He was rooted to the ground.

But it was what he heard next that truly stunned him, that awakened depths of horror in him that he didn't know he had. It was Michael's voice, bellowing a challenge. Michael's voice, cursing the monster in their backyard.

Oh, no, thought Vander Meer. *No no no no no . . .*

Michael had opened the door, perhaps to distract the Ursa in an attempt to save his sister. The monster roared even more loudly than before, and a male cry of pain was added to the hideous, discordant opera playing out behind Vander Meer's house. A thud. A series of wet chomping sounds. In his mind's eye, Vander Meer saw the Ursa feeding on the remains of his son.

Please, he thought, not sure whom he was pleading with. *Please let me go back to them. Please let me get back inside without the monster catching sight of me.*

Then he heard plaster and metal splinter. Glass broke. The creature was attacking the house itself or had crashed into it. Whatever was happening, Vander Meer knew the Ursa was after Natasha and Skipper.

His wife's cry came as a grim confirmation. *Run,* thought Vander Meer. But no one ran out of the house, and the creature didn't come out, either. At least not until sometime after someone had gotten hold of Vander Meer and dragged him away.

His family. His flesh and blood. *No,* he thought. *It can't be.*

Trey Vander Meer wept, great sobs of pain erupting from his chest, and kept on weeping for a long time.

Bonita Raige's squadron arrived too late to help the family whose home the Ursa had invaded. She could see that as they arrived in their vehicle. The creature was busily consuming the remains of its victims, half in and half out of the ruined house, seemingly oblivious to everything else.

However, they could help the man who was standing in the middle of the street, staring at the house, frozen by fear. It wasn't until they had dragged him inside their vehicle and begun treating him for shock that Bonita realized who he was.

Trey Vander Meer. The guy who had started the movement to pare down the Rangers. *And here the Rangers are, saving his skin.* The irony didn't escape Bonita.

Vander Meer moaned something she couldn't make out, at least partly because she was keeping one eye on the Ursa. "What did he say?" she asked Yang, who was administering to Vander Meer.

Yang looked up at her. "My wife . . ."

Bonita glanced at the home the Ursa had broken into. Was it Vander Meer's? She gritted her teeth. It looked like whoever was inside would be way past help—hers or anyone else's. Nonetheless, she had to try.

"Danuta, you're with me," she snapped to a woman with thick red hair twisted into a braid. "Yang, you'll stay here with your patient. Bolt, Kromo, Carceras—evacuate the other houses." There were six of them left in the development. "Get people to the shelter on Buckingham."

Normally, she wouldn't have risked prying people out of their homes. But if there was one thing they had discovered, it was that the Ursa were quick learners. Once this one realized there was food inside these structures, it wouldn't leave the area until it had emptied every last one of them.

The Rangers acknowledged Bonita and spilled from the vehicle to follow her orders. As she swung around the house to get a better look at the Ursa, she wished she had a weapon in her hands that could put the thing down. After all, it would be an easy target as long as its attention was focused on its prey. But their pulsers weren't going to kill it; squads of her fellow Rangers had learned that the hard way. The best they could do, even at a dozen feet, was keep the Ursa off balance.

Moving past the corner of the house, Bonita caught sight of the beast just as it shoveled a bloody limb into its fanged maw. It made some wet crunching sounds, and blood dripped carelessly down its chest.

Bonita could feel her gorge rising, and she swallowed it back. *No time to puke. Not now.*

Behind her, her team was banging on doors and shouting orders. She could hear the footfalls of people as they emerged from their homes and responded to the Rangers' authority. They, at least, might be safe from the Ursa's predation. Meanwhile, the thing wasn't raising its head. It was as if it hadn't noticed Bonita or Danuta. Bonita kept moving, her goal to take a position behind it. Then she could look into the house through the hole the Ursa had made and get an idea if there was anybody left inside to save.

With every step she took, she imagined the Ursa turning and charging at her. But it didn't. It was too busy feeding. Finally, Bonita was directly behind the creature. Looking past it, she couldn't see anyone who hadn't already been ripped apart. But that didn't mean there wasn't someone hidden in there, someone praying that the monster would finally go away.

"Orders?" breathed Danuta.

Bonita cast a glance over her shoulder. As long as the thing didn't delve any deeper into the house, it made sense to wait and give her Rangers time to get the neighbors as far away as possible. So she waited.

But all the while, she couldn't help thinking she had a chance to take the thing out. After all, it hadn't reacted to her presence behind it. What if she were to take the offensive and get as close as she could and hit it with everything she had? Would her pulser do any more damage at close range?

Even before the neighbors were gone, Bonita had made her decision and communicated it to Danuta via hand signals. When the last of them vanished from sight, escorted by Bolt, Kromo, and Carceras, she began counting to fifty. Fortunately, the Ursa went on feeding, undisturbed by her presence behind it.

And it kept on feeding after she reached fifty and began advancing on it, pulser in hand, covered by Danuta. Her heart was pounding so hard that she couldn't believe the Ursa didn't hear it, her breath quick and uneven in her throat. She forced herself to calm down, to concentrate on the task at hand.

Step by step, Bonita came up on the creature. And it didn't move. It was as if she were in its blind spot, though it didn't make sense that a beast without eyesight could have a blind spot—did it?

She would leave that question to the Savant's people.

Her job was to do as much damage as she could to the monster before it went after anyone else.

She was ten feet away. Eight. So close now that she could almost reach out and touch the Ursa's hindquarters. Six. Four. As quietly as she could, she took aim at the back of the thing's head . . .

And heard the scream.

She didn't turn to see which neighbor it was whom her people had missed. It had to be a neighbor, she was certain, because none of her Rangers would scream that way. Therefore, she didn't turn, because it wouldn't tell her anything she didn't already know.

But the Ursa did.

Bonita found herself looking directly into its maw, a dark hole full of pointed teeth from which bloody flesh and gristle hung in tatters. And in that moment she knew the monster was looking back at her, realizing—if it hadn't already—that she was close enough to be a threat.

Fire!

Even as the command exploded in Bonita's brain, she depressed the trigger mechanism on her pulser and a bolt of fusion force buried itself in the Ursa's face— carving out a bloody gash every bit as deep as it was wide.

A moment later, Bonita realized she was lying on the ground, pinned under the creature's weight. But she was alive.

She couldn't breathe with the Ursa on top of her. It was suffocating her, crushing the life out of her. But at least for the moment she was alive.

As for the Ursa . . . she couldn't tell. She felt something hit it from the side, then a second time, and a third. Finally the thing began to stir. It was alive. And the impacts Bonita had felt? They had to be Danuta burying burst after burst in the creature.

Bonita had only one chance—to slip out from under the thing as it went after Danuta. But as the Ursa rose, it planted one of its massive forepaws on her face. Then, as if it were no more than an afterthought, it used the other forepaw to gut her like a fish.

As Bonita lay dying, she tried to yell to Danuta to get away while she still could. But there was too much blood gurgling up into her mouth, choking her, making it impossible for her to utter a sound. So all she could do was think it: *Danuta—run!*

CHAPTER THIRTEEN

Wilkins was reviewing telemetry in the command center when she overheard Hāturi speaking to someone over a voice line. He didn't sound happy. In fact, he sounded positively grim.

Who? was the question that came to mind. Not *What?* Field casualties had become as common as sand fleas, as common as skipjacks on the western flats. These days, the only question was *Who?*

As she moved closer to Hāturi to find out more, he cast a glance in her direction. His eyes were red and wet. It shook Wilkins to see him that way, to see Hāturi, a rock of a man, caught in the grip of such emotion.

The Prime Commander waited until Hāturi had ended his conversation. Then she asked the question.

His voice was husky with mourning. "It's Commander Raige, ma'am."

It felt like a physical blow. Wilkins grabbed the back of her chair to steady herself. After all, she was the one who had sent Bonita into battle despite her injury. She was the one who had put her friend in harm's way.

But she'd had no choice. Bonita was a good Ranger. She had been needed in the field. And she'd asked, for heaven's sake. She'd *asked*.

Hāturi gave her the rest of the report. Danuta had died as well. But most of the people they were trying to save had reached a shelter. Their mission had been a success, as much as any mission could be a success these days.

The Ursa had claimed four civilian casualties. It was still alive, still seeking prey. *Hardly a surprise.*

Wilkins absorbed the news. As it spread from Ranger to Ranger, a hush descended over the command center.

"Get me Torrance Raige," she told Hāturi. "I'll be in my office."

She knew Torrance was in an infirmary, recovering from the injuries he had sustained the other day. The damage wasn't bad. He'd be sidelined for a week. But Wilkins had a feeling he'd want back into the field sooner than that when he heard what she had to tell him.

Conner was just getting ready to go out on another food-gathering detail when Wilkins appeared at the entrance to his barracks.

What's she doing here? the cadet wondered. The Prime Commander didn't just show up in the barracks unannounced. Something was up.

Wilkins didn't say anything. She just scanned the barracks, obviously looking for something—or someone. As Conner watched, he wondered who it was. He was still wondering when the Prime Commander's eyes found him . . .

And stopped.

Conner felt his throat constrict. The look in Wilkins's eyes . . . it was the same one she'd had when she'd told Chen about his mother the day before. Even before Wilkins crossed the room and took hold of his shoulder, he knew what she was going to tell him. He just didn't know which member of his family she would name.

"Ma'am?" he said, trying hard not to let his voice crack.

"I have bad news, son. Your aunt Bonita . . ."

Wilkins didn't have to say any more. "Yes, ma'am. I understand. Thank you, ma'am."

Wilkins looked at him a moment longer, her brow creasing. She looked as if she wanted to say something else, but she didn't. She just smiled sadly, turned, and left Conner standing there.

With his grief.

Lyla Kincaid considered the device she had made in her lab a month earlier. An eternity ago, or so it seemed. After all, that was before the Ursa had landed on Nova Prime. The device was tiny, half the size of her fingernail. She tossed it in the air and caught it. *Light, too.* It was also durable, made of materials that were built to last.

And it helped people hear when nothing else would.

The scientists of Nova Prime had made remarkable strides in medicine since the Arrival hundreds of years earlier. For instance, back on Earth, people had had to put up with hearing impairments, some of them congenital, some the result of injury, and some inflicted by disease.

Not anymore. In most cases, the causes of the impairments had been eliminated. In the rest, the Savant's engineers had invented devices to address the problem. That was where Lyla's work came in.

The device she held in her hand was designed to be surgically implanted in the inner ear, where it would effectively take the place of an eardrum. Without it, certain individuals would be unable to hear. With it, they could hear perfectly.

Like Pietro. A good thing by all accounts.

But there was nothing revolutionary about it. *Nothing revolutionary at all. It just works a little better than the model before it, which worked a little better than the model before that, and so on.* But the Savant had asked

Lyla—like all her fellow engineers—to come up with a tactical application.

"A *tactical* application," she repeated to herself, and laughed at the idea.

Were the Ursa vulnerable to certain sounds the way human beings were? Did the creatures even *hear* in the first place? Despite the best efforts of those who had observed the beasts, there was no conclusive evidence either way.

Lyla frowned at her device. It was nothing like Jack Kincaid's concept for the F.E.N.I.X. projectile system he had introduced hundreds of years earlier. A projectile that used magnetic fields to transform itself into a number of different shapes, one after the other. Now, *that* was an innovation.

Yet the concept originally was shot down by the Savant of that era, who, ironically enough, happened to be a Kincaid as well. In fact, Bree Kincaid, a brilliant woman in her own right, was the very *first* Savant. Like everyone else at the time, Bree had grown up with fusion-burst tech. She had come to depend on it. When it didn't work against the Skrel, her first thought was to find a way to improve it, not to chuck it out the window in favor of something new and untested.

Of course, there was another reason Bree Kincaid took the conservative approach. The office of Savant was so new that the people still didn't know what to make of it. One wrong move, Bree had noted in her journal—which had become required reading for engineers ever since—and the colony might have decided to get rid of the Savant. That would have been a blow to scientific progress from which the people might never have recovered.

To avoid such a disaster, Bree had decided to build methodically on what had come before and in that way gain the colony's trust. The last thing she wanted to do was make the people think they had entrusted the office of Savant to a rebel.

So she tossed her cousin Jack's idea on the trash heap.

It was only after the Rangers had gotten hold of a Skrel vessel and determined the nature of its shielding, which could withstand fusion-burst blasts no matter how much the colonists amped them up, that the Savant gave in to her cousin and allowed him to try out his F.E.N.I.X. system.

From the beginning, it worked like a charm. One by one, the Skrel ships were destroyed. And from then on, Jack Kincaid's F.E.N.I.X. system became the preferred defense option on Nova Prime.

But now they had a problem that they'd never had before, and neither F.E.N.I.X. nor fusion burst was proving useful in stopping the Ursa. The Savant, unlike Bree Kincaid before her, had asked them to look for answers in a wide variety of research projects. *That was to his credit,* Lyla thought.

She didn't think the project she was working on would be very helpful. However, she had a feeling that something else might. It wouldn't hurt to pursue that option as well—to take the idea just starting to take shape in her head and see where it might lead her.

After all, you never know.

Trey Vander Meer sat in the shelter on Buckingham Street with Yang, a Ranger with a smooth scalp and cheekbones so prominent that they looked like they could cut glass.

"You don't have to leave?" the commentator asked.

Yang shook his head slowly from side to side. "I'm here as long as you need me."

"That's kind of you," Vander Meer said. "Very kind."

His brain felt sluggish as he tried to process what had happened earlier that day. He had walked out the door a proud husband and father. Now he was bereft of his family, alone in the world. The Rangers had responded. They had saved his neighbors and—he thought, though he wasn't sure—hurt the creature that killed his family.

But where were the Rangers when he needed them? When the beast was tearing . . . was grinding—

He couldn't go on, not even in the deepest recesses of his mind. He had to stop and gather himself.

"Are you all right?" Yang asked.

Vander Meer nodded. "Fine. Thank you."

Yang was a good man. But neither he nor the other Rangers had been there when Vander Meer needed them.

I should have stayed, said a voice in Vander Meer's head. *I should have argued with Natasha a little longer. I should have stayed and talked to Michael before I walked out the door.*

A series of missed moments, time he would never recover.

Were they even having funerals for the victims? He couldn't recall. Suddenly, he remembered that Pham was waiting for him. Waiting . . . at the studio. *Yes.* But Pham would understand. He always understood.

I'll take some time off, Vander Meer thought. *It's only reasonable.*

After all, he had lost everything dear to him. And what had the Rangers done to help him, vaunted defenders of the colony that they were? He kept coming back to that, kept thinking that if the Rangers had only done their jobs, he would still have a family around him.

It isn't my fault that they're gone, he thought. *It's the Rangers'.*

That was the *real* problem, wasn't it? The Rangers had failed the citizens they were supposed to protect. He wouldn't forget that.

Not ever.

Torrance Raige hadn't taken the news about his wife very well. The only way he could deal with it was to get back in the field. Knowing him as well as she did, Prime

Commander Wilkins had approved the idea. But there were fields, and there were *fields*.

I should be out there. I'm a trained Ranger, dammit. What am I doing here defending a supply depot when there are more important things to be attended to? This is insane. It's madness.

Bonita. Oh, God, Bonita . . .

Torrance used his uniform sleeve to wipe away the sweat beading on his forehead. *Get your head out of your ass and into the game.*

Back to basics. Back to basics.

One of the first things the Rangers were taught as part of their training was that when matters seemed to be spiraling out of control, the wise thing to do was to take a knee and focus one's energies. It had been a long while since Torrance had done so, but he could not recall the last time he'd been faced with a situation quite like this one.

He went down to one knee.

Focus on your surroundings. Root yourself in this present moment.

The smart fabric that lined the walls of the supply depot fluttered in the stiff breeze coming in from the north. The structure was ringed by a squad of Rangers, a number of whom, like Torrance, had been injured in the field. Since the medics had judged that their assorted injuries would slow them down in battle against the Ursa, an inconvenience that could easily prove fatal, they had been given duties that probably would prove less of a threat to their lives.

Torrance's wound was still throbbing; the synthoheal that the medics had spread on it had been only partly successful, for the wound was still red and swollen and was beginning to feel hot to the touch (or at least it seemed hot to Torrance). The medics had sternly informed him that if he felt faint, he was to report back to the medicenter immediately.

Torrance would be damned if he would do something

like that. He was going to be out here fighting the Ursa until the last shreds of life had fled his body.

Shut out the distractions. Pain is of no use to you. You know the injury is there. Ignore it.

He shut down the discomfort the wound was giving him. It wasn't all that difficult, really. *Just part of the training.* Pain was never insurmountable. It was simply something else to be dealt with. Torrance gathered all the anguish he felt from his wound, isolated a section of his brain where he could place it, as if in a lockbox, and then sealed it off. When it was contained, he was aware of nothing beyond a faint, dull ache instead of a steady stabbing sensation.

He reached out with his finely honed senses but couldn't perceive anything that posed a threat, most notably the Ursa. It was, however, disconcerting to know that the damned things could practically be breathing down the necks of the Rangers on duty and they wouldn't know it until it was too late.

"Taking a knee?"

He didn't even bother to open his eyes and look to his right. He was fully aware that Marta Lemov was standing a few feet away. Marta had joined up with the Corps the exact same time Torrance had. They'd come up through the ranks together and often had wound up teamed on various squadrons. At one point they had even had an ill-advised and short-lived liaison (before he'd hooked up with Bonita) that they still occasionally kidded each other about.

Marta was tall and lanky and had received any amount of teasing about her "manly" hands and feet. Her head was bandaged, but she didn't seem the least bit bothered by it.

"The old ways work because they're tried and true," Torrance said.

"That's certainly circular reasoning."

"Shut up," Torrance said dismissively before adding, "You okay?" He indicated the bandaged head with a tilt of his chin.

"This?" Marta pointed at the bandage. "It's nothing. The medics made some noises about concussion, but . . ." She waved it off dismissively.

"You're out of your mind. You should be in for observation."

"*I* should be in? Torrance"—all the sarcasm and irony was gone—"Torrance, my God, your wife is barely a couple of days gone and you're back out here."

"You suggesting I should abandon my people in a time of need? You have me confused with someone who doesn't give a damn."

"I'm not even going to try to argue with you about this."

"Wise move," he said.

The half dozen other Rangers were paying little to no attention to the conversation between Torrance and Marta. They were far too busy surveying the surrounding area, searching for any sign, any warning of a possible threat. They had sustained varying degrees of injury, but to a man they were dealing with the pain and shunting it aside much as Torrance had.

"Hey!" came a shout. Several men were approaching. Torrance recognized them by sight if not by name. One of them was a technician; two more were farmers. The technician, for no reason other than that perhaps he was the most articulate, appeared to be the spokesman. "Hey!" he said again. It did not appear to be a jaunty greeting.

Nevertheless, Torrance, as the senior Ranger on station, provided a cheery "hey" right back at him. *Keep this calm. He clearly has something on his mind. Let's hear it. Perhaps, whatever it is, it won't be any sort of issue that could—*

"Step aside. We want access to the supplies."

So much for that hope.

"I'd love to, but everything's being meticulously rationed," Torrance said patiently. "The Ursa are tearing through everything, causing random destruction. So what we have left, we have to carefully—"

"You think you're telling me anything new, Ranger?" Torrance wasn't thrilled with the way he was saying that word, *Ranger*. As if it were an epithet. The technician pointed at the two farmers. "My friends here were telling me how one of those things came tearing through his farmland. *His* farmland."

"The farmland is shared by all—"

"*Shut up*," the technician snapped, so angrily that Torrance immediately realized he had erred. Focusing on the philosophy of joint ownership, of shared need, had been the wrong angle to take. He should have been reacting instead to the fact that the farmer probably had been scared witless and was damned lucky to be alive.

Meanwhile, the technician was still ranting. "Thank God that these men's fathers and their fathers' fathers had the initiative to build their own bomb shelters after the first Skrel attacks! No Rangers helped them do that; no, sir. And so when the Ursa attacked, they had somewhere to take refuge and hide so those creatures couldn't sniff them out."

Torrance noticed that the technician was wobbling slightly. It was clear to him now what had been happening. The three men had gotten to talking while having drinks together somewhere—tossing back a few in the face of impending disaster—and a session of mutual frustration had morphed into a call for action, even if it was misguided action.

"These men have paid more than their fair share into a system that's completely breaking down! They had to save their own lives because you damned Rangers were nowhere around, and now they can't feed their own families from the fruits of their labors while you people get to decide how much or how little is being handed out to others!"

Torrance kept his voice level and did his best to try to sound sympathetic. "Gentlemen . . . I understand what you're going through . . ."

"Do you?" said one of the farmers challengingly.

"Yes, I do. The Rangers weren't there for you. We're

stretched thinner than we've ever been before and . . ." *And we have no idea how to fight these things.* ". . . and we can't be everywhere, as much as we'd like to be. But the fact is that we have an order to our society. A way we do things. Don't you see that the Ursa were sent here by the Skrel not just to kill us but to shred the fabric of our society? The rationing system has to be carefully maintained. Our way of doing things has to be maintained. Because if that doesn't happen—"

"Look out!" came the startled cry from Marta, but it was too late for Torrance to react.

When the rock bounced off the side of his head, he was caught completely off guard. It hadn't come from the technician or the two farmers facing him. While he'd been distracted by the three of them, others had been approaching from the side. No one had spotted them because they'd all been distracted by what Torrance had been saying to the technician.

The rock had hit him just above the right temple. Dazed, he went down to one knee, just as he had a few minutes earlier.

"Get the food!" shouted the technician, a defiant rallying cry, and there were more shouts from the other direction as well.

Everything was coming unraveled too quickly for Torrance to follow. He couldn't tell if this had all been some sort of masterful game plan—the technician and farmers had been an advance guard to draw their attention so that others could sneak up and get into position—or if everything had just unfolded spontaneously and Torrance had had the lousy luck to be at the eye of a rapidly approaching hurricane. Except there was nothing remotely peaceful about this particular eye.

The technician tried to shove past even as the world spun around Torrance. He was suddenly blind in one eye and didn't understand the reason for it until he realized in a distant manner that blood was pouring into that eye from a cut in his head. The technician swung a kick at Torrance for good measure as he went past, but that was a mistake, as Torrance's training and reflexes kicked in.

He caught the technician's leg in a perfectly executed cross block, guided the force of the attack past him, and shoved hard. The overbalanced technician lost his footing and came down on the ground with his legs in a split. He screamed in pain. *With any luck,* thought Torrance, *the bastard ripped a muscle in his crotch.* Torrance swung a roundhouse that caught the technician squarely in the face, and the man fell over without another sound.

Marta and the other Rangers were tightening their circle, but Torrance could see the hesitation in their eyes. The Rangers had been trained throughout their existence for one mission: to preserve humanity. Not to battle against it. To use force of arms against their own people was counterintuitive, especially in a situation such as this one.

These people weren't lawbreakers. They were desperate, frightened, just trying to survive. How much easier would it be to just get the hell out of their way?

The blood was now pouring from the wound in Torrance's forehead and didn't seem to show the slightest inclination to slow down. He tried to wipe his eye clear as he shouted, *"Stop them!"*

The Rangers formed ranks and battled back, but only hand to hand. To a man, they would not use potentially lethal force against their fellow human beings. This restraint on their part didn't make the Rangers any less formidable. But for every Novan one of the Rangers managed to take down, two or three more took his place.

Apparently word had spread with the speed of light that there was a massive assault at this supply depot. People were coming from everywhere, and not a single one of them was showing up to fight on the side of the Rangers.

Worst of all, Torrance had to think that this wasn't an

isolated incident. Panic and desperation weren't going to remain confined to this one particular depot. If this kept up, the Skrel weren't going to have to do much more than sit back and wait for humanity to tear itself to pieces.

People were converging from all sides. Torrance fought back, his hands moving so quickly that they were little more than blurs. Someone came in at him fast. He recognized his attacker: the curator of the local history museum. He could talk for hours about such items in his collection as an actual vintage copy of *Moby-Dick,* a first edition acquired by Forever Books in the year 2032 AD. The sweetest, gentlest man anyone could hope to meet. And there was murder in his eyes.

"Weapons!" Torrance shouted, because there was no choice. "Half power!"

The Rangers unholstered their pulsers and opened fire.

The barrage of silver-blue blasts ripped into the attacking citizenry. The impact was akin to being struck in the chest by a bag full of rocks. People were knocked off their feet, crying out in pain, and for a few moments it seemed as if the Rangers were going to stem the tide.

But then the attackers rallied, redoubling their efforts. Wholly unintentionally, the people toward the front of the mob wound up being human shields, absorbing the brunt of the pulsers' punishment and then slamming forward into the Rangers. Torrance and the others continued to fire into the crowd. Had their pulsers been at full power, the entire area would have been stacked high with corpses.

But they treated their panicked brethren with mercy and thus paid for it.

"Hold ranks! Hold ranks!" Torrance shouted, and then his wound started bleeding again, even more profusely. He was completely blinded, and before he could clear his vision, he was borne to the ground. He fired unseeing into the crowd, and then his pulser was kicked away. Instinctively he threw his arms around his

head to protect himself. Someone drove a kick into his stomach, and he gasped. Then his world began to blacken, and he realized it wasn't just from the blood in his eyes.

Bonita . . . damn . . . I'd have been safer hunting the Ursa.

And then he was out.

CHAPTER FOURTEEN

It is Gash.

It does not call itself that.

It has no name for itself.

It has no awareness of itself.

It has no capacity to wonder what is happening on this world or ponder why it has come to this place and this time.

It only knows what is hardwired into its very essence.

It knows that it must eat.

There are others of Gash's kind around. They are hunting in pairs for the most part, but Gash hunts alone. The others irritate Gash. Gash is bigger, stronger, faster than any of them. They slow Gash down. They diminish him.

At the moment, Gash is curled up in an alleyway, shaded from the warmth of the twin suns overhead. Gash finds the warmth irritating. Its skin ripples several times, from head to tail, trying to shake off the annoying sensation, yet it cannot seem to do so. Some of the time the heat vanishes, the lights in the sky departing to whatever holes they emerge from, so that Gash may be provided some temporary relief.

Gash hates this world. The world Gash had before was contained and dark and quiet. The world Gash had before was the epitome of peace.

Then Gash was evicted from that world and thrust into this one.

Here it is hot and irritating. Here it is painful. Gash's

long tongue emerges from between its lips and slides across the injuries it has sustained, particularly the long, blistering slice across its skin that has earned it the name it doesn't know it has.

It received the injury—the gash—in an encounter with the smell things. That is how Gash has come to think of them. If a thing smells a certain way, it can be eaten. It is therefore Gash's quarry. If it does not smell a certain way, it can be ignored.

But the smell things do not allow themselves to be eaten without a fight. They try to hurt Gash. The last time Gash ran into them, Gash believed it had found easy prey. Gash had killed and begun to consume two of the smell things, one of them very small and unsatisfying, before a third one attacked Gash.

That was the smell thing that dealt Gash its injury. It hit Gash with a terrible force, a force that made Gash stumble and fall. But only for a breath. Then Gash recovered its senses and killed the smell thing. Gash—

—freezes in place.

Another of the smell things is nearby.

Whether it is looking for Gash or not is completely beside the point. It is meat. It smells like hunger abated.

The smell thing draws nearer. Gash realizes there is a second one with it. Two smell things are even more irresistible than one.

Gash waits until the first one is almost on top of it, and then Gash is on its feet, letting out a thunderous roar.

The smell thing has seen Gash, heard Gash. Gash is certain of it. Gash has a clear "view" of its target, "sighted" to within eighty percent of certainty. But eighty percent isn't good enough. Gash wants more.

So Gash advances toward the smell thing before Gash bellows its defiant cry. The thing's aroma is now so pronounced that it is driving Gash to the brink of madness.

Gash runs it down. Gash rips it apart. Gash devours a mouthful of it, blood and flesh and bone all at once.

The other smell thing—there are two; Gash was correct—seems unable to move. Gash leaps, its paws out and forward, and lands squarely on the smell thing's upper body. The smell thing is screaming. Gash pushes down hard, and its front paws crush the smell thing's upper torso. It crunches like a brittle stick, and there is blood everywhere.

Gash laps up some of the blood. Then Gash proceeds to devour the rest of its two victims. Eating the corpses of these revolting creatures is the one thing on this world in which Gash can take pleasure.

Once Gash has finished, it settles in. It will digest its meal and then will continue on its way.

It will head toward the sources of meat.

And it will consume them one by one.

Because that is the only thing it can think of to do.

Theresa Raige had been on her knees in a tiny stone room praying for the salvation of Nova Prime, just as she had prayed the day before and the day before that, and so on, ever since the coming of the infernal beasts known as the Ursa, when she heard the announcement that there were Rangers in the building, seeking asylum.

The building—a towering spire of rock called the Citadel—had been home to the Primus and the augury since the Arrival. In all that time, no Ranger had set foot in it. If they were doing so now, there had to be a good reason for it. Theresa, whose prayer room was on one of the Citadel's highest floors, hurried down the long, winding stairs of the immense retreat to its ground-level entrance hall. There she saw the ones who had sought asylum.

The Rangers were covered with bruises. Several were bleeding from cuts on their faces. Uniforms were torn, and one Ranger was moaning softly, clutching at a shoulder that clearly was dislocated. Two of them looked dazed, as if they weren't quite sure how they had gotten to the Citadel in the first place.

Theresa couldn't help looking around to see if one of them might be a member of her family. Though poor Bonita was gone, her brothers and her nephew were still fighting the Ursa. But as it turned out, neither Frank nor Torrance nor Conner was among the half dozen Rangers she saw scattered on the floor, lying on blankets brought to them by augurs who were already attending to their injuries.

Nonetheless, she knew one of them: Marta Lemov, who had gone out with Torrance at one time and was serving under him the last Theresa had heard. Marta's head was bandaged, but it looked far more professionally done than anything they could have accomplished at the Citadel. It was obviously an older injury that medics elsewhere had attended to already.

Marta was sitting on the floor, utterly unmoving, staring off into space. Her eyes might have been open, but she was clearly looking inward. Theresa approached her tentatively and whispered her name.

Marta's gaze flickered over to her, and at first she didn't seem to recognize her. Then her eyes widened and the edges of her mouth upturned ever so slightly. The lower half of her face was bruised—someone clearly had punched her in the side of the jaw—and there was a dark red spot on the bandage that Theresa thought might actually be widening. "Hey. You look good," she told Marta.

Recognition dawned in the Ranger's eyes. "Really? You look like crap on a crap cracker." Then she chuckled softly, which set off a coughing fit that took thirty seconds to get under control. Once she had managed to do so, she put out a hand. "Good to see you, Theresa."

Theresa knelt beside her and took her hand in hers. "What's happening out there?" she asked. In other words: *Why are you here?*

"Insanity," said Marta. "Madness. People going crazy." Disgust was etched on her face now. "It's unbelievable. We're destroying one another. We should be united against the Skrel, and instead we're ripping one another apart. And some of us are too stupid to . . ." She growled low in her throat, like an animal. A caged animal.

"Too stupid to what?"

"To realize how much the others hate us. Your brother Torrance fought right beside me, and he wound up here along with the rest of us. And with all his injuries, he refused to stay here. Right now, even as we speak, that blind fool is out there, determined to keep fighting back against those devouring animals. Fighting against them in order to save a bunch of traitorous bastards who aren't worth saving . . ."

And then another voice spoke.

"Losing faith?"

Both Theresa and Marta looked up in surprise.

Primus Leonard Rostropovich was standing a few feet away.

Marta, who had shown very little interest in moving until that point, was suddenly on her feet so fast that Theresa was almost knocked aside. *"You! This is all your fault!"*

Had it not been for Theresa, Marta would have been across the room and upon the Primus in a heartbeat. And it was only because Marta was in a weakened state that Theresa could stop her, grabbing her across the chest and around the shoulders and pulling back as hard as she could. If Marta had been herself, there would have been nothing Theresa could do.

Still, Marta struggled. Theresa pleaded with her to stop even as Marta kept bellowing, *"Your fault! Yours, you sanctimonious prick!"*

The Primus didn't move, didn't even look surprised. Instead he simply stood there, his fingers interlaced in front of him.

"Marta, calm down!" Theresa chided, and then, with even more force, she shouted, *"Calm down!"* and jammed her knee into the back of Marta's leg. Marta went down, Theresa on top of her, trying to immobilize her.

She could not, however, stop Marta from blaspheming against the Primus. "You're the one who turned the people against the Rangers!" Marta snapped. "You're the one who kept telling everyone we weren't needed! We're being eaten alive out there! By those creatures! By one another!"

"Devoured," the Primus said mildly. They might have been having a purely academic discussion for all that he showed of his emotions. "Devourers. Isn't that what some people are calling them?"

"Let go," Marta said to Theresa between gritted teeth. "Let go. I'm gonna—"

"Attack me?" The Primus's face remained impassive. "You have taken an oath to protect humanity. Is this how you're going to fulfill it? By assaulting someone who is just standing here?"

Before Marta could respond, they heard the sound of approaching voices—belligerent voices, presumably those of belligerent individuals—coming from the direction of the Citadel's front door. The injured Rangers in the room looked at one another with concern and alarm, because the repeated refrain from outside was "Bring them out! Get them out here!" And there was little doubt as to the identity of the "who" that was being demanded.

A couple of augurs came running up to the Primus, clearly agitated. They talked over one another, competing to explain to their leader that a mob was outside the Citadel, a mob that was insisting that the Rangers be turned over to them.

Marta was still on the floor, her body entangled with Theresa's. With cold fury, she snarled, "The Skrel are out to destroy us, and thanks to you, Novans are blaming us for it. Congratulations, Primus. Because of you, down is up and black is white. Why not go out there and take a bow for your mighty achievement?"

The Primus, unfazed by the pure, shocking hatred in

Marta's voice, said with seeming indifference, "I believe that's an excellent idea. Wait here." Theresa noticed the arrival of the Primus's guards, who were armed and ready to defend the guardian of Nova Prime's soul. However, the Primus casually waved them away and, when they appeared dubious, was more insistent. "Stay back," he said. "I will attend to this. And you," and he turned to Marta.

Then he hesitated.

"Me what?" Marta said challengingly.

The Primus bowed slightly. "Thank you for your service."

As Theresa watched, he went to talk to the people.

Farmers, the Primus thought as he looked out on the gathering protesters who were angrily demanding to be allowed entrance to the Citadel.

The Primus's guards who were customarily on duty outside were still at their posts, warning the crowd to stay back. Thus far the farmers had attended their cautions even though they far outnumbered the guards. They didn't look like they meant to rush the Citadel, although they seemed to harbor quite a bit of hatred for the Rangers who had been dispatched to guard the colony's emergency food stores.

And whose fault is that? Whose fault?

Even though the mob wasn't trying to force its way in, it was still making a hell of a ruckus—right up until the Primus made his presence known. The moment he did that, everyone immediately fell silent.

The Primus scanned the audience with an air of indifference, as if he could not possibly have cared less whether they were there or not. *As a mob they are formidable, unthinking. Break them into individuals.* "Farmers," he said quietly after a long pause. "Service workers. Artisans. So many of you, from many different disciplines. What would you have me do?"

There was hesitation. Then one of them managed to cobble together some arrogance. "There're Rangers hiding in there!"

"They are within, yes," the Primus said mildly. "They are guests of the Citadel."

"They attacked us!" shouted another, and choruses of agreement sounded from within the mob.

"How now? From my understanding, you attacked them first."

"We want justice! They were keeping us from what was rightly ours!"

"Rightly yours?" The Primus insinuated a sharpness into his voice that hadn't been there before. "We are as one on Nova Prime. The resources provided by one serve all. You know that. You all know that. So by what right do you demand to take back that which you provide by custom and law?"

"Things are different!"

"Because the devourers have come," said the Primus.

They didn't have to ask to whom or to what the Primus was referring. They knew all too well. They nodded almost as one.

The Primus took several steps forward, his hands draped casually behind his back. The crowd took the same several steps back.

"When the Skrel attacked us in force," he said, "we pulled together. All the factions of Nova Prime were as one. Together we were unbeatable. And now here we are, turning on one another. The Skrel sent the devourers, and we wind up devouring each other. I suppose, in a way . . . they followed us. Followed us from Earth. Followed us from the earliest days of our people.

"It's all there in the old writings. I've studied them, you see. I've studied them all. Christians routinely referred to Satan, the ultimate evil, as the Devourer. But it goes back even farther. Ancient Egyptians had a creature they called Ammit—a beast composed of equal parts lion, hippo, and crocodile. I suppose, in their fear and superstition, they chose those three because they were the three most fearsome, voracious animals in their experience. And Ammit, well . . . he was the guardian of their place of death." The Primus's voice rose and dropped steadily in a singsong tone that he customarily adopted when he was acting in a teaching capacity. "When the dead would arrive for judgment, the Ammit would determine whether or not the deceased was worthy of advancing along the path to their version of heaven. And if they were found unworthy, why . . . the Ammit would devour their hearts. The Egyptians called it the second death.

"And we should know about second deaths, should we not? After all, our planet died. Earth died all around us because we were greedy and uncaring and faithless. Our souls"—his voice began to soar—"were traded for credits, our aspirations replaced by rapacious greed. Our better angels were destroyed by our inner demons. And God saw that we were no longer deserving of the paradise that He had given us, and God drove us away. We were punished for all that we had done wrong, and we deserved that punishment.

"And after centuries of wandering we were brought here because God forgave us. He saw our penance and was pleased, and so He delivered us to a new world. Not a paradise, to be sure"—he looked around ruefully—"but we did not deserve to have paradise handed to us, for we had failed to protect the one we had. So instead we were given this world to make *into* a paradise. That was the new mandate, the new goal for humanity.

"And now look. Look at what has been sent down upon us.

"Devourers. As voracious as anything the Egyptians could have concocted. As evil and devoted to destruction as Satan ever was."

The Primus abruptly pointed a finger at the crowd, his voice rising with loathing and condemnation, as if the crowd were an abomination in his eyes. *"The explanation is obvious! We have failed in God's eyes! He has looked into our souls and found us wanting! He has sent us a test, and we have failed! And you dare—YOU DARE—to come here to the Citadel and demand justice of me? There is your justice!"* He turned his finger upward and stabbed it at the heavens. *"There is your justice, for He is bringing His heavenly retribution down upon us, and instead of standing here like mewling sheep, you should be at home with your families, praying for forgiveness! Now go! Go to your homes and pray for God's mercy, for you all know in your hearts what sins you have committed to warrant His fury! Go, I said!"*

They went. A few hesitated, but they saw the anger in the face of the Primus, and none of them was strong enough to stand up to it. Within moments the entire area in front of the Citadel was devoid of people. Even so, the Primus stood there for long minutes, saying nothing, doing nothing.

Then he turned and walked back into the Citadel.

"The mob is gone," he said to everyone within hearing. "You are free to leave if you so desire. Or you may stay here for as long as you wish. Either choice is acceptable."

He started to head up the stairs toward his sanctum, and then the Ranger named Marta called out, "Not that I'm knocking the fact that there's no longer a bunch of people out there shouting for our heads, but telling them they brought this all down on themselves? That's rough. You don't think it would be better to tell them something that will give them hope at a time like this?"

The Primus studied her silently. "What would you have me say? That I hope their deaths are quick and easy?"

Marta had no response to that, and the Primus went upstairs in silence.

* * *

Conner's squad, in which he was one of only two cadets, was patrolling the North Side, where an Ursa had been sighted by his father's pilots only minutes earlier, when he saw a cageball court up ahead.

It caught him by surprise.

Conner had been focusing on rooftops and alleyways, anywhere an Ursa might hide. Not the street ahead of him. And surely not the open area of a cageball court, where nothing could conceal itself.

It wasn't the court where he had seen Lyla Kincaid, but it might as well have been. He thought about the way she had looked that day, the way she had smiled when she watched her twelve-year-old client dribble the length of the court. It made him smile, too, even now, even in the middle of a perilous hunt for a deadly predator. He wished she would have stayed a little longer.

But he understood why she had bolted. She was Lucas's sister, and Lucas hated Conner's guts. And the shock of recognizing Conner after all those years . . .

He must have changed. *She* had—that was for sure. She wasn't a skinny kid with scabs on her knees anymore. She wasn't running to her parents, tattling on Conner and Lucas for getting into some scrape.

She was . . . pretty. Really pretty.

Too bad, he thought.

Suddenly, Conner's squad leader got a call on his comm unit. "Rivers here," he said. "Uh huh. Right. Copy that."

Everyone in the squad looked to him.

"Our Ursa's been spotted heading south," said Rivers. "Too far from here for us to pick it up. Another squad's been assigned. Looks like we're off the hook for now."

Everyone in the squad breathed a sigh of relief. It was noticeable even though none of them would have wanted anyone to notice it.

"We continue to patrol the area," said the squad leader. "Just in case. Slowly. With eyes open."

The rest of the squad nodded or muttered in agreement.

"Let's go, then," said Rivers.

Everyone fell in, Conner included. He took one last look over his shoulder at the cageball court and remembered the color of Lyla Kincaid's eyes. Then he left it all behind.

CHAPTER FIFTEEN

Cecilia Ruiz hated every moment of being where she was and doing what she was doing, but she had absolutely no choice.

She had no idea if she was wasting her time. Everything she had heard, everything she had done, had been through third parties and even some outright rumors. People might well have lied to her. Perhaps she had walked into a setup. Perhaps the man she was supposed to meet didn't have the goods. It was simply impossible to tell until it actually happened.

The spot where she was supposed to be meeting her contact was on the western border of the Inner Wilderness. The terrain was fairly flat; it was easy to see in all directions. That was by design as far as her contact man was concerned. Being able to see for kilometers in all directions reduced the likelihood of *his* walking into a trap.

"A man in his line of work is, naturally, concerned about that," is what Cecilia had been told. She had nodded. If anyone was going to understand that, she would.

As Cecilia paced back and forth at the meeting place, her movements displayed an almost balletic grace. She had a head full of thick black ringlets; she'd actually been rather surprised when her hair grew in that way. She'd had a buzz cut for as long as she could remember, and every so often she would run her fingers through her hair in wonderment, as if she had accidentally put on someone else's head that morning. Her face was angular and an odd combination of dark skin and freckles.

She was wearing very tight black shorts, an undershirt of such thin material that it was practically seethrough, and a pair of boots that reached to midcalf. The outfit made her feel extremely self-conscious. Even on the hottest days Nova Prime had to offer—and they could pack some formidable temperatures—Cecilia wasn't accustomed to displaying that much skin. But she'd had no choice; it had been mandated by the man she was meeting. He wanted to make sure she wasn't packing any weapons out of fear that she might try to rob him.

"Be happy he didn't make you show up naked," she'd been told by the contact who had set up the meet.

It was an effective strategy. Her old pulser was much too big for her to carry and have it remain unseen. Such weapons were designed for power, not concealment. It didn't mean that she had to go into the situation completely unprotected, though. She had a long serrated knife concealed in the top of her boot out of habit. It gave her some measure of protection against her contact should he try something, plus she had her Ranger training.

However, she wasn't sure a knife would do a thing against an Ursa (not even pulsers appeared to be accomplishing anything). And it seemed lately that the damned things were everywhere. Even that impression, though, was taking a toll. On hot days when the air would shimmer, as it was wont to do, it was easy to be startled because it seemed that one of the beasts had appeared and was about to charge. On dark nights, as the shadows would stretch, it often seemed that an Ursa was concealed in the shadows, waiting for the perfect moment to strike.

Cecilia leaned against the landmark the man was supposed to be using to meet her: a single spire of rock that through happenstance of nature stretched ten feet in the air like a dusty red monument. She kept glancing around, Ursa on her mind. What if one attacked her now? She wouldn't last a second against it. She'd never return home. "What happened to Mom?" her children would ask, and her husband would have no answer. They might find some tattered remains of her body, but there was no way to be sure of that. Her disappearance would simply be another unanswered question in the history of Nova Prime.

Then, in the distance, she heard a whistling of wind. She turned immediately to face it and saw a skipjack heading her way. A skipjack was a single-person vehicle, similar to an Earth bicycle except airborne. It was extremely maneuverable and solar-powered, and so it was very quiet and, thanks to its size, not easy to spot. Consequently, it was a favorite of black marketers because it was easy for Rangers' scanning equipment to miss.

There was a man astride it with a pair of goggles drawn over his eyes. Even more encouraging, Cecilia saw several large sacks dangling off the back of the skipjack, as if the fellow were some sort of bizarre latter-day Santa Claus. She waved to him. He didn't wave back. Instead he executed a slow circle, doubtless making sure that there was no one within the area. Once he was satisfied, he glided to the ground and settled in. Then he swung his leg around and off the skipjack and stood to face her. Cecilia was pushing six feet, but this guy was taller than that. Slowly he walked toward her, taking measured strides, seemingly appraising her with every step. Cecilia could feel her heart pounding in her chest. He didn't need her, but she sure as hell needed him and didn't know what she was going to do if this didn't pan out.

He looked vaguely familiar, but she wasn't sure why. His clothes indicated that he was a farmer by trade, although who knew for sure if that was the case. He might indeed be a farmer who had conspired to keep his crops hidden from collection for the common good and was instead trying to profiteer despite all Nova Prime laws to the contrary. Or he might have taken the clothes from a farmer. He might have been part of one of the raids on the storage depots that she'd heard about.

It didn't matter to her, and it grieved her that it didn't matter. Because once upon a time she had stood for something, and now she was consorting with this . . . this person. She felt unclean.

But her family was counting on her. That was all that mattered.

"Turn around," he said.

She didn't like the sound of that. Presenting her back to this guy? Nothing good would come of that. "I think I'll stay facing you if that's all right."

"You'll do what I say. I want to make sure you don't have anything behind your back."

"I don't," she said firmly.

"Look, lady." He took two more steps toward her, his eyes narrowing. "If you want any taste of what I've got on the back of my vehicle, then you'll do exactly what I . . ." His voice trailed off.

Recognition suddenly seemed to glint in his eyes. "Oh, you gotta be kidding me. How stupid do you think I am? Deal's off." He pulled out a pulser from a holster on his hip. It was an older model, larger and clunkier than what Rangers carried. But it was still lethal, and Cecilia was standing there flat-footed. "In fact, I should just put a shot through you on general principles." He started backing up hurriedly.

"Wait!" she said, and started following him. "I don't understand!"

He fired a warning shot directly at her feet. It kicked up dirt and rock right in front of her. She froze. He raised his voice, and it echoed across the arid plains. "Any of you try anything and she's dead!"

Remaining where she was, she said in frustration, "What are you talking about? Who are you talking *to*?"

"Do you think I'm stupid?!"

No, but I wouldn't put much stock in your sanity.

"There's no one here except you and me," she said with forced patience. "You saw it yourself."

"And I saw *you* myself, too. Back when you arrested me nine years ago. I had a good thing going on a weapons racket, and you and your Ranger pals put an end to that! You look different, but I never forget a voice."

Oh, shit. That's why he looked familiar.

He was continuing to back up, keeping the pulser leveled on her. At that moment she realized she was faced with a hopeless choice. She had to try to convince him of the truth. Except the only thing that was preventing him from shooting her was the belief that he had wandered into a trap. If she managed to make him believe her about the truth about her living situation, she might well be rewarded with a blast to the face.

But she didn't see herself as having an abundance of options.

"Look," she said desperately, "I'm not a Ranger anymore!"

"Sure—"

"I'm not. Look." She held out her right hand flat, palm to the ground. It was trembling, shaking steadily as if she were palsied.

The black marketer stopped and stared at it. "What's that supposed to mean?" he said warily.

"Nerve damage," she said. "Sustained in the line of duty." She pointed to the lengthy scar that ran along the inside of her forearm. "Can't hold a gun steady. Can't aim. If you can't aim, you have no business being a Ranger. And if I had taken the desk job they offered me, it would've meant just sitting around watching my old friends do what I couldn't anymore."

"My heart bleeds," he said with a sneer. Then, intrigued in spite of himself, he asked, "They couldn't fix it?"

"They did. It was worse than this before." She lowered her arm then but kept both her hands out, palms up. "I got married to a great guy. He was a factory worker. But the factory cut back, and he was asked to find work elsewhere. With the drought, easier said than done."

The Novans had experienced droughts before, but never like that one. It had lasted for months, and eaten deep into the food surpluses the colony had put aside. It had sent the Savant's meteorologists scurrying for explanations, spurred new research and new conferences. But mostly it had left people hungry and miserable.

"We have two children," Cecilia continued, "and we're both out of work . . ."

"You're telling me your life's story?" The black marketer chortled. "Oh, this is great. This is too much."

"I know you don't care—"

"No, no, go on." He gestured for her to proceed. "I'm loving this. It just doesn't get any better, you standing there telling me why I should feel sorry for you."

"Look," she said with growing urgency, "whatever else you may be, you're still human, just like me. And we should be standing together against these creatures that are trying to wipe us out, not standing in each other's way as we try to survive."

"Yeah, that's a great sentiment, princess." There was nothing but contempt in his voice. "Except if you hadn't gotten your arm messed up, and you were still wearing your Ranger uniform, and I told you some long sad story about my personal problems, what would you do? I'll tell you: You would throw my ass in Ranger lockup. Yes? Am I right?"

She couldn't look him in the eye. "Probably."

"Probably?"

"Definitely," she said with a sigh.

He bowed slightly, although it seemed more mocking respect than anything else. "Thank you for your honesty."

And then he turned and started walking away. He kept the oversized pulser in his hand, not holstering it.

"Wait!" she cried out after him. "Please, sell me the food. We need the grains, the greens . . ."

"You?" He whirled and leveled the gun at her. "You're damned lucky I don't kill you where you stand! Only reason I don't is that I want you to remember what it was like for a woman like you to come begging to a guy like me! I want you to—"

A cold fury was swelling up within her. She still had the knife in her boot. She was calculating whether she would have the time to draw it, pull back her arm, and throw it with enough strength and accuracy to bury it in his chest. Could she stoop to that? Could she become a murderer? Was she that desperate?

Then she realized that the black marketer had stopped talking. His face went deathly white. Then he brought the pulser straight up and fired right at her . . .

No. Not at her. Above her.

And from behind her, in the distance, came an infuriated roar of anger and annoyance.

She didn't even have to look. The instant the Ursa bellowed, she ran straight toward the man who had opened fire on the creature. Her arms pumping, she sprinted right past him as he continued to fire the pulser. He seemed rooted to the spot, and the only thing he could do was keep blasting away.

She felt the ground thundering under her. The Ursa was charging, closing the gap. She had no chance against the thing, she thought, as she heard the high-pitched scream of terror from the black marketer, followed by the sounds of bones crunching as the Ursa leaped on him. *I never even knew his name,* she realized abruptly.

She knew that as long as she heard eating noises from behind her, she had time. She prayed desperately as she sprinted toward the skipjack that it would be enough time.

When she was within a couple of feet of the skipjack, the slurping and bone-crunching noises ceased. Terror slammed through her, and it served as a propellant, sending her leaping onto the skipjack and gunning it to life.

Unfortunately, it also served as a beacon and a spur to the Ursa.

It pounded toward her as the skipjack lifted into the air. She had just enough time to glimpse the ruined body of the black marketer nearby, and then she whipped the skipjack around in a fast one-eighty and started to tear away from the area. *Thank God they can't fly . . . can they?*

Suddenly the skipjack was yanked sideways. She shrieked and looked down, knowing what she was going to see. The Ursa was on its hind legs, and it had sunk its claws into the sacks that were dangling from behind the vehicle. It was shaking the skipjack like a cat worrying a mouse. Cecilia hadn't had time to belt herself in, and she was holding on to the handlebar controls desperately to avoid being thrown off.

The monster was growling furiously, trying to use the bags to drag the skipjack to the ground. It outweighed the small vehicle so vastly that the skipjack didn't have a chance against it. Cecilia had altitude, but that was all, and it wasn't going to last very long.

The skipjack was now tilting at forty-five degrees, and Cecilia was in danger of losing her grip. If that happened, she would tumble straight down into the jaws of the Ursa.

She did the only thing she could. Releasing her grip with one hand, she yanked her dagger out of her boot and then bent backward. The only things keeping her anchored to the skipjack were her legs clamped around the seat and her feet wedged into the stirrups.

She swung the knife almost blindly and sliced through the rope that was keeping several of the bags attached to the skipjack. The rope obediently parted, and the Ursa fell back, clutching three of the four bags in its claws. The cloth got hung up in the creature's claws, and with a frustrated snarl the Ursa tore away at it, sending food spilling every which way.

Cecilia slung herself forward and grabbed the handlebars once more. A single sack of food was dangling from behind. She kicked the skipjack into top speed and tore out of there, the lone remaining sack of food dangling behind her.

Sparing herself a glance over her shoulder, she saw the infuriated Ursa stomping around on the food that had spilled all over. Cecilia wanted to sob seeing the much-needed food being destroyed under the paws of the creature. She realized that she had no business complaining; but for a bit of luck, it might well be her carcass it was stomping.

She supposed she should have felt sorry for the black marketer. She allowed herself to wonder briefly if he, too, had a family, people who would now wonder what had happened to him.

Then she stopped worrying about it. She was alive, and that was all that mattered. That evening, with the bag of vegetables Cecilia had managed to salvage, she and the neighbors made soup for everyone. It seemed the best way to share the bounty she had happened upon. For the most part the soup consisted of water with vegetables sparsely distributed through it. But it was just enough to provide some decent taste for the soup, and all the neighbors greatly appreciated the thoughtfulness of the Ruiz family.

Her husband, Xander, pulled her over as the children were feasting. The adults were all watching solicitously, waiting for the children to eat their fill before helping themselves to it. "Do I want to know where you got all this?"

She kept a smile fixed on her face. "No," she said. "Don't ask again." And he didn't.

CHAPTER SIXTEEN

Trey Vander Meer had lost track of time.

It could have been a week or a month since his family was slaughtered. He knew it wasn't yesterday, but beyond that, things were fuzzy. Each time he closed his eyes, he heard the screams in order: Elena's, Michael's, Skipper's, Natasha's. Every time he tried to sleep, he remembered the nice bald-headed Ranger consoling him, checking his vitals, sitting with him in the shelter.

At some point an augur had appeared to take the Ranger's place. He had prayed for Vander Meer, staying with him, making sure he washed, ate, and at least had the opportunity to sleep. The poor fellow had put up with Vander Meer's ravings, which must have been many and awful to contemplate.

Pham had visited as well. He had come to comfort his friend, he had said, though Vander Meer had never really thought much about their relationship before. They had been coworkers, certainly. They had discussed matters honestly even when they didn't see eye to eye on an issue or a method. But friends? That was a new concept for them and one Vander Meer wasn't sure he could accept. It felt too much like pity.

Everything else was a blur.

He remembered someone saying that their part of the city had been abandoned by the Ursa, that the beasts had plagued other parts instead. He didn't recall who had said it but was sure he had heard it. *Too late,* Vander Meer thought at the time. *Too late, I'm afraid.*

Friends and neighbors braved the streets and came to see him in the shelter. The augur, whose name Vander Meer kept forgetting, guarded the door and would admit only those Vander Meer approved with a nod.

Most of them just came to sit and hold his hands or share stories about his family that he might not have heard before. Friends of Michael and Elena turned up, too, feeling a need to be there, maybe just so they could accept that the kids were gone. The young ones had little to say to Vander Meer, maybe a mumbled word or two, but he accepted their clammy handshakes and awkward hugs. The augur encouraged them to go home as soon as they could, while there were Rangers available to provide an escort. He also watched to make sure they didn't take any food, because the shelter barely had enough for those inside it.

One morning the augur helped Vander Meer wash, shave, and dress. Then the two of them went to the nearest house of worship—one that was only a block away—where services were held for the newly dead, including Vander Meer's family. He sat in a haze, repeating the words of devotion by rote memory, aching from his loss and feeling little else. Burial, he was told gently, would be at another time. The bodies would remain refrigerated until the Ursa threat was over.

"Would that be by next week?" he asked the augur in his fog. "It will be Michael's birthday then, and we can have a party." The look in the man's stricken eyes kept Vander Meer from asking again.

A day or so after that, he asked to visit his studio. The augur brought him to the front door despite the danger involved. The young man was prepared to wait until Vander Meer wished to leave and then walk him back to the shelter.

But Vander Meer thanked him for his time and effort and sent him away, saying he should tend to those in greater need. "I'll be fine here at the studio," he said, "where I can resume my work."

Pham was at his accustomed post when Vander Meer walked in. He looked surprised to see his partner.

"Trey," said Pham. "What are you doing here?"

"I could ask you the same thing."

Pham shrugged. "I felt like people should have some comfort. Some contact. And I only live a couple of blocks away; you know that." He smiled. "You . . . you want to record something?"

Vander Meer took a chair. "Not today, thanks."

"Okay," said Pham, "whatever you say," and returned to his work.

The hours stretched on. Vander Meer watched the news feeds and noted that though the Rangers continued to fight the Ursa, both Rangers and citizens alike were dying. The alien creatures seemed invincible.

There were runs on supplies. Even the relief drops from New Earth City were not proving to be enough. People were starving, and the tripartite leadership seemed incapable of staying on top of the crisis.

The Prime Commander refused to help people who wanted to flee the city. Her concern, as she had expressed it on several occasions, was that the Ursa would follow them and hunt them down and become aware of New Earth City in the process. The people of Nova Prime City might have understood and maybe even agreed with Wilkins's judgment, but they still felt like sacrificial lambs.

As day turned to night, Pham seemed to want to head home. However, he hesitated when he saw that Vander Meer was still watching the news.

"How'd you like to come home with me?" Pham asked. "Can't offer you much in the way of a gourmet meal, but at least you'll have company."

"No, thanks," said Vander Meer. "I'll be fine here."

He watched the news throughout the night, and with the passing hours he absorbed the personal accounts of Ursa sightings, the acts of individual heroism, and the stories of tragedies not unlike his own. Even through the veil that clouded his mind, he could see the mounting stress on the systems that maintained society. It was clear to him that the Ursa were winning. In his mind, he could see a clock counting down to the death of Nova City in the corner of every screen.

Vander Meer reached conclusions that once might have seemed radical to him but seemed perfectly rational now. He began formulating a commentary in his mind, and as the first hints of dawn appeared in the window, he delivered the commentary to the mirror where he was used to putting on his makeup.

Not good enough, he thought.

He made some modifications, adjusting the order of things, and then repeated the piece. By the time Pham arrived early for the workday, no doubt out of concern for his friend, Vander Meer was ready.

"I have a commentary to record and broadcast as soon as possible," he said by way of greeting.

Pham broke into a grin. He handed Vander Meer a container of coffee and a sweet roll that he had brought from his dwindling supplies at home. "I'll go clear time on the schedule." He hurried off.

A short time later, after Vander Meer had eaten and drunk without tasting what he was eating and drinking, he applied his makeup. Then he went to sit in his familiar spot in front of the camera. Pham took the controls.

Vander Meer saw him switch on a fail-safe app that would cut off the signal immediately if the commentator said something he didn't think advisable. Vander Meer smiled. In his estimation, Pham wouldn't need to do any such thing.

The red light went on, telling Vander Meer it was time for him to speak.

He didn't sit in one spot, though. He wanted to convey the magnitude of the problem, and so he got up and paced for a moment. Pham, as astute as ever, widened the angle and swiveled the camera to capture his movements.

Finally, Vander Meer turned to the camera and spoke.

"My friends," he said, "I want to thank you for taking time from your own worries and concerns to express your sympathies regarding my loss. Of course, the tragedy that befell my family is no different from what so many of you have experienced. I am still hurt and grieving. But just as there is no time to bury the dead, there is no time to mourn them. We need to focus on the immediate danger.

"I have seen the savagery of the Ursa firsthand. They are killing machines, make no mistake. They elude our best efforts to find and track them. They withstand our pulsers for the most part. They need little rest, if any.

"So we sit huddled in our homes and shelters, and starve, and watch as our families are destroyed. We cower like scared children, worrying about the monster under the bed. Meanwhile, the Ursa run free.

"But they can be defeated—and we are the ones who can defeat them. Now, I do not have the magic bullet, the solution to our woes. But we are a people that found the wherewithal to build arks and escape a toxic world. We are the people that time and again devised ways out of dilemmas that seemed certain to crush the spirit.

"Sometimes we need inspiration.

"Clearly the Rangers are in over their heads. They need our help.

"Sometimes we need motivation.

"Let me motivate you, my friends.

"I will post an award of a million credits, which is everything I have left in the world. To claim it, all you need do is be the first to bring me an Ursa corpse. No, not even an entire corpse—just its head. Bring it here to the studio, prove you killed the monster to which it belonged, and the reward is yours.

"There are nearly three dozen Ursa stalking our city, so there is plenty of opportunity. But you don't need to kill them all. Just one. *One.*

"I will remain camped here at the studio, awaiting the person who comes in first to claim his or her prize. Good hunting, my friends."

And the red light went off, Pham knowing him well enough to time it just right.

Vander Meer sat down, exhausted. Apparently, he still had a way to go before he got his strength back. But he had had enough to deliver his message.

Pham toggled off the camera and the lighting, jaw agape.

"Do you think anyone heard me?" Vander Meer asked.

Pham nodded. "I'm sure of it. And those who didn't hear you firsthand will get wind of what you said soon enough."

Vander Meer closed his eyes. The monsters would pay. His family would be avenged.

Lyla had never listened to Trey Vander Meer's broadcasts, and she was even less inclined to do so now that she was so focused on turning her research into the kind of weapon the Savant had asked for. But thanks to the banter of her colleagues over the Savant's comm channels, she was aware that the broadcasts were continuing unabated.

The Prime Commander had considered shutting the commentator down for morale reasons, apparently, but had opted not to do so. Vander Meer was too resourceful, his broadcasts too well known. If his broadcasts suddenly vanished, as critical of the Rangers as they had been, it would prompt the citizenry to think that he was making valid points that the Rangers were afraid to have out there.

So Vander Meer, despite the annoyance of a number of people in the Rangers organization, was being allowed to speak. From what Lyla's colleagues were saying, the commentator believed that the Rangers were overwhelmed. He talked of how the situation was rapidly descending into every man for himself. He talked of how he was going to continue to provide a bounty for every Ursa head brought to him because he, Vander Meer, was the only one capable of getting Novans to stand up and do what the Rangers couldn't do.

Lyla studiously ignored the controversy. She had work to do.

But as Cecilia Ruiz sat in her small home and looked at the last remains of the vegetables she'd managed to salvage from her misbegotten adventure with the black marketer, she heard Vander Meer's words.

And she started *listening*.

Conner could have sat in the barracks with the other cadets and listened to another of Trey Vander Meer's diatribes, but he couldn't stomach the idea. Before, Vander Meer had angered him. Now, with his call for ordinary citizens to fight the Ursa, Vander Meer had gone from despicable to dangerous.

Unfortunately, Conner couldn't do anything about him. Apparently, no one could.

In his downtime—the first he had gotten in days—he chose not to remain with his fellow cadets but rather to see his aunt Bonita one last time.

He couldn't speak with her again. He couldn't hug her. But thanks to the footage taken by one of the colony's satellites, which tracked every Ranger maneuver visible from orbit on a line of sight, he could sit in a room in the command center and watch her die.

It wasn't easy. But it was *her*. It was what she had done in her last moments of life. So Conner watched and did so gratefully.

He wasn't expecting to get anything useful out of it. Not even remotely. Therefore, it came as a surprise when he realized that his aunt had done something he wouldn't have thought possible.

Despite the creatures' acute sense of smell, she had snuck up on one of them. She had gotten close enough without its noticing to hit it point-blank with a pulser blast and leave a gash across the creature's hide just above its gaping black hole of a mouth.

More important, the Ursa had faltered. For four or five seconds it had been stunned. And if it hadn't fallen on Aunt Bonita, driving her to the ground with its weight, she might have pressed her advantage.

But she couldn't do that because she was pinned. Given time to recover, the beast had risen up and killed her.

Conner sat back in his chair, his mind racing. His aunt had knocked the Ursa out. He had seen it even if the Rangers who had served under her hadn't noticed. She had *stunned it*.

He recalled what he had done in the war game, how he had taken advantage of Lucas Kincaid's aggressiveness to sneak up behind him. That was what his aunt had done with the Ursa.

At least, that was how it had looked to him.

Maybe he was completely and utterly mistaken. Maybe he was just a cadet jumping to conclusions, which was what people would certainly say. But there was a way to find out.

CHAPTER SEVENTEEN

Three weeks of this. Or is it four? God, how much longer can this go on?

Torrance Raige felt as if he were going out of his mind. His wife was gone. All around Nova City and its outlands, Rangers were falling under the relentless assaults of the Ursa. The entirety of Nova Prime was slipping into the kind of despair he never could have imagined.

Where is it going to stop?

His injuries had healed, and he had been put back out into the field, part of a search-and-destroy team that consisted of ten Rangers. With that many of them operating in such close proximity, the major concern was getting in one another's way, so they had to remain ultra-aware of the location of each teammate. It was of particular consequence since the Ursa had a terrifying habit of appearing out of nowhere, often in the middle of a crowd. In a way, they were representative of humanity's existence on Nova Prime in microcosm. One minute everything was fine; the next, the Skrel showed up and all hell had broken loose.

You're drifting. Stay focused.

They were making their way through a rugged, mountainous area. No one had ever bothered to name it, which was odd since humans had a tendency to slap names on practically every damned thing. There wasn't an ounce of green anywhere on it, just brown scrub here and there. It alternated between twisting paths—

sometimes so narrow that people had to walk single file—and plateaus and cliffs. To make matters worse, it was studded with caves. It was effectively a sandblasted maze of brown rock filled with countless twisting curves and holes where an Ursa could be lying in wait.

Why were they there? Because, contrary to what they had thought, a couple of Ursa had gone that way. They didn't know why, but now they were sure of it. And they wanted to know why. The fear—and it was a *huge* fear—was that they might be up there breeding. Maybe some of the Ursa were specifically designed for that, the Savant's people were speculating.

Or maybe something else. They just needed to know. And if Torrance's mission was a success, they would.

He heard the sound of a Ranger skimmer, a large, boxy aerial vehicle, roaring overhead, scanning the general area and giving an eyes-in-the-air aid to the forces on the ground. Their report crackled over the comm unit of every Ranger in the area. "No sign of the bastards."

"Doesn't mean we lower our guard," came Marta's reply. She was about ten yards back, and Torrance could hear the determination in her voice. She had recovered from her injuries just as he had and had reclaimed her place as a Ranger in the field.

But she had recovered *more*, it seemed to him. "You going to be okay?" Marta asked, still worried about how the death of Bonita had affected him.

Torrance glanced at her and just for a moment allowed the frustration and gnawing sense of dread he'd been feeling in the past weeks to show through. "Are any of us?"

"Yes," she said with the certainty in her voice that always lifted him. "Yes, we're going to be okay. The Skrel tried to wipe us out ages ago, and we survived. And we will survive again. Because they keep underestimating us. They think we're nothing but ants for them to stomp on, and sooner or later they're going to get the message."

"And if, upon getting that message, they simply decide to destroy the world entirely?"

"If they were going to, they would have done so by now," Marta said firmly. "There's something here they want."

"Then why don't they just tell us what it is?"

"Because they can't communicate with us, or maybe they feel they shouldn't have to. They just figure we'll leave. But they've misjudged us."

"Sector 11 clear!" crackled the voice of Freeman, one of their fellow Rangers. They had broken up the area they were exploring into sectors, going through them methodically one by one to ensure that there were no Ursa hidden there.

"Sector 9 clear," came Swan's report.

There was silence then over their comm units. Marta drew closer and said into hers, "Sector 10, report in."

Marta and Torrance stared at each other nervously as she got no response. *They* were in sector 10.

Torrance immediately spoke into his unit, "Norris? You there? Status report." The longer the silence continued, the more worrisome matters became. "Norris! Dammit, report!"

Marta started tapping into the naviband she wore on her forearm. A light flashed back. "I've got his location." Quickly she relayed it back to the other Rangers in the vicinity, and then they sprinted forward.

Torrance heard the rest of the squadron pounding up behind them. At least he had people covering his back. He had his pulser drawn, ready for anything they might encounter.

What do you mean, "anything"? There's only one thing we have to worry about encountering, and damned if you can ever really be ready for that. His lower jaw tightened. *Except I can be. I'm Torrance Raige, dammit, and there hasn't been a thing in the history of humanity—including the loss of the Earth itself—that my family hasn't been able to handle. And that's not about to change now.*

The narrow path opened out onto a plateau. "He's just ahead," said Marta. Her voice was steady, but there was a slight edge to it.

"Nobody move," Torrance said sharply. "Because I'm not seeing him." His gaze swept over the area in front of them, and indeed there was no sign of Norris. There didn't seem to—

Then he spotted it. At the far end of the plateau, he saw Norris's hand.

Just Norris's hand, lying at the base of a couple of rocks. His naviband was flashing red, indicating that it was still functioning.

No way. No way in hell did the Ursa plant that here to lure us. Impossible. It . . . My God, it must have swallowed Norris whole. Almost whole. I can see it now, the serration ending just above the wrist. It just scooped him up, swallowed him, and, as Norris tried to climb out, clamped its jaws shut. Any screams would have been muffled.

All this went through Torrance's mind in a second. His gaze swept the plateau. There was nothing there. The Ursa was gone.

No—it's here, he thought. He heard its growl, chilling him to the bone.

"It's here!" he called out.

A moment later the monster bounded into view. It seemed to hesitate for a moment, apparently trying to decide who to attack first.

"Fire!" Torrance yelled.

Pulser blasts rained down on the Ursa, but they weren't seriously hurting it. They were, at most, annoying the crap out of it. *No surprise there.*

Suddenly he saw, to his horror, that Marta was advancing, trying to get closer. Hoping, no doubt, that a closer shot would have a greater impact.

"Fall back, Ranger!" Torrance shouted. *"Fall back!"* He never stopped firing as he grabbed her by the elbow and pulled her away from the creature.

The Ursa's head snapped around. Its nonexistent eyes settled on him. It roared. It charged.

In an effort to draw it off from the others, Torrance ran along the edge of the plateau, all the while continuing to fire. The Ursa's head swiveled to track him, turning it away from the rest of the Rangers. They converged on it as one, pouring on a barrage from all directions. The Ursa felt the concentrated firepower and, still facing Torrance, roared in pain.

Its mouth was wide open, and Torrance took aim. *Let's see how invulnerable these bastards are on the inside,* he thought.

But before he could fire, it swiped at him. He leaped backward quickly enough to avoid the worst of the blow, but it still sent him flying.

He somersaulted in midair and prepared to land on his feet. But when he tried to plant them, he saw there was nothing beneath him—nothing but empty air.

The Ursa had knocked Torrance clear off the plateau. Below him was a fall of several hundred feet to the ground. The only thing that went through his head was, *This is how I die? This? How incredibly stupid.*

Then he plummeted. He heard a scream—Marta's, not his own.

Marta watched Torrance plunge to his death, and her mind shut down. Heedless of her own danger, heedless of anything except the need to put down this monster, she advanced on it with a continuous barrage. She knew no fear. She knew nothing but pure unadulterated fury.

"Die, you son of a bitch!" she screamed.

The Ursa whirled and roared, its foul breath washing over her. She continued to fire, hoping she would stop it despite everything she knew about it, but it didn't stop. It coiled and sprang.

A blast from overhead with far greater power than anything the handheld pulsers were packing ripped through the air and struck the Ursa broadside. It was the Ranger skimmer, diving down in an attack pattern that had enabled it to strike the Ursa in midleap. The impact was so fierce that it sent the Ursa flying sideways toward a wall of rock.

Unfortunately, Marta was between the Ursa and the wall of rock.

She tried to move, but everything was happening too fast, and the Ursa crashed into her with horrifying impact. The Ursa didn't appear to notice that it had crushed anyone, which wasn't surprising. The thing's hide was so thick that it was shrugging off pulser blasts at point-blank range, and so there was certainly no reason for it to be aware it had crashed into a person.

The skimmer dive-bombed toward the Ursa, continuing to fire. Marta sank to the ground, barely hanging on to consciousness, her arms and legs splayed in angles that shouldn't have been possible.

The Ursa didn't seem to be aware of her. Instead, it was focused entirely on the skimmer that was coming toward it. The creature might not have had any eyes, but the pounding from the heavy-duty pulser cannons was serving as a guide, and the noise of the skimmer was more than enough to cement the Ursa's ability to track it.

With a howl of fury, the Ursa leaped for the skimmer. The skimmer pilot made a quick course adjustment, but the boxy vehicle wasn't a Kelsey flier. It was designed for transport, not battle. The cannons had been a recent add-on, an attempt to convert the skimmer into a fighting vehicle. It wasn't designed to make swift aerial maneuvers, and that lack of ability cost it.

The Ursa landed on the front of the skimmer, just above where its cannons were mounted. Its back legs scrambled, and its talons found purchase. It shoved its way onto the top of the skimmer and started both clawing at and pounding on the top. The skimmer canted sideways and then performed a barrel roll to try to shake the monster off. The maneuver did no good at all.

The creature's talons were sunk right into the hull of the skimmer; the Ursa wasn't going anywhere.

There was no way for the Rangers on the ground to fire on the monster, not without doing damage to the skimmer. From what Marta could see as she flitted in and out of consciousness, it seemed certain that the skimmer would be the only thing that *would* be damaged by the pulser blasts, since the Ursa had been more or less shrugging off everything they had to throw at it.

Suddenly, the skimmer straightened out and hurtled past the Rangers on the plateau. It was moving so quickly that it was only a matter of seconds before the vehicle and the Ursa were far from sight. Even in the ocean of pain that threatened to overwhelm her, Marta couldn't help noticing that the pilot had flown in the exact opposite direction from Nova City.

Good, she thought. Then she passed out.

Cecilia Ruiz remembered the superb target range to which she'd had access back when she was a Ranger. Electronic targets had enabled her to determine down to the centimeter how precise she had been in her aim. She had always taken pride in the fact that she was in the top 3 percent when it came to accuracy.

She was as far from those glory days as she could possibly be. Now she was standing in a field behind her house, although *field* might have been far too generous a word. *Field* summoned images of vast swaths of green. This field had a few patches of brown scrub, but that was about it.

Holding a rock in the palm of her hand, Cecilia walked to the central post of a wire fence that wrapped around the border of her family's meager property. She couldn't even remember at this point why Xander had erected the stupid fence in the first place. *Something to occupy him,* she thought. *Something to keep him busy.*

It wasn't bad enough that he'd been out of work since

the Ursa arrived. Truth be told, they hadn't been doing so well even before then, but at least they'd put food in their kids' mouths, and there had been the prospect of Xander getting a job in the new energy plant made necessary by the growth of Nova City and its population.

Now there wasn't even that.

Then Xander had been injured in that food riot. He hadn't even been one of the guys trying to attack the Rangers who were guarding the place; he had far too much respect for the Corps and the job they were trying to do. He'd just been in town looking for work and wound up getting trampled when Ranger aerial reinforcements sent the crowd running.

His leg had been twisted so badly that his hip had popped out of the ball socket, yet he had managed to make it back home. When Cecilia had found him lying at the threshold of their house, mangled and battered, she'd been filled with such outrage that she wanted to find a random crowd and open fire. She'd dragged him in and popped the leg back into place, eliciting a scream that she would never forget. Their son and daughter, John and Abby, age six and four, respectively, sobbed when they heard their father in such agony. Now he was on crutches and feeling more useless than ever . . .

Cecilia pushed all that from her mind. Instead she counted back thirty paces, took aim at the rock, and tried to steady her hand. She reached around with her left hand and gripped her right wrist, trying to prevent it from trembling. She was only partly successful. Instead of stilling her trembling right hand, all it did was leave her left hand shaking.

Nevertheless she did everything she was supposed to do. She aimed as best she could, took a deep breath, exhaled slowly, and fired.

The first silver-blue pulse blast sailed to the right by at least six inches. She tried to readjust, and the second missed by even more. The third struck the fence and knocked it over, sending the rock tumbling to the ground.

"Fantastic," she muttered. Once upon a time she would have been able to shoot the rock off the fence from twice the distance she was standing at now. For a moment anger flashed, and she just wanted to throw the pulser down and stalk away. But that wasn't going to accomplish anything.

And she most definitely had things that required accomplishing.

CHAPTER EIGHTEEN

Lyla Kincaid took a breath and let it out. Then she watched the holographic screen floating in front of her go live with an image of the Savant's deputy.

"Good morning," said Vincenzo.

"Good morning," Lyla replied.

"I wish I had time for pleasantries," Vincenzo said, "but I don't. Your research has been in the area of hearing augmentation, correct?"

"Yes," said Lyla.

She transmitted the file that contained the results of her efforts to translate her research into a weapon. Then she watched the woman scan it. She didn't look very enthusiastic.

"It amplifies sound to create a . . . well, a louder sound," Lyla said. "I thought if the Ursa had eardrums . . ."

It was a pretty poor effort—the engineer was aware of that. But then, she had started with a sound amplifier, for God's sake. People put them in their *ears*.

Vincenzo was frowning as she looked up at her. "This is the best you could do?"

"With what I was working on," Lyla said a little defensively, "yes. But to tell you the truth, I didn't see a whole lot of potential in that approach."

"It wasn't your job to make that judgment. Your job was to find an application that would help us fight the Ursa."

"I know," Lyla said. "Which is why I eventually put

that technology aside and went to work on another one. More specifically, the one my ancestor Jack Kincaid came up with."

Vincenzo's frown deepened. "You mean F.E.N.I.X. tech?"

"Yes."

"We talked about that in the briefing. F.E.N.I.X. tech was a helpful approach when we were dealing with aerial attacks. But the Ursa are a different kind of problem."

Lyla leaned forward. "Of course they are. But if we adapt F.E.N.I.X. tech the way I indicate here, I think it can be as effective a solution today as it was in Jack Kincaid's time."

And she sent Vincenzo the file with her *other* plans in it.

For a moment, Lyla thought the woman would reject the design out of hand. But she didn't. She took the time to go over it. And she kept on going over it, her brow crinkling, long after Lyla would have thought she'd stop.

Finally she asked, "What do you think?"

Still examining the design, Vincenzo shook her head. "I don't think it will work."

Lyla felt her throat tighten. After all the work she had put in, she wanted to protest. But she couldn't. It was the Savant's deputy.

However, there were lives at stake, her brother's among them. She ventured to ask, "Is there a flaw?"

"There are a few of them," Vincenzo told her.

A *few*?

"First off," said Vincenzo, "the shielding is insufficient to protect the user from the nuclear reaction. We don't want Rangers succumbing to radiation sickness the first time they take one of these things into the field. On the other hand, adequate shielding would make the weapon too heavy to carry, much less to wield.

"Second, you're limited by the speed of human reaction time. In projectile form, F.E.N.I.X.-tech adaptations follow preset patterns; in hand-to-hand combat, the rate of adaptation would depend on the commands of the Rangers. And by the time they input those commands, they would be Ursa meat.

"Third," Vincenzo continued without missing a beat, "you need more superconductors for something this size. Otherwise, the quantum field is too unpredictable and the device will blow up in your face."

Lyla didn't think so. But then, she wasn't the one whose decision mattered.

"But the real question," said Vincenzo, "is whether a hand-to-hand weapon is the answer. I mean, how close do we want to get to these monsters?"

"The problem," Lyla explained, "is that the Ursa are on top of us before we know it. How close we get usually isn't up to us."

The Savant's deputy seemed to absorb the information. "I wish we didn't have limited resources," she said at last. "Unfortunately, we've got to be careful where we place our chips. We can't spread ourselves too thin."

The engineer swallowed her disappointment. She thought she had come up with something worthwhile. Obviously, Vincenzo felt otherwise. But Lyla wasn't going to give up on her idea. It could still do the job, she thought. She could still give the Rangers the weapon they needed. She had already resolved to disobey the Savant's deputy and pursue her concept on her own when Vincenzo said, "Work on it."

Lyla looked at her. "Work on it?"

"Yes. Let me know when you've addressed my concerns."

The engineer smiled, though it was mostly inside. "I will. Thank you. Absolutely."

"No thanks necessary," said Vincenzo, and her image vanished from the holographic screen.

Lyla felt a surge of triumph. *Yes!* she thought.

But she had a hell of a lot of work ahead of her. If she couldn't take care of the problems Vincenzo had noted, her great idea would amount to exactly nothing.

* * *

"Cece? What the hell?"

Cecilia thought she'd been quiet as she'd rummaged around the small warehouse in the back. It wasn't actually a warehouse; that was a term left over from an earlier time. It was simply a storage area where they kept most of the tools they used for building.

Building a life together. That's what we've been building, really. And I've got to do something to maintain it . . .

She turned to face Xander, a machete in her hand. There were spots of rust on it, but it was solidly constructed and still had some life in it. Xander was standing there, leaning on his crutches. He seemed unable to process what he was seeing. His straight brown hair hung down in front of his face, and he flipped his head to one side to clear his vision. "You're not serious about this."

She had a tool pack lying on the floor. There was a hammer, a screwdriver, a length of rope, a handful of nails. She had a few items of practical equipment such as binoculars. Also a meager supply of dried foods that weren't especially tasty but would suffice and a small clear bag of what were clearly energy pills. A bottle of water was dangling from her left hip; her pulser was on her right. Briskly she closed the bag and slid the machete into a loop on the bag's side. "We've been over this . . ."

"I didn't think you were *serious*," Xander said. "I just thought you were thinking out loud."

"I don't have time for thinking out loud. None of us does. I have to take action."

"Cece"—he was the only one who ever called her that—"Vander Meer is nuts. He's an opportunistic blowhard. It's completely insane to stake the future of our family on—"

"*We don't have a future.*" The words had torn out

of her, and she closed her eyes, fighting to regain her calm. When she was sure she had, she opened her eyes and saw the look of hurt on his face. She brushed it off. There was no time for hurt feelings. "Our family is foundering, Xander," Cecilia told him. "It's not your fault. I don't blame you. I love you. But we need credits—and besides, this isn't about Vander Meer. It's . . . it's something else."

"Something risky."

She sighed. "No more risky than starving to death. That's what we're doing, isn't it?"

"Like everybody else," he said in frustration.

She shook her head. "Let them starve, then. I'm not going to let that happen to *us*."

"But what about the Ursa? People say we're not going to survive them, that they're unstoppable no matter what we do or what we throw at them. That's what you hear everyplace."

"Then you need to start listening to other people and other places."

"But what if it's true?" There was desperation in his voice. "Shouldn't we be spending our last days as a family?"

"You mean huddling all together, crouched in a corner, waiting for an Ursa to come crashing in and eat us all? Is that what you want for us, Xander?"

"Cece—"

"Do you really want the last thing our children see to be their parents being devoured, knowing that they're next? Knowing that we failed in the simplest, most fundamental job of a parent: protect our children?"

"Cece, listen—"

"Stop calling me Cece! I'm not twelve!"

She headed toward the door, and Xander moved to block her. She stopped and stared at him incredulously. "Seriously? All I have to do is knock one of your crutches out from under you. You'll be flat on your face. Now please, honey, step aside before you hurt yourself."

Xander clearly didn't know how to respond. After a few moments, he hobbled aside, and Cecilia moved past him. "What do you suggest I tell the kids?" he asked.

She paused, her back to him so that he didn't see her closing her eyes in pain over the prospect of the children being informed of her absence. "Tell them," she said steadily, "that Mommy will be back as soon as she can."

"And if you don't come back?"

This time she did turn to face him, and she said heatedly, "You know, you could show just a glimmer of support. I'm doing this for *us*, Xander. For our family."

"No. You're not," he shot back. Xander had always been the most easygoing man she'd ever met. The fact that he was raising his voice to her now startled her. "You're doing this for you. I've never been enough for you, and neither have the kids. If it weren't for you being booted out of the Corps, you'd never have married me, never been a mother. This is about your pride and about you wanting to go down fighting. That's what it's about. So don't make it about any of us because you need to take care of whatever needs you have that the kids and I aren't fulfilling. Okay? So we're clear on that. Now why don't you just go?" When she remained where she was, he practically bellowed at her, *"Go!"*

She swallowed once, a gulp, and then nodded. She reached out to embrace him, but he managed a step back and turned his head away.

"Okay," she said. "Okay."

As Cecilia left, she could hear Xander mutter one final barb under his breath: "Once a Ranger, always a Ranger."

The medicenter had been overwhelmed for days, and it was only getting worse. Doctors were at their wits' end because painkillers were running low and the constant moaning of the victims was starting to become overwhelming. The doctors were in the horrific position of having to determine who was genuinely in the most pain so that they could be allotted painkillers and who would be denied them because they weren't in *enough* pain.

There was, however, one individual who was in huge amounts of pain and would have been a certain candidate for them.

She simply refused.

The beds in the medicenter were packed so closely that there was scarcely room between one and the next. Yet they had managed to get a small amount of distance between Marta Lemov and everyone around her. That had been because Marta had proved to be singularly unsympathetic to her fellow patients.

A man with half his skin torn away during an Ursa attack was lying there bandaged from head to toe. Every so often he would groan a little, but even that relatively minor acknowledgment of his agony was greeted with nothing but impatience from Marta. "Shut up. Stop whining. You don't hear me whining," she growled, and the man with the shredded skin ceased immediately.

When he died of his wounds a half hour later, Marta didn't acknowledge it.

She did, however, glance up when she heard a soft "Oh, my God" from nearby. Her gaze flickered to the source.

"Theresa," she said. She didn't smile. There was no humor left in her.

"I heard you were here." Theresa tried to cover the dismay she felt as she stared at Marta's broken legs and the arm she had up in a sling. "I spoke to the doctors. They said you're lucky."

"Did they?"

"They said that even a few decades ago, injuries like this . . . you'd never walk properly again. But with modern bone reknitting and neural repair for your spine, you should be at about fifty percent capability within a month. That means you'll be able to get around—"

"And fight?" she said tightly. "Do they let you fight Ursa at fifty percent?"

"I . . . I don't know . . ."

"I do. They don't let you. They don't let you do anything except watch your world collapse around you."

"Marta . . ."

"I was supposed to compete in the Asimov Games; did you know that?" Marta made no attempt to keep the bitterness from her voice. "Two years. Two years I trained for that. Not enough that they had to cancel the games because of the Ursa. God had to make sure that I'd never have the opportunity to compete should we survive all this and the games get rescheduled."

"Marta, why won't you take any pain medication? The doctors said you must be hurting."

"I'm in agony. Look at my lower lip."

"It looks . . ."

"Chewed through? Yes."

Theresa grimaced, though she was no doubt trying not to. "That's how you're dealing with pain? By abusing yourself?" The augur's voice softened, and she reached for Marta's free hand. Marta, without even realizing it, pulled it away.

Theresa stood there for a moment with her hand extended and then withdrew it. "Marta . . . you shouldn't feel guilty because you survived . . ."

"I'm not guilty," she said flatly. "I'm angry. I'm angry that these things are killing good Rangers. I'm angry that two members of the Raige family are gone. And I'm angry that all I've got is this broken body to deal with it."

"There's more to life than anger, Marta . . ."

"Don't you dare . . ."

"Marta—"

Marta looked like she was ready to leap out of the bed and assault her. But Theresa didn't move. She remained precisely where she was.

In a voice that trembled from the strain of keeping it at just below a whisper—as if she didn't trust herself—Marta said, "Don't you dare start telling me some kind of augur crap about belief in something bigger than ourselves. Don't give me garbage about being tested or something."

"I wasn't going to—"

"*You* haven't seen these things in action. You haven't looked into those eyeless faces or seen your friends disappear down their gullets."

"My brother—" Theresa protested.

"Is dead," snapped Marta. "And I'm sorry for you. But you weren't there to see them die, so you don't get it. This is it. This is the end of days. Those things are going to keep on coming, and they are going to wear us down. Sooner or later, every damned Ranger in the Corps is going to be lying dead and there will be nothing to protect you from the Skrel and their pets. And then they will feast on you, on all of you. And here I am, and I can't do a damned thing about it. I'm a warrior trapped in a useless body. Better that the creature had killed me."

She had spoken with deep, powerful intensity. But now she allowed her head to slump back onto the pillow. "Better that I had died," she whispered, and turned away from Theresa.

The augur's impulse was to walk away so as not to irritate Marta further. It seemed hopeless; the poor woman was lost in a mental labyrinth of frustration and despair. Who could blame her, really?

Theresa even started to turn away. Then she thought about Torrance. She couldn't bring him back. God had taken him. But a little of Torrance survived in each person who had known him, and Marta had known him better than most.

Therefore, instead of leaving the woman lying there, Theresa looked back at her. "I'll be back tomorrow," she said with quiet determination. "And however many tomorrows it takes."

"You're an idiot," said Marta.

"Yes. I know." Then Theresa left her, but only for the time being.

CHAPTER NINETEEN

As Yang led the way down the narrow street, he wished again that Wilkins hadn't given him Bonita Raige's squad.

In the brief time he had served with Raige, he had come to appreciate her confidence, her tenacity, and her ability to coordinate the team's efforts. It wouldn't be easy to fill her boots, especially when he was leading the men and women he previously had fought alongside. Still, he imagined Wilkins knew what she was doing. She had seemed confident when she took Yang aside at headquarters and gave him the assignment.

At the time, Yang's thoughts were still in the shelter with Vander Meer. His heart went out to the man no matter what he had said about the Rangers. *No one should have to endure a tragedy like that one.*

Not that Yang approved of the bounty Vander Meer had posted. He couldn't imagine where *that* would lead. Vander Meer's broadcast had aired just once, but it had gone viral quickly. It had become a vid that was talked about everywhere, even on the largely deserted streets.

"Look alive," Carceras said as they approached an intersection.

He wasn't talking to his fellow Rangers so much as to the two cadets on the team. Yang wasn't thrilled about taking cadets with him, but he understood the need for them. Wilkins was running low on Rangers, so many of them having been lost in confrontations with the Ursa. She had to do something. Besides, these cadets were supposed to be two of the best.

Yang wasn't familiar with Ditkowsky, the woman. However, he knew the other one—the Raige kid. Hell, who *didn't* know him after he had almost single-handedly won the last war games exercise? Word traveled fast among the Rangers when it came to the war games, since they had all taken part in them as cadets, and it traveled even faster when someone pulled a stunt like the one Conner had.

Of course, Wilkins wouldn't expect Yang to give the kid special treatment. Not even if he bore a close resemblance to his uncle Torrance with his broad shoulders, dark eyes, and even features. Much more so, in fact, than he resembled Frank Raige, whom Yang had trained under, though Conner had Frank's close-cropped thicket of sandy brown hair.

As they approached the intersection, Bolt and Kromo went ahead to make sure there wasn't an Ursa waiting around a corner. Then they signaled for the others to advance. No one had seen one of the beasts in that part of the city in days, but they had to stay alert. Otherwise, there would be even fewer Rangers for Wilkins to work with and a couple fewer cadets as well.

The next intersection didn't give them any problems, either. It was the third one where things began to get hairy. It was there that Bolt and Kromo spotted the ragged mob of men and women carrying shovels and rakes and implements of destruction.

In other words, out hunting Ursa.

Yang eyed the mob as it got closer. He counted twelve or thirteen Novans, all of whom eyed him back. *Looks like Vander Meer's offer got some takers.*

"They're going to be eaten alive," Bolt observed.

"Yes, they are," said Yang.

"How do we save them from themselves?" Carceras asked.

"Let's see how far talking gets us." Knowing that he made an imposing figure because of all the time he spent in the gym, Yang went ahead of the squad and planted his booted feet in a stance that suggested he wasn't moving.

The mob slowed down warily but didn't stop.

"I need you to go back home or somewhere safe," Yang said in a deep baritone that echoed on the long, narrow street. "This is no place for civilians."

"Why?" called a man. "So you can get the bounty for yourselves?"

"We're just doing our jobs," Yang told them.

One of the women laughed derisively. "Like you've killed any of 'em! Step aside and give *us* a chance."

"They're out of their minds," Kromo said. He came up behind Yang's right shoulder, helping to create a human barricade. A moment later, Arce came up on his right.

The mob kept coming.

"They're nuts," Carceras whispered.

"They're scared," Yang said. "And the bounty is tempting."

"What do you want to do?" asked Kromo.

The last thing the Ranger wanted was to fight his own people. With just a few yards separating him from the mob, he took out his pulser, put it on its lowest setting, and aimed it at the street in front of the mob. Then he fired.

The shot of silver-blue energy did what words could not: The civilians stopped in their tracks. A man who had a pitchfork in his hands raised it defensively.

"Hang on," said Yang. "Let's be reasonable about this. Is a farm implement really going to do a better job than a pulser?"

That gave the assembled Novans pause. But before any of them could respond, there was a war whoop from above. Yang turned and followed it to a man on one of the roofs.

"I see an Ursa two blocks over," the guy cried. Then he darted across the rooftop in the direction of the creature.

The mob turned and ran, leaving the Rangers slack-jawed—but only for a heartbeat. Then Yang said, "Pulsers on high. Let's move!" The team took off after the retreating citizens, hoping to catch them in time to keep them from engaging the Ursa.

The mob, or at least part of it, moved faster than Yang would have guessed. It seemed like all he and his Rangers could do was keep pace. But after a while, the citizens ran out of steam and Yang's squad caught up to them. It was no time for niceties. As Yang went by each bounty hunter, he shoved him to the side. More often than not, the civilians lost their footing and rolled. The others followed his lead, and in short order the way was clear ahead of them.

That was the good news. The bad was that an Ursa charged out from an alley up ahead, its bulk nearly filling the narrow street.

"Fan out!" Yang commanded. "Fire at will!"

The air was electric with the ripping sounds of multiple energy bursts, all concentrated on the Ursa. Unfortunately, they couldn't get around it to hit it from all sides, which was something that seemed to at least slow the things down. Still, it was distracted by the collective power of their pulsers long enough to pause in its tracks, toss its eyeless head, and roar in defiance.

Dammit, thought Yang, *what's it going to take to kill one of those things?*

Far from dying, the Ursa began to advance on them. Fortunately, the bounty hunters had begun to run, not so brave now that they had seen their target for real. Worst came to worst, Yang's squad could retreat without fear of leaving a civilian in harm's way.

"Fall back!" Yang bellowed. He looked around and counted Rangers to make sure none of them had fallen without his knowing it. But he counted only five. His heart sank. Who was missing?

It took him a moment to figure it out: *Raige.*

Where had the kid gone? There weren't any bodies in the street, either Rangers or civilians. So where—

Then he saw it. Somehow Raige had gotten behind the monster. He was standing there in the street, aiming his pulser at it. *Good work,* Yang thought. *We've got it surrounded.*

The Rangers had seen from experience that that was only a temporary solution, that the creature eventually would shrug off their blasts and come after them. But maybe this time the tactic would work. With the ordnance they had, there wasn't much else they could do.

The only problem was that Raige wasn't firing his pulser yet, which meant the Ursa could continue to advance on the squad, unaware that there was a threat behind it. And eventually that advance would turn into an outright attack. Yang didn't get it. What was the kid waiting for?

Then he saw something he would never forget as long as he lived.

With about sixty feet between Raige and the Ursa, the kid broke into a dead sprint in the monster's direction. Like a long jumper, he waited until the last moment and then used his momentum to leap into the air—and land right on the creature's broad, sinuous back. Feeling Raige's weight, the Ursa whipped its head around—

Just in time to take the cadet's silver-blue pulser burst squarely in its face.

Suddenly, Raige was flying end over end through the air, flung off the Ursa's back. Yang watched the cadet hit the ground hard. Somehow he had managed to hang on to his pulser, but he looked unconscious—or worse.

Stupid! Yang thought as he rushed to Raige's side. After all, the kid was defenseless. The Ursa would make a meal of him if it didn't meet some kind of resistance. But as the squadron leader reached Raige and whirled to meet the Ursa with a burst, he realized there was nothing to meet. The monster was still standing in the same spot. As Yang watched, scarcely able to believe his eyes, the Ursa shuddered.

"Hit it with everything you've got!" he roared.

And they did. He and his four remaining squad members blasted away at the creature, advancing step by step, their barrage making the Ursa's skin seem to writhe like a watery surface in a strong wind.

Until that same skin blackened and cracked and bled something that looked more like crude oil than blood and the beast crumpled to the ground, and even then they kept up the barrage. Finally, once Yang was as sure as he could be that the thing was dead, he told his Rangers to stand down.

Bolt took a reading with his mediscan. "Looks dead to me," he said.

But it was an alien creature, and they wouldn't take anything for granted until a science team had confirmed Bolt's finding. In the meantime, Raige was stirring, trying to get to his feet. Yang went over to see to him.

"Did we get it?" the cadet groaned.

"Don't move," Yang said. "You may have broken something."

Raige glared at him as if to remind him that he was Bonita's nephew and that he had a score to settle. "With all due respect, sir, *did we get it?*"

Yang smiled. "We got it."

Carceras and Kromo exchanged high fives. And why not? It was the first Ursa they had taken down since the things had infested Nova City.

And it was all the kid's doing.

Conner stood in Prime Commander Wilkins's office, his arms at his sides, and waited patiently for her to recognize him.

Wilkins shook her head. "What is it with you Raiges? Don't injuries mean anything to you people?"

Conner had landed funny after the Ursa had thrown him off its back, but it wasn't anything serious. He couldn't run, but he could still walk. And if he could walk, he was going to talk to the Prime Commander.

That was why he had left the medicenter, made his way across the Ranger compound, bypassed Wilkins's surprised adjutant, and planted himself directly in front of Wilkins's desk.

"Sorry, ma'am," said the adjutant, a couple of seconds behind Conner, "but he just—"

Wilkins held up a hand and said, "Understood." Then, with another gesture, she dismissed the man, leaving Conner standing there.

"Prime Commander," he said, "I know you asked me to wait at the medicenter and it's my duty to follow your orders. But if our positions were reversed and you told me you were in possession of something that could save human lives, I wouldn't ask *you* to wait. I'd want to hear what you had to say before I took another breath."

For a moment, he was sure she would punish him for his impudence. After all, what kind of cadet did what he had just done? *Somebody insane, maybe. Somebody who had lost his last marble.*

But Wilkins didn't give him any indication that she was going to punish him. Instead she smiled and said, "Actually, I was about to go see you, now that I've gotten the Ursa's carcass to a secure location. After all, we don't know if the creatures are cannibals, and we didn't want to risk one of the other Ursa consuming it before we got it under wraps."

Conner hadn't thought of that.

"But now that you're here," said Wilkins, "why don't you tell me what you did and why you did it. And don't worry; I'm not going to make you file a formal battle plan."

He nodded. "Thank you, ma'am. As far as what I did . . . it was the same thing my aunt did just before she died."

Wilkins leaned forward. "Your aunt . . . ?"

"I went over the satellite-to-ground footage," Conner explained. "I know you've got other people doing that, but I had a reason to go over this particular footage more carefully. After all, it was the last time anyone saw my aunt alive."

The Prime Commander nodded. "And you found something?"

"I did, ma'am. I noticed how close my aunt was able to get to the Ursa."

"It was feeding, as I recall."

"That's true. But what if that wasn't the reason? What if the creatures have a blind spot directly behind them—a blind spot in their *sense of smell*? We've been giving them credit for an extraordinary sensory range despite the fact that they're eyeless. But what if they don't have the kind of range we've assumed?"

"A blind spot," she echoed.

"Everyone's got one," said Conner. "Lucas Kincaid did in that war game. That's how I was able to get behind him. After I saw my aunt's footage, I figured the Ursa had one, too."

"So you went out and tested that theory?" Wilkins said, a note of disapproval in her voice.

"It was on my mind," he admitted. "But to be honest, I didn't think I'd get the *chance* to test it. And then I did. And at that point, I had no alternative but to check it out."

"Why didn't you discuss it with me first?"

"Because you wouldn't have assigned me to a squad. You would have let someone else risk his or her life to see if I was right. And I didn't want to be responsible for someone else getting killed."

"Noble," said Wilkins. "But dumb. Someone more experienced would have had a better chance of making it work. But be that as it may, you've provided us with a valuable insight. Except . . ."

"Ma'am?" said Conner.

"I'm not ready to bless it until we've had a chance to test it in different circumstances."

"I've already tested it," he insisted.

"Understand," said Wilkins, "that I've got responsibility for the entire Corps. If I send out every squad we've got and we've misinterpreted the data, that's it. The Skrel and their monsters will have won. So I need to test it one more time."

Conner bit his lip. "No problem. I can take a squad out as soon as—"

"*You?*" said Wilkins.

He hadn't thought about it. It had just come out. "I just want to be part of the squad," he said more reasonably.

The Prime Commander shook her head. "No. This has got to be a squad of veterans, Cadet Raige. I'm not risking a cadet. Especially one that's hobbled the way you are."

Conner felt a surge of disappointment. "But ma'am—"

"Look," said Wilkins, "you've made what I hope will be a huge contribution to the defense of this colony. But this mission is going to be one of the most important we've ever carried out. I'd be derelict in my duty if I didn't assemble a team of the most experienced Rangers we have—and that includes *me*."

"With all due respect," he said, "experience is great. But it's not a matter of how *much* experience. It's a matter of what kind. I was the one who caught on to the Ursa's weakness, ma'am. I know what it takes to capitalize on it."

"So do I," said Wilkins, "now that you've shared your observations with me." She got up, came around her desk, and put her hands on Conner's shoulders. "Relax, cadet. When we come back with a dead Ursa in tow, you're the one who's going to get the credit."

Credit? "It's not about that," he blurted, feeling the heat rise in his face. "Not at all. I—"

Wilkins held a hand up. "Sorry. Bad choice of words—I've been doing that a lot lately. I didn't mean to imply that that was the first thing on your mind. But you *will* get the credit. Hell, you'll deserve it."

On that note, she showed him the door. Conner noted a spring in her step that hadn't been there when he walked in.

"Smile," said the Prime Commander. "If your theory pans out, you'll have done this colony a great service. Now get some rest. We may need you again before this is all over."

He was bitterly disappointed, but he had pleaded his case as hard as he could. "Yes, ma'am. Thank you, ma'am."

"You're welcome, Cadet. Carry on."

As he left Wilkins's office, he couldn't help feeling good about what he had done but also bad in that, in his estimate at least, he could have done so much more.

CHAPTER TWENTY

Conner was surprised when he answered his vid tablet and saw who was trying to contact him. Of all people, it was his father.

"Morning, Cadet," said Frank Raige.

They hadn't spoken in such a long time, Conner didn't know how to respond. He still felt the sting of what his father had said to him that day outside the command center.

"I said, 'Morning, Cadet.'"

"Morning, sir."

"Listen, I've only got a minute while Smitty replaces a mag coil. But I got a call from Meredith Wilkins. She tells me you killed an Ursa."

Conner felt a flush of pride. "Not just me, sir. I was part of a squad."

His father's brow creased. "You calling the Prime Commander a liar, Cadet?"

Conner was caught off guard by the question. He was about to protest until his father cracked a smile and Conner realized he was joking. It felt good to see him joke. It had been a long time.

"No, sir," he said. "I wouldn't do that, sir."

"Glad to hear it. Conner . . ." Silence for a moment. "I'm hoping what you figured out about the Ursa will make a difference. But Torrance is gone, and Bonita is gone, and . . . well, you can never tell who's going to make it back from a mission and who's not. So I want you to know"—his voice cracked as Conner had never heard it crack before—"what I said at the command center that day, I wouldn't have done it if I hadn't seen something in you, something that's just beginning to show. You know, I've always talked so much about family tradition, you probably wondered if you could ever live up to it. Let me let you in on a secret, son—you don't have to *become* a Raige. You've always *been* one."

Conner felt his throat constrict.

"You're a fine, fine Ranger," said his dad, "and I am as proud of you as I can be. Always remember that."

Conner nodded. There were tears standing in his eyes, but he didn't wipe them away. "Thanks, Dad."

Someone off camera said something, and Conner's father glanced that way. Then he turned back to Conner and smiled. "Good luck, son."

"Rangers make their own luck," said Conner. It was something Frank Raige used to say a lot when Conner was growing up. *Rangers make their own luck.*

"I've heard that, now that you mention it. See you soon, son."

"You bet, Dad."

And his father's image winked out.

Trey Vander Meer sat in the studio, in Pham's office, and watched the news feeds on a bank of holographic screens. All over Nova City, people were rising up against the Ursa, even if it was only with farm implements in their hands. His offer of a bounty had gotten some traction, just as he had hoped it would.

Ordinary citizens were doing the job the Rangers already would have completed if they were anywhere near as prepared as they should have been. The people, who had always been the strength of the colony, had taken up the fight with their own hands. When they did that, there was no monster, from their own world or any other, that could stand against them.

Vander Meer scratched his face. He hadn't shaved in

a while; he didn't really know how long. *Maybe I'll grow a beard,* he thought. *Natasha always kids me about my b—*

He stopped. *Natasha . . .*

He would shave. It was just a matter of finding the proper tool. Maybe I'll ask Pham to bring a shaver with him tomorrow. Or the next day. No hurry, really.

The people were on the job. It was just a matter of time before they erased the Ursa from the face of the planet. Just a matter of time . . .

The air had become positively stale as Cecilia Ruiz sat there on the edge of Nova City's outlands. She'd been walking for two days and thus far had encountered nothing untoward. But at least she wasn't feeling over-taxed. Her body hadn't betrayed her; she was in as good shape as she had been nine years ago. *Not bad for having had two kids,* she thought proudly.

She was armed with two pieces of electronic equipment that she prayed would give her the edge she needed in tracking down an Ursa.

First was her old naviband.

Technically, she should not have had it. It was a piece of equipment that was supposed to be turned in when one left the Corps. But Cecilia had had a long-standing and very positive relationship with the quartermaster, and so when he had asked for the return of her band, which performed the function of communications as well as navigation, she had just given him a look of carefully crafted chagrin and told him that tragically, she'd lost it. He'd simply studied her, his face deadpan, and then said, "If it turns up, bring it back."

If he had wanted, he could have used the band's tracking function to find it. But out of kindness he hadn't.

Cecilia hadn't done anything inappropriate with it since then. It was just that every so often she liked to find a nice private spot, turn on the link, and listen to the cross chat of various Rangers. It made her feel ever so slightly as if she still belonged, even if she could only listen in from afar and live vicariously through the Rangers' communications.

The second piece of equipment was an electronic map. It was displayed on a small pad, and she was using it as a point of configuration to see if there was any rhyme or reason to the manner in which the Ursa were making their presence known. Thus far, she had been unable to find any kind of pattern. She wasn't sure whether to be relieved or frustrated by this. The frustration would stem from the fact that the random nature of their movements made it impossible to determine where they might strike next. But it was something of a relief because it meant that the monsters weren't intelligent enough to form a coherent plan of attack. Animals that could strategize were certainly the last thing anyone needed.

Cecilia studied the glowing dots that indicated all the places the Ursa had struck recently. She noticed that there was one area, about fifty kliks north of her current location, that seemed to be without any sort of reported Ursa sighting. "Seems as good a place as any to look around," she muttered, and so north it was.

She continued to run through her head what she had discerned about the creatures during her one brief encounter with one. Its behavior didn't make sense to her. It had had her dead to rights, attacking her from behind. She'd been oblivious to its presence. But it had gone right past her and attacked the gunman.

Why?

Well, there were only two explanations. The first was that it actually had discerned the shooter as the greater threat. He had a weapon in his hand while she was weaponless, and so from a strategic point of view, it made sense to incapacitate him before her. The second explanation was that it simply hadn't seen her. What better reason to bypass her than if it didn't know she was there?

No eyes. The fact that it has no eyes must be the clue.

Perhaps it's telepathic somehow. Or maybe it has some sort of built-in radar. Or it could be that it's able to detect heat signatures and it's following those. It could even be something as simple as smell: that our scents draw it to us. If only I knew which of those it was, I might be able to exploit it as a weakness and defeat it.

The problem was that she didn't have a lot of latitude for experimentation. She could come at the Ursa with an attack designed to target a weakness that it might or might not have. Judging by the creature's track record, she wouldn't get a second chance.

Cecilia continued to negotiate terrain that at certain points was jagged and challenging. One would have thought the Northern Plains, which she was currently making her way across, would have been nice and flat. Not so: There were plenty of ups and downs and several places where the land was so uneven that she nearly fell. That could well have been catastrophic. If she'd injured her ankle, she would have been alone and vulnerable in the middle of nowhere. It was an unsettling realization.

Maybe if you'd given this any damn thought ahead of time, you'd have had the brains to remain at home. Was Xander right? Is this all about me and nothing to do with trying to help my family?

She tried to push those concerns away, but they dogged her as she continued her trek.

The suns continued their circuit across the sky. At the hottest point of the day, she found shelter inside an empty cave, but not before she took the precaution of firing in a few pulser shots to make sure there was nothing hiding within it. Only then did she crawl in and remain there until the heat was less blistering. The entire time she remained at the ready, sitting toward the mouth of the cave with her pulser resting on her lap.

She speculated about how wonderful it would be if an Ursa went slinking past below while she was sitting in the mouth of the cave. She'd be able to send a steady stream of pulse blasts at the monster before it even knew what had hit it. With luck, a lot more than the

Rangers in the city had had, she would be able to kill the thing without putting herself at risk.

Without any luck, it looks up, sees me, and I'm dead.

Cecilia was becoming frustrated with herself. This was not the attitude a Ranger displayed in contemplation of battle. This was the sort of negative thinking that got one killed.

She pulled her binoculars from her pack and surveyed the area. As she panned across the uneven terrain, she suddenly swung the binoculars back and zoomed in on something she hadn't noticed before. It appeared to be a mining colony. She vaguely remembered hearing about such an endeavor out here but couldn't recall much in the way of details beyond that.

Cecilia decided to head in that direction, which seemed as good an idea as any. Perhaps they would be able to tell her something. Perhaps they'd seen something.

Perhaps they're all dead.

She growled angrily at herself. *Again! Again with the negative thinking. Stop it. Not everything is a worst-case scenario.*

Mentally scolding herself the entire way, she set out for the colony.

Back in the days before humankind left Earth, there was a city called Newcastle in the middle of a big coal-producing region in a country called England. Newcastle needed lots of things, but coal wasn't one of them, and so when people wanted to describe an utterly useless activity, they said it was like bringing coals to Newcastle.

That was how Frank Raige felt as he plied the air over Nova City in his flier and, in fact, how he had felt every day since the Skrel ship had crashed outside Nova City and unleashed its plague on humanity.

Unfortunately, he didn't have the option of doing anything else.

He had suggested to the Prime Commander more than once that he would be more useful leading ground patrols, but she wouldn't go for his suggestion. She had insisted that he was doing his fellow citizens a service by looking out for Ursa in the streets and that he was saving lives by continuing to fly. But it sure didn't feel like he was saving lives.

What it felt like was gratitude on Wilkins's part for the good turn his father had done for her. That had been Frank's theory until she told him she was going to let Conner go on a mission.

Until then, the boy had taken part in civilian evacs and little else. But a ground mission was serious business, and if Wilkins would let Conner go on one, she wasn't operating out of gratitude to the Raige family after all. Maybe, he had to allow, she really believed that Frank's flying over the city was accomplishing something.

An opinion he didn't share. "Coals to Newcastle," he grumbled.

He would have gone on grumbling except for what he saw on a rooftop coming up on his right. Banking and slowing down as much as he could without losing altitude, he peered over the side of his flier and spotted a bunch of kids—six or seven of them; it was hard to tell—waving their arms at him as if they, too, wanted to take flight.

What the hell were kids doing outside when there were Ursa roaming the streets? It wouldn't be any big deal for one of the creatures to bound up onto the roof and make short work of the youngsters.

But he couldn't yell at them from where he was. He would have to contact Hāturi and get some orders relayed to the nearest ground patrol.

Frank already had opened a channel to Hāturi's office when he saw the reason the kids were up on the rooftop. An Ursa was slinking alongside a building with a human body in its maw. And as Frank flew past, he could see that a wall of the building had been broken in. Instantly, he reconstructed what had happened. The Ursa had gotten into the place, and one or more of the adults had tried to stop it while the kids escaped to the roof.

It didn't matter if he was right. All that mattered was that the Ursa was following the half dozen kids and that before long it would consume them as it already had begun to consume the adult.

Unless Frank did something about it.

Banking sharply, he came back at the creature with his flier's pulsers spitting silver-blue destruction. It didn't stop the Ursa. It got its attention.

That had been Frank's purpose all along. The Ursa tossed its head and roared at him and maybe would have gone after him if he hadn't been out of reach. As it was, it resumed its pursuit of the kids.

Unfortunately, they had about reached the end of the roof, and there was no way they could leap over to the next one—not across the width of a whole street. All the Ursa had to do was leap up and take them. Frank couldn't let that happen. But what could he do? He couldn't scoop the kids up, and he couldn't stop the creature with his fusion-burst fire.

That left him one option.

Banking again, he came around for another pass— just in time to see the Ursa do what he had feared it would do. With a push of its powerful back paws, it propelled itself onto the roof, the human corpse still in its mouth.

The kids crowded the edge of the roof, screaming. But if they jumped, it would be to their deaths. In no hurry, the Ursa advanced on them.

Frank knew what would happen to him if he carried out his plan. He did it anyway.

As the Ursa gathered itself to do to the kids what it had done to its first victim, Frank aimed his flier at it. Then he plowed into it at full speed.

The thing was heavier than it looked but not so heavy

that the impact didn't sweep it off the rooftop. Frank braced himself for the crash that he knew would follow as he and his flier hit the ground, a crash he couldn't reasonably expect to survive.

But as he fell along with the Ursa, the creature hugged the flier to its pale, sinuous breast. And as luck would have it, the Ursa took the brunt of the fall.

Still, the collision with the ground nearly snapped Frank's neck. Too dazed to move, he watched the Ursa shove the flier off it, get to its feet, and toss its head. Up close, it was even more alien, more terrifying. Frank tried to get out of the flier, but he couldn't. Its cockpit hatch was jammed, no doubt a result of the fall.

The Ursa tilted its eyeless head as it approached him and roared so loudly that he thought his eardrums would burst. Then it smashed the cockpit, driving shards of shattered plastishield into his face and arms and chest. Consumed by pain and barely able to move, Frank had no illusions about what the thing meant to do with him. Its maw opened, and it smelled worse than the worst rotting meat Frank had ever had the misfortune to smell.

But he wasn't going to go down without a fight. Pulling out his pulser, he set it for maximum force and fired directly into the creature's maw. But nothing happened. The weapon didn't discharge.

Frank looked at his pulser. *Must have been damaged in the fall.* It figured.

Then the thing came at him a second time, and this attack was more successful. Before Frank knew it, the Ursa's talons had ripped his chest open. He was spurting blood like a fountain.

I'm done, he had time to think.

His only consolation was the knowledge that he might have saved the kids from the same fate.

CHAPTER TWENTY-ONE

Conner stood in Prime Commander Wilkins's office. Commander Hāturi loomed over Wilkins's desk, looking too big for it by half.

His words fell like hammer blows: "I didn't think it was fair for you to wait until Prime Commander Wilkins came back."

Conner nodded. "Yes, sir."

"Your father was a brave man, Conner. He didn't go without a fight."

Dad . . .

Conner nodded, feeling his eyes fill with tears. "Yes, sir."

"When we notified your aunt Theresa, she said she would hold a memorial service. Not just for your father but for your uncle and aunt as well."

Conner drew a ragged breath. His mom was strong. She had known there might be a day like this.

Later, he would sit with her and they would grieve together. But for now, she would want him to help the colony. His dad would have done the same thing if their positions were reversed.

"My place is with my squad," he told Hāturi.

The Commander's brow knit. "Permission to remain with your squad is denied. We need you, but we need you with a clear head. Go home. Clear it. Then come back to us."

"Sir—"

"That's an order, Cadet." Hāturi's tone left no room for disagreement.

"As you wish, sir," said Conner.

It was only when Cecilia drew close enough to the mining colony to see the razorbeaks pinwheeling in the air that she realized her most dire imaginings were far more than just worst-case fantasies.

The razorbeaks were analogous to Earth birds called vultures. However, their skin was far more leathery, and their wings, more bat-shaped than birdlike, were about six feet long from tip to tip. On seeing them for the first time, Novans had named them for the obvious reason that their beaks were exceptionally sharp. They rarely attacked humans, or at least healthy humans. But when they did, they could be nasty, even dangerous.

She spotted the first corpse, or at least what was left of the corpse, at the perimeter of the colony. A razorbeak was picking at it with the point of its beak. It noticed Cecilia coming its way but seemed indifferent to her.

Cecilia felt her gorge rise as she saw it nibbling on its putrid treat. Forcing the nausea back down, she pulled out her pulser and fired. Her hand trembled, but it didn't matter. If she hit the thing, fine. If she didn't, the bursts would be enough to scare it away.

At least that was her theory.

The actual practice of it worked out a bit differently. Her blast kicked up dirt to one side of the razorbeak. The creature leaped upward with an alarmed squawk, its wings beating the air, and then it angled around and barreled straight at Cecilia, its beak aimed at her like a spear.

She backpedaled, unleashing a silver-blue barrage. The razorbeak darted swiftly around it with ease. *Aw, crap,* Cecilia thought as she swung the pulser back and forth in a continuous arc.

Her inability to keep her hand steady turned out to be her salvation. It added a randomness to her shots that the bird could not anticipate, the result being that it flew right into one of her pulse streams. It clipped the razorbeak on the right wing, and the creature spiraled out of control, then hit the ground not ten feet away from Cecilia.

It skidded past her, and before it could leap to its clawed feet again, Cecilia opened fire at point-blank range. Even her trembling hand was up to the task of finishing off a downed razorbeak. A minute later it was nothing more than a twitching mass of flesh.

She heard a distant *caw* in the sky and looked up. Three more razorbeaks were heading her way. Quickly Cecilia backed up, keeping the pulser leveled as best she could at the incoming creatures. The razorbeaks angled downward but displayed no interest in Cecilia whatso-ever. Instead they landed atop the fallen razorbeak and started devouring it.

Nice to know they don't discriminate, she thought with grim amusement, and holstered her pulser.

As she made her way into the mining colony, it oc-curred to her that the Ursa responsible for the carnage was still somewhere in the camp. If it came leaping out at her, she should have her weapon at the ready. But she decided to keep it holstered, confident in her ability to draw it quickly. After all, she'd been the fastest draw in the Corps. Her hand might tremble, but she hadn't lost a second off her ability to pull a weapon and have it ready. If, however, an Ursa leaped out at her and star-tled her, she could very easily lose her hold on the gun if it was in her hand. Thus, holstered was preferable.

The mining colony was deathly still. Nothing more than a collection of ramshackle shelters. Most signifi-cantly, there were spatters of blood everywhere. If there had been the slightest doubt in Cecilia's mind that an Ursa had torn through there like a sandstorm of de-struction, there was no longer any left. Bits of bone, muscle, and internal organs were on view everywhere.

She forced herself to detach her mind from the devastation she was witness to. *Give the devil its due: The creature's thorough,* she thought grimly. There was clearly nothing left alive in the whole—

"Don't move."

She started at the command but instantly regained her cool.

"Turn around," came the next order.

She swallowed once and then spoke in what she hoped sounded like a conversational tone. "Can't exactly do both," she said reasonably. "Want me not to move? Or should I turn around?"

She heard a low and slightly confused exchange of hushed voices. *More than one. Okay.* Then one of her new friends said, "Just turn. And keep your hands where we can see them."

Cecilia obediently kept her hands raised as she turned to face the people standing behind her. There were three of them, three men dusty and scruffy from the road. And one of them was holding a knife within a couple of inches of her throat.

She knew the type: vagrants, nomads who preferred to live outside the laws of Nova Prime. They had no interest in contributing to the commonwealth; instead, they kept on the move, grabbing what they could, thinking only of themselves.

It was an attitude that disgusted her. Had they learned nothing from the lessons of the past? Didn't they understand that humanity's only hope of survival was pulling together, everyone striving toward the shared goal of keeping humankind alive? That every man for himself was an outdated mode of thinking?

Obviously not.

Their hair and beards were unkempt and caked with dirt. They looked as if they hadn't showered in weeks, if ever. "Are you miners?" she said, already knowing the answer.

"No," said the tallest of them, who might well have been the leader, assuming creatures such as these had leaders. "No, we're not from around here." He chortled softly at that, and the others followed suit. Then, more seriously, he said, "We found the supplies here fair and square. So you keep your hands off 'em, understand?"

Supplies. Of course. The miners would have had food-stuffs and such of their own. With the place devoid of life, that would have left it easy pickings. And apparently these three had decided to settle in.

"I don't care about your supplies," she told them. "Keep them, enjoy them, choke on them. All the same to me. All I care about is the thing that did this," and she tilted her head toward the remains of one of the miners. "You seen any sign of it?"

"You mean an Ursa?" The leader wasn't stupid, so that was something. He laughed nastily. So did the man with the knife, with a funny catch in his laugh that made Cecilia wonder if he was more than a little crazy.

Great, she thought.

"Don't rightly think we'd still be alive if one of those things was wandering around," said the leader.

She hated to admit it, but what he was saying made sense. Rather than hanging around an area, it seemed more consistent with what they knew of the Ursa for the creature to destroy whatever it encountered and then keep going.

"I suppose you're right," she admitted. "The fact that you're still alive is as convincing an argument as any-one's going to find. So I'll just keep going, then. Have fun . . . or whatever it is you do."

The leader's eyes drifted down to the pulser on her hip. As far as Cecilia could tell, they weren't packing anything like it. "Pretty nice gun you have there," he said. "Mind if I take a look at it?"

Right, because I'm sure you'll hand it right back. "Rather not."

"I'd rather you did," said the leader.

The guy with the knife touched its point to her throat and pressed ever so gently.

"Take it slowly out of the holster," said the leader,

"and toss it on the ground. Oh, and whatever else you got in that pack. We want that, too."

"That'll leave me nothing," said Cecilia. "Doesn't seem fair."

"We're the law around here, sweetheart," said the leader. "We're the ones who decide what's fair and unfair. Now give it here. Now." When she didn't react immediately, he repeated—louder and more threateningly—"*Now!*"

The knife point pressed harder into her skin, maybe hard enough to draw some blood.

Without a word, Cecilia pulled the pulser from her holster. She didn't have time to raise it and point it at the leader, so she did the next best thing. She shot downward at what she thought would be the vicinity of the knife wielder's foot.

Of course, if she missed, it would probably mean her life. But she had resolved to adopt a more positive attitude, hadn't she?

"*Eyeaaghh!*" cried the knife guy, hopping backward in pain.

That gave her all the room she needed to take out the leader. As he flew backward, a bag of broken bones propelled by the force of her pulser burst, the third guy went for her throat. He was quicker than he looked— quick enough to get within a few inches of her before she caved his face in with her next shot.

That left the knife wielder, who was still hopping on one foot, clutching at the one Cecilia had broken. As she watched, he fell down, raising a puff of dust around him. Then he lay there on the ground, his eyes wide, no doubt wondering how she planned to kill him.

"Here's what's going to happen," she said. "You're going to stay there and not move a muscle. I'm going to go over to where the provisions are and take what I want. I will then leave a booby trap so that if you try to raid them, you'll be blown to bits. I will also inform the Rangers of the situation out here so that they can give your poor-bastard friends a proper burial.

"By that point, you will be long gone. If you have to crawl, crawl. That's entirely up to you. Do we understand each other?"

He managed a nod.

"Then go."

He started crawling.

Cecilia sat down and watched him, careful not to look at the two corpses she had made. She waited until he had crawled over a ridge and was out of sight.

Then she went to her knees, leaned her head forward, and vomited violently. The contents of her stomach, as meager as they were, exited with velocity, and it took a few minutes to recover her composure. Finally she managed to do so, but her throat remained raw. She rubbed it delicately and then took a gulp of water to try to ease the pain. She was only partly successful, but partly was better than nothing at all.

Cecilia staggered to her feet and then went to find the storage bins. When she found them, she stocked up on everything she could comfortably carry. She didn't really have anything to rig a booby trap with, but she supposed that fear alone should be enough to keep raiders away from the rest of it. She also found a few other things in the stores of the miners that she felt could be of use and tucked them away carefully in her pack.

Finally she put out a general call to the Rangers without identifying herself. She hadn't hesitated to grab some of the stuff for herself, but she reasoned that the rest should go into the general stores to help everyone on Nova Prime.

Just before she left, she caught a glimpse of her reflection in the metal surface of one of the canisters. Her hair was disheveled; her eyes looked sunken, as if she hadn't had a good night's sleep in days. Which was more or less accurate. Blood was spattered on her right cheek, and she hadn't even realized it was there. She wiped it away as best she could, but there was still a faint red tint.

She wondered whether when she came back from this trip, her family would even recognize her.

Then she realized that her coming back from the trip was itself more of an *if* than a *when* but immediately dismissed that from her mind. *Think positively,* she reminded herself.

Music came up, mournful and dignified. It was a signal that resounded throughout the Great Hall.

Conner, who was sitting next to his mother, felt her slender hand slide into his. He grasped it, the same way she used to grasp his when he was little and needed comforting.

Conner's hand wasn't as big as his father's had been. But then, no one's was—literally or figuratively. There had been only one Frank Raige. *And he's gone, like Uncle Torrance and Aunt Bonita and all the others.*

It was hard for Conner to comprehend, hard for him to wrap his mind around the concept. *Gone. And they'll never be back. And if we don't figure out how to beat the Ursa, the rest of us will be gone, too.*

Hundreds of years earlier, the arks had settled on the red sand of Nova Prime, embracing a bright promise and a new world. Had the people who disembarked from the arks ever envisioned a time like this? Had they ever imagined that the human species, which had survived in space for a hundred years, would be erased from existence by a few dozen alien beasts?

As Conner pondered the question, a robed figure came out onto the platform. It was wearing a brown robe, not the dark blue of the Primus. *Aunt Theresa.*

Part of Conner was angry. The Primus had conducted so many memorial services. And after Conner's father, his aunt, and his uncle had given their lives for the colony . . .

But another part of him was glad it was Aunt Theresa who would be conducting the service. After all, she was family. Coming from her, the words that were spoken would mean something.

Conner's aunt looked out at what must have seemed like a sea of mourners. But she didn't seem daunted by the sight. She seemed as comfortable as if she were standing in her own kitchen with a few good friends.

She didn't say or do anything right away. She just stood there and smiled. Then she raised her hands, the sleeves of her robe sliding back to reveal her arms almost to the elbows. Almost immediately, the talk in the hall hushed to a whisper and finally to nothing at all.

Aunt Theresa put her arms down. "Today," she said, her soft voice filling the hall, "I'm not just an augur leading a memorial service—I'm also the *sister* of the deceased. So when I say I know how you feel, I do. I know *exactly* how you feel.

"I feel cheated of the years I wanted to share with my brothers and my sister-in-law. I feel lost without their wisdom to guide me. I feel empty, scoured out inside, as if my life will never be the same."

She drew a deep breath, let it out. "Though I'm supposed to give you solace and perspective and lend meaning to what happened, I find it hard to do so. For all my learning, all my faith, I'm not sure I can find solace and perspective even for myself. And meaning? Well, I'll do my best.

"Our brothers and sister have been taken by a higher power. I know that with the same certainty that I know the suns rise in the west. I know it as surely as I know the beating of my own heart.

"We might ask how such a thing could happen when we need them among us here and now, when we need them as we have never needed them before. Even if we were privy to the answer, I doubt that we would be happy with it. For those of us who watch our loved ones go on while we stay behind, no answer can be sufficient. No reason anyone can give is enough to take away our pain.

"But Frank and Torrance and Bonita leave us each

with our memories, with priceless glimpses of who they were and what they stood for. A memory of brave people, proud people, who loved their family and their friends without stint or qualification. Memories of Rangers in the finest meaning of that word, who would—and did—give their lives for those they swore to protect.

"How can we honor their memories? By remaining strong in the face of the alien scourge. By not giving up no matter how hopeless the situation may seem at times. By hanging on to our faith in the midst of adversity because our faith will see us through, as it has so many times since we set foot on Nova Prime.

"Neither Frank nor Torrance nor Bonita can carry on the fight any longer, may their souls rest in peace. But we can. And we will."

Conner nodded. He would carry on the fight. But it would be harder than before, much harder. After all, he had lost more than his father. He had lost his father's wisdom, his father's way of looking at the world.

He had been happy to become a cadet, to take on the same responsibility that his father, his uncle, and his aunt had taken on before him. But in the back of his mind, he had known that he could fall back on their experience and expertise, that he had a safety net if he ever needed one. Now the safety net was gone.

It was just him out there, all alone, to stand or fall. And if he fell, it wouldn't just be a cadet named Conner who screwed up. It would be Conner *Raige*.

Whatever he did would reflect on the whole Raige tradition, starting with the first of his ancestors who had put on the rust-colored uniform of the Rangers back on Earth. It was a big burden for an eighteen-year-old to shoulder.

Not that he had a choice. He was who he was, and he would be who he would be.

When the service was over, Aunt Theresa came down and hugged them—every one of them who had come to the service. Then Conner and his mother went to the door, where a squad of Rangers was waiting for them with a couple of ground vehicles.

"Conner," said his mother.

It had been a long time since they had spoken, and it seemed even longer than that. Like everyone else, Rebecca Raige had a few extra lines in her face.

"Are you all right?" she asked him.

"I'm fine," he said, all the while knowing she would see through his denial. Then he added: "I gave Prime Commander Wilkins an idea. I'm hoping it works. But—"

"But what if it doesn't?"

Conner nodded.

His mother studied him for a moment. Then she asked, "Do you remember what Dad used to tell you when you played cageball?"

When I played cageball . . . ? "No."

"Come on—when you were a little boy? And your team was trying to hang on to a lead?"

Then Conner *did* remember. "The rhythm thing."

His mother nodded. "Every game has a rhythm. In some games, you build up a big lead. You feel like you're going to win going away."

"Then the other team comes back. It comes back with a *vengeance*. And when that happens, you're on your heels. You forget how you ever built up a lead. You feel like you've got no chance."

He could see Frank Raige towering over him. He could feel the weight of his father's hand on his bony young shoulder.

"When that happens, all you can do is hold on," said his mother. "Just hold on and do your best. Because if you do, the other team will eventually run out of fuel. The tide will turn your way again. And in the end, you'll come out on top."

Conner shook his head. "It's not a game, Mom. People are dying, Rangers especially."

"You know your father. You think he was talking about a game?"

Actually, Conner *had* thought that.

"Conner, everything he did, everything he said, was to prepare you for life. Of course, he didn't know the Ursa were going to descend on us. How could he? But he knew there would be challenges ahead, and he wanted you to be ready for them—or at least as ready as you could possibly be."

Conner nodded. That sounded like his father, all right.

"We built a civilization here," said his mother. "We got ourselves a nice big lead. Now the Skrel and the Ursa are trying to take it away from us. They're charging hard. We're on our heels. It feels like we can't win, like we never had that lead in the first place.

"But we didn't get to where we are by not being good, by not being tough and resourceful and determined. We can beat the Ursa, Conner. We can beat *anything*. We just have to hold on and do our best until the tide turns back in our favor."

The words were coming out of his mother's mouth, but Conner could hear his father saying them. And if he were there, he would have. Conner was sure of it.

"So all I've got to do is hold on," he said.

"That," said his mother, wiping a tear from her eye, "and forget about dribbling with your right hand. You know how lousy you are at dribbling with your right hand."

He couldn't help smiling. "Thanks, Mom."

She pulled his head down with both hands and kissed him on the forehead. "Don't thank me. Thank your father."

CHAPTER TWENTY-TWO

Prime Commander Wilkins might have been the leader of her squad, but she wasn't its most important member. Not by a long shot.

That distinction went to Rita Norman, the gold medalist in the long jump at the last Asimov Games, who also happened to be a veteran Ranger. Norman's job was to do what Conner Raige had done when his squad took down that Ursa: get as close as she could to the creature and blast it from behind.

Wilkins was just one of the nine Rangers whose job it would be to distract the Ursa while Norman did the real work. It was just as well. Wilkins had been a pretty good athlete in her day, but that day was long past.

Now she prided herself more on being a tactician. As such, she had picked nine of the coolest, most disciplined, and most battle-ready Rangers she could find. And she had picked herself to lead them because she was cool and disciplined as well.

Not because she had been outmaneuvered by the Primus into looking like a fool on Trey Vander Meer's broadcast and as a result been forced to give up the Rangers' satellite monitoring function. Not because the engineer on that critical shift had failed to detect what the Skrel had done to their satellites. Not because Wilkins had something to prove, especially to herself, after she had failed her Rangers and her colony.

No, that had nothing to do with it. She had elected to lead the mission because she was the best leader she could find even if she had to keep telling herself that to make herself feel certain of it.

After all, there was a lot riding on this mission. *I want everything to go right,* she thought as she checked the fusion chamber in her pulser for perhaps the sixth time since she'd left the Ranger barracks. *Everything.*

She had barely looked up again, satisfied that her pulser was in perfect working order, when she saw the monster show up down the street. It was huge, alien, its maw a black hole surrounded by rings of jagged teeth. The holovids didn't do it justice.

For a fraction of a second, as the Ursa rumbled and tossed its head and started in their direction, Wilkins felt a spurt of panic. Then she reminded herself who she was and why she was there, and she was able to tuck away the panic in a place where she didn't have to deal with it.

She was, after all, the Prime Commander of the Rangers.

"Positions," she snapped into the receiver in her comm gear. Her Rangers responded smartly, spreading themselves across the width of the street. Norman was on one end of the formation, where she would try to slip by the monster and get behind it.

As it stalked them, remaining in the middle of the street, that was exactly what Norman did.

Wilkins nodded to herself. *So far, so good.*

"Hold your fire until I give the word," she said, amazed at how calm she sounded.

They all held their fire.

She waited until the Ursa had advanced to the point where it was surrounded by them. "Now," said Wilkins.

As one, they began blasting away at their target. The Ursa halted in its tracks, turned this way and that, and made a ripping sound in its throat. Obviously it didn't like being scalded by pulser fire from every direction. *Or rather,* Wilkins thought as she watched Norman crouch the way she had at the Asimov Games, *nearly every direction.*

"Maintain fire," Wilkins said.

Everyone except Norman maintained his or her fire. Norman, pulser in hand, took a breath, shot forward, raised her head, and leaped.

Wilkins held her breath as she watched. *A great jump. No—a perfect jump.*

But the Ursa didn't remain distracted by Wilkins and the other Rangers. It whirled before Norman could get off a shot—and before Wilkins's horrified eyes tore Norman out of the air with a sweep of its razor-sharp talons.

By the time Norman hit the ground, she was a mess of blood and bone and not much else. But the creature didn't stop to satisfy its hunger with whatever meat still clung to Norman's bones.

Instead, it continued to advance into the midst of Wilkins and her Rangers. The Prime Commander felt her teeth grate. *That's all right,* she thought; *it's not over.*

But in her heart, she knew it was as over as it could get.

Gash regards the creatures converging on it—or at least regards them as clearly as its sightlessness permits.

It stops a moment to remove the grime that has collected on its paw. It licks it experimentally. It always licks experimentally. It never knows exactly what it is that it's going to be stepping on. The liquid is warm, although that warmth is quickly fading. There is a faint taste of something: salt, perhaps.

The creatures—the smell things—are advancing. They are coming together as one and in that action perhaps believe that they are capable of triumphing over Gash.

They are wrong.

One of them comes up behind Gash, but Gash is

aware of it. Gash whirls and smashes the smell thing out of the air with a sweep of its taloned paw. Then, as the smell thing shrieks, Gash tears the smell thing apart.

Gash keeps going, assailing two more simultaneously. It stretches its body, ripping apart one smell thing while sinking its teeth into the other. More of the blood taste floods through Gash, energizing it, bringing it to new and more enthusiastic life.

Then Gash lets out a roar. It is an ear-splitting transcendent noise, and for just a moment all the smell things freeze. Then Gash is everywhere, bounding back and forth. The smell things try to take aim at Gash, but they fail. Gash is here, then it is there, then it is elsewhere. Their energy beams spear the air but are unable to spear Gash.

Thirty seconds. That is all the time it takes—not that Gash is timing it—to rip apart all save one of them.

Gash turns to face the sole surviving smell thing. It fires at Gash, and this time it strikes its target.

Gash staggers a little, and it fires again. And again. It annoys Gash, this barrage. It reminds Gash of the other time a smell thing fired at it and left Gash with a scar over its maw. Gash does not like the feel of its scar, and it certainly does not want another.

The smell thing—a female it, it seems—probably thinks it has Gash at a disadvantage. But there is only one smell thing. With no others to distract Gash, no noise to turn Gash's concentration elsewhere, Gash knows exactly what to do.

Suddenly Gash breaks right. The smell thing swivels her gun to continue firing, but she is too slow, for Gash's move was a fake. Gash cuts back left, leaps toward her. She tries to bring her gun around to strike Gash again, but it is too late. Gash's vault carries it over her shot, and Gash lands on her. Gash's claw wraps around her weapon, and Gash shreds it.

Then Gash shreds her.

Gash first slices through something thin and metal. A nameplate—Wilkins—but, to Gash, all it is is an impediment to the viscera beneath. Then Gash continues tearing away at her, and she struggles for as many seconds as she can before she stops moving.

The smell thing is dead.

Gash eats her slowly. Gash wants the satisfaction of eating to last, and it does, until Gash loses interest and leaves the smell thing's half-eaten corpse behind.

Gash has other things to do with its time.

Conner had just come back from a shelter on the South Side, where he and a squad of cadets under Yang had delivered a pitifully small supply of food and water rations, when he saw the crowd gathered around the entrance to the command center.

Wilkins, he thought excitedly.

Instead of retreating to his barracks and getting out of the suns, he headed for the crowd, picking up his pace little by little until he was almost running at the end. Carceras, a Ranger who had fought alongside Conner's aunt Bonita, was the first face the cadet recognized. He put a hand on the man's shoulder and said, "What's going on?"

Good news, he thought. *Give me good news.*

But when Carceras turned to look back at him, there was anything but good news written on his face. "The Prime Commander," he said flatly. "She's dead."

Conner felt a pit open in his stomach. "Wilkins . . . ?"

Carceras nodded soberly. "Wilkins. She and her squad encountered an Ursa down by the Citadel. It got her and two others. The rest were lucky to get away with their lives."

Those were the wrong words. "Wilkins," Conner echoed, unable to accept what he'd heard, unable to make it real.

"Yes," said Carceras, a note of annoyance in his voice. "You all right? You don't look so good."

Conner muttered something, then walked away on legs he could barely trust to carry him. *Wilkins. Dead.* And it was his fault. *His.*

His plan had failed. *But how?* he asked himself. *How?*

CHAPTER TWENTY-THREE

It was late. The stars were out in full force.

But Conner wasn't going to sleep anytime soon. He sat there in his chair at the cadet study center, staring at the satellite feed of Wilkins's battle with the Ursa, trying to figure out what had gone wrong.

But all he saw was the Ursa cutting through Wilkins and the others with appalling speed and ferocity. There was blood, so much of it that Conner felt his stomach start to betray him. There were silent screams of horror and pain. There were mangled heaps of flesh and exposed bone where there had been whole human beings seconds earlier.

I don't get it, he thought. *It should have worked.* The Ursa should have been dead, and the Rangers should all have been alive to celebrate their victory. *It should have worked.*

But it had gone wrong.

He remembered what Wilkins had told him the day of the war games about his talents as a strategist. She wasn't one to throw around compliments. She had been impressed with him, with what he could do.

And what had he done? He had gambled with the lives of good men and women so that he could show everyone that he was right. And those good men and women, all of them experienced Rangers, had paid for his arrogance with their lives.

Suddenly he didn't feel so talented anymore.

So what are you going to do? he asked himself. *Wallow in self-pity? Or figure out what went wrong?*

There was only one answer to that question.

There was no point waiting any longer.

If Lyla had had years to perfect her handheld F.E.N.I.X. weapon or even months, it might have been a different story. But she didn't have that long, so she had to show the Savant's deputy what she had accomplished so far.

Vincenzo's image floated in front of Lyla on a holographic screen. "All right," she said, sounding even more tired than the last time they had spoken, "what have you got?"

Lyla bit her lip and sent the file. "As you can see, I've addressed the areas you were concerned about."

Vincenzo examined the contents of the file. She took her time, too, just as she had before. Finally, she looked up at Lyla and said, "This is better. Much better."

Much better was a start.

"You've taken care of the shielding issue, though I didn't think you could."

Yes, I have.

"You've put in more superconductors. And you've simplified the reaction sequence. Not bad."

There was only one problem. Lyla figured it would be better to get it out in the open now than to give the Savant time to find it for herself. "There's a glitch in the scythe function," she said.

Vincenzo glanced at her. "What kind of glitch?"

Lyla wished she had found a way around it. She had tried several different approaches, but none of them had worked. Therefore, as much as she wished it were otherwise, there was only one thing she could say.

"It makes the device explode."

Vincenzo's eyes narrowed. "Explode?"

Reluctantly, Lyla nodded. "Completely. The fusion

chamber remains intact, but the metal components go flying apart exactly ten seconds after the scythe function is activated."

"That's some glitch."

Lyla swallowed. "I was thinking that even without the scythe function, the device would still be useful. Certainly a lot better than what the Rangers use now."

"That may be," the Savant's deputy said. "But if they touch the wrong stud . . ." She didn't have to complete the sentence to make her point. "Can't you just leave out the scythe function from the design?"

"It's not the scythe function per se," Lyla said. "The pressure is the problem. If it wasn't the activation of the scythe that triggered it, it would be the activation of something else."

"I see," said Vincenzo. She didn't sound sanguine about it.

If only Lyla had had more time. Or more experience. Or more . . . something. She knew the problem could be fixed. She just didn't know how to do it yet.

"I can't authorize the production of a weapon that might explode in the hands of the Ranger using it," said Vincenzo. "Sorry."

So am I, Lyla thought.

Conner pounded the table and felt it shiver under the force of the blow.

He had gone over the satellite feed for what seemed like the thirtieth time, gone over every last detail from every possible computer-generated angle. But he still couldn't see the flaw in his plan.

Norman had done exactly what she was supposed to do. *Exactly*. But the Ursa had detected her approach. Why? What had Conner done that she hadn't?

He forced himself to keep his eyes trained on the screen, to keep on tormenting himself. *A hundred times more, if necessary. A thousand.* He owed it to those who had died depending on him.

And then he saw it.

Conner pushed himself away from the table. He had sat there for so long that his eyes felt scoured with sand. *But it was worth it.*

He had been right.

His plan had been sound. It was just the execution that was flawed. *It wasn't me.* He closed his eyes and heaved a sigh, feeling as if the weight of the entire planet had been lifted from him. *It wasn't me.*

Not that he was celebrating. How could he when Wilkins and two other Rangers had died trying to carry out his scheme? But he knew now that he could follow the same strategy and make it work. And if it did, that first squad wouldn't have died for nothing.

He would ask for another shot.

But this time, he wasn't going to let someone else lead the mission. He was going to do it himself.

Conner stood in front of Tariq Lennon's desk and waited for a reaction to his proposal.

"A squad," said Lennon.

"That's right, sir," Conner said.

"So you can attempt to execute your plan again. Except this time you're going to be the one giving the orders."

"That's correct, sir."

Lennon scowled. "Forget it."

Conner bit the inside of his lip. "I'm telling you, sir, it will work this time."

"It was supposed to work the *last* time, and we know how that turned out. You made a mistake, Raige. Accept it and move on."

"There was a mistake, sir," Conner said, "but it wasn't mine. It was Prime Commander Wilkins's."

"I see," said Lennon. "Let's blame it on the Prime Commander."

"Sir, if you'll look at the satellite footage—"

"I have. And there's nothing there that makes me want to change my mind."

"Sir, I've analyzed what happened out there step by step. I know what went wrong, and if I'm in charge, I can make it go right."

"*You,*" said Lennon, an unmistakable note of disdain in his voice. "A cadet. *You* can make it work where the head of the entire United Ranger Corps couldn't." He made a sound deep in his throat. "I'd heard you were full of yourself, Raige, but this . . . this goes beyond arrogance."

"It's not about *me*, sir," Conner insisted. "It's about getting rid of the Ursa. I can do it—if you give me the chance."

Lennon shook his head. "That's not going to happen. At least not on my watch. You're dismissed, Cadet."

Conner felt the anger building inside him, threatening to consume him. But it wasn't going to do him or anyone else any good if he lashed out at Lennon. He clamped his teeth together as best he could and left the office.

As far as Lennon was concerned, Conner had gotten his chance and had blown it. It didn't look like he would get another one.

At least not from Lennon.

CHAPTER TWENTY-FOUR

By the time Conner entered the barracks, he already had made his decision.

As he went inside, he could feel the scrutiny of his fellow cadets. They had all heard about Wilkins's mission and Conner's part in it, and they all wanted to know what had happened in Lennon's office.

But Blodge was the one who actually asked the question out loud. "Did you see Lennon?"

"I did," Conner said.

"And what did he say?"

"He said he wouldn't do it—not at all and certainly not with me in charge."

"Did you tell him you had gone over it and you could make it work this time?"

Conner nodded. "It didn't help."

"But you killed an Ursa. Who else has done that?"

"Still."

"That stinks," said Blodge.

"It does," Conner said. "Because now I'm going to do something my dad would have killed me for even considering."

"What are you talking about?" Gold asked.

"Yeah," said Cheng, "what?"

Conner scanned their faces. How could he ask them what he was about to ask? *For only one reason: the survival of the colony.*

"Lennon told me he wouldn't authorize the mission. That's not going to change. But there's a lot more at stake here than the Rangers' chain of command. We're fighting a war against the Ursa, and we're losing. The only way we can turn that around, I believe, the only way to get the command center behind us is to try what Wilkins tried. Except this time do it right."

"But if Lennon—"

"We're not going to ask Lennon's permission," Conner said. "We're going to do it on our own."

He let his words hang in the air as their meaning slowly sank in. Little by little, the expressions of his fellow cadets reflected their reactions.

A handful were horrified. But not everybody. Most of them looked like they might—just *might*—be ready to hear more.

"Just to be clear," Conner said, "I'm talking about disregarding orders. That's not a trivial offense."

"Damned right it's not," said one cadet.

"Rangers have been court-martialed for less," Conner continued. "We've seen it happen."

No one spoke out against the idea. But then again, no one spoke for it.

"Who's with me?" Conner asked hopefully.

"Me," said Blodge, raising his hand.

"Me, too," Gold said.

Conner looked around. No one else seemed ready to make the leap of faith he was asking of them.

That's it, then, he thought. He looked at Blodge and Gold. *Three of us.* But with only three, he couldn't do what he wanted to do. They'd be doomed before they started.

Conner's heart sank. They had a chance to beat back the Ursa, and they weren't willing to take it.

Then he heard another voice behind him: "*I'm* with you."

Conner turned to see whose it was and found himself staring into the face of Lucas Kincaid. "*I'm* with you," Kincaid repeated in case there was anyone who had mistaken his words or where they had come from.

Why? Conner asked himself. Why would Lucas Kincaid of all people decide to back him up?

"Because," Kincaid said, as if he had heard Conner's silent question, "we can't sit around and wait for the Ursa to wipe us out one by one. I've heard Raige's plan. It worked once. It'll work again if it's carried out right."

"You saying Wilkins didn't carry it out right?" one of the other cadets asked. "The *Prime Commander*?"

"Not as well as Raige will," said Kincaid.

It couldn't have been easy for him to make such a statement, but he had made it. Everyone respected Lucas. Because of that respect, they seemed more open now than they had been before. Conner would be damned if he wasn't going to take advantage of it.

"Remember why you wanted to be a Ranger?" he asked, eyeing each cadet in turn. "It wasn't just to wear the uniform, right? You wanted to do something for the colony. Well, now's your chance. The question is, what are you going to do about it?"

It wasn't an easy step to take, not for any of them. It would involve repercussions—Conner had said so himself—even if they were successful. But to his mind, they didn't have a choice.

He just hoped the others saw it the way he did.

Primus Rostropovich was in his sanctum, standing near the altar at which he prayed first thing in the morning and last thing at night. He regarded his augurs with a look of confidence but also disappointment. The disappointment was in them and in the people of Nova Prime, or at least that was what he intended to convey.

His disappointment with God he intended to keep buried deep within him. That was for another, more private, inner discussion. One that he hoped he could resolve to his satisfaction.

A dozen expectant faces were upturned toward him. The room was circular, and there were no chairs. Everyone was sitting cross-legged on thin carpets, looking up at him and waiting to hear his words of wisdom.

Words that will ring hollow unless I make every effort to convey my belief.

He stood before them, his fingers interlaced. "The attendance at this morning's service was, to put it mildly, a disappointment. We had our few but faithful; that much is true. But I have been noticing a steady lessening of our ranks, and this is a bothersome development."

"Maybe they're being eaten."

It was a sharp, angry comment from Augur Winton. One of the younger men in the order, he had a probing mind and was not afraid to ask difficult questions. Normally the Primus found that commendable; now, less so.

"Was that intended to be funny, Augur Winton?"

"No, Primus," said Winton. "No, but I consider your attitude funny. We're being ripped to pieces by the beasts. You want the people of this city to bow down and ask for God's mercy and guidance, and yet we're being eaten alive and God is nowhere to be found."

"There's another explanation for the dwindling congregants," said Augur Theresa. "People are simply afraid to leave their homes. And who can blame them, especially when they're being *told* to stay within. If that's the case, there's only one option: We have to take the word of God *to* them."

"That"—the Primus smiled—"is exactly the sort of spirited attitude that I want to see from—"

"Are you *out* of your *mind*?" Winton was on his feet. It was a serious breach of protocol, standing up in the presence of the Primus in his own sanctum. It implied that the augur believed himself to be on a level of spirituality with the Primus himself, and that was blasphemous since the Primus was the holiest of holies.

It was obvious, though, that Winton didn't give the slightest of damns. "Don't you understand what's happening? Don't you see? These beasts have been unleashed upon us, and nothing is stopping them. Nothing.

There's only three possibilities: God doesn't care, God wants it to happen, or there is no God. No matter which of those is the case, *what the hell are we doing here?*"

"Sit down, Winton," the Primus warned him.

Instead, Winton ripped off his augur robes, exposing his simple street clothes. As he did so, he stared deep into the Primus's eyes, which the Primus found more than a little disconcerting.

"You know," said Winton, "I can see it. You have no more faith than I do anymore, just a greater taste for hypocrisy." He dropped the robe to the floor. "If you think I'm going to go around from home to home trying to foster faith in the hearts of credulous individuals rather than tell them the truth—that we're all doomed and damned—then you are insane. I am going to spend what may well be our last days providing emotional support and comfort to my wife and son. What you do with that time, I honestly don't care."

"Winton," said Theresa, reaching out to him. "The Primus merely—"

But seconds later he was gone.

There was a deathly silence in the sanctum for long moments. All eyes were on the Primus, waiting to see what he would say.

As if Winton had never spoken, the Primus said, "Theresa, be so good as to work with Augur Parkin." He nodded toward the stocky augur off to the side. "Put together a schedule. I want this visitation program implemented immediately."

"Of course," said Theresa, ever the most willing of Rostropovich's flock, ever the most devoted to the augury and all it stood for.

The Primus bowed to the augurs, and they responded in kind. This was the traditional way of indicating that the meeting was over. As they filed out of the sanctum, the Primus turned his back to them. He didn't want them to see that he was inwardly shaking with rage and mortification.

How dare he? How dare Winton speak to me that way!

But he knew his anger was misplaced, or at least the reason for it was. He wasn't angry because Winton had addressed him in such a defiant manner. He was angry because it was as if Winton had ripped open the top of his head and exposed the thoughts in his head to public scrutiny. It made the Primus feel as if he had no safe place, not even in his own mind.

He abruptly became aware that someone was standing behind him. He turned and saw Theresa looking up at him. "I believe I've given you your assignment," he said.

She averted her eyes and spoke so softly that he had to strain to hear her. "I wanted to thank you for providing a place for Marta here."

"You're quite welcome," he said.

There had been no place to put Ranger Marta Lemov after her condition stabilized. After all, the medicenter needed her bed for those requiring immediate treatment and the Rangers' infirmaries were full of the maimed and the dying.

Marta had expressed the desire to be taken home, but that had become problematic when the doctors learned that she had no one to care for her there. "You need someone to attend to you," they had told her. "Otherwise . . ."

She had made it clear, in extremely florid style, that she didn't give a damn about "otherwise."

Theresa had brought the situation to the Primus's attention, and the Primus had promised her that he would attend to it. What was more, he had been as good as his word. At one point, Marta had drifted into a deep sleep, even though she had no idea why. When she came to, she discovered that she'd been relocated.

Technically she'd had no reason to complain; her new facilities were far superior to where she'd been. Instead of being crammed into a single overlarge room with dozens of moaning patients, she had her own room in the Citadel. Small, to be sure, but very private.

Yet when she'd awakened and seen Theresa standing there, watching her with an assured and happy smile, she had let out a string of invective that had mortified the augur. So much so, in fact, that Theresa had not returned to Marta's room since that first encounter.

Or so the Primus had heard.

Now Theresa was standing there thanking him for providing Marta with a room. But it was clear to the Primus that there was something else on Theresa's mind, and he gave her leave to speak about it. No reason not to. Considering the rank disobedience that one augur had displayed this day, it seemed a wise course of action to reward those who had acted more reasonably.

"Go ahead," he prodded.

"I . . . I was hoping you could speak to Marta."

"Ranger Lemov? I rather thought that you were going to be attending to her. She is your family's friend, after all."

"But part of your flock as well. One who is severely grieving and won't listen to me. I was hoping that perhaps you could reach her in a manner that I'm unable to. She . . ." Theresa hesitated. "She also grieves the loss of her Ranger friends. She's convinced that those who have survived are helpless in the face of the Ursa."

She's not the only one who feels that way. With superb self-control, the Primus kept that sentiment carefully buried. "And you believe that I can somehow convince her otherwise?"

"I think," Theresa said with total conviction, "that there is nothing you cannot do, Primus, when it comes to matters of faith."

Oh, you poor, sad, pathetic wretch . . .

"Of course," said the Primus. "I'll see to it."

* * *

As it turned out, Conner was right about Wilkins's mistake.

Two hours into their patrol, he and his squad encountered an Ursa on O'Hara Street, not far from the jewelry store where Blodge had bought his girlfriend a necklace. The thing wheeled and roared and attacked them as soon as it spotted them; probably it had been denied a meal for too long.

Conner's squad spread out across the thoroughfare just the way it was supposed to, surrounding the Ursa and then battering it with pulser bursts from all sides. But that wasn't all they did. They also yelled at the tops of their lungs, yelled like banshees—exactly as Conner had planned it. The creature's head tossed this way and that, fixing on one target after another. Its teeth gnashed.

And all the while, Conner looked for his opening.

It was the same thing he had done to Lucas in the war games—invite his enemy to focus on something else and then hit that enemy from behind. When he saw his chance, he didn't hesitate. He got a running start, leaped onto the Ursa's back, and took his shot.

Please, he thought, *let this work.*

Not just because his own life depended on it but because they needed a shred of hope. Until that point, it had all gone the Ursa's way. The Rangers needed to turn that around.

At the last moment, the Ursa's head swiveled, and Conner found himself looking down its maw. He fired at it point-blank, just as his aunt had fired at the monster that killed her, just as he had fired the last time he had faced one of the creatures.

As Conner rolled off the monster's back because he knew better now than to hang on any longer than was absolutely necessary, he thought it again: *Please.*

Then he hit the ground, and rolled to his feet, and

took aim again in case he hadn't accomplished what he had hoped to accomplish.

But he had. The Ursa was folding before his eyes, its legs giving out beneath it. A moment later it hit the ground. Then Conner's teammates approached it and poured on a barrage of pulser fire to finish it off.

But not all of them.

Even as Conner fired at the Ursa, celebrating his success, he noticed that two members of his squad were stretched out on the ground. The one lying face up with her chest torn open to the bone was McKinnon. The other one, whose head had been torn half off his body, was Bashar.

They had yelled like everyone else, distracting the Ursa, because that was what Wilkins's squad had *failed* to do. The Prime Commander had been so focused on taking advantage of the creature's olfactory blind spot that she had forgotten that it had other senses.

A sense of hearing, for instance. The kind that would allow it to detect someone sneaking up on it from behind even if it couldn't smell that someone. The kind that had discerned Norman's approach while her squad mates watched silently, holding their collective breath.

But if an Ursa's sense of hearing was confused as well, Conner's plan could work. And it had. And because of that, the cadets had won. They had eliminated one of the monsters that had been slaughtering their people and, more important, confirmed that there was a way to eliminate others.

But, Conner asked himself as he gazed at McKinnon and Bashar and would continue to ask in the days that followed, *at what price?*

CHAPTER TWENTY-FIVE

The first place Conner headed for after he turned over the Ursa's corpse to a *real* Ranger squad was Tariq Lennon's office in the command center.

It was bad enough that he had defied Lennon's decision. He wasn't going to add insult to injury by making the man come looking for him. He was going to give himself up.

When Conner had taken out his squad of cadets against the Ursa, he hadn't harbored any illusions. He had fully expected that he would pay for his transgression eventually and that those who had followed him into battle would do the same.

In his mind, it had been a done deal. No getting off the hook, no way out, regardless of the results.

So here I am, he thought.

There was a cadet sitting at Lennon's desk, his back to Conner, peering at the commander's monitor. *A cadet,* Conner thought. Not even one of the more *experienced* cadets but a guy so new that Conner didn't recognize him.

"Be with you in a second, sir," said the cadet, his voice high and frazzled, so intent on the monitor that he held a hand up instead of turning around.

Conner stood there for a few seconds before the guy put his hand down and turned to face him.

"What can I do for you, s—?" he started to say. Then he seemed to realize that Conner was a cadet just as he was, because he simply repeated, "What can I do for you?"

"I'm looking for Commander Lennon," said Conner.

"He's not here right now," the cadet said. "Sorry."

"When will he be back?"

"He wasn't very clear about that." The cadet made a face that suggested discomfort. "To be perfectly honest, I haven't heard from him in several hours."

So there was no guarantee he'd be back at all, Conner thought grimly.

"I know," the cadet said, wiping perspiration from his forehead, "it's crazy. A guy who signed up a few days ago running Commander Lennon's office. If someone had told me last Sunday that I'd be sitting here in this chair, dispatching emergency response teams . . ."

"Well," Conner said, "if you do hear from the commander, let him know that Conner Raige is back. And so is my squad."

The cadet looked puzzled. "*Your* squad?"

"I know," said Conner, "crazy." And he turned to leave.

"Wait," the cadet said. "Did you say your name was Raige . . . ?"

Normally, Conner would have stayed and endured the expressions of admiration for his family, admiration that he himself hadn't earned. But at the moment he was too tired to be polite.

So all he said was, "Thanks, Cadet. I'll be in the barracks."

He could have gone to see Hāturi in Wilkins's office—or rather what had been Wilkins's office—but Hāturi had to be busy with more important matters. If he wanted to punish Conner and the others, he could do so any time he wanted.

As Conner emerged from the command center, Lucas and the others were waiting for him. "What happened?" Lucas asked.

"Nothing," Conner said. "Nothing at all. Lennon's in

the field, so there's no one to take us to task for what we did."

"So . . . that's it?" Blodge asked, looking as drained as Conner had ever seen him. "We get away scot-free?"

"At least for now," Conner said, pulling off his head-gear and running his fingers through his thick, sweaty thatch of hair.

None of them seemed unhappy about the outcome, temporary though it might be. But then, they had plenty to be unhappy about already. They had lost two of their fellow cadets, after all.

Objectively speaking, their mission had been a success. But if this was success, Conner didn't know how much more of it he could take.

Marta moaned softly when she saw the Primus himself approaching her. This had Theresa's fingerprints all over it. *"What?"* she said curtly.

The Primus didn't seem the slightest bit put out by her attitude. "I'm told you have a great deal on your mind."

"I've been listening to the news."

He gestured around them. "This is a place of peace. There are no intrusions from outside. No screens. There is no news here to interfere with your contemplation . . ."

Marta shook her head. "If that's what you think, Primus, then you don't know people very well. There's more to news than what shows up on screens or wends its way through the ether. There's what people say as they come in and out of this place. They keep talking about Gash. That's all anyone talks about."

"Gash—?" The Primus shook his head in confusion.

"Gash." Marta did nothing to mask her annoyance, as if she could not believe that the Primus could possibly be this clueless. "Gash, the biggest, most dangerous Ursa of all. The body count that one Ursa alone is racking up is beyond anything we could possibly have been ready for."

"And people speak of this?"

"Hell, your own people speak of this. Your augurs speak to one another in hushed whispers so as not to catch your ear or disturb worshippers. Don't you know the hearts of your own people, Primus?"

The Primus sidestepped the question. Instead he said, "I know *your* heart, Ranger. I know there is a darkness in it that goes beyond grief. It partakes also of . . . guilt. You believe there is something you could have done to keep your friend Torrance Raige alive."

Marta winced. "And you're going to tell me that's not so, are you? You're going to tell me I'm free of blame even though you were sitting here in your blessed Citadel at the time, not within ten kilometers of us?"

The woman's tone was insulting, calculatedly so. And the Primus had borne enough insults for one day from Augur Winton.

He had been named Primus for his depth of spirit, for the generosity of his soul. But he wasn't feeling especially generous at the moment. In fact, he was feeling downright cruel.

"Me?" he said in answer to the Ranger's question. "I would presume to do no such thing. As you say, you were there and I was not."

He left Marta Lemov sitting there, wallowing in her guilt—and incapable of doing anything about it.

Conner was sleeping, grabbing as much rest as he could before his next assignment—whatever it was—when he felt a hand on his shoulder. Looking up, he found Commander Hāturi looking down at him.

"We need to talk," Hāturi said.

That's it. I'm going to be court-martialed. Conner was ready to pay that price.

Rubbing sleep from his eyes, he pulled on a clean uniform and followed Hāturi into the command center. When they got to Wilkins's office, the commander closed the door.

"At ease," he said.

Conner was grateful. It was hard standing at attention when his muscles were so sore. "Permission to speak, sir?"

"Go ahead," said Hāturi.

"What I did," Conner said, "I did on my own. The others . . . they shouldn't be held accountable. I convinced them to come along."

"So the responsibility is all yours."

"Yes, sir. All mine."

Hāturi harrumphed. "Exactly what I thought you'd say. Which is why I woke you in the middle of the night. You see, I need help, and you're the one who can give it to me."

Conner didn't understand. "Help, sir?"

The commander nodded. "I'm no Prime Commander, Cadet Raige. Never was, never will be. I'm great at putting out fires, getting things done here and there. But I'd be lying if I said I was cut out to be the brains behind the operation."

Conner had always imagined otherwise. Who was more efficient than Elias Hāturi? He'd been Wilkins's right-hand man.

"I mean, I could take over for the Prime Commander. I *could*. And if we weren't in such a bind, I guess I would. But even then I'd be exposed as someone who's better at taking orders than giving them, at least at this level.

"But *you* . . . you're the real deal. A leader if ever I saw one, maybe even better than your dad. You should be the Prime Commander, no doubt about it."

Conner wondered if he was dreaming. "Me, sir?"

"You."

"The Prime Commander?"

"That's right. In fact, I've got half a mind to recommend it. On the other hand, you're only . . . what? Eighteen? People wouldn't see in you what I see. All they'd think about is your age, and then they'd tell me I was crazy."

I might be one of them, Conner reflected.

"So here's what I'm going to do," Hāturi said. He leaned forward. "I'm going to take the job of Prime Commander. Officially, that is. But I'm going to lean on you, if you know what I mean. I'm going to lean as hard as I can. That all right as far as you're concerned?"

"It's fine," Conner told him.

"I had a feeling you'd say that. But before you answer, I want you to know what I mean by *lean.* I'm not talking about a little counseling. I'm talking about you taking charge in every way that matters—including dealing with the Primus and the Savant. You still want to say it's fine?"

Conner took a deep breath. It was insane for Hāturi to place such a huge responsibility on him. No question. But at the same time, he knew he could do it.

He had felt what it was like to lead. He had been successful. And he knew somehow that he could be successful at what Hāturi was asking as well.

Conner nodded. "I'm your man, sir."

CHAPTER TWENTY-SIX

Conner sat forward in Prime Commander Wilkins's chair, his elbows planted firmly on the desk in front of him. *No,* he thought; *too eager.* He leaned back in his chair and crossed his arms over his chest. *No, too complacent.*

Somewhere in between, then, he thought. He tried to achieve such a position, but it felt awkward. Then again, *any* position was going to feel awkward to him.

He wasn't used to even *attending* meetings with people outside the ranks of the Rangers, much less *conducting* such meetings. And it wasn't just any two people he had asked to join him in the Prime Commander's office.

It was the two most important people in the colony.

As he thought that, Blodge opened the door and walked in. "They're here," he said.

Conner nodded. "See them in."

Blodge smiled and said, "Good luck." Then he went back outside.

A moment later, Conner's guests arrived. They walked in one right after the other, first the Savant and then the Primus. The Savant finished a remark to the Primus that he evidently had begun outside.

Conner had seen the two of them many times, especially the Primus. But he had never spoken to them in person.

Until now.

"Thank you for coming," he said.

They looked past him. Clearly, they had been expecting to see Hāturi. "Where is the Prime Commander?" the Primus asked.

Up close he looked heavier than he did from a distance, thicker around the middle, though his robe did a decent job of concealing it. And his skin, pale for the most part, was a blotchy red in places, something else Conner hadn't noticed before.

"The Prime Commander has work to do," Conner said in as even a tone as he could manage.

Flint scowled. "No more than I do. Is he on his way?"

"No," Conner answered. "I'm here instead."

The Primus smiled. "Very amusing, my child. But we're busy people, as you can imagine. Is the Prime Commander coming or is he not?"

"He didn't ask you to come," said Conner. "*I* did."

"The message was from the Prime Commander's office," the Savant insisted.

"I know," Conner said. "I sent it."

The Primus's expression stiffened. "I didn't come here to meet with a cadet."

"Nor did I," said the Savant Flint.

"I don't know about you," the Primus said to Flint, "but I'm leaving." He eyed Conner. "If the Prime Commander wants to see me—at my convenience—he can make an appointment with my clerk."

The Savant looked ready to go as well.

Conner saw his initiative falling apart before his eyes. Without the support of the Primus and the Savant, he wouldn't be able to accomplish a thing.

He got to his feet. "If you're smart," he said, "you'll sit down."

Both the Primus and the Savant looked shocked, but only for a moment. Then the Savant said in a voice as cold as ice, "To whom do you think you're speaking?"

Conner didn't flinch under the Savant's scrutiny. "I *thought* I was speaking with two of the people entrusted with looking out for this colony, people capable of putting their egos aside for the good of Nova Prime."

He expected the Savant's jaw to drop. It didn't. "Those

are big words," he said. Then something changed in his expression. "Raige, isn't it?"

He nodded, grateful that the Savant, at least, had recognized him. "Conner Raige."

The Primus's eyes narrowed. Apparently, he knew the name as well, if not the face. But if his continued scrutiny was any indication, he was starting to pick up on the family resemblance.

The Savant chuckled. "Only a Raige would have the nerve to sit in the Prime Commander's chair before he even became a full-fledged Ranger."

"Things have changed," Conner told him. "They've had to. Prime Commander Wilkins is dead. So are more than seventy percent of the Rangers."

"So you've staged a coup," said the Primus, making no effort to hide his disdain.

"Not at all," Conner said. "I haven't displaced anyone. I've got the support of all our highest-ranking officers, Commander Hāturi among them."

"Which doesn't make it any less of a coup," the Primus insisted.

"Look," Conner said, "we can argue legalities here or we can put our energies into something constructive."

"I'm not engaging in 'something constructive' with a *child*," said the Primus.

"Do you want to survive the Ursa?" Conner asked him. "Because the only way you're going to do that is if we work together."

"The Ursa," said the Primus, lifting his chin as if addressing his congregation, "are a sign of something greater than humanity in the universe, something granted superior power by the One who is *most* powerful. The majority of my fellow colonists seemed to believe that we would remain preeminent forever. But those of us who have taken the time to think about such things have always known that we would eventually encounter a species we couldn't master, a species we couldn't control—and now we have. It's prideful to think that the outcome of this encounter is in our hands. If we on

Nova Prime are *meant* to survive, we will do so. If not . . ." He shrugged.

Conner turned to the Savant. "Do you feel the same way?" he asked, rooting desperately for the answer to be "no."

"In terms of the wisdom of following an eighteen-year-old?" said the Savant. "Absolutely—no matter what he's accomplished." He glanced at the Primus. "But not in terms of our survival. As the Primus knows, I believe that our fate is squarely in our hands."

The Primus harrumphed. "Of course you do."

Conner was glad that the Primus had said what he'd said. The more he pushed the Savant away, the easier it would be for Conner to win him over.

Besides, the Savant was devoted to logic—he had to be—and so was Conner. His initiative was based on a scientific approach: observation and the testing of hypotheses. The Primus, in contrast, saw only what his faith allowed him to see. And the more pronounced his resignation to the colony's fate was, the more eager the Savant would be to find an alternative.

At least, that was Conner's *hope*.

The Savant eyed him. "Talk. I'm listening."

Inwardly, Conner was pumping his fist in celebration. Outwardly, he remained cool, like a veteran of such meetings instead of a neophyte.

"One thing we need to discuss," he said, "is the deployment of Rangers around the colony. There just aren't enough of us to go around anymore. We're stretched too thin."

"What do you suggest?" the Primus asked. "That I have my augurs pick up fusion-burst rifles and start hunting Ursa?"

Conner didn't take the bait. "What I'm suggesting is that your people—and the Savant's—help with the non-combat tasks normally assigned to the Rangers. For instance, evacuating the population where there are Ursa sightings. Or distributing food and medical supplies wherever they're needed."

"My augurs are helping the people already," the Primus said. "They're giving comfort and solace to the fearful and the bereaved."

"That's great," said Conner. "Then they won't mind giving out supplies as well."

The Primus's eyebrows jumped in indignation. "I'll be the arbiter of what they mind and what they don't mind."

The Savant, by contrast, didn't seem perturbed at all. "I'll dispatch everyone I can spare."

"And I'll give you all the information you need in order to do that," Conner said. "Speaking of information, you've been dissecting the Ursa we killed. Is there anything you can tell us that we don't already know?"

"Actually," Flint said, "there is. Just this morning, my man Rambaldi finished his analysis. The report was sent to Commander Hāturi, but I suppose I can share it with you. Especially the good news—there's no evidence in the creature of reproductive organs."

That *was* encouraging. Critical, in fact. They were having a hard time dealing with the Ursa as it was. If the creatures had the ability to reproduce . . .

"Which," the Savant continued, "supports our suspicion that the Skrel *designed* the Ursa as opposed to plucking them out of nature."

"Designed them to destroy *us*," Conner said for the Primus's benefit.

"Exactly," said the Savant.

The Primus dismissed the implications with a flip of his hand. "That doesn't change my theological position on the matter. What does it matter if the Ursa are naturally occurring creatures or laboratory creations? They are here for a reason. And their fate, and ours, will be determined by One greater than either of us."

"My mom mentioned an old saying once," Conner said. " 'God helps those who help themselves.' "

The Primus held up a finger as if he were teaching a class. "When He is inclined to do so."

Conner gave up on that front and turned back to the Savant. "What else did your people find out?"

"Well, there's support for your theory about a directional blind spot in the creature's ability to smell. It's not that the Ursa can't smell anything behind it. It's that all things being equal, its brain recognizes the smells in front of it much more strongly than those in back. The smells in front *drown out* the others, as it were."

Good to know, Conner thought. "Maybe we can refine our approach, produce stronger smells . . ."

"Except, as you discovered, the Ursa don't rely solely on their sense of smell. So it's not that simple."

"Nothing is," the Primus said. "There are mysteries within mysteries."

"And it's up to us to solve them," Connor told him.

"But Rambaldi's most interesting finding," said Flint, ignoring the Primus now, "is that the Ursa's hide is reinforced with metal alloy. Not a surgical insertion, as you might expect, but an integral part of the creature's physiology, as much so as its teeth or its talons. We're calling it *smart* metal."

That was *interesting,* Conner thought.

"Which," the Savant continued, "is why pulsers haven't had much effect on the Ursa. The smart metal protects them."

"But we've *killed* Ursa with our pulsers," Conner pointed out. "Two of them now."

The Savant shrugged. "A function of the prolonged nature of your attack. You poured on so much firepower that you eventually damaged some of the creature's organs. But it's only possible to do that if you've stunned the creature to begin with, and from what I understand, that's not so easy to do."

True, Conner thought. Even when his squads were successful, the death toll was horrific. "You have something else in mind?"

"Nothing specific. But ideally, it would be something intrusive. Something that can find one of the spots in the Ursa's anatomy unprotected by the smart metal and take advantage of it."

Conner recalled something. "You and Prime Commander Wilkins discussed weapons development—it was in her notes."

"You've been reading Wilkins's *notes*?" the Primus said. He shook his head disapprovingly.

"That's right," said Flint, responding to Conner's comment rather than the Primus's. "I had my deputy, Leslie Vincenzo, task our people to come up with something more effective than pulsers. Unfortunately, they haven't had much success." A pause. "One approach seemed promising for a while, but it ultimately proved untenable."

"What was that?" Conner asked.

The Savant described it to him and told him as well why it couldn't work. "Not a trivial flaw, as you can imagine. Maybe with more time," he said. "A *lot* more time . . ."

"Well," said the Primus, "good luck with that." He rose and straightened his robes. "I'll be in the Citadel if you need me."

Conner was disgusted, even angered by the man's haughtiness. But it wasn't his job to reform the Primus. His job was to save lives.

"I'd like to look at your engineers' weapon concepts," he told the Savant. "Especially the one you described."

The Savant's expression hardened a bit. After all, Conner was intruding on his territory. But Flint didn't chastise him.

All he said was, "Suit yourself."

Lyla had tried to forget about Conner Raige.

After all, Lucas had told her the guy was a hothead and a know-it-all and hadn't been very popular with his fellow cadets for a long time as a result. And he had brawled with her brother in the barracks.

And she hadn't expected him to be little Conner Raige.

Then, weeks later, Lucas had changed his tune. Suddenly Conner was a leader of men, a brilliant tactician, a guy the other cadets wanted to follow, Lucas among them. In fact, the whole colony had pinned its hopes on Conner lately.

Lucas wasn't the type to give out a lot of praise. If he was endorsing Conner, the cadet must have become everything Lyla had heard about him.

But that day at the cageball court he had been just another cadet. When had he changed? When had he become this wunderkind who could kill Ursa and live to tell about it?

She would have a chance to find out for herself. After all, Conner was scheduled to arrive at her lab in a minute or so.

Lyla looked around. She had cleaned up her coffee cups and food wrappers and wiped all the counters clean. *Why? He's just Lucas's little pal. It's not as if I have to impress him or anything.*

And her invention had hit a wall. It was flawed, unusable. So Conner wasn't going to be hanging out very long. But—

Her thought was interrupted by a knock on her door. She crossed the lab and opened it.

It was Conner. And he had changed, all right.

She couldn't put her finger on *how.* He wasn't any taller. He hadn't put on any weight. Did he look more like his dad? *Maybe.* Or maybe it was just the way he carried himself, as if he'd been in charge not just for a few days but for a long time.

"I heard you were working on a weapon," Conner said, smiling despite what had to be a lot of pressure on him these days. "A hand-to-hand version of our F.E.N.I.X. projectiles if I'm not mistaken."

He was not going to mention that embarrassing moment at the cageball court, she thought. *Good.*

"That's right," Lyla said. "Come on in." She indicated the stool she had set up for him. "You can sit there."

As he took the seat, she activated the holographic array. A moment later, a mock-up of the slender silvery device was hanging in the air in front of Conner.

"What do you call it?" he asked.

"A cutlass."

Conner glanced at her. "Like what the pirates used back on Earth?"

She returned the look. "How did you . . . I mean, yes."

"I liked pirate stories, too," he said. "What does it do?"

She showed him.

"Nice," he said. He got up to walk around the hologram. "I mean *really* nice. I've never seen anything like it. And it cuts through anything?"

"Almost anything. But it's got to be in its blade formation. Then it's just a single molecule thick at the forward edge."

He nodded approvingly.

"Just one problem," Lyla said. "It blows up."

"Yeah. The Savant mentioned that."

"Every time you hit the scythe function."

Conner continued to study the holographic cutlass. "But only then, right?"

"Right. But if you hit it by accident—"

"As you say, it's a problem. But Rangers are trained to do a lot of difficult things. I don't see why we couldn't avoid a particular function."

"Even in the heat of battle?"

He nodded, throwing her another smile. "Even then."

Lyla was surprised. The guy didn't *seem* like a hothead *or* a know-it-all—not even a little. In fact, he seemed respectful of her expertise and her hard work, and he hadn't said or done a thing to suggest that he wasn't in control of his emotions.

Then again, Lucas had his own agenda sometimes.

"If I told you I wanted this," Conner asked, "how

long would it take to make a hundred of them? Working models?"

She hadn't even considered the possibility. "I don't know. A week? Two?"

"Lives depend on it," he reminded her.

"I'll get them to you as quickly as I can."

"Thanks," he said. He looked her in the eye. "This could be really important. I've got a feeling about it."

It took her a moment to look away, to return to her control panel and deactivate the holographic display. The cutlass vanished as quickly as it had appeared.

"I hope you don't mind," Conner said, "if I come by from time to time. Check up on you . . . I mean, on your progress."

Is he hitting on me? Lyla wondered. *No. Can't be. He's just being diligent.* "Of course."

"Good. I think this will work out." And with another smile—a shy one, she thought, as crazy as that sounded—he left.

As the door closed behind Conner, Lyla took a deep breath. She was excited that he had thought enough of her cutlass to put it into production. If it turned out to be the weapon the Rangers needed, that would make her proud—damned proud.

But she couldn't help thinking about Conner himself. She hadn't been nervous in the least, just as she hadn't been nervous around him when she saw him at the cageball court. But she had been . . . She looked for a word. *Aware* of him?

Connected?

Is it just because I don't get many visitors? No, it was more than that. There *was* a connection between them.

And she was sure he had felt it, too.

CHAPTER TWENTY-SEVEN

Conner had visited Lyla Kincaid as he had promised, daily in fact.

He kept telling himself that he was going only to see how the cutlasses were coming along. In reality, he knew it was more than that.

That day at the cageball court . . . he had felt something for her. Then he had realized that she was Lucas's sister and that she was uncomfortable with the idea of even speaking with him, and he had done his best to put her out of his mind. If he hadn't seen her again, he might have succeeded.

But he *had* seen her—had been *forced* to see her because her cutlass meant so much to the defense of the colony in his estimation. And at that point, there was no denying his feelings.

He had thought about following through on them and rejected the idea. They were at war with a dangerous enemy. He had too much responsibility to be pursuing a romance with Lyla. And she had too much responsibility to be pursuing a romance with him—even assuming she was tempted to do so.

Then came the day when the cutlasses were supposed to be ready. Conner didn't go to Lyla's lab that day. He went to the factory where Lyla was overseeing the production run.

He found her hunched over a monitor in the factory's back office, her hair drawn back into a poorly fastened ponytail. She looked tired, as if she hadn't gotten enough sleep.

"Lyla?" he said. Then a little louder: "Lyla?"

She sat up abruptly. "What—?"

"Are they ready?" Conner asked as gently as he could, though he was barely able to contain his eagerness.

"Did I *say* they'd be ready?" Lyla asked him, straightening out her hair.

"Actually," he said, "you did."

"Then they're ready."

She walked out of the office and across the factory floor. Then she opened a drawer and with both hands removed something from it.

A cutlass, he thought.

The weapon glinted in the light of the overhead fixtures, a grooved silver cylinder almost the length of Conner's arm. It looked bigger than he remembered, both longer and thicker. Or was it his imagination?

"Here you go," said Lyla, handing it to him. "Hot off the assembly line."

"Did you make any changes in it?" he asked.

"Not one," she assured him.

Conner took the cutlass from her and felt his trepidation melt away. It wasn't heavy at all. It was light, well balanced. In fact, it felt as if he had been born with it in his hand.

"Nice job," he said.

She shrugged. "We did our best. When are you planning on field-testing it?"

Conner frowned. Part of him wanted to find an Ursa then and there. But it wouldn't be fair to his cadets to send them out with the cutlasses until they'd had some time to get used to them.

"Day after tomorrow," he decided.

"Will they be ready by then?" Lyla asked, her brow crinkled with concern.

"They'll have to be. Of course, I'll have to be ready first."

"So you can show them how it's used. And how to avoid that pesky scythe function."

"Exactly."

"Well, then," said Lyla, "let me show you."

She held out her hand, and he laid the cutlass in it. Then she slid her hands along its length and tapped it once. Instantly, the cutlass grew a blade on either side. Then she did the same thing, except with two taps, and the blades transformed into spears.

"Okay," Conner said. He came around behind her and put his hands alongside hers on the central cylinder of the cutlass. "Now do it *with* me."

Standing with her back to him inside the circle of his arms, Lyla took his hands and slid them apart. "Now tap here," she said, "with the middle finger of your left hand. Just once."

He tapped. The blades re-formed.

"Slide again and tap twice—right here."

He let her slide his hands again. Hers were slender and cool to the touch. Conner liked the way they felt on his. Liked it a lot, in fact.

"And the scythe function?" he asked.

He felt Lyla's arms, her shoulders, her back, pressing gently against his chest. He smelled her hair, remarkably fragrant considering she had spent the night working in the factory.

They didn't get to the scythe function. At least not yet. Instead, Lyla turned in his arms and looked up at him, looked into his eyes. Hers were light-colored, open, vulnerable.

The next thing he knew, he was kissing her. Her lips were pressing against his, and they were soft and warm and yielding, and he was kissing her as he had imagined he would do someday.

He hadn't planned it, hadn't intended it. In fact, he had resolved to keep their relationship strictly professional until the Ursa were gone, however long that took. But in that single confusing moment, with her eyes pulling him in, he had been helpless to resist.

"Conner," she said in little more than a whisper.

"I know," he said. And he pulled her even closer. They stood there for a long time, Conner holding the cutlass in one hand and Lyla in the other.

Finally she said, "If we stop the Ursa—"

He smiled. "*When* we stop them. You've got to think positively."

She smiled back. "I'll remember that."

And he would remember her smile, he told himself, until the time came when he could do something about it.

Despite the way it might look to the public, Elias Hāturi had done the right thing in turning over the reins to Conner Raige. He was as sure of it as he had ever been about anything in his life.

Especially since it left Hāturi free to do what he did best. Under Meredith Wilkins, he had been the guy who was everywhere, the guy who got things done. Now he could be that guy again.

He was just putting together a squad to respond to an Ursa sighting in the Outlands when he heard a knock on the door. "Come in," he said.

He wasn't sure who he was expecting to see, but it certainly wasn't the Primus. Yet that was just who walked in. Out of respect, Hāturi got to his feet.

The Primus smiled the way he did on public occasions. If he looked that way when he addressed his congregation, Hāturi wasn't aware of it; he wasn't a religious man and never had been.

Nor had he ever regretted that fact less than in the time since the Primus had taken Vander Meer's side in the commentator's attacks on the Rangers.

"No need to stand on my account," the Primus said, his voice full of gentleness. "All I need is a moment of your time."

"Of course," said Hāturi, trying his best to be civil. "What can I do for you?"

The Primus wagged a finger at him the way somebody might wag a finger at an unruly child. "You can take command of the Rangers, that's what you can do."

Ah, Hāturi thought. "With all due respect, why would I do *that*?"

"Because with all the casualties we have suffered in our struggles with the Ursa, you are the highest-ranking Ranger left to us. Not the overly ambitious, full-of-himself cadet who stands in charge now but *you*. It's not Conner Raige's place to make decisions when it comes to the defense of our beloved colony—it's yours."

Hāturi chuckled. "I'm sorry, Primus, but I made the only decision I had to. And I didn't do it lightly, if that's what you're thinking. I brought to bear every bit of experience I had under my belt, every bit of wisdom I'd ever learned from any Ranger I'd ever served under. It all pointed in one direction and one direction only, which is why I gave Conner Raige my full support."

The Primus shook his head disapprovingly. "Do you know what you're doing, my son? You're making a mockery of the position of Prime Commander and every courageous, dedicated soul who has ever held it."

"Maybe so," Hāturi allowed. "But I'd be mocking them even more if I were to claim the job knowing I'm not the best man for it."

"You're too modest by far. You have the respect of the other Rangers. I know you do; I took the trouble to ask around."

In other words, Hāturi reflected, he'd been poking around where he didn't belong. "Now, that was kind of you, Primus, especially when you've got your hands full keeping up the people's morale. I'd hate for somebody to do something desperate because his spiritual leader was polling Rangers instead of providing comfort."

The Primus's eyes narrowed. "Now," he said, his voice taking on an edge, "it's not just the Prime Commanders you're mocking."

"My apologies," said Hāturi, "if it sounded that way." But the truth was that he *meant* it to sound that way, and they both knew it.

"I thought I might find a willing ear here," the Primus said. "I see that I was mistaken."

Before Hāturi could respond, he left.

Hāturi had friends who would be appalled if they found out how he had spoken to the Primus. That was all right with him. If they had the right to embrace the truth as the Primus saw it, he had an equal right to think the Primus was full of horse manure.

And low-grade horse manure at that.

Conner looked out at the assembled Rangers. There were more than a hundred of them standing in the empty theater, which was the only place that could hold all of them without exposing them to the Ursa.

Most of them were cadets.

Except they didn't look like cadets anymore—not after they'd been out hunting Ursa over the last few days, employing the tactic Conner had tested in the field. They looked like Rangers.

It was evident in their posture, in the cast of their eyes. *Definitely Rangers.*

But with every Ursa they had taken down, there were fewer and fewer of them. They couldn't afford to play a numbers game any longer. And if Lyla's weapon was the godsend Conner thought it was, they wouldn't have to.

"Listen up," he said, his voice sounding big in the theater.

The Rangers listened.

"I've got something to show you," Conner said. "Something that's going to help us in our fight against the Ursa."

It had been a long time since anyone had introduced a new weapon to the Corps. Hundreds of years, in fact.

Conner wondered how the Prime Commander at the time had felt as he showed *that* weapon off.

His name was Patrick Wulf. Conner had looked it up. He was a mild-mannered man for a Prime Commander, a peacekeeper at a time when the colony desperately needed one. Unfortunately, there wasn't a whole lot more that was known about him.

Had Wulf been a Raige like his immediate predecessor—or, for that matter, like his successor—Conner would have known his cap size, his favorite color, and how he liked his coffee. After all, Conner's dad had known every detail about every Raige back to the launch of the arks from Earth, or so it had always seemed.

Then, too, the Skrel had been a problem, albeit a different kind. All they had attacked with were ships, and little ones at that, although they were pretty frightening to a colony that had never run into even a hint of alien life before.

Until the colonists came up with the weapon they needed, they saw a lot of misery, a lot of destruction. They were desperate for an answer. But then, as now, there had been some controversy over what that answer might be.

Was Wulf's announcement met with cheers or skepticism? Did he find support right away, or did it take time for people to get used to what he was proposing?

Conner had no way of knowing and therefore no precedent to learn from. In effect, he was on his own. He picked up the cutlass prototype from the table beside him and turned the weapon over in his hands. It looked so simple, so unassuming, not like a weapon at all. But the fate of Nova Prime rode on it.

He hoped the other Rangers looked at it the way he did.

"Up until now," he said, "they've had the advantage. But this is the day we start to turn things around." He produced the cutlass and held it out for them to see. "With this."

The cadets eyed the device with curiosity. Except for

Lucas, Blodge, and a couple of others, of course. They had seen it before.

"What is it?" asked a Ranger named Bolt, who had served under Conner's aunt Bonita.

"It's called a cutlass," Conner said, "and it's designed specifically with the Ursa in mind. In other words, for close quarters."

"Thank heaven," said another Ranger, a fellow named Yang.

"It's about time," someone else said.

"How does it fire?" Bolt asked.

"It doesn't," Conner told him. "It makes use of F.E.N.I.X. tech to change its shape."

He performed the requisite slide and tap, and the cutlass morphed in his hand, becoming a double-ended blade. Then he carried out another maneuver, and it transformed itself into a mace. The others looked on, mesmerized.

"So it's not just one weapon," Conner continued, "it's a number of them, and in any given encounter an Ursa won't know which one it's going to get."

"Interesting," said Ditkowsky.

"There's just one glitch," Conner said, and he told them what it was.

"You're kidding," said Erdmann, probably speaking for every Ranger in the place.

"I'm not," Conner told him. "But don't worry. It's easy to avoid."

"What if we don't *want* to avoid it?" Yang asked.

Conner hadn't anticipated such a reaction. *But I should have.* "What do you mean?"

Yang shrugged. "One for one? That's not bad, considering how many people each of these monsters has killed already."

"You're talking about suicide," said Lucas.

"Damned right," Yang said, his eyes like steel.

"No," Conner said firmly, putting an end to the idea. "That's *not* an option, especially when we've got so many other possibilities available to us in the cutlass."

Yang nodded, though he looked reluctant to give in. "Whatever you say, sir."

"All right, then," Conner said. "Watch closely." And, re-creating the rest of the demonstration Lyla had given him, he showed the others how to operate a cutlass.

CHAPTER TWENTY-EIGHT

As Conner lay in his bunk, going over his battle plan, he got the feeling that something was wrong.

Then he realized what it was. There was always a sound in the cadet barracks. A cough, a laugh, a whispered bit of gossip. Sometimes even a warning to cut out all the other sounds, with a promise of the measures that would be taken if the warning wasn't heeded.

But not now. It was perfectly quiet. Like a tomb.

Conner thought he knew why.

He had been so focused on preparing his squad for the logistics of the battle, he had lost sight of something else, something just as important if not more so.

They were scared.

None of them was likely to admit it, not even on pain of death, but it seemed to him that they *were*. After all, with the dawn they would move out into the embattled streets of Nova City, and they would face the stuff of their nightmares.

It was a natural response, nothing to be ashamed of. But if they had been more experienced, they would have known what to do with their fear, how to turn it into motivation.

Conner's cadets didn't know that trick. For them, fear was a burden, a weight that might drag them down when they needed most to move freely.

He had to do something about that or he wasn't much of a leader. But what could he do? Give them years of training and experience overnight?

Then it came to him.

He went into the command center, into Wilkins's office, and fabricated something. Eight somethings, in fact, since he had determined through his studies of the Ursa that eight was the maximal number of Rangers in a squad. Then he returned to the barracks and one by one woke up the members of his team.

"I want to talk with you," he said after they had joined him outside. He turned to Blodge and asked, "Who are you?"

His friend smiled at him. "Are you kidding?"

"I asked you a question, Cadet."

Blodge's smile faded. "I'm Raul Blodgett, Blue Squad."

Conner shook his head. "No. From now until we come back tomorrow with a dead Ursa, you're Sam Dardanopoulos."

Blodge looked confused. "Sorry," he said, "but I don't know—"

"Sam Dardanopoulos was a baker on the North Side," said Conner. "He had a wife, two daughters, and six grandchildren and a reputation for making the best galaktoboureko in the colony. That is, until he went out to raid his bakery for food three nights ago and an Ursa caught him."

He had Blodge's attention. And not just Blodgett's but that of the rest of his squad. *Good,* he thought. *It's working.*

He took a translucent piece of plastic out of his pocket and handed it to Blodge. It bore the likeness of Sam Dardanopoulos.

"Sam couldn't do anything about what happened to him," Conner told his friend, "but *you* can. You can be Sam's eyes and ears and the hands he used to make those delicious custards. He couldn't do anything about the Ursa, but *you* can."

The look in Blodge's eye said that he understood now. He nodded and put the piece of plastic in his pocket.

Conner turned to Lucas Kincaid. "Who are you?"

Kincaid's lip curled. "I think you're about to tell me."

"You're Amaya Nakamura. She lived on the South Side with her parents and her two brothers. She was six years old, on her way to a shelter, when she was attacked by an Ursa. Three children died that evening. Amaya was one of them."

He handed Lucas a plastic card with Amaya's likeness on it. "Who are you?"

"I'm Amaya Nakamura," Lucas said, as if he had been saying it all his life. "Amaya Nakamura." He put the card in his pocket.

Conner then turned to Gold. "Who are you, Cadet?"

"I *was* Danny Gold," he said.

"Maybe so," Conner said, "but now you're Archie Banuelos. A week ago, Archie was driving a building supply truck to a medicenter that had been the site of an Ursa attack. When he saw a bunch of construction workers trapped by an Ursa, he tried to use his truck like a battering ram. The Ursa survived the impact. Archie didn't." He handed Gold a plastic card. "Who are you?"

"I'm Archie Banuelos," came the reply.

Conner nodded. "Damned right."

Ditkowsky became Tonia Malley. Augustover became Randall Butterfield. Erdmann became Kalman Ben Jacob. Cheng became Mustafa Ryder.

"What about you?" Lucas asked Conner. "What's your name?"

"Frank Raige," said Conner. "I'm Frank Raige."

"Hell of a coincidence," Lucas commented, "you having the same last name and all." He smiled a tight smile. "And a hell of a name to live up to."

Conner was thankful for the kind words from a guy he once had considered his enemy, but all he said was, "Don't worry. I'll live up to it."

As he stood in the cadets' midst and looked around, Conner saw that they were different. They didn't look scared. After all, they weren't fighting for themselves anymore. They were fighting for someone else, which was really the way it had been all along.

And there was no longer any need for them ~~~ about dying: The pieces of plastic in their poc ~~~ proof they were already dead.

Ever since Lyla's cutlass had become the focus of Conner Raige's attention, she'd had an escort to and from her lab and, more recently, to and from the factory where the cutlasses were being manufactured.

His name was Bolt. He didn't talk much in her estimation, but he seemed to know what he was doing.

Either way, Lyla had felt guilty about having him. After all, Rangers were needed in so many other places, especially seasoned Rangers like Bolt. However, she understood the need for Conner to protect her. She held the fate of the colony in her hands. Wasn't that how he had put it? "The fate of the colony . . ."

Someone like that had to be preserved at all costs.

Except now Lyla was done making the cutlasses. She could go back home and contact the Savant and see what project she might work on next. Even if the cutlasses worked, and there was no guarantee that they would, there had to be plenty for an engineer to do at a time like this.

Lyla was wondering what it might be when she caught a glimpse of someone walking toward her from the other direction. It was rare to see anyone else on the street, and so she took more than a little notice. But really, it would have been hard for her to miss someone as prominent as the Primus of the entire planet.

He was wearing a majestic navy-blue robe that looked like it had been cut from the night sky, a stark contrast to the plain brown robes and rusty uniforms of the augurs and Rangers who surrounded him. In all, there had to be eight or ten people in the Primus's entourage.

It made her feel a little better about having Bolt with her.

Where was he going? Lyla wondered as the Holy One

came closer and closer still, so close that she could see the red blotches on his face that the cameras never picked up. As far as she knew, the Primus had remained locked up in his Citadel ever since the Ursa's arrival. What was so important that it had drawn him out into the streets, escort or no escort?

She was so busy thinking about it that she barely noticed the shadow that passed over her, blotting out the sunlight for a fraction of a second. But she didn't miss the descent of something big and pale just behind the Primus, something that decidedly didn't belong there in the heat of a lazy late afternoon.

An Ursa, Lyla thought, her heart climbing into her throat.

The creature was immense, wide enough to fill the street from one wall to the other. Rather than a finished organism, it looked like something that had been forcibly turned inside out, all ghostly white flesh and blue-gray smart metal. Any one of its four long, angular limbs was powerful enough to tear her apart if the news accounts were the least bit accurate.

But the most hideous part of the thing, the part that sent chills up and down the rungs of Lyla's spine, was its face—because strictly speaking, it didn't have any. In its place yawned a black hole, and in the center of that hole a maw full of sharp black teeth chittered like an army of hungry wet insects.

My God, she thought. *My God my God my God* . . .

She had never imagined anything like it, not even in her worst nightmares. She was paralyzed by the sight of the thing, rooted in place.

But the Primus wasn't rooted at all. He and his entourage came charging toward her, their robes aflutter, all of them except for two of the Rangers who had been part of the Holy One's escort. Except that for whatever reason, the Ursa wasn't interested in the Rangers. It came bounding past them, ignoring their barrage of silver-blue pulser bursts, intent instead on the Primus and the rest of his group.

"Move!" Bolt yelled, and shoved her behind him.

Lyla began to run.

It didn't seem right for her to abandon him. He was risking his life to save hers, and she knew from Conner's accounts that his pulser wasn't going to help him.

Glancing back over her shoulder, she saw Bolt train his weapon on the Ursa and fire. His fusion burst struck the creature head-on with enough force to collapse a wall. But it didn't stop the monster. All it did was slow it down for a moment.

Putting its head down, it came charging at them with renewed fury: Lyla, the Primus, his augurs, and his remaining Rangers. In another heartbeat it would be on top of them.

Lyla ran for all she was worth. But she had barely taken three strides before she felt a hand on her shoulder. *Not Bolt's—it can't be. Then who?*

She felt the hand clutch at her, pull her back, and then, joined by a second hand, throw her to the ground. She barely caught a glimpse of the person the hands belonged to, but she saw enough to know that she had been betrayed.

Since she had been a little girl, she had believed in God and believed almost as much in His emissary the Primus. But it was the Primus who had dragged her down from behind, his eyes wide with fear, his mouth gaping as he gasped for breath.

It was the Primus.

Lyla was almost trampled as the others went by. But she was still able to get to her feet and run after them.

It didn't matter. She knew that. The Ursa would get to her first. That had to have been the Primus's thought all along: to give the creature what it wanted so that it would leave the rest of them alone.

Behind her, the Ursa was getting closer. She could hear the scratching of its claws on the ground, the gnashing of its teeth, the rumbling in its throat. It bounded awkwardly, but with its long limbs it was faster than she was.

Lyla had seen the news coverage of the Ursa's victims. It never zoomed in on the details, never gave too precise a picture of the remains. But there was always blood—blood everywhere—painting the ground and the walls of nearby buildings and everything else in sight.

And soon it would be *her* blood.

It was hard to believe, hard to wrap her mind around the idea as she ran. But the thing behind her was real. Its hunger was real. And her death? In a minute, maybe less, that would be real, too.

As she sprinted, her breath burning in her throat, she saw the Primus ahead of her. He had bought his life with hers. The Holy One, the voice of heaven on Nova Prime, had sacrificed her so that he could live.

It was a bitter thought.

Then Lyla had no more time to think, no more time even to breathe, because the Ursa was almost on top of her. *Conner,* she thought, wishing she could see him one last time. *Conner . . .*

The world filled with the Ursa's roar. *My God,* she thought.

My God my God my God . . .

Gash perceives, in the same way it always does, a smell thing in front of it. Another female, of a certainty. And for a moment—just a moment—it considers skipping over her.

Gash has no idea why that thought comes to it. It is counterintuitive.

Gash must kill.

Gash must destroy.

And yet, as it advances on her, it cannot help but notice an oddity about her.

She has stopped moving. She is lying there, waiting for . . .

. . . what?

Her end? Her demise?

Gash senses bodily functions from her, yet she is not resisting in the least.

Gash crouches over her, its claws at the ready.

And still she does not respond.

Gash stops. It does not look down at her, for it has no eyes. Yet there is something about her that draws Gash's attention.

At first the smell thing does not seem to be aware that Gash is simply standing there, regarding her with what amounts to curiosity. Then, very slowly, she looks up. Does she realize that Gash has not yet attacked her, that it is simply studying her, trying to discern more about her?

And then she speaks to Gash.

It is the first time Gash has ever heard one of the smell things speak. Scream, shriek, howl . . . these Gash knows. But the simple spoken voice is different somehow. Gash can't say exactly how, but it is different.

"Please," the smell thing says, her voice barely above a whisper. "Make it quick."

Gash doesn't know what the sounds are supposed to mean, but it does not have a lot of patience. It has had enough.

Gash's mouth lowers, envelops the smell thing's head, and clamps down. The smell thing shudders and stops moving.

Interesting, Gash thinks. But that is all it is: a brief moment of interest.

Gash consumes the smell thing's body, or most of it. Then it leaves the remains there and moves on. After all, Gash has other smell things to kill.

The Primus, Leonard Rostropovich, disappeared from his apartment that night.

He opened a secret door in his bedroom and followed an equally secret staircase down into the bowels of the

Citadel, where food and drink awaited him. And he hid there because he could not bring himself to do anything else.

The Primus knew what his duties were at this critical time in the life of his people. He knew what his flock expected of him, what it needed from him.

But he couldn't face another human being. Not now. Not after he had flung that girl to the ground, and felt the crunch of her bones as if they were his own, and seen the spray of her blood, and heard the wet chomping sound the creature made as it fed.

Even now, his stomach churned at the thought. Why had God let him feel and see and hear that? Hadn't he always sought to serve Him? Hadn't he always done his best to be God's voice on Nova Prime?

Why had God brought him so close to death, so very close?

He would not even have considered exposing himself to danger if he were not doing heaven's work. He had been on his way to present Conner Raige with a Writ of Objection, a legal document that enabled any leader of the tripartite government to temporarily disqualify a colleague if that colleague was patently unsuitable, and to the Primus no one was less suitable than Raige.

Unfortunately, such a writ could not be delivered electronically. It could only be handed to Raige in person. And the Primus was about to do that very thing, in God's name, when he and his entourage were attacked.

But why would his deity do such a thing to him? He couldn't get the question out of his head. Why would God place him in so terrible a position?

There was only one answer: God had abandoned the colony. Not through any fault of the Primus, of course. But it was clear to him now that that was what had happened.

God has abandoned us. Abandoned me.

So what else could he do but hide? He was only a

man, after all, and men were frail. Especially in the face of something as hideous and powerful as the Ursa.

Once again, despite himself, he saw the creature tear the young woman apart. Unable to stand the sight, he closed his eyes and jammed his fists against them.

"So very frail," he moaned.

CHAPTER TWENTY-NINE

Conner sat at Meredith Wilkins's desk with his head in his hands.

He had received any number of condolences in the aftermath of Lyla's death.

Of course, none of the people expressing them knew how Conner felt about her. All they knew was that he had worked closely with her on the cutlass project.

Hell, even Conner didn't know how he felt about her. He just wished to heaven he had had the chance to find out.

Lyla . . .

Lucas hadn't said a word since his sister was killed. *Not a syllable to anyone.* But he was taking out his grief on Ursa after Ursa in patrol after patrol after patrol.

"Sir," said Dolpa, the adjutant who had worked for Wilkins and now worked for him, "I have someone to see you. An augur."

Conner looked up and gathered himself. He had made a promise to Hāturi to lead. He couldn't renege on that promise now no matter how he felt.

"See the augur in."

Conner didn't know why such a person would ask to see him. To comfort him, maybe? It would be a comfort, he thought, to know the Primus would be more cooperative with his initiative.

As he thought that, the augur walked into his office. But it wasn't just *any* augur. It was his aunt Theresa.

She took a seat opposite him. "Before you ask, nephew,

I'm not here on personal business." She sighed. "The Primus has disappeared."

It took a moment for the words and their import to sink in. "Disappeared," Conner echoed.

"Yes. He doesn't answer my calls or, for that matter, anyone else's. And his apartment is empty."

Perfect timing, Conner thought. *As if I didn't have enough on my hands.*

Then he stopped himself. It was his job to see to the welfare of the colony's citizens, and the Primus was no less a citizen than anyone else. No sense complaining about the problem, even to himself.

"Where was the Primus last seen?" Conner asked.

"In the Citadel, by some of us augurs. But that was yesterday. No one has spotted or heard from him since."

Conner nodded. "All right. I'll send out an alert. If anyone catches so much as a glimpse of him, it'll be reported."

"I was hoping you could send out a search detail," Aunt Theresa said.

"I wish I had that luxury," Conner told her, "but I don't. We have too few boots on the ground as it is. I can't redeploy them for a search detail regardless of who it's for."

Theresa looked disappointed, but she didn't argue with him. "Very well. We'll pray for the Primus's safe return to us. Heaven forbid that anything has happened to him."

Conner couldn't join her in that invocation. But out of respect for her, he didn't say so.

There were eight of them. Three—Blodge, Ditkowsky, and Augustover—had remained with Conner. Four others—Lucas, Gold, Erdmann, and Cheng—had come around the block and were advancing from the other direction.

And between the two groups, thunder erupting from

its throat, or what passed for a throat in its alien anatomy, was an Ursa.

It was massive, powerful-looking, and utterly unaware of how important the next few minutes of its life would be. Because if Conner and the rest of his squad took it down, it would mean that Lyla's cutlasses had made the difference humanity needed. And if the monster prevailed, it would mean that their last, best hope had been dashed.

The Ursa swung its head back and forth as if it were trying to decide which morsels of flesh and blood and bone to go after first. But it didn't look daunted. Why should it? Everywhere it turned, there was prey.

"All right," Conner said into his comm gear, "just like we practiced it. Cheng, Erdmann, Gold, Ditkowsky—deploy hooks. Everybody else is showing blades. On my—"

Suddenly Lucas interrupted him with an urgent yell: "Raige, behind you!"

Conner looked back over his shoulder, wondering what could have made Lucas cry out that way—and saw the last thing he wanted to see. A second Ursa was lumbering toward them from the other end of the street, its open maw saying loud and clear that it was glad to see so much meat in one place even if there was a chance it might have to share some of it.

Damn, Conner thought, his mind racing. *That changes everything.* In less than a heartbeat, the encounter had gone from a controlled experiment—albeit a potentially deadly one—to a free-for-all.

He had only a hot instant to review their options. One was to split up the team and fight both Ursa at once, but he didn't like that idea. Even with cutlasses, it would be hard for four Rangers to take down one of the monsters. Their other option was to keep the second Ursa busy while the majority of the team went after the first one.

Conner liked that idea a lot better.

But whoever was asked to keep the second one at bay

would be taking a huge risk. He couldn't ask anyone in his charge to face that kind of jeopardy.

That was why he would take on that assignment himself.

"Everybody," he barked into his comm gear, "we've got two targets now. Lucas is going to lead the assault on Target One, our original objective. I'm going to engage Target Two, slow it down."

"Not without help," said Blodge, loyal as ever.

"That's an order," Conner insisted.

Then the time for talk was past because Target Two was bearing down on them, gathering speed as it came. Conner pelted forward a half dozen steps to meet it before it reached the rest of the squad.

Having watched hours of bloody combat footage, none of which ended happily, he knew the Ursa would try to pounce on him. It was a successful tactic when its prey was running away, which almost invariably had been the case. But Conner knew better than to run away.

He slowed down for just a fraction of a second to make the monster think he was going to retreat. Then he ran at it even faster so that when the Ursa sprang, he was able to dive in below it, twist his body around until he was facing upward, and take a rip out of its belly.

He had hoped that the damage would be enough to disable the creature, maybe even kill it. But it only made the Ursa more ferocious.

No sooner did it land on the ground with nothing to show for its attack than it whirled and launched itself at Conner a second time.

And a second time he sprinted forward to dive underneath the thing. Except this time when he twisted and used his cutlass to cut a furrow in the Ursa's underside, the wound he made was deeper, deep enough to release a spray of thick black ichor.

I hit something important, Conner thought as he got his feet beneath him. *An artery or its equivalent.*

But he knew better than to become overconfident.

The Ursa was still moving, still baring its teeth at him, still every bit as deadly as before.

But it no longer seemed as eager to spring at him. It was advancing on him slowly instead, its shoulders and haunches close to the ground, as if it had learned the error of its ways.

Conner had no choice but to back off, matching the Ursa's pace. Switching to a pike, which offered him more length, he poked at the creature. It roared and tossed its head but didn't stop padding toward him.

Suddenly it reached out and swiped at him with one of its paws. Conner saw that he had miscalculated, allowed the thing to get too close. To keep from getting raked by the Ursa's talons, he had to fling his arms up and backpedal like crazy.

As it was, the thing sliced the front of his uniform to ribbons and came within a hair of shredding his chest as well.

Still, he would have been all right if the road behind him hadn't been so full of debris. As he retreated, his eyes fixed squarely on the Ursa, he felt his heel catch on something heavy. Before he knew it, he was going down, sprawling unceremoniously on his back.

The Ursa didn't hesitate to take advantage of the fact.

Conner hugged the cutlass to him, careful not to stab himself with its pike, and rolled as hard as he could to the left. A fraction of a second later the Ursa's paw came down in the place he had vacated, ripping up the ground.

Scrambling to his feet, Conner went quarterstaff. Then he held his cutlass up in both hands to ward off the Ursa's next blow, because he *knew* there would be a next blow. The cutlass took the full impact of the creature's attack, exactly as it was designed to do.

But unlike his weapon, Conner wasn't made of superstrong metal alloys. As much as he hated to admit it, he was only human. When the Ursa's paw hit his quarterstaff, it ripped it out of his hands.

Leaving him completely and utterly defenseless. The

monster seemed to know it, too. With renewed fury, it flung itself at him.

Conner managed to dodge its rush and watch it crash into the wall behind him. Without respite, the Ursa attacked again. And again Conner threw himself out of the way.

But as he got to his feet, he knew he was a dead man. The Ursa was too fast, too strong, and Conner's muscles were burning, his breath coming in huge searing gasps.

He wasn't going to win this fight. All he could do was prolong the inevitable.

As he thought that, the Ursa rounded on him and opened its maw, and out of it came a great and terrible rumbling. It seemed to be saying, *You thought you could stand against me? You're meat, nothing more. You're what I rend with my talons and grind between my teeth.*

Conner bit down on his fear. The Ursa might kill him, it might tear him apart, but it wasn't going to make him beg for mercy—not even in the privacy of his own mind.

Suddenly, the Ursa lowered its head and charged him. Conner braced himself, ready to try to throw himself out of harm's way one more time if he could.

But before the monster could reach him, something happened—something long and bright, glinting in the light of the suns and burying itself in the back of the Ursa's neck.

Forgetting about Conner, the creature spun and looked for the source of its pain. Conner looked, too, and found it in the form of an empty-handed Raul Blodgett. Nor was he alone. Six other Rangers were trailing behind him, their cutlasses held aloft, the black blood of a dead Ursa spattered across their uniforms.

The dead Ursa in question was stretched across the street behind them, motionless, nothing more than a pale lump of alien flesh.

But the live Ursa, the one Blodge had wounded with

his cutlass, was starting after him. Conner couldn't let that happen.

"Hey!" he yelled, picking up a chunk of debris and flinging it at the creature. "I'm still here!"

The debris hit the Ursa in the back of its head. Enraged, it turned on Conner again. He started to fall back, wondering if he had paid for Blodge's life with his own.

Then another silver shaft hit the monster and stuck in its back. And when it whirled, a third one lodged in its face, just above its maw.

The creature writhed and rolled and swiped at the third shaft but couldn't get it out. In the meantime, Conner's squad went blade and started hacking at the Ursa from behind.

The Ursa roared, turned, and snapped at its tormentors. But they weren't there anymore. They had spread out on either side of the thing and were wreaking havoc on it.

Little by little, the Ursa succumbed. First it crashed to its knees. Then it dropped its head. By the time Lucas drove his blade into its neck, it was all but done.

As the monster breathed its last, Conner looked into the faces of his squad. He saw pride there and hope. They'd done what they'd set out to do.

Now others could do the same.

Marta Lemov experimentally moved her new wheelchair back and forth. Her one good hand rested on the small switch that maneuvered the wheelchair, and she used it as deftly as she could. Nevertheless, she still kept miscalculating and banging into walls in her small room. Marta was impatient under the best of circumstances, and these were hardly the best.

She heard a knock at the door and with a sigh of frustration turned to see Theresa standing there.

"I should have known," Marta said, thumping the

wheelchair with her fist. "When I woke up and this thing was just sitting here, I should have known you were responsible for it."

"I see you got into it all by yourself. You could have asked for help, you know."

"I prefer doing things on my own."

"That's the difference between us, I suppose. You never ask for help, and as an augur I do nothing *but* ask for it."

"Yeah? And who did you ask for help with *this* thing?"

"Him." Theresa chucked a thumb toward the door. "Or, more accurately, *them*."

Marta glanced with only mild interest toward the door, but when two men entered, she actually gasped in surprise.

One was Donovan Flint, the Savant. He nodded toward the wheelchair and said calmly, "Don't let the learning curve deter you, Ranger. You'll get the hang of it in no time."

What had he done, build the chair himself? But Marta figured she could ask that question later. At the moment, her attention was focused on the man *next* to Flint. Her reflex to stand to attention was so ingrained that she automatically tried to get up out of the chair. "General Hāturi," she said. Then she quickly corrected herself. "I mean Prime Commander Hāturi."

"Let's stick with Commander," said Hāturi. "And please, sit back down. We don't need you injuring yourself even further."

Marta did as she was instructed. Hāturi seemed slightly amused. "You seem surprised to see me, Ranger."

"With all respect, sir, I'm a grunt. But you . . . I mean, after the death of Prime Commander Wilkins, you've had so much dumped on you. I just figured that you had far more important things to do than visit me."

"Nothing's more important than my people. And Savant Flint feels the same way. That's why he put this chair together for you."

So he did build it.

"Thanks," she told Flint. "But—"

"But why did we bother?" Hāturi asked. He glanced at Flint, who nodded in confirmation of something Marta could only guess at. "Well, as it turns out, we can use your help."

"My help?" It was hard for Marta not to laugh. "Commander, I'm in a wheelchair. A fine wheelchair," she acknowledged in Flint's direction, "but a wheelchair nevertheless."

"Yes. And you're going to need it to get around," said Hāturi.

"Around where?"

There was momentary silence as if the three of them hadn't decided who was going to broach the subject. It was Theresa who finally took a step forward and said, "I proposed to the Primus that the augury embark on a program where we bring comfort and reassurance directly to the people of Nova City."

"You mean like . . . what? House calls?"

"That's exactly right," Theresa replied. "They seem reluctant to come to us, so I thought we should go to them. And at first the Primus agreed to it. He declared it to be an excellent idea. And then, shortly afterward, he suddenly canceled the program. The ostensible reason was that he had decided it was simply too dangerous out there for us."

"Yeah, well," said Marta, who was not the least bit surprised, "I never thought I'd say this, but the Primus is one hundred percent right."

"Still," Hāturi said, "Augur Raige's idea is a good one. But with the Primus missing, there's no one to approve it. And therefore no augur to carry it out."

"All right," said Marta, who was still feeling as if she had walked into the middle of a play. She sensed that she was supposed to have some sort of function here, but she couldn't imagine what it was. "But I'm still uncertain what bearing this has on me."

"It's about faith," Flint told her.

"I thought you were a man of science," Marta said.

"There are all manners of faith, Ranger. I have faith in our ability to survive and overcome. I have faith that through our science and in our force of arms we will triumph. Many, though, need something more than that. They feel they have to place their faith in something greater than themselves. And frankly, anything that will keep the people calm and confident in the proposition that we will conquer these monsters rather than giving up and sliding into total anarchy—"

"Which simply makes *our* job harder," put in the commander.

Flint continued, "—is the kind of faith we need to triumph over our current circumstances. That, Ranger, is where we'd like you to come in."

"Meaning—?"

"The augurs need guidance," Theresa said. "They are on the whole decent and caring individuals. And they excel at doing what they are told. But without strong leadership, they find themselves uncertain and afraid."

"So *you* take control," Marta told Theresa.

The augur shook her head firmly. "I am one of them. They will not respond to me, nor will they obey my commands, in the way that we would want them to."

"That, Ranger," Hāturi explained, "is why we need *you*. I am giving you the field promotion of Commander, effective immediately. Your assignment is to work with Augur Raige here to implement the door-to-door visitation plan she developed. You will oversee the augurs and coordinate their activities with a squad of Rangers who will escort them."

"And when the Primus surfaces?"

"As he will," Theresa said with unflinching faith in him despite everything.

"I will have a chat with him at that time," Hāturi said. "We're walking a delicate line, *Commander*," he continued, putting a delicate emphasis on Marta's new title. "The last thing we need is for the Primus's lack of faith to go public. You understand?"

"You mean you're worried that if people have seen that the Primus himself has lost faith, it may seem pointless for anyone else to maintain theirs."

"Exactly right, Commander," said Hāturi. "The only question is: Are you up for this endeavor?"

Marta remembered how recently it had been that she'd felt nothing but contempt for the Primus. Now she actually felt sorry for him. "Am I being given a choice, General?"

"Not really, no."

"Then I'm up for it."

The general snapped off a salute, and she returned it even though it was with the wrong hand. "And General . . ." she said.

"Yes, Commander?"

"Thank you," she said in a voice both formal and sincere, "for giving me a purpose again."

"We all have a purpose, Commander. Every so often, though, we lose sight of it. So just consider this a vision adjustment."

"Yes, sir," she said.

Conner sat in the same chair from which he had watched his aunt Bonita die under the talons of an Ursa and watched Lyla do the same thing.

He wanted to turn away. He wanted to scream, hit something, cry. But he didn't. He sat there and watched the satellite feed.

It didn't show him everything, but it showed him enough. When he had seen as much as the footage would reveal, he knew who had killed Lyla.

It was Gash.

The monster that had destroyed his aunt after her pulser blast had left it with a livid scar over its mouth. The killing thing that had taken the life of Meredith Wilkins as she tried to test Conner's theory, along with the lives of too many other Novans to count.

But Gash's story had grown bigger than the thing itself.

People talked about its ferocity in whispers to keep from scaring their children. Those who prayed asked God that some other Ursa kill them, just not the one with the scar. They even speculated that the other Ursa were scared of Gash, giving it a wide berth so it wouldn't rip *them* apart, too.

And now the thing had claimed Lyla.

When Conner had accepted Hāturi's offer to serve as the de facto Prime Commander, he had given up the right to pursue personal quests. He would honor that agreement, at least until the colony had turned back the Ursa threat.

Then, if Gash was still alive at that point, Conner would find it and *destroy* it. Not as part of a squad, either. He would do it with his own two hands.

Cecilia Ruiz was as close to giving up as she'd ever been.

Even with having restocked at the lost mining colony and even with careful rationing, her water supply was getting dangerously low. She knew she was becoming dehydrated, but there was very little she could do about it. At least second sun was setting, with the stars creeping up on the horizon.

She'd heard so much about constellations back on Earth. The ancients had gazed up at the stars and seen all manner of things: a warrior with a belt, an archer, and an assortment of animals both real and imaginary.

The array of stars she gazed upon now were not remotely the stars her ancestors had gazed upon. And no one on Nova Prime had the time or the patience to look to the skies and draw imaginary pictures on them. The stars were simply stars and nothing beyond that.

She wondered if it was a case of something trivial and childlike being left behind in the inevitable march toward adulthood for the human race or if something truly wondrous had been tossed onto the scrap heap as if it were useless when it was in fact a testimony to humankind's boundless imagination.

Finally she decided that such musings were above her level of philosophy.

In any case, it wasn't visions among the stars that occupied her mind. It was a vision of Xander: the hurt look on his face, the expression that said he was never going to see her again. Perhaps there had been even more to it than that.

All I've done is underscore his sense of helplessness, she thought. *How could I not have realized it? He's sitting at home right now believing that if only he'd been a better husband, a better provider, I wouldn't be out here risking my life. The guilt that I've dropped on him must be driving him insane.*

What have I done to him? To my family? All because I thought I could solve our problems in one stroke.

"That's it," she said. They were the first words she had spoken in a while, and now as she looked out on the red plains before her, she was startled by how gravelly her voice sounded. It was a sign of just how parched she was. "That's it," she said again with a pronounced croak. "I'm going home. Enough is—"

That was when her naviband crackled to life. The stern voice of a Ranger dispatcher—she didn't know which one it was, but it didn't matter—advised that there was an Ursa sighting in the Cray farming colony. Apparently, unlike other colonies, Cray had actually set up a lookout in a high tower that they thought was safely above an Ursa's perception range. And the lookout had spotted something he believed was one of the creatures.

He had sent out word without a moment's hesitation. All the farmers in the Cray colony—about ten or so, plus their families—had been advised to seek immediate shelter and await the arrival of a Ranger squad.

Excitement rising within her, Cecilia checked the distance to the Cray colony on her electronic map. She couldn't believe it. She was ten minutes away from it.

Ten minutes away from finding an Ursa.

Ten minutes away from the confrontation she'd been seeking for days now, after it was beginning to seem to her as if the Ursa had somehow conspired to find shelter any time she was in the area.

Ten minutes away from death . . . ?

She shoved the notion clean away and set off at a rapid trot. She was on foot, and the Rangers no doubt would have high-speed vehicles. They'd be able to cover in no time the area that she'd needed days to traverse.

But it didn't matter. None of it mattered.

This was her chance. And she had picked up some items at the mining colony that she prayed would be just what she needed to finish the damned thing off. All thoughts of Xander's words and her children's needs were forgotten. She cared about one thing and one thing only:

Do the job.

CHAPTER THIRTY

Cecilia approached the Cray farming colony from around the back of one of the barns. She smelled something foul wafting from one of them and peered carefully between the folds of smart fabric that composed the sides. There were red splotches on the cloth, which she knew instantly were blood. Within the barn itself, aside from various tools, was a cow. Farmers cherished their cows and did their damnedest to breed them, because growing them from the DNA samples that had been on the vessels that had carried them to Nova Prime was always a hit-and-miss operation, even after all this time. Natural breeding was far preferable.

This cow had been gutted. Worst of all, the poor thing was still breathing. How it was possible Cecilia couldn't even imagine.

She used one of her daggers to cut aside the smart fabric, insinuated herself into the barn, and put the barrel of her pulser against the poor animal's head. It looked at her with its saucerlike eyes, and there seemed to be a flash of gratitude in them. Then she squeezed the trigger once, hoping that the fact that she had jammed it against its head would muffle the shot. She certainly didn't need to alert the Ursa to her presence. The cow shuddered once, and then it was gone.

She crossed the barn, trying to determine the stealthiest way to approach the thing.

That plan went right out the window when she heard the unmistakable roar of an Ursa, accompanied by the terrified screams of several people, including what sounded like a young girl.

With no thought of her own safety, with no thought of anything save what needed to be done, Cecilia charged out of the limited shelter of the barn and slapped on a pair of infrared goggles so that the darkness wouldn't impede her. Then, while still running, she unslung her pack and started fishing in it for the items she had taken from the warehouse back at the mining colony. She saw the Ursa from behind, maybe a hundred yards away. It was smaller than the one she had encountered what seemed like an eternity ago, but it was still large enough to swallow her in one gulp.

The monster had torn up what appeared to be a trapdoor sunk into the ground. She realized immediately that it was an old bomb shelter, constructed to withstand Skrel aerial assaults. But it could not withstand the close-up attack of the Ursa. The creature was reaching down into the shelter with one of its claws, trying to extract the people within like a child trying to pull fruit filling from the middle of a pastry.

Cecilia brought up her pulser and started firing. Her hand was shaking, but it didn't matter because the Ursa was more than enough of a target. Pulse blasts ricocheted from all over it.

The thing whirled to face her and bellowed in anger. It didn't look at all as if she was managing to hurt it, but she definitely had gotten its attention.

Cecilia stopped and did the only thing she could think of: She roared back at it. The Ursa actually seemed taken aback by her response. It paused for a moment, processing it.

Then it charged, its claws spitting up pieces of dirt as it came at her.

There was no further time to rummage in the bag. In desperation, she dumped everything out and saw, rolling around her feet, two blast charges she'd gotten from the mining colony. Each one consisted of a small block of explosives with a timer attached. The miners used them to clear away stubborn sections of underground caves, but Cecilia had a different use in mind. She also yanked out the machete, shoving it into her belt.

The creature came straight at her, roaring again, its mouth wide open. The timer usually was set to something along the lines of twenty minutes to make sure everyone had time to get clear. Cecilia had no such luxury; she set it to five seconds and threw it straight at the creature's open maw.

Her shaking hand betrayed her. The blast charge glanced off the Ursa's open mouth and struck the ground directly in front of it.

An instant later, it exploded—just as the Ursa passed over it.

The blast sent the creature spiraling through the air, carried by the force of the detonation. It hit the ground about ten feet away, landing heavily, and lay there for a moment looking stunned.

The force of the blast had knocked Cecilia off her feet as well. She tried to stand up and cried out in pain. She'd been twisted around by the impact of the landing and had managed to torque her knee. It was hardly a life-threatening injury unless her inability to move quickly enabled the Ursa to leap on her and dispatch her easily.

The explosion must have been heard by the farmers because a moment later they opened the trapdoor and came pouring out of the shelter. When they saw the Ursa lying there, they recognized their opportunity. With a collective shout of defiance the farmers charged the beast, waving pitchforks, scythes, and anything else with a point or a sharp edge that could serve as a weapon.

"No, wait!" Cecilia shouted. She grabbed the second blast charge and looped the rope around her shoulder. "It's only stunned! Be careful—!"

They didn't attend to her words, possibly because they didn't hear them since they were so busy shouting imprecations at the Ursa. But by the time they got near it, the creature had recovered and was on its feet, turning to face them.

Cecilia limped frantically in their direction. The pain was so severe that tears welled involuntarily in her eyes. "Encircle it!" she yelled. "Come at it from all sides! Strike and fall back!"

Now they heard her, or at least they chose that moment to pay attention to her. A dozen of them were surrounding the monster, taking turns stabbing and thrusting with their makeshift weapons and then jumping back whenever the Ursa turned its attention to them.

It was an effective tactic for a short time, but then the Ursa lashed out with its claw and slashed open the chest of a man wielding a pitchfork. Cecilia heard a woman cry out his name in a way that indicated that she was his wife. *Now she's his widow,* Cecilia thought grimly as the man fell backward, dead before he hit the ground.

"You son of a bitch!" the widow screeched, and came at the Ursa with a sickle. The Ursa bit down on and through her weapon-wielding arm, and she shrieked as the limb was bitten off with a sound like a drawer slamming shut. Blood fountained from the truncated arm, and the woman collapsed in shock. The Ursa spit out the sickle and the arm that was still gripping it.

Cecilia, limping wildly, started firing again. She was desperately worried that her erratic aim would cause her to strike some of the farmers. She needn't have been concerned; the farmers were doing their best to get the hell out of the Ursa's way.

Attracted by the bursts of pulser energy, the monster zeroed in on Cecilia and charged again. At that moment, providentially, Cecilia's knee gave out, and as she collapsed, the Ursa overshot her. For a second the creature's underbelly was directly above her.

Without realizing she was doing it, she shoved the machete up into its gut. Fusion-burst pulses might have ricocheted off it, but the serrated blade penetrated the Ursa's hide.

The creature let out a howl of fury, and that was

when Cecilia heard a chorus of angry shouting. The farmers were attacking once again, battering the Ursa from all directions with their tools. The humanity of Nova Prime, harkening to its most basic instincts, looked like its prehistoric ancestors attempting to take down a mammoth with nothing but spears.

Cecilia, still lying beneath the creature, saw her opening. She thumbed the second blast charge to life and blindly set the timer. She didn't know whether she'd set it to detonate in seconds or hours and was unable to check because there was no room to do so. Instead, she did the only thing she could: She thrust the blast charge up into the Ursa's gut.

The Ursa bellowed so fearsomely that Cecilia's mammoth-hunting ancestors could have heard it. Then the beast bounded away from Cecilia, the source of its discomfort.

The farmers pursued the Ursa but only until it whirled to face them, at which point they fell back in pure terror. Then the monster locked onto Cecilia once more. Baring its double row of jagged teeth, it advanced on her. Her pulser was once again in her hand.

"Go to hell," she snarled between bloodied lips, and fired. As the pulse blast struck the charge in the creature's gut, it detonated.

The blast lifted the Ursa several feet into the air and landed it on its side. But it still wasn't dead. Its belly was a mess of black gore, but it still had the strength to roar at the farmers and struggle to its feet.

But the farmers weren't going to let it go far. Using their tools, they stabbed at it and hacked at it and pummeled it until the thing collapsed. Even then it snapped at a farmer, nearly taking his leg off, and so they kept stabbing and hacking and pummeling until the Ursa stopped moving.

It took a long time.

A young girl knelt next to Cecilia, who was still lying there, pain turning her leg into an appendage that was good for nothing except keeping her boot on. "That's

some gun!" she said in admiration, apparently under
the impression that the pulser was responsible for the
Ursa being blown apart.

Cecilia was about to tell her the truth when she heard
a tremendous yell of triumph. One of the farmers, using
a scythe, had chopped the Ursa's head off. "I got it!" he
shouted. "Wait'll Vander Meer gets a load of this! I'm
gonna be rich!"

Oh, you bastard, she thought, and she tried to stand
up, but her knee betrayed her. "Like hell!" she managed
to grunt. "It's mine!"

No one heard her. The farmers, having completely
forgotten about their savior, were busy arguing with
one another. It was clear that Cecilia wasn't the only one
who had heard Vander Meer's offer.

"Keep away!" said the man who had the head, and he
actually swung it around and knocked over some people with it, black Ursa blood flying everywhere. Then
another farmer came up behind him and slammed him
with a hoe in the back of his skull. The head tumbled
out of the first man's arms, but he wasn't unconscious.
Turning around, he slugged his assailant in the face.

The grisly trophy bounced away, and people stumbled over one another to get their hands on it.

Cecilia lay there, with the young girl trying to find a
way to position her leg so that it wouldn't hurt.

"What's wrong with them?" the girl asked. Her eyes
were filling with tears. It was clearly horrifying to her to
see the adults, covered in black blood and filth from
battling the Ursa, turning against one another.

Cecilia watched the display. She saw the fury on their
faces and the lack of humanity. They seemed ready to
kill one another. Only moments earlier they had been
united against the common enemy; now they found an
enemy everywhere they turned.

She thought of what she had been like when she had
killed the men back at the mining colony. She had done
it in self-defense and thus had been ruthlessly efficient

in doing it, yet even then the violence had sickened her. It was one thing to be part of the Rangers, but this?

The worst thing was that she knew that if her leg were functioning properly, she would be right in there with them. She would be wrestling for the proof of the creature's death, and she might even be desperate enough to start shooting.

What good would I be to my family like that? Is that what the children deserve? A mother who's thrown fundamental human decency out the window? Who'd be willing to slaughter her own people not to protect her life or the common good but out of desperation? Is that who I want to be?

The little girl was still looking down at her. Cecilia wiped the tears from her eyes and whispered, "They don't know any better."

That was when another, even more devastating roar sounded across the colony. Everyone froze at the sound. Two men had been struggling for possession of the head, but they both dropped it.

It was another Ursa, eagerly advancing on them. It roared again, and it was impossible to tell whether it was angry over the loss of one of its kind or if it didn't give a damn and was simply informing them that it was going to kill them all.

Before the farmers could decide whether to come together as one or run in a burst of every-man-for-himself, the Ursa decided it for them. It charged into their midst.

Oh, God . . . it was all pointless, Cecilia thought, and that was when she heard a triumphant hum: a fleet of Ranger skipjacks.

A Ranger on a skipjack descended from overhead, coming in fast. A dozen other Rangers were right behind him on similar vehicles. Undaunted by the Ursa's strength and teeth and talons, the lead Ranger leaped off his skipjack and fell toward the creature.

He had something in his hand that was like nothing Cecilia had ever seen. It was some kind of staff, except it looked like it was constructed of intertwined strands of silver metal. At the end of the staff, there was a vicious-looking blade.

As Cecilia watched, spellbound, the Ranger landed on the back of the startled Ursa and drove the blade into the back of its head.

The Ursa roared and twisted, throwing the Ranger off. He hit the ground and rolled to his feet, but before the monster could reach him, the other Rangers had hit the ground and begun thrusting at the Ursa with their own strange bladed weapons.

Cecilia had been incredibly lucky with the thrust of her machete; if she hadn't been as close as she was, it was likely that the blade never would have penetrated. And how often could one reasonably expect to get that close to an Ursa?

But the attacking Rangers didn't appear to require that proximity. They moved around the Ursa in a continuous circle, spearing, slicing, and moving lightly out of the way before the Ursa could counterattack. Everywhere they struck, their blades penetrated with such ease that they might as well have been assaulting a gigantic stick of butter.

And it wasn't just blades they were using. They had pikes and spiked balls and hooks on the ends of their weapons as well. But—and Cecilia didn't know if she was hallucinating this part—it wasn't that each weapon was different. It seemed to her that each one was transforming itself from one shape to another as she looked on.

One thing she was sure of was that she knew one of the Rangers: Commander Hāturi. Despite his age, he was attacking shoulder to shoulder with the other Rangers, maneuvering as ably as any of his subordinates. With a roar of rage, the Ursa swiped at the commander with its talons, but he retreated in time to keep from being cut to shreds.

It was the last offensive move the creature would make. The Rangers piled on, moving in a fluid and coordinated manner. The minutes seemed to take an eternity to tick away, but when it was over, the Ursa lay on the ground, cut to pieces. There was no question in any-one's mind that it was dead.

"Sweep the area," Hāturi ordered. "Motion sensors on full. I don't want anything getting this near again." Then Hāturi turned his attention to the farmers. "Everyone here okay?"

The little girl, who hadn't budged from Cecilia's side, called out, "This lady could use some help."

Seeing the mess Cecilia was in, Hāturi called, "Medic!" and walked over to her. As he did so, his blade trans-formed itself into something blunt and inoffensive. A medic came in right behind him, and Hāturi knelt next to Cecilia. "You're going to be all right, Miss . . ."

Then his face darkened. His gaze had fallen upon the pulser in her hand, and there was genuine threat in his voice as he said, "Where did you get that?"

She would have laughed, but she was starting to feel pain in her chest as well. It was possible that she had broken a rib, but that was a problem for later. She winced as the medic started examining her knee, but she man-aged to get out, "Cecilia Ruiz, formerly Ranger Cecilia Sanchez."

Recognition dawned on Hāturi's face. "Sanchez? I re-member you. Some sort of nerve injury, yes?"

"Only to my shooting hand."

"Yes, yes. Of course. You're a farmer now?"

She managed to shake her head. "No, sir."

"Then what the hell are you doing out here?"

"Killing Ursa, sir."

Hāturi studied her for a long moment. The man wasn't stupid. She knew that he was figuring it all out. She found that she couldn't keep looking him in the eye. She felt ashamed, as if she had betrayed some deeper meaning of the Ranger oath she had taken so long ago, the oath that, thanks to her injuries, she had left long behind.

"I *thought* I saw people fighting over the head when we were coming in." He eyed her. "The reward credits are that important to you?" he asked, removing any doubt that he hadn't seen through her purpose.

"Taking care of my family is."

He looked back in the direction of the Ursa's carcass. "Makes you sick, huh?"

"Yes, it does."

"And I assume you were the one largely responsible for killing the beast?"

The little girl spoke up. "Yes, sir. She was. She blowed it up good."

"Indeed." His eyes narrowed, and there was anger in his face. "I don't approve of Vander Meer's methods, but fair is fair and a reward's a reward. I'll make sure you'll get the head—"

"No, sir," Cecilia said quickly before he could stand and move away. Then she let out a sigh. The med tech had injected her with painkiller, and the ache was fading to something manageable.

"Why not?" Hāturi was clearly confused.

"Because . . ." She tried to frame the thoughts tumbling through her head. "I don't know." She couldn't take her eyes off the weapon that Hāturi was holding. Before he could press the subject, she said, "What *is* that?"

"Well"—he held it closer—"the unofficial name for it is a cutlass, although I'm sure we'll come up with a better name before long. It's a new weapon developed by an engineer named Lyla Kincaid, may she rest in peace. As you can see, rather formidable and much more effective against Ursa than pulsers."

"Definitely."

He studied her a moment and then slid his hand along the thing and tapped it. Instantly, the cutlass grew a blade at either end. He handed it to her. "Give it a try," he said. "Just don't tap it. You might get a nasty surprise." With a gesture of his head, he indicated to the med tech that it might be a good idea to back up.

Cecilia swept the cutlass back and forth with facility.

It felt comfortable in her hand. Natural. Remarkably light but also obviously devastating in a battle.

Hāturi was now standing, and he addressed the farmers. "Ladies and gentlemen," he said in a formal voice, "the United Ranger Corps thanks you for your cooperation. It has come to our attention that this young woman has personal needs that you can attend to. As thanks for her aid to you, you're going to gather a considerable amount of food and present it to her for her to take back to her family."

One of the farmers tried to protest but wilted under Hāturi's gaze. "How much?" was all he managed to say.

"We'll tell you when it's enough," Hāturi said coolly. As if that ended the discussion—which, as far as the commander was concerned, it clearly did—he turned back to Cecilia. "So what do you think of the cutlass?"

"Incredibly maneuverable," she said. "Been field-testing it long?"

"Long enough. We've killed dozens of the damned Ursa with it. It's devastating. We've got enough DNA samples of the things that the Savant is in heaven, or at least whatever he believes heaven to be. We haven't gotten that bastard Gash yet—the biggest Ursa you've ever seen—but we will. We're closing in on putting an end to these bastards."

"Well, that's . . . that's great to hear."

She offered the cutlass back to him. Hāturi studied her and then said quietly, "Of course, even when we kill the last of them, there's no guarantee there won't be more. In fact, I'm sure there will be. The Ursa represents a sea change in Ranger preparedness."

"Okay." She shrugged; there didn't seem to be much else to say.

"I suspect that the cutlass is going to become the primary weapon of the Rangers, especially when it comes to combating those things."

"That makes sense."

"And I can't help but observe that you seem to be holding it reasonably steadily."

"Yes, I suppose I—"

Her voice trailed off as the significance of what he was saying began to settle in. He reached down and took the cutlass back, and as he did, he said, "It would appear to these eyes that the small muscle control that you don't possess to wield a pulser accurately really isn't an issue when it comes to a cutlass. Would your family be upset if you had a regular job again?"

"No, sir. Not at all."

"Good. Because we're sorely in need of Rangers, especially experienced ones. This bunch with me are all cadets, believe it or not."

Cecilia had thought they looked a little young.

"And although the economy is a little soft right now, I'm sure we can find some credits to cover back pay for the years you missed. Right now, though, you'll return home, get some rest, and prepare some nice meals for your family, thanks to the generosity of these farmers, before reporting for duty." He saluted her. "Welcome back to the fight, Ranger."

She returned the salute. "Glad to be of help, sir. Um . . . I hate to seem ungrateful . . ."

"But?"

"Do you think you could give me a ride home?"

Conner stood in the Ranger supply depot and counted out two dozen salt tablets on the table in front of him. Out in the desert, he wouldn't last long without them.

Of course, if he had been the Prime Commander in name as well as in practice, someone would have been available to count salt tablets for him. But even then, he would have done it himself. *My life. My responsibility.*

It was something his father had taught him, one of many things.

He had barely counted the last tablet when he heard a

knock at the open door. He turned and saw Blodge standing there. "Come on in," he said.

Blodge joined him in the depot. "I know you're busy getting ready and everything, but I've got to ask: Are you sure this is a good idea?"

Conner picked up the tablets and poured them into a Ranger-issue waterproof container. "What do you mean? My going after Gash?"

"Your going after Gash *alone*. I know you've got a plan, but what if something happens to you? What are the Rangers going to do for a leader?"

Conner smiled to himself. "They'll find somebody. They always have."

"But this is a bad time to settle for *somebody*."

"Is it? Gash is the last Ursa we have to worry about. If I don't get him, someone else will." In fact, he had already begun thinking in terms of that possibility, even down to the question of who would lead the squad that came after him. "Don't worry; I'll make sure of that."

"I'm not talking about Gash," said Blodge. "I'm talking about the Primus."

Conner looked up. "The Primus is missing. Unless you know something I don't . . ."

"No. But he'll turn up; everybody says so. And even if he doesn't, there'll be somebody else. Vander Meer, maybe. Or some other Primus."

Conner saw what his friend was talking about. "And I've stood up to them. But you think somebody else won't be able to."

"Even Wilkins was having a hard time with this stuff, and she was hard as rocks. She had to give in on the budget, right? All that stuff about cutting back; it was destroying the Rangers, making us an afterthought." He jerked a thumb over his shoulder. "What do you think will happen if you get killed out there? You think people are going to take it easy on your replacement? Someone will try to bury us all over again.

"And this time," Blodge continued, "there'll be no one to fill the breach. Hāturi, maybe, but he's already as much as said he'd make a lousy Prime Commander. Kincaid? He's a bigger hothead than you are. They'd be no match for someone who knew how to work public opinion."

"True," Conner conceded. "But then, *I'm* not ready to take on someone like that, either."

Blodge looked shocked. "What are you talking about? You've got the public eating out of your hand."

"Sure, because our campaign against the Ursa has been a success. People are grateful. They think the Rangers are heroes. But what happens when the Ursa are all gone? People have short memories. They'll forget what the Rangers did for them. They'll start to feel cocky. And they'll listen when Rostropovich or someone else starts talking again about cutting our funding."

"All the more reason to have you around to remind them."

"Me?" Conner laughed. "I'm eighteen. Why would they listen to me?"

"Without you we would never have gotten rid of the Ursa. We'd be hiding in our houses, waiting for the creatures to kill us."

"*You* know what role I've played in this, and so do the other Rangers. But who knows outside of the Corps? Not many. The Savant, sure, but he's not going to pin any medals on me. So really, what am I? Just an eighteen-year-old who did a good job filling in for his superior. A Raige? That's nice. Always did like those Raiges."

Blodge held his hands out, seeking understanding. "What are you saying?"

"That I'm expendable like anyone else." He thought about Lyla. "And that I've got no choice."

Blodge looked at him for a while. Then he said, "Guess I'll see you before you go, then."

"I'm counting on it," said Conner.

He waited until his friend left. Then he went back to packing his salt tablets.

CHAPTER THIRTY-ONE

Desert sunsets were beautiful, Conner thought as he hummed across an expanse of red-clay flat on his skip-jack in the last rays of second sun. In fact, he couldn't imagine anything *more* beautiful.

When he was little, he and his family had gone out from Nova City and camped out in the desert, finding themselves in the embrace of the land. They had made fires and huddled around them against the evening chill, and Conner's mother had sung funny songs.

It seemed like a long time ago.

But then, the Ursa had changed so many things. Now Conner meant to change them back.

Gash was more than a predator engineered to destroy, if the Savant had it right. It had become a symbol of death and misery and despair, no doubt exactly what the Skrel had intended when they had sent the Ursa to Nova Prime. Humanity wouldn't be free of its nightmare until that symbol was destroyed.

I'm coming for you, Conner thought.

There had been reports of an Ursa—a big one, bigger than any of the others—heading out that way. It had to be Gash. It was the only one of its kind still unaccounted for, the only one that had escaped the scrutiny of the Savant's scientists.

Of course, it might take a while for Conner to find him. That was all right. He wasn't in a hurry. In the cities, people rushed back and forth. *But not out here in the desert.*

In the desert, you took your time.

* * *

A few hours after full dark, Conner landed the skipjack and laid out his bedroll. Then he set up a ring of monitors around him that would wake him if anything got close.

Considering the reputation of the monster that shared the desert with him, he might have had a hard time sleeping. But he slept soundly and without dreams.

After all, he cherished simplicity. The Primus made his life complicated. So did Vander Meer. So did the intricacies of a hundred Ranger personalities that he had to fuse into one purpose.

But hunting Gash? What could be simpler than that?

In the morning, Conner ate and drank and took a salt tablet. Then he stood up bare-chested in the cool, still air and checked his cutlass. He turned the weapon in his hand, and it glistened in the soft pink light of first sun, long and slender like its namesake. Long and slender and deadly.

Sliding and tapping, he turned its business end into a blade that shone in the pristine light of first sun. Then a pike. Then a hook. And so on.

Lyla was a genius. She was also beautiful, as beautiful as any woman he had ever seen, but as soon as the thought entered his head, he thrust it away. He couldn't be thinking about Lyla now. He had to focus on the task at hand.

On the Ursa. And on the cutlass he would use to destroy it.

It was light, so light that he felt it was part of his hand. Perfectly balanced for optimum maneuverability.

Of course, there was that *one* slide-and-tap combination he had to be careful of, the one that activated the scythe function. The one that would cause the cutlass to fly apart in a million directions, his own included.

Lyla had *agonized* over that failing. That one failing out of everything she had accomplished in engineering the cutlass. If he hadn't gotten involved, the Savant wouldn't have let the cutlass out of Lyla's lab.

But it wasn't a failing. It was an *asset*. Yang was the one who had pointed that out to him. And if Conner got the chance, he was going to use it to good advantage.

No, he thought, wiping a bead of sweat from his forehead. *Not if. When.*

It was almost midday when Conner came in sight of another chain of mountains, smaller than the one into which Nova City had been built. It was called the San Franciscos after a chain back on Earth that was also rust-colored, though the one on Earth apparently had been bigger and more impressive.

He didn't know why Gash would have ranged so far from Nova City if the Ursa was engineered to attack human beings. However, there was plenty of game in the San Franciscos. Maybe Gash, unlike the rest of his kind, had more of a yen for other kinds of prey.

Not all humans were alike. Maybe the same went for Ursa.

As Conner closed the distance between himself and the San Franciscos, something occurred to him. Something grim and a little frightening.

If he died on this mission, the Raige bloodline would come to an end. After all, Grandpa Joshua had died when Conner was twelve, and he'd had only one grandchild—Conner himself. Uncle Torrance—for reasons Conner never had learned—had not had any children, and Aunt Theresa didn't seem likely to have any, either. She had celebrated her fiftieth birthday recently, and as far as Conner could remember, she had never had a boyfriend, much less a husband. She had always been too devoted to her faith to think about romance, even before she became an augur—or so his dad had told him.

Of course, Conner had plenty of cousins on his mom's side of the family. Rebecca Raige had been born one of four sisters, and each of them had given birth to at least a couple of children. But none of them were Raiges. They couldn't carry on the name.

That leaves just me, Conner thought. *And if I make one mistake, one wrong move . . .*

He shook his head. *A world without Raiges.* It was unimaginable. All those sacrifices over the long history of humanity on Nova Prime, all those acts of heroism . . . gone. Not completely, of course, but nobody would attend to the family history the way the Raiges themselves had.

Was he the first Raige who had ever faced such a possibility? He wished he knew. Of course, it was too late to go back through the family archives and find out. He could do that only after he returned to the colony.

If he survived.

No, he thought. *I can't let myself think that way. The Ranger who worries about being beaten is already beaten.*

A Raige had said that, he recalled with a smile. Carter Raige, who had become Prime Commander hundreds of years earlier. He was talking about the Skrel and how as a child he had gone looking for one of the alien ships without regard for his own life.

In the end he found the ship and gave the Savant of that time a chance to figure out how its shields worked. And the colony survived. All because one little boy had the guts to take a chance.

The Ranger who worries about being beaten is already beaten. It was good advice. He would do well to remember it rather than fret about his family coming to an end.

Conner leaned into the wind on his skipjack. The air was warm and dry on his face. *Soon,* he thought.

He didn't have any way of knowing for sure, but he could feel it in his gut. *Soon.*

Late in the afternoon, with first sun dropping down in the sky, Conner reached the San Franciscos. He heard the wind howl through the smooth red rock formations, hooting as if it were amused. But then, it had never before seen what it would see if Conner was right about Gash's having holed up there.

The problem was that the mountains were rife with overhangs that obstructed his view. He wouldn't be able to find Gash unless he got off the skipjack and continued his search on foot.

He would be a lot more vulnerable on the ground. But then, the same thing went for the Ursa. After all, the mountain passages were narrow. It would be difficult for Gash to maneuver.

With all that in mind, Conner landed the skipjack on a shelf of rock. Then he took his cutlass in hand, climbed down from the shelf, and found a cleft that wound its way through the range.

First sun dropped out of sight as he negotiated the cleft. Then second sun followed it. And no sign of Gash.

Conner was eager to confront the monster, but he didn't want to do it while he was sleeping. If he didn't find Gash soon, he knew, he would have to double back to his skipjack, which had his sleeping gear and his perimeter monitors, and resume the search in the morning.

But he still had half an hour at least. He stopped for a moment, just long enough to pull a drink of water from his canteen. *Maybe I'll get lucky.*

Suddenly, Conner realized something with terrible clarity. He wasn't the hunter anymore. He was the *hunted.*

Whirling just in time, he caught sight of the Ursa as it emerged from the cover of some rocks. It was huge, pale, with thickly muscled limbs and curved talons the size of Conner's head—easily the biggest, most fearsome-looking Ursa he had ever seen.

There was a livid scar across half its face, or what passed for a face. The scar that gave it its name.

As the monster loomed against the sky, its maw wide, its claws extended, it let loose a roar that Conner could feel in his bones. Then it bunched itself and launched itself at him.

It was faster than he'd expected, faster than any of the other Ursa he had seen. Conner flung himself to one side, careful to maintain his grip on his cutlass.

A claw tore open the front of his uniform and scored the flesh underneath, setting Conner's chest on fire. But it didn't kill him. He rolled to his feet, his cutlass at the ready.

It was a good thing, too, because the Ursa had already landed and was turning in his direction.

It didn't have the same range of senses that humans did. The Savant's people had established that fact. But it knew there was prey within reach. Conner was certain of that. *Dead* certain.

He was certain also of what he wanted to do. Trusting in his ability to manipulate the cutlass, he did it.

As Gash came at him a second time, Conner summoned a blade and slashed at the creature. The move drew a black splash of blood from one of its forelegs.

Just as important, Conner ducked back beneath an overhang before Gash could return the favor. But he was out again a moment later, pressing his attack before the monster could whirl in the tight space afforded it.

He called up one function after the other so quickly that Gash had all it could do to adapt. First the spear. Then the mace. Then the hook. Then the blade again.

But the Ursa avoided them, every one of them, as if it knew they were coming, as if it had a crude animal sense of what Conner would do and when he would do it. Of course, that was impossible. It was just a beast, wasn't it?

You've just got to be faster, Conner told himself.

He gritted his teeth and attacked with redoubled speed, not just with single blows but also with combinations, coming at the creature from every angle he could manage. It didn't seem to make a difference. Gash was a step ahead of him. Conner began to see how this Ursa had earned its reputation as the most deadly of its kind on Nova Prime.

Doesn't matter, Conner thought.

His muscles screamed. Sweat fell from his forehead, found its way down the sides of his face, and dripped from his chin. Lean and fit as he was, he felt his throat burn like a furnace as he pulled in breath after hot salty breath.

Because he wasn't just fighting the Ursa. He was fighting the desert as well. And of course fighting *himself.*

Every part of him wanted to stop, to give up, to go home. But he couldn't do that. *Wouldn't* do that.

Except little by little, Gash was forcing Conner to retreat. And with each step backward, he was less protected by the rock formations around him. With each bit of ground he yielded, he emerged onto a flat plateau where the Ursa had a decided advantage.

He tried to take the offensive again, to push Gash back into the cleft. But he couldn't. He was faltering, his arms and legs growing leaden despite his determination to destroy the creature. And the more he faltered, the closer he came to the edge of the plateau.

Worse, the rock was smooth there, worn down by the elements. *Don't slip,* Conner thought.

But Gash seemed to have other ideas. The beast gathered itself and sprang at him, filling Conner's vision with its bulk. All he could see for a moment was its maw, huge and black and full of teeth.

Except it had slipped on the smooth surface of the plateau, and its attack fell short. Instead of landing on its prey, it landed just in front of him.

It was all the opening that Conner needed.

He pulled his cutlass back and swung at Gash's head with all that was left of his strength, hoping to slice the creature's throat open. But the cutlass never connected with its target—because Gash ducked underneath it.

And looked up at him.

Too close, Conner had time to think. *Too close.*

He was less than an arm's length from the monster's maw. If Gash was quick enough, it would reach out and disembowel him. Or rip his legs out from under him. Or kill him in a half dozen other ways.

But the Ursa seemed as surprised as Conner by its proximity to him, because it didn't do anything right away. It just continued to stare at him.

He would never get a better shot.

His jaw clenched, Conner forced himself to slide along and tap the handle of his weapon exactly as he had done a hundred times in practice. Then he reached into the monster's slimy black maw and shoved the cutlass down its gullet.

Got to get away, he thought wildly.

Except before he could do that, he felt Gash's teeth close on his hand. The pain shot up his arm, forcing a cry of pain from his throat.

But he couldn't let Gash keep him there—his cutlass was set on the function that made it explode. And it would do exactly that in just a few short seconds, destroying anything and everything within ten meters of it, Conner included.

He tried to yank his hand free to no avail.

Then Gash solved the problem for him. With a wrench of its head, it tore off the last two fingers on Conner's hand.

The pain was indescribable, but Conner was free. Pulling his mangled, bloody hand into his chest, he whirled and scrambled away as fast as he could.

Gash flailed at him, raking his back with its claws, but the monster failed to get a grip on him. *Ten seconds,* Conner thought, dropping back down into the cleft.

He could see Gash's shadow stretch out past him, falling in disjointed sections on the formations in front of him. The creature was coming after him, cutlass in its throat and all. But then, as the Savant had told him, it didn't breathe the way people breathed. The cutlass might not be an impediment.

At least not yet.

Eight seconds, Conner told himself.

He ran as he had never run before, careful not to trip, because if he did, it would be his last act. The mountain air was like fire, burning the lining of his throat. It didn't matter—it was fuel. He drank it down as fast and as hard as he could.

Six seconds.

Was Gash's shadow getting shorter? Was it short *enough?*

Four seconds.

One last burst of speed. It would be for only a little while—a few quick heartbeats, a few frantic strides. Then he would know if he had put enough distance between himself and the Ursa.

Two.

One.

Now.

Nothing happened.

No, Conner thought bitterly. *It's got to work. It's got to.*

He shot a glance back over his shoulder. Gash was still pounding after him, showing no ill effects.

He had given up his cutlass. He had gambled everything on it exploding inside Gash. And it hadn't. It had *failed to fail.* Even in his desperation, he couldn't help seeing the irony.

Now what? He couldn't keep up this pace much longer. But Gash could. It would narrow the gap and—

Suddenly, his ears throbbed like drums and he felt a giant hand shove him forward. He went tumbling end over end so hard that he thought he would surely break his neck.

But somehow he didn't. He found himself lying on his

back in a cloud of dust and debris, looking up at the sky. It was quiet, unnaturally so.

Conner felt something sitting on his shoulder, something soft and wet. He plucked it off him and looked at it for a moment, trying to figure out what it was.

Then he realized: It was a chunk of pale flesh mingled with thick, black ooze. A chunk of *Gash*.

It smelled putrid. But he didn't get rid of it, not right away. He endured the stench long enough to rasp with his raw, dry throat, "Got you, you bastard."

Then he flung the chunk away as far as he could.

Something gnawed painfully at his hand. Looking down at it, Conner saw blood seeping from the ragged wound where two of his fingers had been ripped away.

He rolled onto his side. His chest hurt, too, where the monster had scored him. And it had lashed his back as well.

A small price to pay, he thought, though that didn't make his wounds hurt any less.

With his good hand, he fingered the activation stud on his naviband. A moment later, he heard: "Conner?"

Blodge's voice sounded like it was underwater. *The explosion did something to my hearing.* Temporarily, he hoped.

"I'm here," he said, his voice thinner and wearier than he had expected. "And Gash . . ." He looked around at the splashes of black gore all over the landscape. Gash was still there as well. And *there*. And *there* . . . "Gash is dead."

He heard cheering through the comm link. It was a good sound. A *great* sound. "Any chance you can send out a flier?" Conner asked. "With a med kit?"

His friend laughed, and there were others in the background who laughed with him. "It's on its way. Hang in there, buddy."

Conner grunted, enduring the pain as best he could. "Like I've got a choice."

CHAPTER THIRTY-TWO

Conner inspected his heavily bandaged right hand. A bright red spot where some of his blood had seeped through was the only outward evidence of his injuries.

Of course, the throbbing hadn't quite gone away despite the painkiller the doctor had administered. It felt like a massive toothache. But he had the satisfaction of knowing that Gash's toothache had been much worse.

"That's about all we can do," said the doctor, and sat back on his stool. "Come back to see me in a few days and we'll change the dressing. Till then, just keep it clean and dry—and for heaven's sake, stay away from Ursa."

Stay away from Ursa. It was a joke the doctor couldn't have made even as recently as the day before. But with Gash gone, the colony could breathe easy for the first time in weeks.

"I'll do my best," Conner said.

When the bandages came off, he would be missing one finger and part of a second one, which would hamper his ability to use a cutlass with his right hand. He would have to train himself to be adept with the left, which would no doubt be a long and arduous process. But he would worry about that later.

"Now get going," the doctor said. "When you're ready, we can talk about prosthetics."

Conner shook his head. "Rangers don't use prosthetics. It's a tradition."

The doctor, who obviously hadn't heard of the tradition, shrugged. "Listen, it's my job to make you aware of the options. Which one you choose is up to you."

"Thanks," said Conner, who had a bit more on his mind than a couple of fingers.

"Come in."

The words sounded hollow in the Primus's sanctum. Theresa stood just outside the doorway, reluctant to enter because she didn't know what she would encounter. But she was sworn to obey the orders of the Primus, and so she kept faith with her oath and entered the room.

The Primus was standing at the far end, near his balcony, gazing at the stars. "Augur Theresa. I understand that in my absence, you were rather . . . busy." He let the word hang there like the last leaf on a tree before it released its hold and fell.

She was happy to see that the Primus had reappeared. *But if I had vanished like that, I would be offering an explanation.* The Primus seemed inclined to do no such thing. He was acting as if he had never been away.

"Busy?" she echoed.

"Yes," he said, still giving her his back. "Your little program of going door to door? It's doing well?"

"Oh," she said, "that. Yes, Primus. I'm pleased to report that it is."

"The program that I specifically decided against after due consideration." There was no anger in the Primus's voice; it was as if he just wanted to clarify matters, to make sure they were discussing the same thing.

"You must understand, Primus—"

He half turned to her. *"Must?"*

"A poor choice of words," Theresa said humbly. "I regret them."

"There is no need to apologize, child. You were saying?"

"We didn't know where you were. I even asked my

nephew to search for you. And the people needed comfort."

"Which you gave them. You and Marta Lemov."

"Yes, Primus."

"And . . . the people have been grateful?"

"Very much so. We've reassured them that God is on our side in this endeavor—"

"God allowed this to happen, Theresa. Was that addressed?"

"Of course, Primus. God is testing us, as always. He does not interfere with free will, even if it is the free will of faithless aliens. He is giving us what we need in order to defeat this latest Skrel assault. We will survive and we will triumph as long as we remain in close partnership with one another and do not allow our faith to waver."

"And people believe all that?" the Primus asked.

"Most choose to do so. In these difficult times, who would not embrace something to believe in?"

He grunted. "Who indeed?"

Taking his subsequent silence as encouragement to continue, Theresa said, "It has not only brought a sense of calm to the people but also a newfound determination."

"I see. How . . . admirable. Of course, they will need their Primus to channel that determination, to mold it into something of which heaven will approve." He smiled. "It's good I came back when I did, eh? Perfect timing, you might say."

"Yes," said Theresa, because it was her Primus speaking. "Perfect." But in her heart, she knew that what the people had found in the Primus's absence—one another—was what was truly perfect.

The Primus chuckled softly. "Funny the way things work out. The way God works them out."

Another silence followed. In a soft, even timid voice, the augur said, "If there is nothing else, Primus, I can—"

"You can go," he said, still turned to the stars.

Relieved, she went.

* * *

With Theresa gone, the Primus reflected on his . . . retreat.

For certainly that was what it had been. A retreat from the affairs of the world so that he could contemplate the proper course of action both for him and for the augury. A respite, nothing more.

Of course, Rostropovich had not cut himself off from the temporal world completely. In his place of contemplation, he had had access to a crude comm device. It was through it that he had learned the Ursa were no more.

God's will had prevailed.

And what had happened in that terrible time before the Primus withdrew from the world . . . why, that was a thing of the past, hardly worth remembering. If he was to discharge his office as humankind's liaison with heaven, he had to shrug off such experiences. He had to come to his task new and refreshed.

It was with that task in mind that he activated his monitor and sought information on his colleagues in the Tripartite Council. Finding a comment made by the Savant only a few hours earlier, he played it back.

"Am I going to support Conner Raige?" the Savant asked. "Unequivocally. At first, I was skeptical about the wisdom of putting such a young man in such a critical position. But that was before I'd seen what he could accomplish.

"When he took over the responsibilities of the Prime Commander, the Ursa were rampaging through our city, killing at will. He turned that around. He made the right decisions—better than those I would have made, frankly. That's why the Ursa are gone, the last of them by his hand.

"But I'm not supporting Conner Raige because we need to reward him. There are medals for that. I'm supporting him because I believe he can do the job going forward. And, significantly, so do the people who follow him. They believe in his abilities. They're willing to do anything he asks of them. That says a lot.

"When I assumed the office of the Savant, I knew one thing: I wasn't going to allow myself to be ruled by emotion. I was going to approach the Ursa problem, and every other problem in front of us, from a purely scientific perspective. I was going to go by the facts. And the facts in this case point unwaveringly to Conner Raige being the best person for the job of Prime Commander."

The Primus bit his lip. He hated the idea of the Raige boy becoming a permanent member of the Tripartite Council. He detested the prospect of treating him as a colleague, an equal.

But what choice did he have? He had been in seclusion, and that would be hard enough to explain. The people were taken with Raige, inspired by him. The Primus would only hurt himself by opposing Raige's appointment.

For now.

But in the fullness of time, the Primus would find opportunities to undermine the boy. Perhaps sooner than later, for he was good at finding such opportunities. Little by little, he would get his point across.

And before long, the Primus would be on top again. Surely, after all he had endured, God owed him *that*.

Nova Prime City was out picking up the pieces.

People were on the streets assessing damage, clearing debris, and working with local leaders to get the reconstruction process under way. Those who were not already back to work in factories and farms were volunteering their time to help one another resume some semblance of their lives. Laughter, something lost but lately rediscovered, could be heard in the spring air.

Trey Vander Meer could feel the energy and optimism of his fellow citizens as he walked to work. He had already determined to move to a smaller home, someplace far from where he had watched his family die. He had heard about a nearly completed apartment structure that actually would cut down on his commute. Of course, he needed at least a bit of a walk in his ever-present struggle with his waistline.

That he could even think about his weight was a sign that he was moving past the intense grief of his loss. With the alien threat finally over, the Primus's staff was organizing funerals for the hundreds of dead who had to that point been denied them. Mass plaques and memorials were already being discussed because people didn't want the events of the last couple of months to be forgotten.

As Vander Meer walked past a construction crew clearing what once had been a theater, he was already forming the day's commentary. It would be about Conner Raige.

The day before, the young, newly minted Prime Commander had called Vander Meer into his office at the Rangers' command center for a conversation. His hand bandaged, his arm in a sling, Raige had said, "Your actions while we were working under emergency conditions complicated our ability to do our job in Nova Prime City. Lives were lost—and not just Ranger lives but those of regular citizens as well—because of your bounty."

He's a boy, Vander Meer had thought. *He'll buckle if I stand up to him.*

"The bounty offer," Vander Meer explained, "was intended to motivate civilians and—yes—even the more reluctant among your Rangers to take some additional risks. I don't see anything wrong with that."

"Except," Raige said in the same even tone, "it cost civilian lives and forced the Rangers to redeploy, taking away from our ability to hunt down the Ursa. Under the martial law Prime Commander Wilkins instituted, I could have you arrested and brought before a magistrate."

"You . . . you could," Vander Meer replied, surprised by Raige's tenacity.

"I won't do any of that," Raige said, his gaze steely, "and not because I don't think you should be punished. It's because I don't believe in censoring people—not even you. I'll let the court of public opinion decide when they've heard enough from you."

Vander Meer didn't like losing an argument, especially to a snot-nosed child. Therefore, he had contacted the Primus, having heard that the colony's foremost religious figure didn't approve of young Raige, either.

The Primus had given him the support he expected. Very publically so, though he had begun in modest ways and gained steam only over time. Vander Meer had lost much in the Ursa attack, but it seemed he had gained an ally in Leonard Rostropovich.

Now Vander Meer was returning to the studio, where he had practically lived during the Ursa invasion, armed and loaded for his hunt. It was a new day and time to get back to work.

As he entered the building, Pham was already in place, wearing a new shirt and having had a haircut since they last saw each other. There was time now for the mundane things. Restaurants were coming back. Shops were reopening.

It would take a long while, the colony's chief economist had reported, but Nova Prime was going to thrive again.

"Looking good, Ken," Vander Meer said brightly.

"Feeling good," Pham replied. "You up for a commentary?"

"That's the plan," Vander Meer said as he looked around the station.

"Topic?"

"The Rangers," said the commentator, and saw Pham's eyebrows rise.

"You do know that, right about now, the Rangers are everyone's heroes," the producer said. "They persevered when you wrote them off and, despite their crippling losses, managed to get rid of the Ursa. Right now, Conner Raige could ask for a dozen virgins and probably get them."

"I cannot argue with that," Vander Meer said. "But I do have something I need to say."

"It better be 'thank you,'" Pham told him.

He began setting up to record the commentary, clearly not thrilled about the choice of subject matter. Of course, he was merely the producer of the program. Vander Meer was the one with the following, the one who made the ultimate decisions.

With his fingers, Pham counted down. The red light went on.

Vander Meer smiled at the camera. "Welcome back, my friends. It's a glorious day, isn't it? It feels good to be alive. Walking in this morning, I was pleased to see that things were returning back to what we call normal. Of course, it'll be a *new* normal as every single one of us adjusts to life without our loved ones—a brutal change and one we did not ask for but which we must nonetheless accept.

"It felt good this morning to walk to the memorial for my wife and children and to see the three Ursa heads adorning the plaque which will be erected. I feel like I had something to do with them. As you know, I have paid out most of my personal funds as I promised, and *my* new normal will be—ahem—a significantly more frugal lifestyle.

"But those Ursa heads reminded me of more than *my* contribution. They reminded me that while the Rangers may get credit for destroying the creatures, the *people* were the ones who ultimately got the job done. The *people* killed that Ursa and showed what we could accomplish. Let's never forget that.

"To be sure, the Rangers did their duty and lost many from their ranks. But—and let's think about this—how long did it take them before they wounded an Ursa, let alone killed one of the monsters? A day? A week? Several?

"For a force that professed to be combat-ready, they certainly did not act that way in the field. They tried one tactic after another, groping in the dark, until something worked. It took the Savant's people to come up with the tool we needed, the one that changed the game. The Rangers, led by Meredith Wilkins, were fighting a losing battle while we relied on them to be our salvation.

"Now Wilkins's disciple, Conner Raige, is leading the Rangers. If I called him a young man, it would be an understatement. Many of you are old enough to be his grandparents. I have to wonder . . . If Wilkins was unprepared for what we faced in the Ursa, how prepared will this child be? How much can we really depend on him?

"We have seen that the Rangers need to stay one step ahead of the Skrel. Under the new Prime Commander, can that be achieved? The Primus seems to think otherwise. If you listen to his sermons, as so many of you do, you know that he has, in his gentle and dignified way, increasingly called into question Raige's ability to lead. And who, I ask you, would know more about leadership than the man whose flock includes every last living soul on the planet?"

The commentator leaned in closer to the camera. "It's a new day, Nova Prime. But it's not without a few clouds on the horizon. It may be too soon to tell how much we can rely on the Rangers anymore, but trust me in this: I am keeping an eye on them and will continue to do so until our questions are answered."

So much for the Rangers being unassailable these days, Vander Meer thought with a measure of satisfaction.

Theresa Raige smiled to herself as she cleared the dinner plates in the dining room. In the adjoining kitchen, Conner, only slightly hampered by his sling, and Rebecca were cleaning the pots and cooking utensils. It felt good to Theresa to know the comfort of family. It felt good to know that they could walk the streets again without fear of the Ursa.

For the augur, as for so many others, peace was becoming a realistic possibility again.

Not that her life would ever be the same. It couldn't be. Her brothers and her sister-in-law were dead, like so many others. The last few weeks had cost humanity much. But they had also taught her that their faith was strong and that it would provide them with the courage to go on.

But at dinner, the conversation had gone in a different direction. It had focused on the mundane things such as when professional sports would resume and if there were enough athletes and venues left to hold the next Asimov Games. In place of the seemingly endless drone of news reports that had occupied them for weeks, the skirl of Celtic music had filled the house. It was a welcome alternative.

After dinner, they sat again for a while, the three of them. Theresa listened to Conner's plans to rebuild Nova City and the Rangers in particular. He had ideas for training cadets quickly and efficiently and a sense that they would have no shortage of applications in the wake of what had happened. Then it grew late, and Theresa bid them good night, first with hugs and kisses and then with a short benediction, because she was still an augur first and foremost.

Her place was only a couple of kilometers away, a pleasant walk at that time of night. But she didn't go straight home. Instead, she headed for the Citadel.

It didn't take her long to get there. A handful of augurs remained awake on the first floor, reading the scriptures written by Primuses past. There was a sense of peace in the building. Theresa nodded at one and all as she made her way to the stairs and began to climb.

With the crisis past, augurs no longer were providing around-the-clock security to the Primus. She was able to reach the third floor, which was entirely claimed by Rostropovich's apartment, without any trouble. Of course, the security logs would show that she had seen him at an unusually late hour, but she figured that in a time of recovery, her visit would be one aberration among many and would therefore go unquestioned.

Theresa entered the Primus's bedchamber quietly so as not to wake him. He was asleep under a richly textured quilt the color of sand, a gift from the augury on his last birthday. Then she stood there.

After a while, the Primus seemed to become aware of her. A moment later, he bolted upright in his bed, wide-eyed, mouth open—clearly startled. A small squeak escaped his lips.

"Theresa?" he said, obviously confused. He rubbed his eyes. "What are you doing here?"

What indeed? she asked herself.

She thought about the terrible times they had lived through in fear of the Ursa. She thought about all those who had lost friends and family. She thought about all the people who had needed leadership, reassurance, and comfort and who had received precious little of those things because of the Primus's absence.

She thought about the sleepless days and nights when she had ministered to the people, wishing there were someone who could minister to *her*. Emotions—dread, sadness, resentment—welled up and overflowed from her heart.

"Theresa?" he asked again, this time a little more sternly.

She went to his bedside and sat down beside him. Then, with a suddenness that caught both her and the Primus by surprise, she slapped him across the face. The resulting *whack* echoed in the room as his hand sprang to the offended cheek.

"What was—" he began.

"Support the Prime Commander," she instructed him in a calm voice but one that would tolerate no disagreement. "Not because he's my nephew but because that is your job. Help get this world back to normal."

Rostropovich hesitated.

"Go ahead," said Theresa, nostrils flaring, barely holding back her revulsion. "Turn the other cheek. My other hand is just as strong."

The Primus bowed his head. In shame, apparently, though it might simply have been a ploy to make her leave. But she had made her point, and having made it, she got up and left Rostropovich's presence.

The last blow in the long defense of the colony had been struck. As Theresa left the Citadel, she prayed she would never have to strike another.

EPILOGUE

Warlord Knahs goes berserk.

"They have survived?" he bellows. "The Vermin upon our Holy World have survived and your genetically bred creatures"—he turns his ire on the High Chancellor—"are wiped out? And you expect me to . . . what? Simply accept this development?"

"It is hardly a complete loss," the High Chancellor assures him. "Our telemetry has provided us all manner of information as to the strengths and weaknesses of the Vermin. Yes, granted, they remain on Zantenor's surface, but that state of affairs is not going to continue. The next time . . ."

"No," the Warlord shouts. "No next time! This time!" He stalks toward his warriors and says with a snarl, "Process attack vectors! Prepare for direct attack on the Vermin!"

"Sir," his second in command tells him, "this is a pilgrimage vessel! We do not have the necessary armament to bomb them."

"We're not bombing them! That's already proved inefficient. We're going down there and disposing of them by hand, as we should have done ages ago!"

"But sir!" His second in command is visibly trembling. "The gods would abominate us for our actions!"

"They already abominate us for our weakness!" His fists clenched, he speaks with thunder in his voice. "I will lead the assault myself! We will descend upon Zantenor, and we will lay waste to the Vermin once and for all! And if any of you has anything to say about it, speak up now!"

No one in his crew says a word.

Instead, as one, they pull out their weapons and open fire.

The Warlord never has a chance. He is blown to shreds, pieces of him flying every which way. The mass of charred meat that collapses to the floor is barely recognizable as a member of the Krezateen, much less as the Warlord.

The High Minister and the High Chancellor regard the remains on the floor. "Well, that was predictable," says the High Minister dispassionately. He glances at the second in command. "Set a course for home. And someone please clean up this mess."

As the others scramble to do as instructed, the High Chancellor and the High Minister walk away from the site of the Warlord's ill-advised final stand. "Overall, I thought the creatures performed quite well," the High Minister says consolingly. "We could not have expected the Vermin to develop some new manner of weaponry to counter them. Had that not happened, the Vermin would surely have been annihilated."

"Whatever they develop, we will overcome it," the High Chancellor says with utter certainty. "Let the Vermin celebrate their victory. In the long, storied history of Zantenor, they will be as nothing—not even a shadow of a shadow. We will learn from our experience. What we create will be faster, stronger, more deadly. In the end, we will devise a creature capable of cleansing Zantenor as our faith commands."

"Yes," says the High Minister. "Not just a predator this time.

"*A perfect beast.*"

The Skrel continued to refine the Ursa, making modifications and sending more of their horrid creations to Nova Prime. Each time, the United Ranger Corps fought back, but not without tremendous sacrifice and loss.

Finally, in 980 AE, Ranger Cypher Raige did something no human had ever done before. He mastered his fear so completely, he was effectively invisible to the Ursa. In the following twenty years, six others also demonstrated this skill.

Here are three of their stories.

The remaining three can be found in the *After Earth* novelization.

AFTER
EARTH

Ghost Stories

HUNTED

Peter David

The Earth is a distant memory, abandoned by humanity during a time of ecological catastrophe millennia ago. Humankind's descendants found a new home on a world they named Nova Prime. There they thrived and grew, until the arrival of an aggressive alien species humans dubbed the Skrel, who attacked the survivors relentlessly for years. But humankind fought back with unfailing determination, led by the valiant United Ranger Corps, and resisted the Skrel's best attempts to wipe them out. The war persisted off and on over centuries, and then the Skrel genetically engineered a weapon of mass destruction—one that would test Ranger determination and resourcefulness like no other.

I

The Ursa lunged, its mouth wide and slavering, letting out a deafening roar designed to paralyze its prey upon attack.

On first sight, it seemed to be nothing but mouth. Its gaping maw could easily have swallowed Daniel Silver whole. If chewing was required, that wouldn't be an issue, since its mouth was crammed with massive fangs. It propelled itself forward on twisted, muscular legs, its talons providing it traction on any terrain.

It was the most formidable, devastating predator on the whole of Nova Prime, and it was bearing down on Daniel with the speed and force of a hurricane.

Without hesitation and unfazed by the creature's speed, Daniel brought his pulser to bear. He was in a partial crouch in order to gain greater steadiness, and he held the pulser in a firm, double-handed grip. His eyes narrowed slightly and he fired off half a dozen quick shots. The Ursa attempted to dodge them, but Daniel adjusted without even thinking about it, each blast hitting home with unerring accuracy.

The Ursa flipped over onto its back. Its legs trembled violently as it let out an ululating howl of agony, and then with one final wail, a death rattle sounded in the creature's throat.

Suddenly the Ursa began to flicker. A faint buzzing noise accompanied the flickering.

And the monster disappeared.

Daniel twirled the pulser a few times before sliding it into the holster on his hip. There were a few appreciative whistles and a smattering of applause, and Daniel bowed in response.

There were many sharpshooting ranges throughout the city. It was a leftover from the more militaristic days of Nova Prime, when everyone was expected to be proficient in small-arms fire. Recent generations had come to rely more heavily on the Rangers, whose training had become more refined and Ursa-centric, thus allowing the balance of the population to pursue less violent vocations. Nevertheless, weapons practice was ingrained into the mentality of the Novans; you couldn't be too prepared for an Ursa incursion, after all, and even the Rangers couldn't be everywhere. The range where Daniel preferred to practice was one of the smaller ones in Nova Prime City, but its technology was absolutely state-of-the-art. Like many of the larger ranges, it carried a sizable selection of holographic targets for users to choose from, but there was no denying that the most popular of them all was the Ursa.

Daniel and the other shooters were standing behind a counter that ran the length of the gallery. The holographic targets were on the other side and would snap into existence at random moments, charging at equally random times from different directions. Glowing numbers at the far end of the range displayed each shooter's success rate, and Daniel's was the only one at 100 percent.

Daniel was over six feet tall, so long and lean that his teen years had been hellish. He'd been constantly tripping over his own feet until his body finally got itself sorted out. Now in his early twenties, he had brown hair so long and shaggy that he sometimes tied it back to keep it out of his eyes. He was all wiry muscle that seemed to develop naturally without his doing the slightest thing in the way of working out. His most charming asset was his ready smile, which he flashed now at the others who were complimenting him on his accuracy.

"You are incredible, Danny," one of them said. "No Ursa stands a chance with you."

"I know, I know. It's a gift. What can I say?"

"You can say it doesn't mean a thing."

It was Tucker who had spoken. Tucker, the guy who owned the place. Short, squat, and barrel-chested, he walked slowly toward his customers. He had no choice in the speed of his gait; his right leg was artificial, causing him to lurch sideways. "Sure," he continued, "you can pat yourself on the back and talk about how great you are and take all the bows you want. But all the pulser blasts in the world won't slow down an Ursa. Not in real life. I know because years ago, I was as stupid as any of you, and when I ran into one of those things I figured I could handle it. And I was damned lucky that it only got my leg, because I wouldn't have lasted more than another second at most. And if the Rangers hadn't shown up just before that second, there'd be no one standing here to tell you idiots that you shouldn't get too damned cocky. Fun and games are fine, but this"—he gestured around the shooting range—"that's all this is. So don't any of you get any fool notions in your head about taking on one of these in real life just because you can pop a few good shots in its head in the comfort and safety of a shooting range. Because you know nothing about nothing. Understood?"

Heads bobbed in response and there were mutters of "Yes, sir."

Daniel's smile didn't come quite so readily as he put the pulser down, feeling an unaccustomed sense of chagrin. But he quickly brushed it aside. Daniel had never been much for allowing himself to be brought down, or at least not for long. It just wasn't in his nature.

So his smile quickly returned, and that seemed to annoy the hell out of Tucker. "Did you hear anything I said, Danny? Does anything matter to you?"

And the smile broadened even more. "Ohhh, yeah. One thing. And that's more than enough. In fact . . . I feel like I have to tell someone. So I'm telling you, Tuck . . ."

"Me? And to what do I owe this honor?"

"Because you're the closest thing I have to a friend. So here it is: I'm proposing to Ronna."

"You are?"

"Yup."

Tucker put out a hand and shook Daniel's firmly. "Congratulations."

"Thanks. I appreciate it."

"No problem. Who the hell is Ronna?"

"I've told you about her. You must've forgotten . . ."

"I don't forget a thing, Danny. You've never mentioned a girlfriend. Or a boyfriend. I just figured you were, what do you call it . . . a hermoglodyte."

"I have no freaking clue what that is."

"It's someone who doesn't care about either sex."

"Kind of doubt that, but in any event, that's not me." He paused, his eyebrows knitting. "Did I really never tell you about her?"

"Not a word."

Daniel thought about it and then smiled again. "Well . . . maybe I just kind of liked keeping her to myself. Plus, you know, I tell you about her and then you're always asking how she is, and it becomes a thing."

"A thing?"

"A whole thing, yeah. And time goes by and you're asking me how we're doing, and if we're talking about getting married, and all that stuff."

Tucker stared at him. "Daniel . . . out of curiosity, in your own mind, just how much time do you think I spend giving a damn about your personal life?"

"Probably none."

"Try definitely none. Propose, don't propose. I absolutely could not care less."

"That's good to know, Tuck," said Daniel, and he strode out with that typical sway of his. Tucker watched him go and then shook his head.

"It'll never last."

II

The city was finally shaking off a lengthy heat wave, and consequently a welcome breeze was wafting through and taking much of the humidity with it. The smart fabric that composed the curved walls of the apartment was allowing the evening breeze to flow through it while keeping out the humidity. The apartment itself was sparsely furnished, the living room decorated with simple, curved chairs and a round table in the kitchen area. Daniel was looking in the other direction, gazing out through a window at the glowing residences of Nova Prime City that studded the landscape, a glittering testament to the resilience of humanity.

Across the room, Ronna was sitting at the table, picking at the remains of the dinner she'd prepared. She was quiet this evening, which was rather unusual for her. Normally, she was the chattiest person Daniel had ever known.

Finally, she broke the silence. Sounding as indifferent as someone could when they were relaying information, she said, "Someone called and left a message for you."

"Oh, yes? Who?"

"A guy named Ryerson."

Daniel thought about it a moment. He wasn't familiar with anyone named Ryerson. Except . . .

"Not Sigmund Ryerson."

"That's it. You know him?"

"I know *of* him. He's some well-to-do eccentric guy. Why would he be calling me?"

"He said he heard you were one of the best trackers in the city. He wants to go on an expedition."

"What kind?"

She looked at him levelly. "He said he wants to track down and kill an Ursa. Be the oldest non-Ranger on record to kill an Ursa."

Daniel was having trouble believing what she was saying. "Go out of his way to push his luck with an Ursa? That's nuts."

"You *did* say eccentric. Besides, you're a good shot."

"Yeah, but it's like what Tucker was saying earlier today: Blowing apart an Ursa in the privacy of a shooting gallery is one thing. Going in and maybe getting yourself killed . . . who needs that?"

"Okay, well, I told you that he contacted you, or tried to. The rest is up to you."

"That's fine, but I really don't have any plans to get myself killed, so . . ." He shrugged.

She returned to picking at the remains of her food as if the preceding discussion had never happened.

He couldn't take his eyes off her. Every day that he was with her was a blessing.

"I can't believe I'm lucky enough to have you in my life," he said, giving voice to his thoughts.

Ronna smiled, but it looked strained. She patted the table across from her. "Could you sit down, Daniel?"

"Sure can. My knees bend and everything." He did so eagerly, sitting with his fingers interlaced. "Actually, there's something I want to talk to you about. I've been thinking a lot about our relationship."

"Have you?"

"Yeah. Do you ever think about the night we met? At the bar?"

"Occasionally."

"There was that guy who was bothering you, and I was the bouncer and told him to knock it off. And he beat the crap out of me, which got me fired, and then you took me back here to take care of me . . ."

"Yes, Daniel, yes," she said with vague impatience. "I remember. I was there. Is there a point to this?"

"The point is that even if it hadn't been my job, I'd still have jumped in to help you."

"That's . . ." She closed her eyes for a moment, looking pained. "That's nice to know." He should have noticed it, should have realized that her mind was in a totally different place from his. But he didn't.

"But here's the thing . . ."

"There's a thing?"

"You're not happy."

She actually seemed surprised to hear him say it. "You know?"

"Sure I know. And I know why. It's because I haven't been willing to commit to you. And it's crazy of me not to, because you're the best thing that's ever happened to me."

"No, I'm not," she said, shaking her head vigorously. "I'm really not."

"Yes, you are." He slid the chair back, came around the table, and, to her confusion, dropped to one knee. He took her hand and, with as much reverence as he could muster, said, "I can't afford a ring right now, but listen to me . . ."

"Daniel . . ."

"Ronna, for as long as I've—"

"Daniel, I need you to leave."

He remained exactly where he was, his brain trying to wrap itself around what she had just said. He didn't let go of her hand initially. "You mean . . . you need me to go out and pick up something for you? Because if that's it then, sweetie, you know . . . not the best time because I was kind of in the middle of something here. So if you could just wait—"

"This can't wait, and I know what you're in the middle of. And yes, you're right, I've been unhappy, but it's not why you think." She'd tried to pull her hand away moments earlier but hadn't managed it. This time she did so with much greater force and freed her hand.

He didn't lower his; instead it just remained there in the air, as if he was trying to grasp something that wasn't there.

"Daniel, I've been thinking about this for a while, and we need to stop seeing each other."

He still hadn't fully processed it. "For how long?"

"For good. I need you to move out."

"But why? I mean, I knew you were distant . . . I knew you were unhappy . . . but I figured you were waiting for me to propose or something!"

"If that's what I was waiting for, I would have been dropping hints. I haven't been doing that."

"Okay, but . . . you haven't been dropping hints about *anything*. How was I supposed to know—?"

"You weren't. It's not you, Daniel. I swear it's not you. It's me."

"I'm not stupid, Ronna. Saying it's you is really code for saying it's me."

"Daniel, listen: You're nice. You're sweet . . ."

"Both good reasons to dump me."

". . . but you have no direction! I mean, God, you can't even stick with a hobby!"

He was about to protest that characterization, but in looking around the apartment, he realized he couldn't. There was the half-finished sculpture of Ronna, thick with dust, from the time he was going to be an artist. Also dusty was the violin in the corner, a reminder of his broken resolve to become a musician. These and a dozen or so other unfinished, abortive projects that he'd never seen to fruition.

He gestured helplessly. "To hell with the hobbies. I want to stick with you!"

"So that I can keep enabling you! So I can keep making you feel better about going nowhere. You keep telling me how your parents said that you had no direction, no plan for your life."

"Right! And you said they were being needlessly cruel."

"No. They were trying to help. I see that now."

"Ronna," he said in frustration, "I can change—"

"Don't start, Daniel, because we both know you can't. Or won't. We've had variations of this conversation at least three times in the past year alone, and you nod and smile and say you'll change, and you never do. And you've managed to convince me that you never can."

His eyes narrowed. "Is there someone else? Are you dumping me for someone else?"

"No. But what I'm convinced of, Daniel, is that there's someone else out there for me that I won't have to push into making something of himself, because he'll have the drive to do it on his own." She took a deep breath and let it out slowly. "You're always going to mean a great deal to me, Daniel, but I can't be your support system anymore. It's not fair to you and it's not fair to me. You can send for your stuff once you've settled wherever you're going to be, but I need you to leave. Now."

His mouth moved and finally words managed to catch up. Barely above a whisper, he said, "I . . . I can't believe you hate me this much . . ."

"I don't hate you, Daniel," she said with a sigh. "I just feel sorry for you. Is that how you want to live? With someone who feels sorry for you?"

If it means not losing you? Yes. A million times yes.

But he didn't say that. Instead all he said was, "I have nowhere to go."

"I honestly hope, Daniel, that you find a path because . . . as much as I hate saying it . . . you've been going nowhere for a long time."

Long after he walked out into the darkness of the streets of Nova Prime, those words were still ringing in his ears.

III

Sigmund Ryerson was seated in his office behind his expansive desk, studying requests for funding that had come through the Savant in the Science Guild. He liked science. He liked the discovery of things, and to see what humankind was capable of accomplishing if only given the opportunity to do so.

Then came a gentle knock upon his office door. He did not respond with words, but simply looked up curiously. His gray, owl-like eyebrows knit as he gazed at his assistant, Myers, with an unspoken question upon his face.

"A Daniel Silver to see you, sir."

Ryerson frowned even more deeply and ran his hand along his smooth pate. "That name sounds familiar . . ."

"Your expedition, sir."

"Oh, of course." Ryerson snapped his fingers with impatience. "I swear, I'm going senile, Myers. Send him in, by all means."

At which time the most bedraggled, devastated-looking individual Ryerson had ever had the misfortune to see walked through the door. He looked like he'd gone three rounds with death and come up the loser, but was too blind to realize it.

"Let me guess," said Ryerson before Daniel could even get a word out. "Your girl dumped you?"

Daniel blinked in clear shock. "How did you—?"

"Know?" Ryerson chuckled, a deep, throaty laugh.

"Son, when you've been around as long as I have, there's not much you don't know. Every expression, happy or sad, exultant or devastated, that I've ever seen in my life has—at some point—been on my face as well. That's what you get for living longer than most of your peers. And the she-broke-my-heart look is one I know all too well. Back when I was a young man, Lord knows I saw that expression enough in the mirror. Trust me, when you get older, your priorities change. Sit down, sit down. Make yourself at home."

Daniel slumped into the chair that had been indicated.

"I'm not going to insult your intelligence, son," Ryerson went on, "and tell you that there'll be another girl along, one who will appreciate you in a way that this other girl never did."

"I don't blame her for not appreciating me," said Daniel in a hollow voice that would have been the envy of a spirit emerging from the grave. "I'm not worth appreciating."

Ryerson shook his head and laughed once more. "Boy, she did a serious number on your head. And—correct me if I'm wrong—but I'm guessing that you've come to me because you want to do something about shaking that number out, am I right? Namely, coming along on my little trip."

"How many on this excursion, anyway?"

"Seven men lined up. Some of *the* best sharpshooters on Nova Prime. And me makes eight. Now, I've heard great things about you, Silver. That you are a superb marksman, which naturally is of vast importance. Also an excellent athlete. And, most important, a superb tracker. Ursa have such fantastic powers of camouflage that we need someone along who can tell when we're deep in their territory. From all accounts provided me by various men whose word I trust—men who have hired you for their own hunting expeditions—that would be you."

"Yeah, but I've never been on an Ursa-hunting expedition. Whatever else you may have hunted, I can assure you that Ursa are something else entirely."

"I'm something else entirely, too, Silver," he said with a broad smile. "My preparations will be completely thorough. I've spared no expense. I'm told you have rugged determination, abundant confidence, and a devil-may-care attitude. That's exactly the type of man I'm looking for. And if you were to come along, be our guide, that would make it a nice even eight in the party."

"Eight's my favorite even number, sir."

"I think you'll find my payment quite generous."

"I don't give a damn about your payment, sir. When are we doing this?"

"My little party is set to head out two days from now."

"Then just let me stay here for two days and we'll call it even."

"You, sir"—Ryerson stood up and extended a hand—"have yourself a deal."

Daniel shook it. It was thick and sandpapery, the hand of a man who was not the least bit daunted by heavy labor. For some reason, Daniel took comfort in that. The expedition being proposed was hardly one to be undertaken by a man who had lived a soft life.

"And as for your girl," said Ryerson, "here's my best advice: Don't worry about her. Women are like buses: There's always a new one coming along."

"That's comforting to know, sir." Then he hesitated and said, "What's a 'bus'?"

"Some old Earth thing. How about a drink?"

"That would be excellent."

They drank some of the best alcohol that Daniel had ever tasted. Ryerson's private stock, or so he was told. Feeling the hot liquid burning down his throat, Daniel tried to convince himself that everything was going to be all right. That Ryerson would be correct and a new girl, a better girl, would come along. One who wouldn't shred every bit of his self-confidence as if it were Ursa chow.

And when he finally had had enough to drink and was led to the bedchamber where he would be staying, he collapsed into the bed and resolved to dream about Ronna. Because if he couldn't have her, at least he could dream of her as he had so many times before, even when she was lying right next to him.

There were no dreams of her that night, though, and it was only upon waking in the morning that Daniel realized that she was really, truly, and completely gone.

IV

The Tangredi Jungle was situated on the other side of the planet from Nova Prime City, although high-speed transport made it fairly easy to get to. Normally it was a popular place with hikers and campers, but there had been recent reports of killings that could only be attributed to Ursa. Bodies ripped apart, or devoured with just bits of bone and flesh left to indicate that they had ever been there at all. Consequently, the Rangers had declared the area completely off limits to citizens of Nova Prime. It was an edict that made perfect sense; no reasonable individual would even think of disobeying it. The Rangers patrolled the area with some regularity, so you would have thought that any sort of hunting party through the Tangredi was an act of insanity. If the Ursa didn't get you, the Rangers bloody well would.

This was a prospect that didn't deter Ryerson in the least.

Daniel wasn't quite sure what to make of that. What possible reason could there be for a man as high up on the food chain as Ryerson to risk being arrested, not to mention perhaps slain by an Ursa? It just didn't make any sense to Daniel.

None of which changed the fact that he was busy crawling around on the ground, looking for some sign that an Ursa had been through the area recently; perhaps hours earlier.

Ryerson was leaning over Daniel's shoulder, watching him with intense curiosity. Daniel was clad in an up-to-date camouflage outfit, as were all of them. It seemed only fair, after all. The Ursa were fully capable of blending in seamlessly with their backgrounds, so why shouldn't human pursuers have that same advantage?

Ryerson's hired hunters were spread out through the jungle, but they were not so unwise as to be in a position where the Ursa could pick them off one by one. Instead they were moving in groups of two, covering each other's backs. To counteract the reputed camouflage abilities of the Ursa, each of their pulser rifles—nothing less would do the job—was equipped with a thermal sighting device. This should give the group a drop on any overconfident Ursa operating on the mistaken assumption that their camouflage would protect them.

"You closing in on one of the bastards, Silver?"

"I'm seeing definite signs, sir. Like right here." He tapped a small pile of dirt in front of him.

Ryerson looked puzzled. "Like what there?"

"Ursa bury their feces. Makes them tougher to track, or presumably they think so. The result is little dirt mounds that look just like this. Also I've seen traces of what looks like the talons of an Ursa in the dirt. I could be wrong. It could be some other predator, one considerably less dangerous."

"But you don't believe that to be the case."

"No, sir, I do not," he said firmly.

"Good lad. Looks like I made the right choice," Ryerson said with a degree of self-satisfaction. "You certainly know a great deal about them."

"I read a lot," he said, his voice flat. He paused and then said, "Mr. Ryerson, what are we doing out here? I mean, really? Are you—?"

"Am I what?" When Daniel didn't respond immediately, Ryerson cracked a smile. "Did I just get a diagnosis from my doctor that my time's up? Or am I terminally suicidal and depressed? Something like that?"

"Something like, yeah."

"Sorry to disappoint you, son." Ryerson thumped his

chest. "But I'm in the pink of health. Nothing wrong, at least that I know of."

"Then why?"

"Because it's the next thing."

"The next—?"

"The next thing I want to do. The next challenge that I could find. That's how you get somewhere, son: by seeing what remains to be done and then doing it. I want to be the oldest non-Ranger who has ever managed to kill an Ursa. If you ask me—which admittedly no one did, but that's never stopped me before—the Rangers are a bunch of arrogant, overconfident smug fools. Telling people where they can and can't go. Acting as if they are our only hope against the Ursa. I believe in self-reliance, Silver. Never a big fan of having someone else doing things on my behalf when I never asked them to, and then acting as if I owe them all some huge debt of gratitude. To hell with the Rangers. If you want a dead Ursa, then do it yourself. That's what I say."

"Well, I'll certainly do my best to help you achieve your goal."

"And what about you?"

Daniel was continuing to study the ground and was only listening with half an ear. "What about me what?"

"Feeling better about the girl trying to push you out of her life?"

"I don't care."

"That's the spirit!"

"No, you don't understand." He turned to look at Ryerson. "I don't care about anything. I'm nothing without her. Hell, I was nothing with her."

"Come on, Silver!" He chucked him on the shoulder. "Nothing good ever came from feeling sorry for yourself!"

I don't feel sorry for myself. I don't feel anything. That's the point.

"You're right, sir," he said, trying his best to inject some degree of emotion into his voice. "I'll try to remember th—"

That was when the deafening roar of the Ursa sounded through the clearing.

Ryerson jumped, startled. Daniel remained utterly calm, not providing any sort of visible reaction. To him, there was no reason for there to *be* any reaction. He had expected this the entire time. When you were leading people into the belly of the beast, there was no reason to be startled when the beast made its presence known. Indeed, he found Ryerson's shock and alarm to be mildly entertaining. *What did you expect, old man?*

It was impossible to tell from which direction the animal's defiant roar had originated as it echoed through the clearing. It seemed to be coming from all sides at once. Quickly Ryerson activated the wrist communications unit that would keep him in touch with his hunters. "Nickerson! Philips! Chang! Anyone! Report!"

The response was a babble of shouts, one overlapping the next.

"No sighting yet, but the foliage is rustling—"

"There's definitely one of them out here—"

"Could be two or three!"

"Something's moving!"

"I don't see any—oh my God!"

Shots fired. A truncated scream.

"This is Vale! Creighton's down! I saw it tear his head off!"

"Maintain position, Vale, we're coming!"

"Screw that! I'm out of—!"

The second, higher-pitched scream, Vale's, wasn't preceded by any pulser blasts at all. He hadn't managed to get off any shots. He'd only had time to die.

It was complete chaos. Ryerson was spinning like a top, hearing death and destruction all around him, not knowing in which direction to look. Another roar, two more screams. Marsh and Inigo, by the sounds of it. Ryerson had hired some of the best hunters on Nova Prime, and the Ursa—for what else could it be?—was picking them off effortlessly.

"What the hell is this thing?"

"I am not dying out here!" came a terrified declaration from Chang, right before he was proven wrong. He managed to get off three shots, a personal best for the group, before his death scream erupted over the comm unit.

Ryerson was encountering a severe depletion of nerve. His face was the color of curdled milk, his eyes wide with horror. He fired several random shots around him into the jungle. The only result that came over the comm unit was a startled yelp from what sounded like Nickerson, yelling, *"I'm shot! What idiot shot me?"* right before the roar of the Ursa sounded and Nickerson shrieked like a baby demanding to be fed. Then Nickerson's comm unit went dead, along with Nickerson himself.

"Silver, do something! Get me out of here!" Ryerson's voice was just above a whisper, his throat constricted. Everything was happening so quickly. It had been barely a minute since the Ursa had first made its presence known, and it was ripping through his entire hunting party with hellacious speed. Ryerson clearly hadn't yet been able to fully grasp what was happening.

Daniel simply looked at him with bland disinterest. "What is it about having a lot of money that makes people feel they are invincible?"

Ryerson shook his head in denial. "If that's what you thought, then why did you come? Are you suicidal?"

"No. Not especially." Daniel shrugged.

Suddenly a tree at the outer edge of the clearing shattered into splinters and there was the Ursa towering over them, not ten feet away. Several pieces of human bone were lodged in its teeth, and its muzzle dripped with blood and gore.

In the face of his impending demise, Ryerson—to his credit—did not flinch. The shrieks and the cries of death all around him had been overwhelming when he was dealing with things he couldn't see. Now that he was face-to-face with the foe, Ryerson rose to the occasion. It wasn't bravery so much as it was pure, gut-roiling desperation as he dashed diagonally across the clearing, firing his pulser repeatedly. *"Die, you son of a bitch, die!"* he shrieked as he fired over and over again.

The Ursa seemed more curious about him than anything, as if bewildered by this foolish little creature that thought it had the slightest chance against him. The pulser blasts rebounded off its hide. The direct hits actually left small scorch marks where they struck, but that was all. The beast didn't rock back or acknowledge the impact in any way. It just stood there, absorbing the assault, like a parent waiting patiently for a child to finish its tantrum before taking full control of its errant offspring.

For five seconds that seemed as if they stretched into five minutes, the Ursa simply took it.

Then it disappeared.

Daniel, mildly curious about the outcome, had the calmness of mind to see a faint shimmer rippling across the landscape. Ryerson, by contrast, could not keep his panic and confusion in check. He whipped his pulser back and forth frantically while shouting, "Come out here and get what's coming to you, you bastard! What's the matter? Can't take any more?"

My God, he actually thinks he was doing well against it.

Ryerson never saw the Ursa drop its camouflage and shimmer into visibility directly behind him. Daniel could have shouted out a warning, but he didn't bother. It was just prolonging the inevitable anyway.

Ryerson had no time to react as the Ursa's maw enveloped him down to the waist. His scream was muffled and then silenced as the monster's jaws slammed together with a sound like an ax chopping into the side of the tree. Ryerson was bitten clean in half. The creature tilted its head back and Ryerson's head, arms, and torso all vanished into its gullet. His lower body actually stood there for a moment, looking ludicrous, before it collapsed. It lay on the ground, the remains of Ryerson's internal organs seeping out and soaking the ground in red.

Then the Ursa made a deep coughing sound, like a cat about to toss up a hairball. Sure enough, its mouth opened wide, and it regurgitated Ryerson. The man's upper half had already been partly processed by whatever stomach acids passed for the Ursa's digestive system, and it was scarcely recognizable as human, much less Ryerson.

"Guess it doesn't do well with rich foods," Daniel said morbidly.

The comment caused the Ursa's head to snap around. The creature had no eyes, but it appeared to be looking right at him. It had doubtless reacted to the sound of his voice.

Daniel just stood there and stared at it. He wasn't going to provide the Ursa any more free guidance by speaking, but he wasn't especially concerned by the fact that it was looking his way.

He remembered the stories about how, when death is imminent, your life flashes before your eyes. Daniel waited for that to happen.

And it did, sort of.

The disapproving looks from his parents when he failed class after class. The stern anger from his father when he'd thrown him out once he'd turned eighteen, telling him that if he was going to get anywhere, he'd have to be on his own to do it, because otherwise he had no motivation. His mother standing there, sobbing, but doing nothing to countermand her husband's actions. There he was, crashing with various friends, getting on their nerves with his aimlessness, going from job to job, holding none of them, putting together no savings, wearing out his welcome again and again, always seeing that same look of disappointment.

And he hadn't cared.

The only one he'd ever cared about was Ronna, and eventually that same expression had been on her face as well. It didn't matter what the Ursa did to him; he was already dead, killed by that disappointed look.

Nothing matters without her. And I don't matter; she made that clear.

The Ursa slowly approached him, but it looked confused, as if—without the guidance of his voice—it couldn't tell where he was. Its foul breath washed over Daniel, and it was all he could do not to choke or gag or make some other sound that would surely pinpoint his presence for the Ursa.

Despite his indifference to his fate, Daniel couldn't help but be intrigued by what was happening. He was there, right there, in front of the Ursa, yet it seemed unable to zero in on him. Daniel held his breath, not for fear of being discovered and killed, but out of curiosity as to how long he could elude detection simply by doing nothing at all.

He had no idea how much time passed as they just stood there, predator and prey. The Ursa seemed confused and frustrated, certain there was something there but unable to figure out where it was.

Daniel realized he was still holding his pulser rifle in his right hand. He'd seen close-up how useless the weapon was against the Ursa. No wonder the Rangers used a techno-bladed weapon called a cutlass: The techno-filaments were so sharp that it was claimed a Ranger wielding this weapon could cut off your arm even if his thrust missed; supposedly the wind from the miss alone would get the job done. Daniel doubted this was true, but he knew from what he'd observed firsthand that pulsers did nothing against the creatures, while the pulser-less Rangers had many kills under their belts, so they must be doing *something* right.

Very slowly, just to see what would happen, Daniel leaned left, then right. The Ursa made no corresponding reaction. *My God, it really can't see me. At all.* Emboldened, he cocked the triggering mechanism of the pulser and then lobbed the ineffective weapon to his right. It landed ten feet away and, upon impact, went off.

Instantly the Ursa lunged toward the rifle, landing squarely upon it with its huge, taloned paws. Rather than try to depart the area, Daniel remained where he was, watching the Ursa with something that seemed utterly inappropriate to the situation: amusement.

Suddenly the Ursa's head snapped up. It let out a furious roar and for an instant Daniel wondered if somehow it had perceived him.

And then the entire clearing was alive with activity. It was a squad of Rangers, coming in from all sides, including one who leaped directly in front of Daniel, shoving him off his feet. "Get down!" ordered the Ranger.

"*You* get down! I was fine!" Daniel snapped at him, but nevertheless he remained on the ground. An Ursa he could handle; Rangers were officious jerks. No point in antagonizing them.

The Rangers converged on the Ursa, cutlasses at the ready. The Ursa didn't know which way to "look" first, its head snapping left and right. The Rangers moved with a fluidity that impressed even the cynical Daniel. They slashed, jabbed, attacked, and then retreated while others moved in to take their place. Daniel remembered, in one of the many courses he'd ultimately failed, reading about prehistoric humankind back on Earth, when hunting parties of men would assault creatures many times their size using their spears and their sheer numbers to accomplish their goal. Daniel suspected that it was much like this: attacking from many directions, then pulling back, and then assaulting their prey once more so that the animal wasted its energy defending the feints while being wounded by the strikes that did land.

A dozen seeping wounds had appeared all over the Ursa's hide. It tried to disappear, to hide behind its camouflage, but the Rangers would have none of it, anticipating its path and striking even though they were only approximating where it was. Yet somehow they managed to hit home with their attacks.

Finally the creature let out a roar so thunderous that the ground under Daniel's feet seemed to shake. Then, gathering the power in its haunches, the Ursa leaped straight up, high over their heads, its trajectory carrying it deep into the brush. Seconds later it was gone.

"Secure the perimeter," said the Ranger who appeared to be in charge. "Make sure no other damned fools decide that hunting an Ursa is a game for amateurs." With this comment, he looked disdainfully at Daniel.

"Don't glare at me, big man," Daniel replied laconically. "I was just the hired help. This wasn't my party."

"Then whose?"

"Ryerson."

"Sigmund Ryerson?"

"The very same."

"He's under arrest, then. Where is he?"

"There," said Daniel, nodding in one direction, and then gesturing in the other, "and there."

The Rangers saw on opposite sides of the clearing the regurgitated remains of Ryerson's upper half and what was left of his lower half. Several wrinkled their faces in disgust.

The officer stared at him for a long time. Then he turned to his subordinates and said, "Call in a detail to clean up this mess. And have him"—he pointed to Daniel—"brought to my office."

"Sir, yes sir," they chorused.

Office? Why his office? If they're going to arrest me, why not just clap me in jail and then schedule an appearance before a magistrate? An office makes it sound as if we have something to talk about. What could we possibly have to talk about?

V

"You're a Ghost."

The ranking officer who had told his people to bring Daniel to his office had introduced himself as Captain Freed. He had black hair that was graying at the temples, and the air of someone who looked older than he was. Daniel had chosen to remain standing when Freed had entered and, despite Freed's invitation to do so, Daniel had declined to sit. Freed shrugged when Daniel stayed on his feet, and then went around to the far side of his desk and sat. Daniel considered this a small triumph for some reason. He was standing, Freed was sitting. Freed was in a subordinate position to him. *I win.* It was a small, petty victory, but Daniel took whatever victories he could get. He felt smug and in charge, right up until Freed came at him with this total non sequitur, at which point Daniel just stared at him in confusion.

"I'm a what?"

"A Ghost," Freed repeated.

"Well, obviously I'm not, since I'm still alive." Daniel spoke slowly, syllable for syllable, as if addressing an idiot.

Freed didn't appear to appreciate the tone, but he pushed past it. "Do you know how Ursa track their victims?"

"Since they don't have eyes, you mean? I've read that they have a powerful sense of smell, and that guides them."

"That's more or less correct," said Freed, tilting his

chair back while steepling his fingers. "But if that's the case, why didn't the Ursa catch your scent and attack?"

Daniel shrugged. He really hadn't given it any thought.

"In the case of their prey, Ursa smell the release of pheromones generated by fear. They home in on fear and destroy the source. If, on the other hand, you can completely control your fear—or if you literally have no fear, for that matter—then you can effectively be invisible to an Ursa. It won't be able to perceive you. You'll be like—"

"A ghost."

"Exactly. It's a very rare ability. Our Rangers are as brave as humans can be, but to be able to disconnect from fear . . . it's a rare gift. And it's obvious that for whatever reason—temperament, happenstance, or simply the way your brain is wired—you possess it."

Despite his general distaste for the Rangers, Daniel found himself intrigued by what the captain was telling him. "Yeah? And just out of curiosity, exactly how many people have this gift?"

"Counting you?"

"Sure."

"Two."

Let it be a girl. Let her be gorgeous. Please tell me I have to breed with her to produce a race of fearless baby Rangers. "Who's the other?"

"A Ranger named Cypher Raige."

"Cypher?" Daniel looked skeptically at Freed. "What the hell kind of name is *Cypher*?"

"Well, I suggest next time you see him, you ask him that, and when he pushes your teeth down the back of your throat, you'll have your answer."

He. Dammit. "Is he around?"

"He's patrolling the southern quadrant at the moment. Heavy Ursa infestation there. As many Rangers as we have, we're still spread thin, so we send people where we can. But to get back to the point, Mr. Silver: It's obvious you can ghost. We saw it."

"You *saw* it?" Something suddenly occurred to him.

"You mean the whole time that thing was up in my face, you were just watching to see what happened? Did you just stand by and watch Ryerson die, too?"

For a moment, Freed looked less than comfortable. "We arrived too late to save him, but we got there in time to see you ghosting with the Ursa threatening you. I made the call to keep our forces back so that I could see whether you could sustain that status."

"And if I couldn't?"

"Then we'd have done our best to save you."

"So you risked my life without my even knowing it."

Freed's voice became harsh. "No, *you* risked your life while knowing exactly what you were doing. It's not the job of the Rangers to take responsibility for reckless decisions on the part of the citizenry. If you had died, you would have been just another dead citizen who thought that he knew better than the Rangers of Nova Prime. But if you survived, then you'd be someone who could be of tremendous service to your people. And that's where we stand right now."

"Meaning—?"

"Meaning I'm inviting you to become one of us, Mr. Silver. I'm giving you the opportunity to become a Ranger. I've taken the liberty of pulling your medical records . . ."

"That stuff's supposed to be private!"

Freed smiled thinly and chuckled as if the notion of keeping secrets from the Rangers was quaint. He tapped his monitor screen. "You're in perfect physical health. You have a good deal of stamina. You're athletic. You are, in fact, an ideal Ranger candidate and I'm frankly surprised you haven't enlisted before this."

"Who said I'm enlisting now?"

"No one," said Freed, spreading his hands wide. "I could point out, of course, that by ignoring a priority one Ranger directive you are in fact a criminal. You and your entire hunting party. The others are beyond Novan justice, but you aren't."

"So if I don't join up, you'll prosecute me? Is that it?"

Freed's face was unreadable. *Never play poker with this guy,* thought Daniel.

"No, Mr. Silver," Freed finally said. "I won't have anyone on the Rangers who isn't dedicated to the cause and isn't here of his own free will. And, trespassing aside, your main crime is stupidity. If we start arresting people for that, half the population will be in front of a magistrate. So you're free to go home, Mr. Silver. Just for our records, where *is* home, by the way?"

Daniel opened his mouth and then shut it again.

"Yes, as I thought." He actually sounded gentle, even understanding. "You know, Daniel, the streets can get cold at night. Very cold. There are public shelters, as you know, but they don't always attract the best elements. So as homes go, you can do far worse than the Rangers. Will you think about it? At least promise me that in exchange for my not throwing your ass in a cell."

"Yeah. Sure. Fine. I'll think about it," said Daniel. "But just because I don't have a home address listed, don't think for a minute that I've got nowhere else to go."

"That's good to know," said Freed.

He thought about it for exactly one night. A night when he walked through downtown, the winds whistling harshly through the canyons of the city. He saw the apartment buildings glowing softly against the darkness, imagined people going through their happy lives. Eating, drinking, smiling together. Lovers' bodies entwined with each other. Children sitting at the feet of their parents, hearing stories about the past of Nova Prime.

He wondered if Ronna had found someone new already. Hell, there was probably someone already lined up when she dumped him. She probably felt she had wasted enough of her life with him and couldn't wait to move on.

He took refuge for the night in Tucker's firing range. He'd crashed there a few times, particularly when he'd gotten drunk at a bar—as happened from time to time—and wanted to get sobered up before Ronna saw him; she hated when he was drunk. It was after hours, but Daniel knew the lock's combo and entered, closing the door firmly against the harsh winds.

He sat there in the darkness for a time and then started running a holographic simulation. It involved a family having a picnic that was disrupted by incoming Skrel attack vessels. Daniel rigged it, putting it into a loop so that the Skrel never arrived. It was just the family—father, mother, son—locked into a pleasant outdoor meal, enjoying one another's company, laughing and joking.

It was completely artificial, and yet it was more than Daniel had ever known.

Daniel Silver had never felt more alone in his life than he had at that moment.

The next morning Captain Freed arrived at his office to find Daniel waiting for him.

"I still think you're all a bunch of idiots," said Daniel without preamble, "but I'm starting to think that I am, too. So maybe I'll fit right in."

"Believe it or not, I've heard worse reasons to join the corps." Freed put out a hand and Daniel shook it reluctantly but firmly. "Welcome to the Rangers."

VI

The recorded sounds of trumpets flared across the sky, and Captain Green was reading out the list of names of those who had graduated Ranger training with honors. The loudest applause, however, came for Daniel Silver as he stood resplendent in the white uniform denoting his status as Ghost.

Captain Freed had handed him his cutlass as Green continued to intone the names of the graduates. Daniel snapped off a sharp salute in response. It was impressive that he was receiving so much of an ovation, considering he had no outside friends or family there. The corps was where all his friends were. The corps was his family.

Before Daniel could step farther down the line, Freed leaned forward and said to him softly, "Fastest trainee in the history of the Rangers. You should be very proud."

"Thank you, sir."

"Your parents should also be proud."

"I'm sure they are."

Freed glanced toward the stands. "Are they here?"

"No, sir."

"Why not?"

"They think I'm a bum, sir."

"Do they." He paused and then said, "Silver . . . I can't account for the man you might have been. But I know the man you are now. The one who, as a Ghost, has been monitored over every step of his progress.

Your evaluations indicate the same thing: You started off slowly, but as time passed, your interest in helping your fellow cadets developed very quickly and very naturally. You moved in natural formation, and your desire to protect others in your squad was instinctive. The general consensus is that you see the others, not as your fellow Rangers, but as your family. Feel free to correct me if I'm wrong."

"You're . . . not wrong, sir," said Daniel, his voice husky.

"I never am," said Freed. And he tossed off a brisk salute that Daniel, displaying some confusion, returned.

Minutes later he was standing alone, whipping the cutlass back and forth. He felt a swell of emotion: He had worked toward something and now he was holding it in his hand. He'd accomplished his goal; the cutlass was the proof of that. It created a vicious arc in the air as he snapped it around with expert dexterity. He looked at it with pride.

With accomplishment.

With naked fear.

I'm a fraud, he thought.

He thought of all the times on the obstacle course as he pushed his body to do more than it ever had before. He pounded across it leaping, jumping, and scrambling, avoiding or dealing with anything that they threw at him. With every new challenge that he met, he felt a surging rise of confidence in the things his body was capable of doing.

Fraud.

He took classes in self-defense, in combat, in survival. He further honed his mind and body, faced off against his fellow cadets in sparring duels, each of them wielding practice cutlasses. Daniel took to the practice as naturally as an infant did to breathing: All he'd needed was that initial slap on the behind and then he was doing it as well as anyone and better than most. His mastery of the cutlass, once he had been drilled in the basic moves, was absolute. Long after other cadets had gone lights-out, he would be outside, stripped to the waist and whipping the practice cutlasses around so fast they were nothing more than a blur. His muscle memory became so drilled into him that his reaction time was measurable in nanoseconds. To attack Daniel Silver was to court disaster, because you would have your practice cutlass knocked out of your hand and your back on the floor before you even knew what happened. "Absolutely deadly." "Never make him angry." That was what his fellow cadets would say about him.

Fraud.

He walked across the field, newly graduated, and people automatically bowed or saluted whenever they saw him. No, not him so much as the gleaming white uniform denoting his status.

Fraud, fraud, fraud.

When he'd first undergone his psych evaluation, he had been entirely candid with them. He had told them flatly that he'd had no trouble ghosting because he was indifferent to whether the Ursa attacked him or not. He was worried this would disqualify him or be perceived as suicidal. Instead the conclusion drawn was that he was simply supremely confident, like an old Earth matador or animal trainer. Subsequent testing determined, to the satisfaction of the doctors, that—if nothing else—Daniel Silver *did* care if *others* lived or died. Were he in a situation where other Rangers were depending on him to save their lives, then he could be counted on to get the job done.

He had told no one of his relative indifference during the assault on Ryerson and his crew. He didn't consider it to be of any relevance. They were fools tempting a vengeful fate, and they had done so with an attitude so cavalier that the gene pool was well rid of them.

The Rangers, on the other hand . . .

His earlier contempt for the Rangers had long since dissipated. As one month rolled into another, Daniel became not only more and more impressed by the character and caliber of the Rangers, but thrilled and honored to be a part of the organization.

And the better he felt about the corps, the better he felt about himself. He had become part of a brotherhood, and he now had something to live for: to serve alongside them and help keep them alive to the best of his ability.

Fraud. Fraud. FRAUD.

"You okay?"

An arm draped around his shoulder. It was Martes, who was arguably the best friend he had in his squadron. Martes was tall, lanky, with a sense of humor that was funny mostly to him. When he'd first encountered Daniel, Daniel had been uncertain and a bit standoffish. This had proven an irresistible combination to Martes, who had taken it upon himself, for no reason that Daniel could discern, to drag him, "kicking and screaming," from his shell. Martes, as much as anyone and more than some, was responsible for the Ranger that Daniel had become, the one who had earned such unreserved compliments from Freed. Eventually Daniel and Martes had bonded during a particularly brutal survival training episode, and they'd had each other's back ever since.

The only frustration that Martes had met up with was when he'd tried to get Daniel to consider the romantic possibilities with some of the more comely female Rangers. Daniel had declined all comers. This had prompted Martes to wonder where Daniel's interests lay, but Daniel had informed him that, yes, females were his "outlet" of preference. At this point in his life, though, he just preferred not to. The fact was that Ronna had so destroyed him inwardly, he simply didn't want to open himself up to that kind of heartache anymore.

"Why, don't I *look* okay?" he said to Martes.

"Dan, this should be the best day of your life and you look like you're about to step off a cliff."

Wow. That is so on target it's not even funny.

"I've just got a lot on my mind."

"What else can you possibly have on your mind, aside from the obvious?"

"The obvious being?"

"We—you and me—are officially the hottest things on two legs. You are a Ghost, and I'm the friend of a Ghost, and we are young, sexy, and incredibly handsome. We are irresistible. Which means the sooner you get over your obsession with Donna—"

"Ronna."

"—the better off you're going to be. Because you, my friend, have a lot to live for!"

And that's the problem, isn't it, old friend, old buddy, old pal. What made me of interest to the Rangers is that I felt like I had nothing to live for. And over time, I found something to live for. And because of that, I might well get myself killed. Myself, and others.

Because I'm nothing but a great, big fraud.

VII

In the end, Daniel knew that it had to come back to here, back to the Tangredi. These things have a way of coming full circle. It started here and it's going to end here, too.

It had been a year since there had been any report of Ursa in the Tangredi Jungle. Ranger squads had continued to patrol there regularly for more than two months, but with no further encounters it was decided that—for the time being, at least—the area was clear. The most hopeful interpretation of the Ursa's absence was that the multiple wounds inflicted by the Rangers had done the creature in, but the corpse remained unfound and so it was generally conceded that thinking the creature was dead was, at best, optimistic.

And now it was back. Or, at the very least, something had taken up residence in the Tangredi Jungle. Since the previous incursion, the Rangers had installed pressure-sensitive bio-detectors at random points throughout the jungle. They had remained undisturbed for many months.

But then, exactly two weeks after Daniel and his squadron had graduated, something tripped one of the detectors. To Daniel's imagination, it was as if the Ursa were sending him a message. *Are you ready for me, Daniel? You may have fooled me last time, but now we both know you for what you are. Come to me, Daniel. It's time you joined Ryerson and his little friends.*

As absurd as it may have seemed, Daniel was secretly glad for the opportunity. He still felt as if he needed to prove something to Ronna's voice: the one in his head that continued to berate him and tell him that he would never amount to anything. If he could truly prove himself worthy of the designation of Ghost, the highest rank of the Rangers, then *that* would show her. And him. It would show once and for all that she was wrong to have dumped him and would go a long way toward mending his broken heart.

Martes was with Daniel, as were Rangers Xin, Ephraim, and Bastante. Three others—Calhoun, Ryan, and Stewart—had gone on ahead. He hadn't wanted any of them along; Ghosts typically hunted alone, and he didn't want to risk others in his squad if it wasn't necessary. But they wouldn't hear of it. "You're not going to take down your first Ursa without us around to have your back."

Captain Freed was heading up another squadron operating in another section of the jungle. Daniel desperately wished that Freed were with him, and had even suggested that Freed accompany their squadron, hoping he didn't sound too desperate when he put forward the idea. Instead Freed had clapped a hand on his shoulder and said confidently, "You're a natural at this, Silver. This is what you've been training for. You're going to be fine."

Daniel didn't feel fine. He felt like a liability.

Nevertheless, he didn't allow any of his inner turmoil to show. "We stay together," he informed his squad as they made their way through the jungle. "No splitting up. I'll be damned if this thing picks us off one by one."

"Roger that," said Ephraim. He was clearly somewhat nervous. He'd had as much training as anyone, but there was still that adrenaline-fueled worry when it came to being out in the field, chasing down the nightmare creature whose name was invoked to scare recalcitrant children when they wouldn't go to bed at night. Every single one of the squadron had been told, at some point in their lives, "An Ursa is going to get you if you don't behave."

They reached the clearing that Daniel knew all too

well. With a year gone by, there was no sign of the massacre that had transpired there. Daniel slowly surveyed the area and saw nothing, which of course didn't mean a thing. Yes, he'd seen the wavery image of the Ursa employing its chameleon camouflage the last time, but that was merest happenstance since he'd been staring right at it. He reached out with his senses, his tracking abilities, everything he could bring to bear.

Nothing.

"Keep going," he said tightly.

They moved in their smooth, practiced manner between the trees. They kept a lookout all around, listening for the slightest snap of a branch, the faintest rustling of a leaf. Anything that would betray the creature's presence, give them even as little as a few seconds' warning.

Still nothing.

"Starting to think we're alone out here," said Xin. She was clutching her cutlass tightly. Xin had been one of the most proficient wielders of the cutlass in class, and there was a look of grim determination on her face. It seemed to Daniel that she was actually anxious to take the creature on.

At least one of us is.

Daniel felt his heart pounding so hard that it was threatening to explode from his chest. He'd had no trouble maintaining calm detachment during training sessions where he was facing off against a simulated Ursa. No matter how realistic it was, it was to him no different than when he'd squared off against the holographic Ursa at the firing range. This, though, *was* different. This was people, men and women, depending on him. He wasn't sure which worried him more: losing his life, or letting down the others.

He was sure his knees were shaking. How could they not notice that?

A crack of a branch and everyone jumped, snapping into a ready position.

"Crap," muttered Bastante. He raised his foot slightly to reveal a branch on the ground that he'd just stepped on. Ephraim promptly punched Bastante hard in the shoulder.

"Stay sharp. No screwing around," said Daniel sharply. The others nodded, and there were muttered apologies from Bastante and Ephraim.

They kept moving, checking in with Freed's squad as they did so.

"I smell water," said Xin minutes later. "Up ahead."

She was right. Ahead of them, the ground opened out onto a wide lake. The water was glass-flat with nary a ripple. Under other circumstances, it would have looked inviting.

"Perhaps we should stake this out," suggested Martes. "Even Ursa have to drink, right?"

"I think so," said Bastante, "but you never know for sure with Ursa."

They drew closer to the lake's edge, and Daniel said, "Okay . . . here's what we do—"

He got no farther, however, as the Ursa exploded upward from beneath the water barely two yards in front of the gathered Rangers.

It emerged with such force and velocity that a huge gout of water erupted all around it. The water leaped up like a geyser and then cascaded down upon them with the weight of a dozen anvils, knocking them off their feet.

Daniel was reasonably certain it was the same Ursa that had attacked them a year ago. It sounded the same; he was even sure he could see scars on its hide from when the Rangers had assaulted it.

The Ursa landed squarely in the midst of the startled Rangers and let out a roar. It pivoted and went for Bastante, who was nearest. Bastante rolled backward, came up on his feet, and slashed his cutlass in a figure eight. The Ursa dodged left and then swept one of its talons forward. It sliced diagonally across Bastante's torso from shoulder to waist. Bastante shrieked and went down, blood pouring from him like a river. The Ursa backed up, and one of its hind feet touched up against Ephraim. Ephraim tried to bring his cutlass to bear, but he had no time; the Ursa simply stomped down on his head with its hind foot and there was a noise like that of a melon being crushed.

Everyone else was still trying to get to their feet, but the ground beneath them was soaked and they were slipping helplessly on the mud. The Ursa's head whipped around as it prepared to pick its next victim.

Daniel had managed to get to his knees. He knew the drill: The Ursa would lock onto a target and not be dissuaded from it until the target was dead. *Ephraim dead. Bastante down, likely dead. They're looking to me to protect them, and I can't, because I don't want to die and this thing's going to kill us all . . .*

What do you think, Ronna? Will this make you love me? Am I enough of a man now? Here I am in a steady job where I have to be prepared to die every day I go to work. If you knew, would you give a damn? Probably not.

All of that went through Daniel's head in a split second, distracting him not in the slightest from the situation at hand, and then he shouted, *"Here! Here, you eyeless bastard! Come and get me!"*

The Ursa locked onto him. He swore he could even see the flare of its nostrils. With a roar, the Ursa barreled toward him.

Daniel closed his eyes.

In his mind, the lake was gone. The Rangers were gone. The Ursa was gone. All that was there, against his eyelids, was Ronna.

I don't hate you, Daniel. I pity you. I pity you and myself for spending so much time with an out-and-out loser. Okay? That's what you are. That's all you are. A big loser. And you can say that people change all you want, but they don't. You were a loser when I met you, and you're a loser now, and you're never going to accomplish anything of any worth for anybody.

She had never said anything like that, but it didn't matter. In his own mind, he had built up his rejection to such heights that that's how she had made him feel, even if she hadn't actually spoken those words.

Everything that he'd felt at that moment—the humiliation, the lack of self-worth, the utter despair that overwhelmed him, the sense that nothing else would matter for the rest of his empty life—came roaring back to him. It was all he could do not to start sobbing.

He became aware of the foul breath of the Ursa upon him. He shoved himself even farther into the despair that Ronna had brought down upon him.

Then he realized the Ursa hadn't killed him.

Slowly he opened his eyes.

The Ursa was looking around, its nostrils definitely flaring. It was trying to find him. It was six inches away from him and didn't know where he was.

Daniel's cutlass was retracted. Very slowly, keeping the soul-crushing diatribe of Ronna fixed in his mind, reminding himself that he was a useless loser who had nothing to live for, he positioned the cutlass so that it was directly under the Ursa's jaw.

Then he activated it.

The blade drove straight upward at an angle, under the creature's chin and up through the roof of its mouth.

The Ursa was unable to roar because its jaw was pinioned shut. The creature's strongest muscles were the ones that closed its mouth; the muscles that opened it were somewhat weaker. That served to Daniel's advantage. The creature writhed and its talons flailed in the air as Daniel forced himself to his feet, pitting his strength against the Ursa's massive weight. It should have been an impossible mismatch, but Daniel was operating on pure adrenaline, and he felt as if he were drawing power from an endless supply. The Ursa was shoved upward, off its front paws. Daniel yanked the cutlass apart, activated the other half. He had to pull his arm back quickly because the Ursa's thrashing talons nearly took his arm off at the shoulder. Then, for an instant, he had a clear shot. He took it, activating the other half of the cutlass and driving it directly into the side of the Ursa's head, into its brain.

The beast shuddered violently. Even with its brain bisected, its nervous system was still firing. In its death spasms, it fell forward, and Daniel wasn't able to get away. It landed squarely atop him, and the only thing that prevented it from crushing him completely was the cutlass Daniel had shoved up under its jaw. Thick blood was drooling from its maw, dripping down on Daniel, and he made a sound of disgust.

Feeling Daniel beneath it, hearing his voice, there was no way the Ursa could miss him. It half rolled off him, and its flailing talons threatened to cut him to pieces.

And then the paw went flying, severed from the arm by Xin, who let out a cry of triumph as she swung her cutlass again and this time cut off the arm completely at the shoulder joint. Even as that happened, Martes charged forward and, disdaining to use his weapon, instead plowed into the Ursa like a linebacker. It knocked the creature clear of Daniel, and Xin and Martes quickly helped him to his feet. His legs almost gave way but he managed to maintain his footing. He gasped deeply for breath, and it took long moments for him to steady himself.

"I'm fine, I'm fine," he said brusquely. Then he informed Freed over his comm unit that they had killed the Ursa but had two Rangers down.

Within minutes they were being evacuated to Ranger headquarters. Ephraim was, of course, dead on arrival. Bastante managed to live three more hours before succumbing.

Daniel was at both their funerals. He kept his gaze level, his jaw stiff, and he spoke to no one for a solid week.

And when he finally did speak, it was to Martes, and it was only three words.

"Let's go drink."

Martes was happy to oblige.

VIII

"Hey, don't I know you?"

The bartender stared at the white-clad Ranger, seated next to another Ranger. The white-clad man had short hair, was clean-shaven, and had a look of quiet confidence about him. When the Ranger didn't reply immediately, the bartender said again, "Don't I know you?"

Daniel looked him squarely in the eyes. "No," he said softly, nursing his drink. "No, you don't."

The bartender's eyes narrowed; he clearly felt he was missing something that he should have been picking up on. Then he shrugged to himself and moved down the bar to attend to another customer.

Martes looked sidelong at Daniel. "Okay, where's he know you from?"

"Here. I used to be a bouncer here."

"A bouncer? You're kidding."

"I used to be a lot of things."

They had another drink and then Daniel decided he'd had enough of the place. He'd returned to that bar as much for personal amusement as anything else, but the novelty had worn off. "Let's get out of here."

"You got it, boss."

They slid off the bar stools and headed toward the door, emerging into the cool darkness of the Nova Prime night. As they started to walk away, a startled voice said, "Daniel? Is that—?"

He turned and, sure enough, there was Ronna. Her hair was shorter than he'd remembered, and she looked a bit more haggard, but otherwise she was more or less the same. Her eyes widened in astonishment. "My God, it *is* you. I thought I was . . . oh my God! You're a Ranger?"

"Sweetheart," said Martes, clamping a hand on Daniel's shoulder, "I'll have you know he is *the* Ranger. And who are—?" Then he saw the look in Daniel's eyes, the silent warning. "You're kidding. This is her?"

Daniel didn't have to reply to him; the answer was on his face.

"So . . . Ronna . . . how have you been?"

"Been okay. I guess."

He realized she wasn't looking him in the eyes. "Really?"

"Not really, no," she admitted. "I've been in and out of a few relationships, and, well . . ." She shrugged.

"They weren't going anywhere?"

She looked down. "I guess I deserved that. The truth is, lately I've been thinking about that night. You know: *that* night. And how terrible I was to you. And I was wondering if you're, y'know . . . busy? Maybe we could go somewhere and talk?"

He was silent for a long moment, studying her, thinking about her . . . thinking about what she'd meant to him, what she could mean to him again.

But he also thought about what he himself could mean for Nova Prime. And Ronna could fit into that, yes . . . but not in the way she was thinking.

For his purposes, he needed her to be not what she was now, but what she had been.

Forever.

Without a word, he started to walk away. Martes automatically followed him.

Ronna stood there, stunned. It took her a few moments to find words: "Daniel? Where are you going?"

And the last thing he said, before the night swallowed him and his fellow Ranger, was, "Actually, Ronna . . . I want to remember you just the way you are."

She looked stunned, but his back was to her and he never saw it.

AFTER
EARTH

Ghost Stories

PEACE

Robert Greenberger

"But he hit me!" the six-year-old wailed.

His mother, a stout, stern-looking woman with gray-ing hair tied in a bun, wrapped the crying boy in her arms, soothing him. She made shushing sounds to calm him and get his attention. "What have we taught you?"

"To turn the other cheek."

"And?"

"Not to hit back."

"Ever."

"Ever."

Hands slick with sweat grasped for the metal rungs of the monkey bars, refusing to let gravity win. Kevin Diaz was halfway across, making good time by his estimate, and was determined to finish. There was a bet riding on his outcome, and he meant to collect from Katya.

One bar, then another, as he made his way slowly across the magnetically suspended apparatus. This morning's testing was just one in a long string of mental and physical exercises at which he needed to excel in order to make it to Phase 2: a step closer to being a Ranger.

For as long as he could remember, Diaz wanted to be a Ranger above all else. They were everything he was not allowed to be. As a boy he marched alongside them during parades, his short legs hustling to keep up with the matched precision of the corps. When his parents weren't watching, Kevin would access the image library to watch clips of the Rangers in action. They seemed to be everywhere, and while, yes, there was danger, there was also excitement and adventure.

Being a Ranger was all he wanted to do and it was the one thing his mother and father both objected to. It was not something the family condoned. Peace was a lesson imparted from an early age—and one Kevin remained resistant to learning.

"You yelled at your teacher?"

His father walked back and forth in the kitchen, a tight pattern given the lack of space. He clearly was controlling himself, refusing to let his anger and frustration seep through. It was always about maintaining calmness and inner peace.

"She wouldn't listen to me," the seven-year-old Kevin explained in as quiet a tone as he could manage. Unlike his father, controlling himself had proven to be a problem. There had been previous outbursts and even fights. After each one, the scene would replay itself much as this was happening now.

"And that gives you the right to be disruptive? To show a lack of respect for your teacher? What have we always said?"

"To be humble before one's elders," the boy said mechanically.

"Were you humble?"

"No, sir," Kevin said.

"Kevin, our family left Earth determined to make a clean start. We vowed to do better, as a family and as representatives of humanity throughout the stars, It has been this way for a thousand years. Our ancestors held tightly to these ideals regardless of what has happened. When the Skrel found us. When they sent the Ursa to us. When we nearly had a civil war. We survived a great deal helping colonize this world, and the Diaz family . . ."

". . . is determined to be humble, to embrace peace and simplicity," Kevin finished.

"Were you demonstrating peace or simplicity?"

"No, sir."

* * *

"Have I made myself clear? Now go to your room, and no vids before dinner."

"Who did this?"

There was still blood dripping from Luis's nose as he kept his head tilted back and pushed a cloth against his nostrils to stanch the leakage. His mother held his other hand. She would have been tending to his nose herself, but Luis was a proud young man and insisted on doing it himself . . . although there was still enough of a boy in him to gain solace from her hand against his. Meanwhile, Kevin sat by, staring mournfully at his brother's injured face and flinching every time his increasingly irritated father demanded to know who was responsible. Finally Luis was worn down enough to shrug off the ancient school code of honor that discouraged snitching on one's classmate no matter the provocation. "Colm," he said.

"Colm. Colm who?" Luis and Kevin's father demanded.

"Colm Delahantey. We . . . go to school together."

"Kevin, tell me what happened," their mother said. "I don't understand."

Stifling tears, Kevin moved closer to his parents and spoke barely above a whisper. "Colm was picking on me at the playground," the ten-year-old said. "He followed me around, calling me names, even trying to trip me. I ignored him. Just like you taught me." It was a struggle to keep the bitterness out of his voice.

"So, what, he hit Luis instead?" his father interjected.

"No . . . it wasn't like that. Luis saw what was happening and came over. He asked Colm to stop, but by then Colm's friends were egging him on. They wanted a fight."

"Why on Earth did they want a fight?"

"I don't know!" Kevin screamed, all the bottled-up frustration finally erupting. "He's a monster! He has a disease! He was born evil! I don't know!"

His father softened at the outburst, clearly shaken. "This should never happen," he said in a gentler voice.

"No kidding," Luis said, and was immediately shushed by his mother as she changed cloths.

"I still don't understand. This boy wanted a fight and you gave it to him?"

"No, Dad, it was nothing like that," Luis said. "He was chasing Kev, the others were following him, and they were looking for a fight. I went to stop it."

"Just like you taught us," Kevin said once more and not without a touch of sarcasm, earning him an unhappy look from his father.

"Who threw the first punch?" his father asked.

"I was trying to get Colm to back off, but his friends crowded us . . . someone pushed me into him. He thought I attacked, and then he started swinging," Luis said.

"I think his nose is broken," Marisa said to Juan Carlos. "He needs a doctor."

"Let's go then," he said, rising. "This Colm can wait."

"Dad, it started as an accident, but Colm wouldn't listen. He just hit Luis again and again, and I just watched. I didn't interfere. I practiced our way," said Kevin.

"And you did well by not making a bad situation worse," the man said.

"But Luis has a broken nose. I could have stopped that!"

The father's eyebrows rose quizzically. "You sure of that? Do you know how to fight?"

"No."

"Sounds like this Colm does. Might be, there would have been two broken noses today."

"Dad, it's just wrong! I let my brother get hurt."

"No, you kept things from escalating. When you're ready, we can teach you ways to disarm the conflict."

"I don't want to disarm the conflict; I want to disarm Colm, like rip his arms off!"

Juan Carlos crossed the small space and grabbed his younger son by the shoulders. In a surprisingly soft *voice he said, "No, my boy. We don't fight. We don't strike back. We don't argue. We are better than that. We make our way through life in harmony with the surroundings. Colm was disruptive and will need punishment, but not with a brawl."*

"I know, it's our way. But you know what, Dad? I hate our way."

Diaz stepped out of the testing booth, grinning from ear to ear. "That was a snap!"

Katya Ronaldo, thin, blond, and adorable, smacked his arm in an affectionate way. She was standing in line, waiting for her turn in the chamber where knowledge of Earth and Nova Prime history was examined in addition to general information about the Rangers. The Rangers likewise traced their heritage to just before humankind had to leave their homeworld for good. So certain was Diaz in his facts that he volunteered to go first, wanting to get the testing over with.

Malcolm Velan, the barrel-chested examiner, consulted a small tablet in his left hand and then extended his right hand to the teen. "Nice work, you scored highest in your squad."

Diaz broke into a fresh grin as he pumped the extended hand.

"The highest so far," Velan added and spun on his heel, returning his attention to the next cadet inside the chamber.

"Pretty sweet work," Xan Minh said. The fifteen-year-old towered over Diaz, which gave him the advantage in many of the physical tests. The chamber was all about the mind, and there, Diaz excelled. Normally, he was content to ignore his parents and their teachings, but controlling his breathing, figuring out a plan of attack, and having confidence in himself certainly gave him the advantage at mental activities.

"It's a gift," Diaz said, looking at the worried faces

still waiting to enter the chamber. The randomized oral testing lasted twenty minutes unless the artificial intelligence needed to probe a candidate's knowledge deeper to make a final assessment. The process had been known to continue for around twenty-five minutes; the longest was thirty-seven minutes by a cadet who wound up repeating Phase 1 as a result. Diaz was in and out in just over twenty-one minutes, a personal best after weeks of preparation.

Months later, not long after the grueling Phase 2 trials were completed, Kevin Diaz rolled out of his bunk, careful not to wake Katya, who slumbered beside him. It was the big day and he couldn't sleep, too excited about the ceremony. He felt his pulse race as he anticipated the day, taking his three-minute shower, then carefully inspecting every inch of his Ranger uniform. As he buffed a button with a cloth, Katya, still in his T-shirt, stumbled into the common room.

"You'll blind me with the glare coming off those things," she murmured as she sought a drink.

"Just excited."

"Hunh. Couldn't tell," she said before taking a big gulp. She shook her head, but her close-cropped hair refused to budge. The normally dry air was somewhat humid, unusual for the time of year, and she always kept it short—shorter than even regulations demanded.

"C'mon, wash up and I'll make breakfast," he offered.

"I can unwrap my own protein bar, thank you."

"Well, hurry up then, it's the day."

"No kidding. I get it. Today we become Rangers. The Commanding General himself will be on hand to make a speech and maybe pat us on the head. I get it. Our parents will be there to cheer and snap pics. We celebrate, especially those of us in the top ten percent."

Diaz wanted to be number one, but had to settle for

top ten. He had easily passed the chamber testing and the physical skills. He won the bet and Katya had to actually go out on a formal date and wear her first-ever dress. They'd been together ever since.

He was, though, dunned by Velan for "excessive force" on the firing range. Rather than pick off the holographic Skrel soldiers, he fired a little too often, a little too wildly. Even now he recalled the free flow of adrenaline, the excitement of the adventure, letting himself get caught up in the thrill of the battle. Velan yelled at him for letting the phaser do the talking. Diaz started to yell back but his training caused him to painfully bite his tongue instead. Later that night, Katya teased him for turning beet red in anger, swearing she saw heat waves rise off his head.

That cost him number one, but his restraint kept him a Ranger.

He reached into the cabinet, pulled out the protein bars she liked, grabbed a round, bright red piece of fruit, and set them on the small table. The other cadets were finally stirring, so there was going to be a run on the showers and the food. Being up early had its benefits.

On the other hand, being up early meant having to wait for the ceremony to begin, and he was never good at waiting. He hurried Katya along so they'd have time to walk the grounds, burn off the nervous energy. In addition to the searing heat, there was excitement in the air. Not only did friends and family attend the graduation exercises, but lots of nearby residents turned out. Being a Ranger was prestigious—and it also meant they could glimpse Cypher Raige, the Prime Commander, perhaps the best-known person on Nova Prime.

Diaz and Katya walked the grounds, which were quiet. No one using the equipment, no trainers yelling at raw recruits. The air was still and the heat was rising. Nova Prime turned out to be hotter than anyone expected, and the honeycombed residences, built right into the mountains, offered some respite. But out here, the sun beat down on them, and he could feel the sweat run down his neck and spine.

"My uniform is going to wilt," he complained as they neared the grandstand where the event would commence within the hour.

"Velan will write you up," she teased.

"You think he will?"

"Yes, and then make you do fifteen laps, one hundred pull-ups, and hand sew a new uniform," she solemnly announced. "All before the ceremony."

"You forgot disciplining the insubordinate graduate," he said, reaching out for her, grasping her tiny waist and pulling her close. He took a deep sniff of her hair and was content. She centered him in ways his upbringing failed to do.

They had flirted from the beginning, and the romance was quick to spark. While fraternization was normally frowned upon among Rangers, cadets were given more latitude since they needed to support one another during the training and examination periods. Velan had made it clear that should both become Rangers, they would never be assigned together, kept as far apart as practical so they could focus on the job. If that didn't deter them, then marrying some time later might be acceptable.

Diaz blushed at the notion of marriage. Hell, he was just sixteen; his whole life was ahead of him.

"You're doing what?"

Diaz wasn't even sure if that was his mother or father talking. He had just come back from registering to join the United Rangers Corps on what he considered the proudest day of his life. With enthusiasm, he ran home, entered their apartment, and made the announcement before he could even say hello.

They were reading. They were always reading, stories of the days back on Earth, of peaceful solutions to dif-

ficult problems like when the populace nearly mutinied on the Asimov ark until they had the notion of resurrecting the Olympics, refocusing their energies. All his family had sought through the years was an elegant peace. Well, except for Kevin, who was bursting with enthusiasm.

Marisa, his mother, fell into a chair, her mouth open without a sound. Juan Carlos wrung his hands and then stuffed them into his pockets.

"I want to be a Ranger."

"My son," she began, then hesitated. "We always want what's best for you . . . but in keeping with our family traditions—"

"But the family traditions mean nothing to me," he snapped. "They never have!"

"Watch your tone," Juan Carlos said. He was a little older than Marisa, and with steel-gray hair. He was built to fight but displayed an incredibly gentle persona. "Kevin, you've rejected our ways for years now. There have been fights, incidents we had hoped you'd grow out of. You need to find our family's inner peace, the soothing of the soul that can guide you through life."

"It's never worked, Dad! I get into fights, I argue with people. It's who I am!"

"But it is not who we are. Living simply, without complications, has worked for generations and we've prospered as a family. Look at Luis, a successful architect and never once a bloody nose."

"Not since the fight."

Luis was four years older; he had been apprenticed at fifteen and was living away from home. The brothers had little in common and rarely kept in touch. Whenever an argument broke out, Luis was out the door to avoid the conflict. Just as he'd been taught. Somehow those lessons were lost on Kevin.

"No, not since then," his father agreed. "But since that day, you have ignored our lessons. Only after you have struck first did you then try to reason with people. Has it made you a better person?"

"I'm still growing up, I don't know what sort of a person I am yet. But I know I will be a Ranger."

With a heavy sigh, his father said, "I don't know what sort of person you're growing into. I'm pretty certain it's not one I like very much at the moment, and that pains me."

"Look, Mom, Dad, maybe being a Ranger is the best for me. There's training and a chance to do good."

"We trained you here," Marisa said, gesturing around their neat, Spartan home. "It seems not to have worked. How will they do a better job?"

"I don't know!" he shouted. "But you know it's what I've always wanted."

"And what we've always objected to," Juan Carlos added. "Still, you defy us and sign up."

"I won't quit," he said, gritting his teeth to avoid the tears he felt in the corners of his eyes.

"He signs up the first day he can and expects our support," Marisa said to her husband. Her own eyes glistened.

"I won't stop him," Juan Carlos said. "He's made a decision and has to live with those consequences. We taught him that, too. But Kevin, we cannot support you in this."

"I know, Dad," Kevin said in a strained voice. "But I want you to be proud of me."

"I'm not so sure we can," his father said quietly.

One by one, the cadets were paraded across the platform and given their badge of office. Cypher Raige, resplendent in his pure white uniform, without a drop of sweat despite the heat, shook hands and snapped off salutes. It was all very precisely, efficiently done.

Diaz was thrilled to watch his friends take their turns, although when Katya paused, turned her head toward her family, and flashed them a brilliant smile, he cringed. It was showy and unbecoming of an officer, but it was also a wonderful moment for her parents and siblings. He had looked for his brother, whom he hoped would at least be on hand, but failed at the task. Failing to accomplish something on graduation day was not the sort of harbinger he had hoped for.

Kevin Diaz heard his name and walked toward Raige. A nod, a handover of the badge, then a salute. And within seconds it was over. As he continued to cross, he stole a glance into the audience. Not a sign of his parents or Luis.

Anger and disappointment fought within his heart as he stepped down and resumed his seat, blinking back what he swore was sweat.

Being a Ranger was prestigious, but no one had ever told Kevin how tedious his job could be. There were routine patrols in and out of the city, always on the alert for dangers. For the last two years he'd rotated through the Ranger organization, being familiarized with how every division worked. He loved being on air patrol and hoped to gain his pilot's certification; he disliked patrolling the city perimeter, but enjoyed maintaining the armory, practicing with cutlasses. Kevin continued to dream of earning an assignment to one of the ships making the run to the anchorage on Lycia.

On this day, he was walking through the market, where Rangers were routinely present to keep the peace. While matters could get somewhat more out of control in the outlying regions, crime was ridiculously low in the first city of Nova Prime, so he contented himself with studying the wares out for sale. The craftsmanship reminded him of the straight, smooth lines Luis drew as an architect. Since they were both older now, they had matured and spoke a bit more often. Their worldviews were still far apart but they found enough common ground to get through the occasional meal.

He missed his parents, though. Since snubbing him at the graduation ceremony, the three had barely spoken. Kevin dutifully turned up for family events from holiday meals to funeral rites, but it was cold and stiff between them. Kevin regretted that but saw a chasm he wasn't sure how to cross. He kept hoping one of his parents would make the first move, but then got angry at himself for being a coward.

Kevin shook his head, visibly attempting to erase the sad feelings, when his comm unit squawked to life.

"*All Rangers, attention. We have an Ursa sighting north-northeast of the city. Be armed and alert. Details to follow.*"

"What's armed and alert?"

Kevin looked down to see a little girl, no more than four, in a flowing purple caftan. The girl's father was reaching for her when Kevin crouched to answer her question.

"Does your father tell you scary monster stories about the Ursa?"

She nodded, wide-eyed.

"The Ursa are the meanest, scariest monsters ever. They're real but they haven't been seen for a long, long time. You know why?"

She slowly shook her head.

"Because the Rangers chase them off every time they show their ugly faces. And what am I?"

"A Ranger?" She got the answer more from his prompt than any certainty.

"Yep, so now that they're back, I will chase them away from you and the city. Being armed means we Rangers use our cutlasses to protect people and kill monsters like the Ursa." With that, he withdrew his weapon and held it before the girl's huge eyes.

"And being alert means we keep our eyes and ears open, being on the lookout for the Ursa so we can get you to safety and keep them away."

The father pulled the girl into his arms, nodding in appreciation at how Kevin handled the situation. While Kevin felt good about it, he was concerned. The last such incursion was nearly fifty years ago. A hundred of the beasts had shown up, deposited on Nova Prime once more by the Skrel, and the Rangers lost a lot of good people back then. When everything was said and done, all but a dozen or so of the creatures were dead. The remaining Ursa vanished into the desert wilderness and with few exceptions had not been seen since.

Kevin thumbed his cutlass to life. He was incredibly thankful for the technology, developed centuries earlier before humankind was first threatened by the Ursa. Since the creatures preyed on civilians, ordnances like bombs, grenades, and other standard weapons could not be used. He remembered reading how a projectile incendiary device had leveled a block of homes during that deadly first infestation from space. Hence the shape-changing, powerful weapons were designed, refined, and employed to do the job with minimal danger to anything save the Ursa. He worried this was a new breed, deadlier than the last, instead of just the stragglers. The Ranger awaited detailed intelligence from command, but until then he tried to slow his pace as he made his way through the market toward the edge of the city.

"I'm scared, Mommy," the four-year-old Kevin said from under his bed.

Marisa knelt down and just looked at him with a sleepy expression. It had been the third night in a row she had been awoken by his night terrors. "I'm right here."

"But the monster will get you," he whimpered.

"What a baby," Luis muttered from underneath the pillow.

"Hush," Marisa told him. She redirected her attention to her younger boy. "I'm right here and I am now between you and the monster."

"Aren't you afraid?"

"Of what?"

"Of being killed."

"We all die sooner or later. If it is to be right here and now, protecting you, then so be it. I'd rather not die, though, especially lying here seeing where I missed cleaning."

"Where would you rather die?"

"In bed, holding your father's hand, when I am very, very old. Years from now."

"Then you should go hide."

"What, and let the monster come for you?"

"Well, I don't hear it, so maybe you scared it off."

"That's good to know. It means I've done my job, and see? There was no fighting, no violence. We let life happen."

She helped him back into bed, wrapped him tight in the blanket, and kissed his forehead. He slipped back into more pleasant dreams.

With every step, he had to force himself to slow down, not appear to panic despite the adrenaline coursing through his body. He'd responded to emergencies before, but nothing like this. This was why the Rangers still existed after a millennium away from Earth. They maintained the peace as the colony grew to a city, then on to multiple cities, and at last to exploration of nearby worlds. It was the Rangers who maintained the peace while the Savant and Primus—the heads of Nova Prime's scientific and religious communities, respectively—bickered generation after generation (or at least that was what some Rangers claimed).

Now it was his turn, and he was going to make his commanders proud.

As he moved through the city, he saw that word had spread and panic was already beginning to grip the populace. Shops were closing up, people were scrambling within the mountain homes, a general sense of terror infused the city noise. He glimpsed two other Rangers, also moving, and his training kicked in. Whenever possible they worked in units, not solo.

One turned out to be Minh, who waved with his five-foot-long cutlass; the other was a man he did not know.

"Diaz." Kevin nodded at Minh. The taller man jerked a thumb at the other Ranger and said, "Tanger."

"What do we know?"

"Not much, Diaz. Waiting on the telemetry ourselves. Let's hustle."

"To where?" he asked.

"Wherever the action is," Minh said with a smile. He actually seemed excited by this, not betraying any sense of fear. All Diaz felt was the adrenaline pumping through him and a sense of dread. Ursa had been holographic training exercises, not real flesh, blood, and metal reality.

As they walked, the streets grew emptier, the suns casting long, dark shadows, giving the place a deserted, unwanted feel. It was a few minutes later that their tablets relayed the vital information that at least a dozen Ursa had been located, scattered near and in the city. As a result, the orders were to kill on sight and patrol the perimeter until further instructions could arrive.

"Ever see one?" Minh asked.

"Just vids," Tanger replied. Kevin nodded in agreement.

"Me, neither. But the footage is pretty wicked, worse than any vid imagined."

The streets now had just a few people on them, and the panicky sounds had died down. In fact, Diaz wanted to hear an alien sound, something he could focus on and attack. He wanted to kill an Ursa, make a little history. Make his parents proud.

They continued to patrol through the dust-swept streets, Diaz thankful that the twin suns were finally beginning their descent. Between the tension and the heat, he was uncomfortable in his uniform.

He glanced at his screen for updates and cursed out loud.

"We lost three, west of here."

"We get any of them?" Tanger asked.

"Not yet," he replied grimly.

The mountains that formed the city were now behind them, and the arid expanse of the desert lay before them. They cast deepening shadows as the suns lowered themselves toward the horizon. Three hours had passed since the first alert, and Kevin was already tired. Tense and tired made a bad combination, but until orders were changed he was on duty.

The morning's tedium was long gone as his eyes scanned for any movement. He saw some reptiles near the base of the nearest mountain, a blue bird flying out of reach. To his right were the long stretches of fabric that protected growing vegetable fields from the scorching sunlight. They appeared to be various peppers in a rainbow of colors, wave after wave. Looking at them ripening made him hungry but he knew he needed to conserve the few packaged snacks in his uniform.

"Rangers! Two Ursa at southwest entrance to the city! One Ranger down."

"Rangers! One Ursa has entered the park and is under fire."

"Rangers! Two Rangers down at the north entrance"

"Rangers! Ursa sighted at the south and west gates! Converge on target!"

The staccato rhythm of the voice, speaker unknown to Diaz, conveyed the urgency of the unfolding emergency. Within, he felt each Ranger death, fueling a boiling anger he tried to contain.

"The west gate is a few klicks that way," Minh said, gesturing. "Let's head over."

Cutlasses at the ready, the trio went from a jog to a full-out run toward the nearest Ursa sighting. As they hustled, Kevin tried to recall every shred of data they had on the beasts. They had studied them intensively and while he knew their history cold, he was less certain about the current generation's capabilities.

"These bastards can camouflage, right?"

"Yep," Minh confirmed.

"They can also spit out that black ooze, the kind that can paralyze you."

"Sounds messy," Tanger said.

"More like deadly," Minh said. "And once one gets a scent on you, it'll hunt you until you're dead."

"They can smell your fear," Tanger chimed in. "So stay frigid."

"In this heat?" Kevin joked. But he knew what his comrade meant. Fear was an emotion with a scent, one some animals could sense, including the Ursa. He wasn't afraid—but then again, he wasn't facing one, either. Instead, he was anticipating finding one and engaging it, using the cutlass to slice it apart. Three cutlasses, one six-limbed beast—two apiece.

With every street crossed, there were fewer people in sight. Suddenly this had become a ghost town, and that was obviously for the best. Kevin had never experienced it so empty or so quiet. He wanted to hear something, some clue as to where they should head. Instead, they walked in the general direction of the western entry into the city.

About a kilometer before they reached their destination, the radios squawked once more, reporting additional sightings far from their position. The news also came that another Ranger had fallen.

"We've lost, what, six, eight men so far?" Tanger said.

"And those other bastards are still out there," Minh answered.

"At what point do the odds turn in their favor," the older man wondered.

"It won't get that far," Diaz said with a certainty he wasn't sure he felt. He took no comfort in being accompanied by two other Rangers since regs normally called for a minimum of eight. There was something to be said for strength in numbers, although he wasn't entirely certain just how strong he was feeling. "Anyone call in for reinforcements yet?"

"I bow to my elder," Minh said, literally bowing from the waist.

Tanger snarled while grinning and turned his back to the others to check in and see if more troops could be sent to back them.

"Colonel Green said more help is being dispatched, but there's a lot of demand with a dozen of these suckers all over the city," Tanger reported.

"Not a surprise since they can blend in with the scenery. Hunting them isn't the same as target practice," Diaz noted.

"Damn rude of them," Minh said and then adjusted his cutlass in his hands.

As they rounded a corner, a moving shadow caught Minh's eye. He held up his left hand, stopping the others. A gesture indicated the fleeting shadow but it had moved so quickly, Kevin couldn't confirm whether it was human, animal, or Ursa that had cast the amorphous silhouette. A second gesture had them simultaneously lower their radio volumes so as not to attract attention.

With agonizing slowness, they approached the corner, all senses straining to find something to latch on to, some evidence a predator was nearby.

A shriek provided the evidence they needed.

All three broke into a dead run, cutlasses humming in the still, hot air. Boots crushed pebbles but there was no use hiding their presence. This was to be an attack, not a stealth mission. Tanger fanned out to the right to help flank whatever it was they were approaching.

Kevin was first around the corner and saw the source of the scream. An older woman lay on the street, her blood feeding the ground, the life fading rapidly from her eyes. A leg was missing and her belly was slashed open. Bits of entrails remained visible amid the gore but the organs themselves seemed absent, no doubt taken by an Ursa for dinner. Any thoughts Kevin had of hunger were erased with that image.

While he focused on the woman, Minh was slowly swiveling about, looking for evidence of the Ursa, his cutlass gripped tightly in both hands. Tanger was similarly poised a short distance away.

"There," he called, pointing to darkening red splotches of blood near the base of a structure. The creature had gone that way, likely into the building itself to eat.

Kevin tried to remember Ursa feeding habits, couldn't conjure up the information; all he could think of was the dead woman.

Minh and Kevin joined Tanger, their breathing the only sound they could hear. He pointed at an open doorway, the blood and bits of bodily matter a grisly welcome mat. All checked their weapons, making certain they were fully powered. Tanger selected the sickle configuration as the metal altered its shape so the curved blade reflected the fading sunlight. Kevin briefly considered which of the dozen shapes he wanted to use but went for the basic blade. The thousands of pieces of smart metal reconfigured themselves into a sharp blade, pulsing with nuclear-fission power. Once the cutlass reformed itself, he glanced at Minh to see that he, too, had gone for the basic blade. Nothing fancy needed: just hacking and slashing until the beast was dead.

The stench hit them before the slurping sounds. Raw organs, waste matter, and blood mingled to create a vile odor that made Kevin try to breathe only through his mouth. This was followed by the distinct sound of moist mastication as the Ursa devoured the remains of its supper. The oval maw had only sharp fangs, but they were sufficient to puncture and shred the human organs.

Kevin tightened his grip on the cutlass. The shadowy hall was a shambles thanks to the Ursa's entry. Kevin had no idea what the building was used for, but it was in ruins and would be worse when they finished off the creature. On the other hand, the space was confined enough to make a three-pronged attack impossible. Tanger had a year on them so Kevin deferred to the senior member of the trio. He had been intently scanning the area and gestured toward the beast, then signaled that only one could attack at a time. He was suggesting they thrust and retreat, letting the next man take a literal stab at the Ursa, until it was dead or flushed outside where all three could attack simultaneously.

Kevin wasn't certain that was the smartest plan, but he figured a plan was better than no plan.

The sickle end of Tanger's cutlass swung through the air as the Ranger lunged forward, hoping the element of surprise would help. Instead the sound alerted the Ursa, which swung partway around, a shortened arm pressed against its chest to avoid being cut. With an unearthly shriek, it whirled itself around on its six legs and charged.

The hallway was wide, but not wide enough to let four figures move with ease. Minh and Kevin made it through the doorway, spinning about to stand ready to attack when the creature came out. Tanger was not so lucky.

He slid on the human remains that were in the doorway, losing his balance, which slowed him just enough for the Ursa to scurry atop him.

Kevin and Minh watched, horrified, as the creature dripped the infamous black viscous liquid on Tanger, while its forward talons pierced his uniform. Their fellow Ranger was a dead man, although his cries of pain indicated he wasn't quite gone.

Without hesitation, letting out a war cry of his own, Kevin rushed the preoccupied beast and slashed at it with his cutlass. He managed to cut deeply along a flank—or at least thought he did. There was a distinct lack of blood or scream, but he did capture the beast's attention. Leaving the corpse beneath it, the Ursa scurried over Tanger and headed directly for Kevin. The

Ranger stood his ground, wishing there was time to re-configure the cutlass, but there was none. Instead, he took a two-handed swing toward the Ursa, the charged hum singing through the air.

That at least caused the Ursa to stop its charge, allow-ing Minh to come from the side and take a stab at the beast. Instead of cutting the Ursa, the cutlass's tip glanced off the smart metal infused into the creature's organic structure. The Savant's people were still trying to understand the alien metal and how it was made a part of the Ursa, but that was not an issue right now. Survival was at the top of his mind. It was just him and Minh, a pair of second-year Rangers, both hoping to make it to seventeen.

The Ursa was distracted by Minh's attack, allowing Kevin the chance to strike a second time. With uncanny speed, the Ursa dodged the thrust and charged Minh instead, causing the Ranger to back up, seeking cover. The Ursa bellowed directly at Minh, and Kevin realized the monster must have imprinted on his fellow Ranger. Minh was effectively a dead man.

Oddly, Kevin's mind flashed to a joke from his cadet days. How many Rangers does it take to kill an Ursa? One, but only if you're Cypher Raige. At that time the Prime Commander was the only man known to have killed an Ursa single-handedly. Drinking beer after hours, the cadets marveled at the feat considering the beast's specs and ferocity.

Now Kevin wished the PC were here to lend a hand.

"Oh shit!" Minh cried out, suddenly realizing what had just transpired.

The Ursa scuttled with great speed toward Minh, who was backpedaling but not fast enough, hampered by the hallway's confines. Kevin saw that his friend was in danger and came up from the rear, swinging with all his might. The cutlass cut skin this time but it was also his turn to hit the smart metal, making the ef-fort mostly useless although it did seem to enrage the Ursa. It stopped charging Minh to turn toward him, much as a fly might distract a tiger hunting its dinner. Minh, to his credit, was returning the favor, coming up on the creature, his cutlass raised high for a strike.

The next several minutes—or were they seconds?—were a fast mix of thrusts, parries, retreats, and alien shrieking that hurt Kevin's ears. He took several glancing blows from arms or legs, leaving him bruised and in pain. It felt like a stalemate—but one thing Kevin knew was that Ursa endurance was easily superior to a human's. It could wear them down, then just strike.

It became apparent the rampaging creature had the advantage in the tight space; in addition, everyone who lived in the area was endangered. Diaz wondered if they could survive a jump from the window at the hall's end; they were up just a floor.

"Window!" he shouted.

"Are you crazy?" Minh shouted back to be heard above the creature.

"Desperate to survive and keep that bastard away from people," Diaz replied. "Look, I'll go first, it'll follow you out, and maybe the fall will slow it."

"And kill me first," Minh added. "Go!"

Diaz turned and ran, ignored by the Ursa, which was solely focused on Minh, who continued to swing wildly in the hope of slicing the forelimbs to ribbons. Kevin stopped to look down, saw there was a drainpipe, and reached out for it so he could shimmy down.

The next sounds he heard, as he leaped the final few feet to the ground, were the Ursa's cry and the crashing of building materials. He spotted Minh's head peek out the window; Diaz gestured for him to jump toward the left. Without hesitation, the Ranger came hurtling out the window and tumbled on the ground, his cutlass flying free. Diaz ran to retrieve it just as the Ursa burst through the window, shattering the frame and raining debris over the area.

Minh had already gotten to his feet and looked about, figuring out a route to lead the Ursa away from the area. Diaz tossed him the weapon and watched as his partner darted between two buildings, too tight a fit for the Ursa. It continued to ignore him as it sniffed the air and leaped to its right, in search of its prey.

Diaz noticed the air had finally begun to cool as one of the two suns had slipped below the horizon. The creature was poised to win but Kevin didn't want to die. Not yet.

"Minh, where are you?"

"This structure is empty," Minh radioed back. *"I can try to contain it until help comes. Might be a good time for you to get us some."*

"Roger that," Diaz said, and switched controls, calling in his status to Commander Isinbaeva.

He heard the Ursa break through a door—or wall, or something—and enter the building in search of Minh. Diaz would follow, holding out hope Minh would survive this.

Breathing hard, Kevin approached from the right, certain he alone could not kill the beast, even as it ignored him and focused solely on ripping a wider opening into the building.

He found a spot out of sight of the Ursa, which continued to pound away at the building. Minh had radioed that he was actually moving through the interior, hoping to find a way out that might confuse the creature. All he had to do was remain a moving target, keeping the building as a barrier between him and the Ursa.

"I would, though, appreciate it if the backup would hurry," he told Diaz.

The Ursa forced its way into the building, roaring and leaving behind an obvious trail of destruction. Whoever lived here would have quite a bit of cleanup work to do, Diaz mused, as he carefully stalked from the creature's rear.

In less than a quarter hour three other Rangers arrived: Carla Macionis, a ten-year veteran Kevin had never met before; David Telgemeier, a swarthy hulk of a Ranger; and Donald Varley, a lean, always angry man just a few years older than he was. After a brief round of introductions, Kevin met them by the ripped-open entrance into the building. Minh had successfully made it up two levels with the beast on his tail.

The second sun was now halfway down the horizon and the skies were rapidly dimming, which would only complicate the hunt should the Ursa escape the structure.

"How many entrances?" Macionis asked. Varley consulted his screen and held up two fingers.

"Telgemeier, take the other entry." They nodded and began to move before Diaz interrupted.

"That thing's imprinted on Minh," he said.

Macionis's eyes widened at the news, and one of the men cursed out loud.

"Okay, the priority remains containing then killing that thing. We may need Minh as bait once I figure out a plan."

She grabbed her radio and clicked it on. "Minh, it's Macionis. You okay?" She carefully walked up a stairway, leaving Telgemeier on the first landing as backup.

"A hot shower would be nice. That thing's getting closer and I'm beat."

"I have a plan but need you to be swift."

"Like a rabbit," he replied.

"I need you to expose yourself, make certain the Ursa is locked on to your position, and then lead it away from the building to the granary half a klick behind your position."

"Is that all? I can run pretty fast. Why not finish it here?"

"The PC has studied the attacks and thinks they're hungry. It's been an unusually hot season and their normal prey may have been diminished. These are walking engines of destruction and they need to stay fueled. If they can't eat anything warm and bloody and human, they'll find the next best thing," Macionis told the Ranger. "Besides, people may still be in hiding somewhere and we have no time to do an apartment-by-apartment sweep."

"They've lasted decades out there," Kevin said.

"Our job, Ranger, is to find them and kill them. You up for the task, Minh?"

"No doubt about that, sir," Minh told her, sounding more certain than he could possibly be.

"It can run faster, so be smart. Take a moment to map a route. We'll try and slow it down from the rear."

Diaz whispered a silent prayer for Minh's survival. As he moved, he could hear the Ursa scuttle away up another flight of steps. Minh had clearly been on the move and he heard a roar. Minh was now exposed, his scent carrying through the warm air.

Macionis's planning time got cut woefully short when they heard the sound of cloth tearing, and then something crashing with a metallic sound. Next came the screams, confirming the building was far from as empty as they'd hoped.

Macionis shouldered her way through a doorway and was taking the stairs two at a time, followed by Varley, Kevin once more in the rear. He tried to determine how high up the sounds were coming from, estimating it to be no more than the third or fourth floor.

One shriek was cut off midcry but a fresh one was heard and then the unmistakable sound of crying.

The Rangers arrived on the third-floor landing and saw two hind legs; the rest of the hideous creature was inside an apartment. Once more, it would be close-quarters fighting, which Kevin dreaded. An Ursa, civilians, furniture, narrow spaces, and three, soon to be five, Rangers meant no one would have an advantage. The ferociousness of the Ursa would probably dictate how quickly this fight would turn into raw carnage.

Perhaps sensing trouble was coming, the Ursa swung about, literally ripping through the wall and placing its forward legs into the hall. It roared at Macionis, who stood her ground, aiming her sword-shaped cutlass at the beast.

Kevin could never be certain afterward who charged first: his leader or the Ursa. It really didn't matter because the woman was torn in two before he could move. Her torso was hurled down the hall toward the Rangers while the lower half collapsed in place, her blood splattering the Ursa and walls, pooling underneath.

He imagined its roar was one of triumph.

The next sound was that of his fellow Rangers finally making it to the end of the corridor. Telgemeier cried out, *"You ugly bastard!"* and charged the Ursa, whose back was turned his way, returning its attention to the apartment. The soldier leaped toward the beast, his cutlass shaped like a sickle, and he swung. Amazingly, the weapon cut through the skin only to strike a metallic portion. It still hurt the beast, which writhed and cried out in a terrible high-pitched tone.

Telgemeier landed on one knee, grimacing in pain, but held on to his weapon. The Ursa turned toward him, and as it twisted in the tight space Varley struck with his own cutlass. His attack was met with a razor-sharp talon piercing his chest, nailing him to the wall. The cutlass fell and was quickly covered in its owner's blood.

The wounded beast roared once more and charged toward Minh. The Ranger backpedaled until he found a door to an emergency stairwell. He started up at a scramble and stumbled through a thin, wooden door, leading into a different apartment. The Ursa followed into the stairway where Kevin could hear it head upward. He knew there were just two more floors before the roof. The stairway was wide enough not to impede its progress so he tried to determine if it was smart enough to get to the roof and leap away until it could heal.

Or would it lie in wait? It was, after all, a hunter. It seemed programmed for maximum slaughter. It probably ran to find open space for a better fight, and the Rangers were hellbent on giving it to the creature.

In less than a minute it had killed two Rangers and received little more than a flesh wound. Diaz cursed himself for being in the background, not following through on his convictions, not attacking. What was keeping him from engaging the creature: Fear? Or some vestige of his upbringing?

Minh recovered from his stumble and was on his comm unit, reporting in, begging for more Rangers. What Colonel Green told him was dispiriting. Three Ursa were on the opposite side of the city, and a disproportionate number of Rangers had been redirected in that direction. Being unable to see the Ursa at all times meant the Rangers had to spread themselves thin around the city's perimeter along with the interior. Each Ursa sighting was usually accompanied by reports that Rangers were being maimed or killed, further depleting the ranks. That Minh was still alive felt like a miracle.

They needed a new plan and Kevin Diaz was out of ideas, brilliant or otherwise.

All his life, he seemed to strike first, especially since he'd watched his brother's less aggressive approach fail miserably. Strike first, strike hard, and don't give your enemy a chance to get up. He had used it in simulation after simulation, satisfied with the results.

It clearly wasn't working here when others tried it in a non-simulated situation.

"What next?" he asked Telgemeier, now the senior member of the team.

"Hell if I know," he said, wiping sweat from his eyes. "Follow that sucker and kill it before it gets Minh. Oh, and keep the citizens safe."

"A little weak on tactics but it works for me," Diaz agreed, sounding a little too enthusiastic for someone who hadn't accomplished much in this fight.

The sound of rampant destruction punctuated his comments and both Rangers looked up, concluding that the beast and their colleague had made it to the roof. "It will follow Minh over to the grain storage building since it probably hasn't eaten in, well, minutes," said Kevin with bitter sarcasm.

"We stay together."

"That didn't work terribly well before and we need to keep tracking it," Kevin said, shaking free and ignoring the direct order. He had Rangers to avenge and an Ursa to kill. Somehow.

"Minh, it's Kevin," he said into the comm unit. "Same plan: Lead it to the granary."

"Easier said than done, but it shall be done," Minh replied. *"Since when are you in command?"*

"No one's in command," he insisted. "Just following orders. Out."

As he made his way downstairs, he flashed on the dead bodies, the portions of Macionis that had once been a comrade in arms. He was channeling the anger, trying to control it and let that fill his thoughts instead of the fear that he'd be next.

Turn the other cheek.

His parents' favorite phrase echoed in his mind, but it seemed eminently useless. An Ursa would simply tear any turned cheeks to shreds.

"That sucker is on the roof with me, where the hell are you?" Minh cried.

"We're coming," Diaz said, finally spurred into taking action, leading Telgemeier upward.

By the time they reached the roof, they watched as Minh, choosing to wait no longer, leaped across to the next building, where scaffolding wrapped two sides for maintenance. The Ursa didn't hesitate and leaped after him, but couldn't reach him through the metallic scaffolding. This bought the Ranger time to make it to the street.

Diaz and Telgemeier didn't hesitate, rushing back into the building and leaping down steps to make it to the street, hoping Minh would still be alive when they reached him.

The Ranger had been successful, darting and weaving around statuary, abandoned carts, and even a well. The Ursa made a straight line, but Minh still had the advantage and managed to enter the granary without incident. The others followed close behind.

Night began to envelop the streets and automatic lighting snapped to life, casting new sets of shadows.

The squad followed the onscreen map and made a direct line toward the grain storage facility, which was a mammoth structure.

The remains of a young man's body were a ghastly signpost but the Rangers barely paused to study the corpse. Not far from it was a woman's body. What they were doing outdoors staggered Diaz's imagination, but they had clearly paid too high a price for ignoring the sirens. That neither of the victims let out a cry for help disturbed him and reminded him anew how stealthy the Ursa could be.

Heat continued to radiate from the streets despite the cooling air, and Kevin found he couldn't make himself comfortable. Gripping his cutlass, he forced his feet to keep moving, not letting Telgemeier get too far in front of him.

Kevin turned his back on the pair, slowly circling the area, checking for movement. The empty streets refused to tell him anything, the air still. Two dead bodies and no one to mourn for them. That would have to come later. He wondered how many had been killed, how many Rangers died to protect a city. They had let two people die while he ate and that bothered him, made him angry.

He looked over his shoulder before moving ahead.

Within five minutes they had walked the perimeter of the squat building, seeing no obvious sign of entry. There was also little sign of blood—nothing to indicate the Ursa was actually there.

Wearily, Diaz unslung his weapon and entered the granary. Its automatic lights had gone on when Minh entered so he could see the bins of various grains, most of which had already been processed. This entrance led into the storage facility, which gave Minh plenty of places to hide and confuse the Ursa. Telgemeier followed him inside, Diaz taking the rear position. His stomach rumbled a bit, seeking sustenance, but he had to ignore it and concentrate on protecting the people living in the vicinity. Isinbaeva had made it clear: people first, killing

Ursa second. All he thought about was the bodies left behind.

The first sounds they heard were of the creature gulping down raw, crunchy grain, making slobbering noises in the process. It had somehow entered the building and was stopping to chow down before killing Minh.

"How could that thing still be hungry?" Telgemeier asked.

"It could be they haven't eaten in a while and are gorging. We have no idea how much they can eat or how quickly they metabolize their food," Diaz said. "Besides, if they're used to flesh and blood, grain might not be enough. They need a constant supply of fuel, like the reactors."

"They've been coming here for half a century and we still know jackshit about them, is that it?" Telgemeier said.

"They keep evolving," Kevin reminded them. "And these have been here for decades so who knows how long they live or how they have adapted to the environment."

"Thanks, Professor," Telgemeier said drily.

He pointed inside the building, showing an obvious trail the Ursa had left behind. It made a clear path, easy to follow.

"Spikes," he whispered. Both activated the configuration and within seconds the pair of cutlasses began to re-form themselves into trident-shaped weapons. Four points of entry certainly beat three and could cause far more damage.

Kevin took several deep breaths, steadying his nerves, finding the will to move, forcing his weary limbs to carry him after the beast.

Suddenly he found himself on point, the other Ranger at his side. Various grains he couldn't hope to identify had spilled from their torn containers. Pipes, conveyors, cords, all manner of damage made the trail easy to follow. Every now and then ocher- and maize-colored grain was tinged a dull red with drying blood.

What bothered Kevin the most was that he could not hear the Ursa.

"Shh!" he said. He'd heard something and paused, waiting to hear it again. There it was, grain shifting, as if moved by a four-legged monstrosity. With the cutlass, he pointed in a southwest direction. His partner, bathed in sweat, nodded, going silent.

The Ursa hadn't bothered to camouflage itself, just tore open the top of a grain bin and began shoveling food into its maw. The creature glistened, light reflecting off the exposed smart metal that was fused to the tough hide, making it an ideal target. Diaz spread his right-hand fingers wide, signaling Telgemeier to fan out, surrounding the vast bin. He remained fixed in place, the cutlass thrumming with energy.

Minh was still nowhere in sight, and it was too risky to use the radio. Telgemeier went right while Diaz headed left and then began climbing atop other bins, gaining an advantage over the seemingly oblivious creature. He was halfway up when the creature stopped eating and raised its head. It had smelled or heard or sensed them. Kevin was still uncertain how it functioned, but the Ursa knew it was no longer alone. Maybe it had caught Minh's scent again, Diaz thought.

The Ursa leaped forward and rushed toward wherever Minh was hiding. Diaz and Telgemeier trotted after it, their trident-shaped cutlasses at the ready. Up ahead, Diaz could see Minh panicking, climbing high atop one bin, seeking the next, foolishly hoping to outclimb the beast. The Ursa was pulling ahead of the Ranger duo and gaining on its target.

Minh's cutlass slashed at the leaping Ursa, but its momentum was too great and it fell upon the Ranger. The Ursa easily jumped to the ground, dragging Minh down, its forelegs literally pinning the Ranger. Minh screamed in pain and kicked with his free legs, but the creature lowered itself, dripping that vile black liquid onto his face, pouring it into his sputtering mouth. The black globules burned and hissed, a form of poisonous acid that corroded his skin almost on contact.

Diaz knew Minh was a dead man so he aimed and watched as Telgemeier hurled the cutlass at the creature, hoping the momentum would aid in cutting deep into the alien threat. The cutlass did pierce the skin but not anywhere near as deeply as hoped. The wounded Ursa snarled and turned on the now-unarmed Telgemeier. That it abandoned Minh meant he was dead.

It wasn't hurt enough to slow down for Telgemeier, who was screaming something at the beast when he was cut off mid-yell as his head was separated from his neck with a swipe.

A fresh roar and the Ursa leaped away, skittering away from bin to bin, deep into the recesses of the storage building. The thought of just how much more dangerous a wounded Ursa could be frightened Diaz.

He was breathing hard, his heart pounding in his chest, and the blood rushing loud enough to cloud his hearing. Just like that, his team was decimated and he was the last man standing. He had no idea when the reinforcements would arrive but he also knew he had to contain the Ursa so it wouldn't escape or harm anyone else. He might die in the process . . . but he was kidding himself. Of course he was going to die. The Ranger had to admit he was just stalling the creature until help turned up.

The Ursa no doubt shared a trait with Nova Prime's animal life: A wounded animal was a dangerous animal. They'd nicked it enough that it was probably in pain. Once it mastered its pain, it was likely to come seeking revenge.

Diaz needed to hide.

He gingerly moved away from the corpses and spilled grain in search of refuge. With slow, deliberate steps, he moved between the towering vats of grain waiting to be processed. Then he scanned the area and spotted a maintenance closet. It had a heavy metal door and might provide enough safety until help arrived. It wasn't a cowardly act, but a smart one, staying alive until the odds could be turned in the Rangers' favor. Right now, Diaz was simply Ursa Chow, and that helped no one.

He couldn't hear the Ursa and knew opening that door might tip off his position, but he was tired and worn enough to take the risk. Thankfully they had done a good job of upkeep with the maintenance door so it did not make a sound, swiveling open soundlessly. Locking it, though, made noise, but by then he didn't care. He was inside. He was safe.

Only then did Diaz let the events of the past few hours wash over him. Tears freely rolled down his cheeks, and his body convulsed with emotion. All the training in the world could not possibly have prepared him for this sort of action. The Ursa were the stuff of nightmares, children's stories, and horror vids for the masses. Sure, everyone knew they were out there, somewhere; it added to the stories' sense of danger.

But here, in town, killing with abandon—that was beyond imagining.

He was going to die and his parents would be so disappointed in him. His thoughts began to drift past the fighting to earlier, happier days. Kevin was suddenly reliving his youth when the family gathered to practice meditation, seeking tranquility. Mom's and Dad's voices played in his mind. The sureness in their philosophy, the utter sense of calm that surrounded them. They were happy days, he realized, ones shared by the extended family. Aunts, uncles, cousins all joined in during holidays and birthday celebrations. No one fought, no one argued, and the joy was palpable. The elders ascribed their prolonged lives to the simple way they lived. Diaz wished his future included a long life but he now doubted it.

Diaz continued to let his mind drift back through the years, before Luis came to his defense. He recalled the lessons his father and mother reinforced at every opportunity. Simple phrases, simple exercises, simple life.

Before long, Diaz realized his breathing had slowed and deepened. He was reflexively exercising the controlled breathing that was a part of his training all those years ago. The whirl of horrific images that filled his mind's eye had vanished, replaced with happier days. He felt himself smiling, the tears drying on his face. He concentrated on his parents' faces, playing with his brother, emblematic of the life he so desperately wanted to preserve.

A wave of calm washed over Diaz, flushing away the fatigue, hunger, and emotional pain he had felt the last few hours. Despite hearing the Ursa moving about nearby, seeking him out, Diaz realized the lessons had value. They refreshed him, centered him. This was his place in the natural order of life and he felt composed. At peace. Should he die right now, he would do so content that he had tried his best, honoring all life. Maybe not the same way his parents and ancestors did, but cherishing life in all its ways.

Without realizing it, he emerged from the closet, moving with soft steps toward the great engine of destruction. It didn't hear him, didn't sense him. The Ursa didn't even appear to hear the powered cutlass, still in its trident form.

Diaz stood in place, studying the creature's movements with fresh eyes. It moved more slowly, one limb definitely out of sync with the rest of the body. That was his target, the weak spot he had been seeking to finish the job his fellow Rangers started.

Step-by-step, Diaz drew closer, and still the Ursa remained unaware. For his part the Ranger felt unafraid, supremely confident that he would complete his task. Dead or alive, he was a part of Nova Prime, and it a part of him.

He smiled a warm smile. There was a silly, blissful feeling he maintained as he reared his right arm back, planting his feet. He felt no fear now, nothing for the Ursa's hypersenses to lock onto. It was effectively blind to him as long as he maintained this feeling of calm and control. That was going to give him the edge in this battle.

Then, with one smooth thrust, he struck the oblivious

monster, the cutlass's tips smoothly cutting into the weakened joint. It dug deep, past whatever passed for muscles, veins, and connective tissue. He hit bone then twisted, ensuring maximum damage was done. Its arms and legs thrashed about, one catching him and sending him crashing backward into a metal seed container. The seam ruptured, and yellowish seed spilled outward with a rush. Diaz winced with the impact but pushed himself upright, steadying himself while crunching seeds with every step. He then strode forward and struck again. Once more the cutlass cut deep; black ichor poured from the Ursa's multiple wounds. With grim satisfaction, the Ranger glided back three steps, seeds snapping under his boots.

Diaz watched the Ursa writhe in pain, ignoring the unearthly wail. Instead, he reconfigured his remarkable weapon into a spear shape. He positioned his feet and then with both hands held it steady until the beast whirled about, its maw wide open. The cutlass went right in through the palate, frying whatever passed for internal organs and brain.

In its wild death throes, it knocked Diaz to the ground, and the hard landing knocked the wind out of him. He picked himself up and stepped back, out of range, as the limbs moved more and more slowly, until they ceased moving altogether. The Ursa slumped forward atop enough seed to have kept it sated for days. The seed softly continued to spill from the container, slowly covering and then burying the creature in a harvest shroud.

After the great beast was dead, Diaz exhaled and sat down on the ground next to it.

That's where the Rangers found him less than an hour later. He was carefully taken to the nearest hospital where doctors checked him over, fed him intravenous fluids, and said he was exhausted and possibly in shock from the battle, but basically unharmed.

Diaz was discharged the following morning, brought back to Ranger headquarters by an honor guard of sorts. Everyone wanted to hear how he'd managed to kill the creature, but Diaz wanted to tell the story only once. So he waited until he was standing before the squad commander. He entered his testimony into the record, calmly answering all the questions while his cutlass was studied, its telemetry used to corroborate the report. Not that he wasn't believed.

He wasn't the first Ranger to single-handedly kill an Ursa. Still, it was almost unheard of. The stuff legends were built on.

A week later, after he rested and was returned to duty, there was a ceremony to honor his accomplishment. The shiny medal gleamed in the morning sunlight as Diaz stood before dozens of his fellow Rangers. In the crowd he spotted Katya, who seemed genuinely pleased for him. There had already been memorials for the others—Tanger, Macionis, Varley, Telgemeier, and Minh—and he'd wept in their memory.

But now the Rangers could celebrate. At least two other Ursa had died, reducing the known population on Nova Prime.

He didn't expect his parents to be there, still protesting his career choice, but it no longer made him sad. They did their job, he made his choices, and somehow he managed to blend them into a personal choice that had helped him survive an ordeal. For that, he was content.

Kevin Diaz stood there hearing Commander Isinbaeva repeat his tale and then shaking his hand. A moment later Cypher Raige, the Original Ghost himself, was handing him a medal. It was sometime after he made his report that his actions were described as ghosting, which he dismissed. But he was assured that his utter absence of fear had allowed him to turn invisible to the sightless Ursa. He was indeed a Ghost, the rarest breed of Ranger there was.

"Congratulations," Raige said to him. "Welcome to the club." Diaz had heard earlier that a civilian also managed the feat, so maybe there was hope yet that these beasts could be challenged and then eradicated.

He shook the OG's hand and turned to the crowd to acknowledge their applause. Off to the side, halfway back, Diaz spotted Luis first, then his parents. Their applause was, to him, the loudest of all.

Kevin Diaz was at peace.

AFTER
EARTH

Ghost Stories

BIRTHRIGHT

Peter David

I

Mallory McGuiness lay on her back, staring uncompre-
hendingly at the twin suns of Nova Prime that were
beating down upon her, and she wondered why it was
that Private Lynch had suddenly turned into a mime.

She thought that perhaps she was dreaming. That
would have explained a lot . . . hell, it would have explained everything. The sense of unreality; the fact that
to her senses, Lynch was moving in what appeared to be
slow motion. Lynch's face was smeared with dirt and
what appeared to be burn marks, and there were bits of
dirt in his short-cropped red hair. His lips were moving,
slowly and deliberately, but no actual sound was emerging. His eyes were wide with urgency and Mallory, for
the life of her, couldn't understand why.

*Why is Lynch in my quarters? For that matter, it's
broad daylight . . . why was I sleeping during broad
daylight? Where's Janus?*

In her bewildered, stream-of-consciousness flood of
thought, Janus—her husband of four years—became
the touchstone. Her thoughts locked onto him, as if she
were being swept helplessly down a river and he was a
jutting boulder in the middle that she was able to grab
onto and find purchase.

*No . . . we got up this morning. Janus shook my
shoulder, woke me up. Kissed me lightly on the cheek.
His beard scratched me. His beard grows so quickly
that by morning it's already non-regulation.*

I thought today was our day off. I tried to roll over and

go back to sleep. But no, he reminded me we had a patrol.
No Ursa within the attack perimeter of the city, but that
didn't necessarily mean anything. Damned things turn in-
visible; you never know when they're going to just show
up out of nowhere. "Have to be vigilant," he told me.

"Can't I be vigilant later?" I said. I rolled over, tried
to go back to sleep. I'd slept poorly that night. Kept
waking up. Bad dreams.

He slapped me hard on my bare ass. "We have things
to do."

"I know what I want to do." I pulled him down onto
me. We kissed deeply. His beard still scratched but I
didn't care.

We made love for the last time . . .

What? What the hell does that mean?

Janus?

Jan?

"Jan!" Her voice croaked. There was a coppery taste
in her mouth. She spit out whatever was causing it and
saw a small wad of dark liquid—blood—land on the
ground next to her.

I'm outside? When did I go outside?

"Mallory!"

She heard Lynch's voice. It sounded as if it were coming from very far away, but Lynch was right there.

It's not Lynch. It's me. I can't hear him. There's a
ringing in my ears. Why is there a ringing in my ears?

She tried to sit up and Lynch immediately shook his
head firmly. He told her to lie back down and was saying something about help being on the way. It was hard
for her to be certain. His voice kept popping in and out,
as if they had a bad communications link.

"Jan," she said again, with greater urgency this time.
She tried to push Lynch out of the way, started to move
her right leg, and let out a shriek of pain.

"I told you! I told you to stay down!" he said firmly.

Mallory managed to move her head, and she looked
down in shock. There was a piece of rock buried in her
right thigh. It was a jagged fragment with blood trick-

ling around it. She tried to reach down for it so she could yank it clear.

"No." Lynch grabbed her hand and immobilized it. "We don't know how deep it is. It may wind up being nothing, and you're up and around in a week. On the other hand, if it hit an artery, then the fact that it's in there may be the only thing keeping you alive. You could bleed out by removing it. So we're not taking a chance; we're waiting until we can evac you out of here."

"I don't understand . . . where's—?"

The Ridges. The Golem Ridges, beyond the outer rim. There was once a colony city there whose population the Skrel eradicated during one of their earliest assaults. It was never repopulated; instead it was left alone as a memorial for the fallen. Unfortunately, Ursa have been known to hide there on occasion, waiting for an ill-timed visit by someone making a pilgrimage to the site.

So we sometimes head out there to make sure . . .

And it was routine . . .

Strictly routine . . .

Janus . . .

He was just walking along through one of the many, seemingly endless passages through the ridges, his cutlass slung on his back. I was walking behind him. The rest of the squad was spread out. All eight of us were in constant contact. No sign of an Ursa. No sign of trouble. No sign of anything.

And then Jan's foot—I think that's what it was— I think he . . .

He stepped on something.

I can't remember.

What did he step on?

He was there.

Then he wasn't . . .

"Jan!" and she screamed.

"I need some help over here!" Lynch was looking desperate. He tried to pin Mallory by the shoulders. She thrashed around like a lunatic as Lynch fought to keep her on her back. A second Ranger, Tomlinson, joined him, trying to make sure she didn't keep kicking and possibly dislodge the stone wedged in her leg.

The last thing I saw . . . this look of confusion on his face, and then this burst of light and flash of heat. And then I was flying through the air, my arms waving around as if I could somehow stay in the air by flapping. My back slammed into the upper edge of one of the ridges and then I toppled over. I went from being propelled to tumbling downward, ricocheting off another outcropping of a ridge, falling to the ground about twenty feet below. I went loose, protected my head, landed on my shoulders. The rest of my body struck the ground but I wasn't feeling anything below my neck. I must have been in pain, but I didn't feel . . .

Jan was smiling at me . . .

He was smiling down at me . . .

Our bodies were merged in bed this morning . . .

I would have liked to stay there, find an excuse to get out of the patrol . . .

But we both knew that wouldn't happen. We are Rangers. We have duties. We have responsibilities.

Jan? Jan, you can't be—

The truth came crashing down on her, but before she could get up a true head of steam and start thrashing around once more, she felt a pinch in her upper arm. She looked frantically to her right and saw a woman wearing the colors of a Ranger medtech. The woman had a sympathetic look to her as she extracted the hypo from Mallory's arm.

Mallory started to ream out the medtech with an outpouring of profanity. But instead all she could manage was a confused grunt, and then her head slumped back. "Hate you," she managed to say. "Hate you . . ."

"There's no reason to," Lynch said soothingly. "We're your fellow Rangers . . ."

"Not you . . ." Her voice was little more than a whisper. "Jan . . . for making me think . . . he's dead . . . he'd never do that to me . . ."

And then she was in darkness. Truly alone.

II

She lay in her bed in the infirmary, staring blankly at Colonel Green. The rugged longtime Ranger was seated a few feet away, his face etched with a carefully neutral expression.

"A mine?" Mallory echoed what he had just told her, her voice hollow.

"Or some manner of unexploded incendiary device," Green confirmed. "Left over from a previous Skrel attack."

"But the last direct assault was decades ago." There was no shock, no protest in the observation. "Unless I missed one."

"No, you're quite right. It landed, or perhaps was planted—hard to know for sure—and then through the years, the sandstorms that blow through Golem Ridge covered it over. And it just lay there, undetonated, all this time. It's a miracle no one stepped on it before—" His voice trailed off, and he looked downward. "Sorry. That wasn't exactly the best way to put it."

"Why not?" She said it so indifferently, she could have been discussing a matter of simple academics. "It's what we do, isn't it? We Rangers? We work to keep our fellow Novans safe from the Skrel and the Ursa and whatever other dangers crop up around us. It was a miracle that no one else was hurt by it, just as you said. And because Janus stepped on it, he saved the life of . . . well, who knows who else? A family out for a picnic. An augur off on meditation. The Savant out searching for inspiration that would lead him to some discovery that will improve the lives of millions."

"Lieutenant—"

"Any host of people who would, almost by definition, be much more important than Jan. It's a fair trade."

"Mallory, listen to me. Take off all the time you want . . ."

Without warning, Mallory pulled aside the bedsheet to study her injured leg. She was naked save for the simple hospital gown she was wearing, and that had ridden up to around her hips. Immediately Green looked away, his cheeks flushing slightly. Mallory was oblivious. Instead she was studying her leg with clinical detachment. The thin line that marked where she'd been wounded was bright red, but the intensity of it was already fading. She touched it gently. "It's amazing what medical science can do, isn't it. You know, once upon a time they stitched people together like clothing. No sealants. Nothing like what we have now. It's almost miraculous. Not as miraculous as a bomb waiting years for Janus to step on it, but it's right up there."

"Mallory, for God's sake—"

She lifted the leg, extended it, coiled it so that her knee was almost up to her chin, and then stretched it out once more. "Wasn't an artery, then?"

"No," said Green. "It looked a lot worse than it was; the bone caught most of it. You may have a slight limp for a bit, but nothing permanent. You got off lucky."

She smiled mirthlessly. "My husband's dead, sir. I don't get to feel lucky."

"Mallory—"

"You're right, though. Feels fine. I won't need any time off."

Green stood up, took the sheet firmly, and draped it back over her to cover her. She looked up at him, blinking owlishly, clearly having no idea why he'd done that. "Mallory, this isn't a request. You *will* take time off."

"So I can do what? Lie around? Think about . . ." Her voice caught ever so slightly, but she managed to pull herself together at the last moment. "Think about what happened? Think about Jan dying, not in battle facing a foe like any Ranger would want, but because of some stupid booby trap planted in the sand? The hell with that and, with all respect, Colonel, the hell with you. I should be out doing my job. And once the docs here sign off on my leg being one hundred percent—which they will, because they did too good a job to say otherwise— I want to go back out in the field."

"You need some time to—"

"I need. To do. My job." She paused, gathering her thoughts. "Sir . . . inaction is not an option. If you relieve me of my duties, I'll simply go out on patrol by myself."

"We'll take your cutlass away." The cutlass was the Ranger weapon of choice. A five-foot staff that could morph its shape into a variety of cutting weapons, designed for close-quarters combat . . . and particularly effective against Ursa at close range.

"Then I'll get my hands on a pulser. And if you take that from me, I'll get a kitchen knife. I will go out, Colonel, and I will do my job, even if I don't have it anymore. Because if I just sit around and dwell on Jan, I will go out of my mind."

"I'm not entirely sure you're not out of your mind already, Mallory."

"Is there anything I've said, anything I've done, that would indicate a break with reality?"

"Well, I'm not entirely sure you're in touch with your emotions right now."

"I don't need emotions; I need my work. And I'm going to go out and do it. The only question is whether I'm going to do it on my own or in the company of my fellow Rangers."

Green looked at her steadily. No words passed between them for some time.

"A full psych evaluation," he said finally. "I don't need some suicidal asshole out on patrol, endangering the others in her squad because she doesn't feel like living anymore."

"Is that what you think?" She sounded surprised.

"I'm honestly not sure what to think right now. For all I know, you want to be with your husband and you figure that facing danger—"

"My husband's dead, Colonel." For the first time she sounded harsh, even annoyed. "I've never been much for religion. Or God. I don't believe for a moment that Jan's off on a puffy cloud somewhere waiting for me to join him. Dead is dead and there's nothing after it. Life is for the living and I have every intention of continuing to live for as long as possible. And what I have to live for is my work. Don't . . ." Her voice caught briefly, betraying for a heartbeat the roiling emotions she was dealing with. "Don't take that away from me. Janus and my job are my life, and he's gone and if you take me away from my duties, I really will have nothing. And the nothing will swallow me whole. Do you understand, Colonel?"

"I . . ." Slowly he nodded. "I think I do."

"Give me all the eval you want. Have me run through the cadet training ground if you want. I'll give you all the proof you need that I'm fit. All right?"

"We'll see" was all he said.

She was on patrol twenty-four hours later.

III

The next two months were mind-numbingly boring for Mallory.

Some delivery routes bringing supplies to outlying areas that were supposedly along dangerous paths. And nothing happened.

Responding to skirmishes or brawls or arguments and being tasked with keeping the peace. And they weren't even exciting brawls. The moment the Rangers showed up, everyone involved decided that it was smarter to shake hands and get along rather than deal with the Rangers dispensing their unique brand of hands-on justice. Certainly no one was enthused about the prospect of the Rangers hauling them before a local magistrate.

One easily solved situation after another. That was what Mallory was faced with, and she was beginning to fear that she would go out of her mind.

It wasn't conspiratorial. Sometimes Rangers went through lax periods. Typically they embraced such times as welcome breaks, with the knowledge that all too soon, something catastrophic would happen to disrupt the temporary peace.

But she said nothing to anyone about it. She didn't want anyone reading too much into her state of mind. It was bad enough that, for the first several weeks of being out in the field, it seemed as if everyone was acting as tentatively around her as possible. Even the simple act of making jokes was quickly hushed whenever she was nearby because everyone was obsessed with watching out for her feelings.

Finally she had confronted the whole of her squadron and told them point-blank, "If you people don't stop treating me as if I'm made out of porcelain, I'm going to put a pounding on the lot of you." That had taken care of the immediate problem, at least somewhat.

It still didn't change the fact that every time Mallory was pushed into a seemingly dangerous situation, it proved frustratingly routine. So when initial reports were delivered that an Ursa had set up shop in the Aldrin Forest, Mallory wasn't expecting much. There was always the possibility that there was no Ursa there at all, but instead some other, smaller creature had taken up residence. It was hard to believe that anything else on Nova Prime could remotely be mistaken for an Ursa, but Colonel Green had supposed that anything was possible.

Consequently, Mallory was part of several eight-man squads that were moving through the Aldrin Forest, looking for some sign of an Ursa.

Jan would have loved this, she thought. He had lived for moments like this, for the thrill of the hunt. She had never quite understood why it was that he'd never been able to completely avoid detection by an Ursa: to "ghost," as this accomplishment was referred to. Only someone who was utterly fearless was able to perform that particular feat, and Janus had been as fearless as anyone she had ever known.

The worst thing was that the forest seemed to be determined to put her off guard. The smell of the greenery was pure and pungent. When Janus had been courting her, they'd enjoyed taking walks in places just like this. The pleasant aroma was enough to trigger recollections of her time with him—

"Sector clear" came a report over her comm unit from another squadron. That was the third one stating with utter conviction that there were no Ursa around; not that it necessarily meant anything. The damned things were capable of hiding in plain sight.

"Stay frosty, people," came the brisk command of Captain Terelli, the leader of her particular squad. "It might still be right in our backyard."

They confirmed with a brisk series of "Copy that." Mallory was gripping her cutlass firmly, the bladed weapon secure in her grasp. She swished it back and forth experimentally. She was breathing shallowly. The longer this hunt went on, the more she could sense her heart pounding away. She kept herself icily calm through sheer willpower. It had only been recently that the other Rangers had stopped treating her as if she were liable to shatter from a harsh word. She wasn't about to do anything that prompted any of them to return to worrying about—

A faint snap of a branch nearby was the only warning any of them had that an Ursa was in their midst. And then there it was, the monster revealing its presence accompanied by an ear-shattering roar.

Ursa didn't simply attack; they liked to play with their food. This Ursa roared, then vanished, and as the Rangers whirled to face it the creature suddenly reappeared outside their circle. It leaped upon the nearest Ranger, a new guy, Harrison, who barely had time to react. And the reaction was a scream as the Ursa whipped around a clawed paw and sliced through Harrison's jugular with surgical precision. Harrison went down, blood jetting from his ruined throat.

The Rangers started to move to surround the Ursa. "Stay in formation!" called Terelli. "Hopkins, flank right, maneuver nine-seven—"

Mallory wasn't listening. She was hearing the words, but it was as if they were being addressed to someone else entirely. Someone who gave a damn about maneuvers and training and the signals and orders that Terelli was calling out. Someone who was, in short, not her.

Words were irrelevant to her. All that mattered was what she was seeing. Yes, Ursa had not killed Janus. But their makers sure as hell had. If it hadn't been for the Skrel, the Ursa would never have arrived on Nova

Prime. And the Skrel had also dropped the mine or un-exploded shell or whatever it had been that had blown Janus to pieces.

She stared at the Ursa, saw the direct link between the creature's presence and the alien bastards who had been responsible for her husband's death. And then, without the slightest hesitation, she advanced on the Ursa.

Somewhere in the back of her mind she heard Terelli ordering her to stay back, to remain in formation, to do what she had been trained to do.

I'm trained to kill these things. And that's what I'm going to do.

"Hey!" she bellowed. "*You ugly son of a bitch! Here! Over here!*"

The Ursa's head snapped around. Ursa didn't have eyes, but they could hear perfectly well, and her furious shout had snared its attention.

Mallory advanced on it and wasn't even aware that she was doing so.

Time seemed to slow down. The world was a blur, punctuated by mental snapshots of the other Rangers. Their eyes were wide with shock, their mouths open. Some of them seemed in the midst of forming the sylla-bles of her name.

She ignored them. Nothing mattered except the Ursa, and she closed the distance so abruptly that she was unaware of how much time, if any, had actually passed.

Everything in the Ursa's posture indicated complete bewilderment. It looked in the general direction from which Mallory had shouted, and then she stepped to the side. She didn't speak. The time for words was over.

The Ursa's eyeless head didn't follow her. It snarled angrily, certain an enemy was approaching, and then it lashed out with its claws, missing Mallory by a good two feet.

The full truth of what she was doing did not dawn on her. All she thought was that the Ursa was confused, and she was going to take full advantage of it.

Others started to move in, but Terelli spread her arms

wide, her hands out and flat, indicating that the other Rangers should maintain their positions. Clearly she wanted to see what would happen.

Mallory slowly continued to move, looking for the ideal position. She held her breath, as much from necessity as anything else considering how foul this particular Ursa smelled. It took several tentative steps in the direction she'd been moving, snapped at the air, and suddenly started to "look" toward Hopkins. It was picking up on the fear that Hopkins was unable to control, which was attracting the beast like a beacon.

She made her move before the Ursa could fully lock onto Hopkins or, for that matter, anyone else. She swept in with her cutlass and swung it in an arc. It sliced across the creature's side. Had the Ursa remained stationary, she might well have been able to gut it. Instead it moved ever so slightly, perhaps still trying to locate its attacker, and so her cutlass blade glanced off its rib cage. It was still enough to cause the creature significant pain.

"Oh, you don't like that, huh?" she shouted, tossing aside her earlier resolve to remain silent, and barreled forward. It whipped around to face her, and for a moment she seemed a goner. Then, in a maneuver that would still be discussed years later, Mallory dropped to the ground and slid forward, one leg extended, like a baseball player sliding into second base. The slide took her right under the Ursa as it slammed its feet down; she actually glided between the creature's legs. The rough ground tore at her uniform, but she never slowed. As the momentum of her slide carried her past, she sliced hard with the cutlass and came within a hairbreadth of disemboweling the creature. As it was, it left a gash so deep that the thick, foul liquid that served as the Ursa's blood gushed out by what appeared to be the gallon.

The Ursa let out a roar so violent, so ferocious, that two of the Rangers would later complain of hearing loss. As it reared back, Mallory was on her feet once more, and for all that the Ursa reacted to her, she might as well have been invisible.

That was when the Ursa made the decision that it had had enough.

It leaped to the side. Ranger Tomlinson lunged to the right to get clear of the monster, readying his cutlass to take a whack at it. The Ursa didn't give him a chance. Instead it sped right past, making a wheezing, grunting noise that indicated every step it took was a strain. Seconds later it went camo, effectively disappearing into the brush. Its invisibility wasn't another trick; instead they could hear the brush and trees being knocked aside, the sounds of the Ursa retreating into the distance.

And once it was gone, it left only deathly silence in its wake.

It was Hopkins who was first to break that silence. "Did what I think just happened . . . happen?"

"What happened is that we just lost a man," said Terelli, nodding toward the fallen Harrison. "Let's get him home and bury our honored dead. You: McGuiness."

"Sir, yes sir," said Mallory stiffly.

"Come with me."

She nodded and then glanced at Hopkins. "Nice working with you," she said in a low voice as she prepared to follow Terelli to what she was sure would be a court-martial.

"Are you an idiot?" said Hopkins in a low voice. "You just ghosted. It's like having the keys to the kingdom."

"I . . . *what* did I do?" The full weight of the last few minutes fell upon her. All she had been doing up to now was mentally beating herself up that the creature had escaped. The means she had employed to attack the monster, and its clear inability to perceive her, had not registered on her.

"You ghosted! You just entered a whole new level of—" Hopkins stopped, seeing the look on her face. "Mal, what's wrong?"

She wiped the moisture from her eyes and said softly, "The first thing I thought was, '*Wait'll I tell Jan.*'"

IV

When Mallory began her day as part of a squad hunting for an Ursa, she never would have thought she'd end it in the office of the Savant.

She'd never had an encounter with the Savant before. As head of the Science Guild, he was simply not someone she'd ever cross paths with.

But because of the unexpected manifestation of Mallory's ability to ghost, Colonel Green had brought her straight to the science hall, where she could be subjected to a battery of tests. They gave her a psychological third degree far more comprehensive than anything she'd ever endured. They asked her hundreds of questions; they showed her screens with random blots of blackness and asked her what she saw (her insistent reply of "random blots of blackness" seemed to impress nobody). They drew blood, had her urinate into a container. They did everything short of shove probes up her ass, and she worried that if they didn't like the results of their tests, that would be next.

And when it was all over—she hoped—Colonel Green had ordered her to wait in the Savant's office. She dutifully did as she was told. Despite Hopkins's certainty that she would face no disciplinary action even though she had disobeyed orders, she had still braced herself for the worst when Terelli returned with her to Ranger HQ. But Green had been waiting there for the both of them; Terelli, it turned out, had sent word on ahead. Mallory had received the equivalent of a disciplinary slap on the wrist, and Green had taken over from there.

Mallory had spent the entire day adjusting to what had happened, and yet her mind was still racing. She paced the office, right up until the door opened and the Savant entered. The Savant was remarkably tall, with sparse hair and sunken cheeks. He also had the most piercingly blue eyes that Mallory had ever seen. She'd never considered what perpetual inquisitiveness would look like, but decided it was probably what she was looking at now.

She snapped to attention the moment the Savant came in. Right behind him was Colonel Green.

"Take a seat, Ranger." The Savant gestured to a chair facing his wide desk.

Mallory remained precisely where she was.

"She's too well trained," Colonel Green informed the Savant. "There's a superior officer in the room. She won't sit unless I give her leave to do so."

"Well, then I would appreciate it if you did, because I'm sufficiently old-fashioned that I won't sit while there's a lady standing."

A twitch of a smile crossed Green's face. "I think the lieutenant might take exception to being described as 'a lady.'" When McGuiness didn't rise to the bait, merely stood there and awaited orders, Green said, "At ease, Lieutenant. Take a chair."

She did as he instructed. Her back remained rigid and her hands were flat upon her lap. She waited expectantly.

"So how are you doing, Lieutenant?" said the Savant conversationally, as if they were sitting down for coffee.

"I've been poked and prodded within an inch of my life, sir," she said, making no attempt to mask her impatience. "So with all respect, rather than how I'm doing, I would prefer to know what, if anything, this intrusiveness has revealed."

"Very well," said the Savant. He had taken a seat and leaned forward on his desk, his fingers interlaced.

"To be honest, I initially believed that the explanation for your sudden fearlessness and your clear ability to ghost—anecdotal, to be sure, but confirmed by reliable witnesses—was psychologically based. That the loss of your husband—"

"Caused me to snap? To become suicidal? To not care about my own welfare?"

"Something like that."

That was exactly the conclusion she had feared. It would be one short step from such a diagnosis to being declared mentally unstable. No one wanted to have his or her life depend upon a Ranger who didn't care whether she lived or died, or might actually be courting death. If it stuck, she might be put on indefinite leave. Or, even worse, handed a desk job, which would be akin to dying as far as she was concerned. "Sir"—her response was addressed to Green, not the Savant— "I assure you, I am not remotely—"

Green silenced her with a sharp gesture. "Let the man finish, Lieutenant."

Her mouth remained open for a moment and then snapped shut with a click.

"However," the Savant continued as if she had never interrupted, "I'm reasonably sure, based upon the psych eval we've done here today, that that is not the case. Especially considering that another explanation has presented itself. You see, we've discovered that there've been some fundamental, metabolic changes in both your pituitary gland and your hypothalamus. Consequently, it's created the chemical equivalent of a modified DPD . . ." When he saw her blank expression, he said, "Depersonalization Disorder. At its extreme, DPD makes sufferers feel as if they are moving through a sort of waking dream. The mind feels disconnected from the world around it. In your case, thanks to the chemical imbalance, when faced with a life-threatening situation—"

"Such as an Ursa," Green said, rather unnecessarily.

"—you enter a sort of fugue state. It's a rather fascinating phenomenon, really. If you wouldn't mind, I'd like to study it further and write a paper about it."

"But I don't understand." Mallory was shaking her head in confusion. "My body's undergone a chemical change? Why?"

"It's actually more or less standard for a woman in your condition."

"My what? What condition?" She looked in bewilderment from one to the other.

"Mallory," said Green gently, "when was the last time you menstruated?"

Her face reddened with annoyance. "That's an entirely personal question, sir, and I don't see where your superior rank entitles you to . . ." Then her voice trailed off as her eyes widened.

There was dead silence in the room for a long moment.

"Oh, holy shit," she murmured.

"Tests indicate you're approximately two months along," said the Savant.

"Are you sure?"

"Absolutely."

When she said nothing beyond that for a time, Green—who had remained standing, his hands draped behind his back—said, "Regulations are quite specific on this matter, Lieutenant. A pregnant Ranger may continue to serve at her discretion for as long as her commanding officer deems her physically capable of doing so. Obviously you are, at this point, still fully capable of functioning, and you have the right to do so."

"So . . ." She struggled to find the words. "So you're saying that my ability to ghost comes with an expiration date? That if the baby's gone . . ." Her voice caught on that sentence, and she powered through it. ". . . I won't be able to ghost anymore?"

"I wish I had an answer for that, but I simply don't know," the Savant admitted. "We'd have to wait and see."

"Lieutenant," Green said cautiously, "your phrasing

was . . . rather specific. Are you insinuating that you may not bring the child to term?"

Slowly she got to her feet, standing at attention. She looked straight forward, but not at anything in particular. "Is the colonel implying I do not have that right?"

"Not at all," he said.

"Or is the colonel thinking of ordering me to continue the pregnancy so that he can have another Ghost at his disposal for a—"

"Stow that right now, Lieutenant." Green looked well and truly pissed. "I have said and done nothing, in the entirety of my career, that would remotely imply I would have such a dehumanizing attitude toward my people, and frankly I resent the hell out of what you're saying."

"I'm sorry, sir," she said immediately, and meant it. "It's . . . just a lot to take in right now. I need some time to process it."

"I understand," said Green. "Take all the time you need to decide upon your course of action."

"Thank you, sir."

"You have until tomorrow."

She paused and then nodded. "Thank you, sir." She pivoted on her heel and headed for the door.

Just before she reached it, Green called, "Lieutenant."

She turned back to him.

"Congratulations," said Green.

"We'll see about that, sir," Mallory said, and walked out.

V

Mallory lay in her quarters the entire night, staring up at the ceiling. She kept resting her hand on her belly, trying to sense whatever it was that was going on within her. "Talk to me," she whispered. "Tell me what you want."

The small passenger did not respond.

She drifted in and out during the night, sleeping for minutes at a time. Every time she did manage to slumber, she was pelted with an unceasing barrage of images: her husband, climbing out of the grave, his arms outstretched, falling upon her and clawing at her stomach, trying to rip the infant from her.

When the first light of the twin suns of Nova Prime began to crawl over the horizon, Mallory's eyes were red with strain. Not with tears; she felt as if she had cried herself out after Jan's death. Instead they were red with exhaustion. When she looked at herself in the mirror, she reminded herself of something out of an ancient tale of the undead.

An hour later she was sitting on the edge of her bed. She was wearing civilian clothes and her hair was wet; obviously she had showered and dressed, but she had no recollection of doing so.

Focus. You need to focus.

There was only one thing she could think of focusing on.

Another couple of hours later—because it took her

that long to muster the will to leave her quarters—
Mallory was standing at the site of her husband's grave.

Well, at least he hasn't crawled out of it.

Valhalla Point was the official burial site for the honored Rangers who had fallen in the line of duty. The headstones were simple: small rectangles of rock with the name of the buried individual chiseled into them. Many preferred cremation, but others were more traditional, and the Rangers endeavored to accommodate all preferences.

Mallory was far too practical an individual to think that Janus was "there" somehow. She knew her husband was gone. He would no more hear her at this site than any other. Ultimately it wasn't about him. He was beyond caring about worldly concerns. It was about her voicing her problems and her inner turmoil.

"I don't know what to do, Jan," she said softly. "First of all, I don't know what to do about the baby itself. You were the one who kept talking about having children. You would have been a great father. I don't know what kind of mother I'd make, and without you . . .

"Besides, what kind of world would I be bringing our baby into? Monsters roam, trying to kill us. Aliens attack us from on high. We can never relax our guard, ever. A lousy mother bringing a baby into a lousy environment . . . why should I do that to him? Maybe it'd be better if he was never born . . .

"But . . ." She hesitated, her voice choking slightly. "How can I kill the only part of you that's left? How can I do that to him? How can I do that to you . . . ? Have I spent so much time focusing on killing things that I've totally forgotten how to worry about the living . . . ?"

She sank to her knees in front of the grave. "And . . . what *about* the living? Don't I have a responsibility to protect them? The citizens of Nova Prime are counting on me. And if I have the ability to ghost now, then don't I have the responsibility to use it?

"But . . . then aren't I putting the baby at risk? So

what if an Ursa can't see me? It could still get lucky. A random sweep of its stinger . . . and I die, and your baby dies . . .

"It doesn't even have to be an Ursa. Maybe somewhere there's an unexploded shell with my name on it . . .

"How many lives are supposed to be on my shoulders? How am I supposed to be a good mother, or any kind of mother, if it means abandoning the people who count on the Rangers? But how am I supposed to put my baby at risk? How am I—?"

She lowered her head, put her hands in her face. Her sides shook, and she heaved agonized sobs, but her cheeks remained dry.

"Are you all right?"

She looked up.

There was another woman a short distance away. Dressed in the gray uniform of someone who worked in one of the tech divisions, she was crouching in front of a grave site and laying down a batch of fresh flowers. The fair-skinned, sad-eyed woman studied Mallory with what appeared to be quiet understanding. "Do you want to talk about it?" She did not ask Mallory what specifically the "it" was. She saw an individual in pain and was clearly prepared to listen.

Mallory didn't move from where she was. She didn't feel comfortable approaching. She did, however, tilt her head slightly and nod toward the grave site where the other woman was standing. "Your husband?"

"My daughter," replied the other woman quietly.

"She was a Ranger?"

The other woman nodded. "Killed by an Ursa last year."

"I'm so sorry." She paused and then said, "I'm Mallory."

"Faia."

The name was vaguely familiar to Mallory, but she couldn't quite place it. "That's my husband," Mallory said, pointing at Janus's grave. "I guess we have something in common."

"Members of a club no one wants to belong to," said Faia. "I'd love to tell you it gets easier as time passes. But I'd be lying. All that happens is that scar tissue builds over it. The wound still cuts just as deep."

"I appreciate your honesty." She was still speaking stiffly and formally, not allowing any of her inner turmoil to show.

There was an uneasy silence, and then Faia said, "Okay, well . . . it was a pleasure meeting y—"

"I'm pregnant," Mallory blurted out. "And I don't know if I should keep doing my job." She didn't bring up the fact that the pregnancy apparently enabled her to ghost. She wasn't sure if that was supposed to be classified, plus she wasn't entirely sure that she herself accepted it yet.

"Oh . . . my," said Faia slowly. "That changes everything, doesn't it?"

"Does it?" There was desperate urgency in her voice. "That's what I keep wondering. Whose needs are more important? This . . . this stranger"—she gestured angrily toward her stomach. "Or the people I'm sworn to protect? One life versus countless others? What makes this one life more important than all the others?"

"I don't know. I wish I knew what to tell you . . ."

"This is what you can tell me." She looked her in the eyes. "You lost a daughter. Is there anyone on this world whose life you wouldn't trade to get your little girl back? Is there anyone whom you believe was intrinsically more worthy to live than your daughter?"

Faia looked down, unable to keep her gaze upon Mallory. Very softly, she said, "My daughter died defending the life of her brother. And I can tell you right now: Not a day goes by when my son doesn't just miss his sister, but also wonders why he got to live while she died. Not a single day. Anyone who tells you there's any fairness in life is lying to you. And we look for a reason for things, and we look to ourselves and our personal failures to try and figure out what we could have done to avoid what happened. But all we do is second-guess ourselves. Because the truth is that you can make your-self insane worrying about these things. The harsh truth—as least as far as I'm concerned—is that the universe is indifferent to us. Our endless second-guessing just makes it harder for us to realize that it's all utterly random. And all we can do, in deciding how to live our lives, is to make our best guess and move on."

"I can't move on." She drew a hand across her stomach. "I'm carrying this constant reminder of what could have been . . ."

"It can still be."

"Not with my husband. I can't . . ."

Faia pointed a stern finger at her. "Don't you dare let the next words out of your mouth be *'do it without him.'* " When Mallory said nothing further, Faia continued. "You're a Ranger, Mallory. I've known a few Rangers in my time, including my daughter. I know the type; I know the mind-set. And there is nothing you can't do if you set your mind to it. If some Rangers can stare down an Ursa and be unafraid, I think you can control your fear of an infant."

"It's not just the baby. It's what it represents."

"It represents responsibility. That's what Rangers are all about."

She had been walking steadily toward Mallory, and now she rested a hand on her shoulder. "Look . . . I have no intention of lecturing you."

"I don't feel like that's what you're doing," Mallory lied.

"Well, I'm skirting it, at the very least. Ultimately, I can't tell you what to do. It's not my place and besides, my personal life is so difficult that I'm hardly the person to lecture anyone else. Listen: We both know the pain of losing loved ones. And we also know the incredible demands that a sense of duty places upon us. I may not be a Ranger myself, but my husband wrote the book on the Ranger mind-set . . . literally."

"What?" Then suddenly everything fell into place. "Faia . . . Raige. Your husband is Cypher Raige. The

Original Ghost. The Commanding General. I'm so sorry. I . . . I should have—"

"Should have what? Stood at attention the whole time?" She smiled slightly, but then the smile faded. "I suppose what it comes down to is that no answer is the absolute right one. You have to choose a path, and it's going to be irrevocable no matter what you do. It's always daunting when there's no going back. And there are always sacrifices to be made."

"And who am I"—once more Mallory put her hand on her stomach—"to make decisions that could wind up sacrificing someone else's life without them having the slightest say in it?"

"Making decisions on behalf of your children—some of them life and death—comes with the territory. Less hardy women than you have dealt with it and come through fine. Like I said, there's no easy answer. But I know this: What's the most important thing? Children being born? Or the world they're being born into?"

"So you think I should—"

"I think," she said encouragingly, "that you have to make a decision you yourself can live with. And once you've done that, everything else will fall into place." She squeezed her shoulder in solidarity.

That evening, in his office, Colonel Green looked up from his desk and saw Mallory standing in the doorway. She was wearing her uniform, freshly pressed.

She saluted sharply.

"Lieutenant Mallory McGuiness reporting for active duty, sir. For as long as it's physically possible, at any rate."

He studied her for a long moment. "Are you sure?"

"A Ranger's first priority is to serve Nova Prime. The sooner Junior here learns that"—she nodded downward—"the better off we'll all be."

VI

For this? I went through all that agonizing for this?

Mallory glanced at her two fellow Rangers. Corporal Abbey was tall and powerfully built, and his enthusiasm for his duty as a Ranger was palpable. Private Sutton was wiry and easily one of the most athletic Rangers in the corps. There was nothing wrong with her companions.

What was wrong was the mission itself.

The delivery shuttle skimmed across the Falkor Desert of Nova Prime. Sutton was at the helm, keeping a steady hand. Every so often it bobbed up and down as a powerful gust of wind would endeavor to blow it sideways. The Falkor was renowned for its strong winds; of all the desert areas of Nova Prime, it was most prone toward sandstorms. Why anyone would have the slightest interest in setting up shop out here, Mallory couldn't even begin to fathom.

And yet a group of scientists had established an outpost, and they were in need of help.

Routine help.

Mind-numbingly boring help.

Which was the only sort of mission she had these days.

Colonel Green had welcomed her back to the ranks of the Rangers all right, but since that day, he had been extraordinarily, even insanely, cautious in terms of how he utilized her. She had assumed that she would be thrust into major undertakings involving Ursa. Instead most of her missions were routine patrols in areas where there had been no Ursa sightings.

I should be out there helping. I should be battling the Skrel and their plans and their evil. And instead I'm stuck doing chores that anyone could do. You don't need a Ghost to do a delivery run. You don't even need a Ranger to accomplish it.

Yet that was what she was stuck doing. The past several months there had been almost no rain on Nova Prime, and the population was creaking under the effects of the growing drought. As a consequence, water was being carefully rationed, and the dispensing of it had fallen under the auspices of the Rangers.

Green had selected her to head up this particular run. When she'd received her orders, she had wanted to scream in protest. She'd hoped that Green had finally decided to give her something interesting, but no, he was still keeping her on the shelf. When she'd offered a token protest, Green had simply replied, "I'm utilizing you where I feel you can do the most good, Lieutenant."

She wasn't buying that for a second. It was obvious to her that, despite her value as a Ghost, Green had trepidations about putting her into the thick of things. She had briefly considered bringing her complaints directly to the Commanding General. If anyone should be irritated by a Ghost being underutilized, it would be the Original Ghost.

She couldn't bring herself to do it, however. First of all, how would she broach it? *Hey, General . . . I happened to run into your wife in the cemetery the other day, and figured you and I would have a chat.*

Second, she had far too much respect for the chain of command. She answered to Green, and Green in turn to the man variously referred to as the Commanding General or Prime Commander. She had no business bypassing Green. It wasn't her job to decide where she could best serve the Rangers. It was her job to obey.

So the only option she really had was to continue the way she was going, as her belly slowly began to distend and make the presence of her little parasite known. The bump was not yet having a major impact on her physicality, but she was feeling the beginnings of awkwardness and discomfort, a recurring sensation of being off balance as her center of gravity shifted. She hated it because her body had always been a finely tuned machine and she wasn't appreciating in the least a wrench being tossed into the works.

I hate my baby.

She felt guilty the instant she thought it, but she couldn't help herself. Here the child's presence had apparently made her capable of ghosting, but she wasn't being allowed to take advantage of that status. So all she was left with was a sense of anger and frustration because the infant was crimping her ability to do her job, condemning her to day after day of inconsequential duties. The baby was curtailing her ability to serve, but if she felt any resentment toward it, then she was automatically a bad mother because good mothers didn't hate their children.

I knew this was a bad idea. Jan wanted children, not me. I am going to be a lousy mother. A lousy mother who's always going to resent her baby for—

"Lieutenant, we've got the outpost on our scopes," said Sutton.

Mallory focused herself on the task at hand, however menial it was. In the rear of the shuttle were six large containers of water. It would have to last the scientists for at least two months, so they would have to be extremely cautious with how they used it.

"Inform them of our approach."

"Aye, copy that."

Mallory watched out the forward observation window as they drew closer and closer. It was nothing more than a series of small buildings, each made of fluttering walls and roofs of smart cloth. Their supreme flexibility enabled them to withstand even the most formidable of winds as they roared through. There were also several silver towers. She had no idea what they were for; perhaps they gathered readings for various experiments the scientists were doubtless performing.

Her tolerance for, and belief in, scientists remained minimal. Nevertheless, they were waiting to be helped, and it was her job to attend to their needs. She frowned, though, when long moments passed and they received no response to their hail. "Sutton?" She didn't have to complete the question; it was obvious that she wanted to know why the scientists appeared to be radio-silent.

Sutton shook his head. "Don't know what's going on, Lieutenant."

"Abbey, check the long-range monitors," said Mallory. She had unstrapped from her seat and was pacing the interior of the shuttle. "See if a sandstorm is moving into the area. Perhaps that could be jamming the transmission."

"How would it be doing that?"

"I don't know," she admitted in frustration. "Just check—"

"Already have. True, things can come up quickly out here, but at the moment the screens are all clear."

Mallory studied the image of the outpost as it drew ever closer. She wasn't seeing anything. No sign of movement, no sign of life anywhere. "Where the hell did they go?" she whispered.

"Should we head back, Lieutenant?"

She shook her head. "No. We need to see what's going on. Maybe they're hiding from something."

"Like what?" said Abbey, but he wouldn't have to think terribly hard to imagine what the "like what" might be. It wasn't a stretch for any of them, really.

"We'll find out," Mallory said in a carefully neutral voice.

Moments later, the shuttle had settled onto the ground about a hundred feet away from the encampment. After sending word to headquarters that something appeared to be unusual and they were going to investigate, Mallory irised open the ship's door. The three Rangers carefully emerged from the ship, their cutlasses at the ready.

Nothing appeared to be moving in the area. As near as the Rangers could determine, they were completely alone.

There was no need to spread out. The outpost was small enough that, even with the Rangers staying together, it would only take a matter of minutes to cover the entire area.

"Hello?" Mallory called out tentatively. It seemed absurd on one level to do so; clearly there was no one around. Nevertheless she did it reflexively. "We're Rangers. Is anyone here? Is anyone in need of aid?"

No response. Nothing save a steady breeze rolling in from the desert.

"Lieutenant." Abbey was crouching a few feet away and gesturing for Mallory to join him. "Check this out."

Mallory walked over to Abbey and saw that he was pointing toward something on the ground. There were a few dark red spots, and several small, white fragments of—

"Bone?"

Abbey nodded. His face was grim. "Blood and bone, aye. Something was slaughtered here. And something was eaten by something that didn't leave much of anything behind. I'll bet you if we check around, we'll find a few more bits like this. But not many more."

"Ursa," whispered Mallory.

"And not all that long ago," said Abbey. He dabbed tentatively at one of the red spots. "It's still wet. And out here, in this heat, it would dry out fairly quickly."

Sutton, a few feet away, turned ashen. Mallory understood why. It wasn't that he was daunted by the prospect of an Ursa. No, he was imagining what it must have been like for the poor bastards who had been here to be assaulted and devoured so quickly, they didn't even have time to send out a call for help. Not that anyone would have been able to arrive in time.

Mallory's immediate instinct was to get back into the cargo ship and get the hell out of there. There was nothing more to be done for the scientists. At this moment they were working through whatever passed for an Ursa's digestive tract.

As if reading her mind, Abbey said, "We need to get out of here. That thing could be anywhere . . ."

"And if it is," said Mallory, "it's our job to kill it."

"There're only three of us."

"One of whom is a Ghost," Sutton reminded him.

"Lieutenant," Abbey said, "with all respect, we all know no one was expecting an Ursa encounter. Typical hunting party for an Ursa is eight Rangers. Even with a Ghost, five is protocol, unless the Ghost is extremely experienced. Again, with the greatest respect, you only have one kill—unconfirmed, mind you—to your credit, and since then . . ."

"I've been more or less given easy duties, which makes you doubt our superior's confidence in me? Plus I'm obviously pregnant and it may slow me down or cause me to hesitate in the face of danger? Is that what you were going to say? With the greatest respect?"

Abbey stared at her silently. He didn't answer. He didn't have to. All he was doing was giving voice to the self-doubts she already had.

"Okay," Mallory said after a long pause. "Okay, you can speak freely. How would you like to see this handled?"

Abbey let out a sigh of relief, clearly glad that Mallory had chosen not to cut him off at the knees, which she would have totally been within her rights to do. "We get back in the ship, button her up, then send for reinforcements and remain on station until they arrive."

It didn't sound like an unreasonable plan. There was no one here to save, so immediate action wasn't required. Proceeding cautiously made every bit of sense. Indeed, there was no reason not to do so.

She nodded.

Immediately Abbey headed back to the ship, Sutton following right behind him. Mallory brought up the rear, keeping a wary eye on their surroundings. If there was one thing that was certain about Ursa, it was that just because you didn't see them didn't mean they weren't around.

The ship was sitting there waiting for them, perched on its landing struts.

Abbey was walking up the ramp; on his approach, the hatch irised open. Sutton was right behind him, and that was when Mallory noticed that the shuttle was sitting lower on its struts than it had been before.

She put it together in a heartbeat.

"Fall back!" she shouted.

Too late. The Ursa, perched atop the shuttle, its weight responsible for the craft's visible sagging, shimmered into view and roared. Abbey and Sutton froze in place, fear pumping through them. Within the darkness of the world that the Ursa inhabited, the terror that they radiated would be akin to a lighthouse beacon. The Ursa swept its right claw around and Abbey's head went flying, blood fountaining from his shoulders. Abbey collapsed, his cutlass slipping from lifeless fingers. Sutton instantly stepped back, bringing his cutlass around, and he slashed at the Ursa. The Ursa vaulted over him and, while in midair, lashed out with its talon. The claw slammed through Sutton's back and out his chest. The sight of his innards spilling out transfixed him. The Ursa landed on the ground near the ship, sending Sutton's body tumbling off its ramp.

All of it had happened within barely five seconds, and the entire time Mallory stood there, bolted to the ground, eyes wide.

The Ursa pivoted, sweeping the rest of the area. Mallory stumbled backward, but her shifting center of gravity, courtesy of her expanding belly, threw her balance off ever so slightly . . . just enough to cause her to fall to the ground with a gasp.

The Ursa's head snapped around. Blind it may have been, but its hearing was sharp, and instantly it perceived her presence.

As it turned to face her, she spotted a long scar running along its side, right where she had cut into an Ursa months ago. The same one? Not definitive, but entirely possible.

It advanced upon her, its claws clacking on the arid ground. It knew where she was generally; it just needed her to exude the level of fear it required to zero in on her.

She saw her fellow Rangers cut to pieces, their bodies scattered, and she imagined herself meeting a similar, horrid fate . . .

. . . and she clamped down on her fear. She tossed it aside like it was someone else's problem. She squared her shoulders, faced the Ursa, and thought nothing of its presence. It became little to her, insignificant. It was as if she had disconnected her mind from her body.

The Ursa stopped where it was. It visibly sniffed the air, but it was designed for perceiving endorphins. Other aromas simply blended together into one indistinguishable mass of olfactory input.

Mallory began to circle it. She bent at her knees, providing her more balance, and her feet moved across the ground noiselessly. Her cutlass was at the ready.

Suddenly the Ursa's head whipped around and it was "looking" right at her. She froze, certain that it somehow had zeroed in on her. She waited, her legs flexed, prepared to leap to either side to avoid the creature's inevitable charge.

Then it continued to sniff at the air and kept on turning.

It didn't see me. It doesn't know I was right in front of it.

She had her cutlass ready. Quietly she separated it into two staves with a vicious curved hook at either end. If the creature kept moving in the same direction, it would present its back to her within seconds and she could make her assault. She had it all planned in her head: She would leap forward onto the creature, securing her position with one of the staves buried in its back.

She would then bury the other end squarely into the Ursa's head, driving the blade into its brain.

This one is for you, Jan, she thought.

And the baby kicked.

For the first time.

Very hard.

She had felt faint fluttering in previous days, but nothing like this. A definitive, literal gut punch as if the infant had decided that this was absolutely the perfect time to announce its presence to the world.

Mallory cried out in surprise and shock. Her mind and body reconnected, and one thought galvanized both of them: *I have to save my baby.*

Instantly the Ursa spun and locked onto her.

Mallory turned and ran, slamming the two halves of her cutlass back together as she did so. The Ursa's roar nearly paralyzed her, but she kept on running.

The Ursa covered the distance between the two of them in one leap, and the only thing that saved her was that she swung her cutlass up and back over her shoulder, blindly, praying.

She got lucky. The blade cut into the Ursa's right foot, severing tendons. The creature toppled over, screeching in fury. It thrashed about, trying to lunge toward her but instead falling forward onto its face.

It's a wounded animal. There's nothing more dangerous than a wounded animal. With that thought slamming through her, she ran like hell, hoping to put as much distance as she could between herself and the Ursa before the creature managed to adjust to its injured foot and come in pursuit. Her heart pounded, all thoughts of ghosting gone from her mind. The primal human fight-or-flight instinct had taken over and she could think of nothing but getting away.

There was only one place that she could get to that would provide her any sort of shelter: the shuttle that had brought them here. She cut sharply to the right and sprinted as fast as she could toward the landing point. It may well have been that she was imagining it, but she had never felt so fat, so slow, so clumsy as she did right then.

The shuttle was there, waiting for her, the door still open. And then she sensed, rather than saw, the Ursa coming after her from off to the right. She was closer but it was faster, and it was coming directly toward her on an intercept course.

Mallory drew more speed from somewhere and, with the door just ahead of her, charged through it. She pivoted and slammed the "CLOSE" button on the wall. The door irised shut just as the Ursa got to it. It slammed into the door at top speed, and the shuttle rocked violently. But the door remained closed, leaving the Ursa stuck outside.

She scrambled forward toward the helm controls to try to lift off the shuttle. And then the Ursa was right there at the front observation window, and it slammed forward with far more strength than she would have thought possible. It struck the observation window straight-on once, twice; the third time, cracks ribboned through the window like a spiderweb. Before Mallory could fully bring the engines online, its claw smashed the front window to bits. Mallory fell back, shielding her face from the flying glass, and hit the floor of the shuttle at the far end.

The Ursa brought its injured leg forward, sweeping it back and forth and clearing out the rest of the glass that was impeding its entrance. The space, however, wasn't quite wide enough to allow it easy access. That didn't deter it, though. With Mallory mere feet away from it, it shoved its maw forward. It was a tight squeeze at first, but the monster began to slowly, unstoppably, push its huge head through, like some sick perversion of a human birth.

This is it, she thought frantically, her confidence in her ability to ghost so shaken that the notion of fearlessness seemed nothing more than a pipe dream at that moment. *This is everything I was afraid would happen. I'm going to die. My baby is going to die. For every-*

thing that Jan and I accomplished during our lifetimes, we might as well never have lived at all. I've completely failed.

The Ursa was unable to roar; its jaws were clamped shut thanks to the narrowness of the entrance it was trying to push through. But it was growling furiously between its compressed jaws.

Crouched at the far end of the shuttle, she reached down and slid her hand under her uniform top onto her bare belly. "I'm sorry," she whispered.

And then she felt another movement in her stomach. Not a kick this time. Instead it was pushing back against her open palm.

She couldn't be certain, but it seemed to her as if it was the baby's own hand flat against hers.

And in her mind, it was as if the baby was saying to her comfortingly, *Don't be afraid. I have faith in you.*

For the first time, she perceived the child in a way she hadn't before. She saw it not as a liability or a drawback. She didn't see it as something that was going to drain away her resolve or impede her development as a person, a Ranger, or a Ghost.

Instead she saw her unborn child as a strength. An asset to her life, not a liability.

She also became convinced, for the first time, that it was a girl. A bond had been created between mother and daughter, a connection at a fundamental level that she had never experienced before.

The Ursa's massive head thrust through and it let out a furious, bone-rattling roar. It waited for the expected unleashing of fear pheromones that would serve to draw it directly toward its prey.

Nothing.

The creature bellowed once more and again waited for some manner of response that it could utilize as a draw to the human.

Still nothing.

The human was gone.

The Ursa couldn't fathom how that was possible. It

sensed that the room was an enclosure, and there had been a human there. Yet now there wasn't.

It reached out with all the senses it had at its disposal.

And it was still straining to find its target when the blade of the cutlass was driven straight through the top of its head by a woman who was standing no more than six inches from it and yet was undetectable.

Mallory McGuiness resisted the temptation to cry out in triumph. Instead, with ruthless efficiency, she yanked out the cutlass and then stabbed downward once more. She was holding one of the staves. The blade punched through with a sound like a knife being driven into a melon. Even as that happened, she slid the edge of the other blade under the Ursa's chin, opening up the veins in its throat. It bled all over the inside of the shuttle, so much so that within seconds a pool of liquid ran an inch deep around her boots.

The Ursa trembled violently, and the entire shuttle shook as if it were in the throes of an earthquake.

And then it fell silent.

Dead.

Mallory's baby kicked. Again.

VII

The alarm sounded through Nova Prime City. Children walking home from school froze upon hearing its shriek. They knew it all too well: An Ursa had been spotted within the confines of the city.

And then they saw it, barreling toward them. It had shimmered into existence a short distance away, and the children cried out in terror.

It noticed them, but before it could lock on, a woman hurtled in from the side. *"Found you!"* She was holding a bladed weapon, and she lashed out with confidence. The Ursa danced away, the children forgotten.

Other Rangers were coming up from behind. The woman called out with authority, "Left and right flanks! Surround it and drive it out of the city! Then we'll dispatch it!"

The Rangers moved with practiced efficiency. It took them only seconds to send the Ursa running on the path that would take it away from any civilians.

And then the woman, who was clearly in charge, paused just long enough to toss off a quick salute to the kids before she led her fellow Rangers in pursuit of the Ursa.

"She saluted at us!" one of the boys said.

A little girl said proudly, "Nuh-unh. She was saluting at me. That was my mom."

"Get out!" said one child, and another said, "Janny, are you kidding?"

"Nope. She's one of the seven Ghosts."

There were impressed murmurs from the other kids. "How'd she learn not to be afraid of anything?"

"I asked her that once."

"What'd she say?"

"She said I taught her," said Janny. And she smiled her father's smile.